WEIGHED IN THE BALANCE

Praise for

Weighed in the Balance

"Highly entertaining."

—Milwaukee Journal

"An excellent exploration of the classic closed-door mystery. In addition, Perry had really done a good job of providing both the Victorian atmosphere and the air of suspense of a hard-fought courtroom trial."

—Pittsburgh Post-Gazette

"Take[s] the reader clue-hunting through the glittery courts of Venice, London, and a never-never-land principality. It's all rich as a warm scone slathered with jam and clotted cream."

—St. Petersburg Times

"As always with Anne Perry, readers get a wealth of colorful characters, social and political details and mores, and a fascinating plot."

—Alfred Hitchcock Mystery Magazine

"The novel springs to life in the courtroom scenes, where careful investigation and astute teamwork produce some astonishing revelations that presage the end of Victorian propriety and an era's pretense of innocence."

—Publishers Weekly

BY ANNE PERRY

FEATURING WILLIAM MONK

The Face of a Stranger
A Dangerous Mourning
Defend and Betray
A Sudden, Fearful Death
The Sins of the Wolf
Cain His Brother
Weighed in the Balance
A Breach of Promise
The Twisted Root
Slaves of Obsession
Funeral in Blue
Death of a Stranger
The Shifting Tide
Dark Assassin
Execution Dock

FEATURING CHARLOTTE AND THOMAS PITT

The Cater Street Hangman
Callander Square
Paragon Walk
Resurrection Row
Bluegate Fields
Rutland Place
Death in the Devil's Acre
Cardington Crescent
Silence in Hanover Close
Bethlehem Road
Farriers' Lane
Hyde Park Headsman
Traitors Gate
Pentecost Alley
Ashworth Hall
Brunswick Gardens
Bedford Square
Half Moon Street
The Whitechapel Conspiracy
Southampton Row
Seven Dials
Long Spoon Lane
Buckingham Palace Gardens

THE WORLD WAR I NOVELS

No Graves as Yet
Shoulder the Sky
At Some Disputed Barricade
Angels in the Gloom
We Shall Not Sleep

THE CHRISTMAS NOVELS

A Christmas Journey
A Christmas Visitor
A Christmas Guest
A Christmas Secret
A Christmas Beginning
A Christmas Grace
A Christmas Promise

The Sheen on the Silk

WEIGHED IN THE BALANCE

A WILLIAM MONK NOVEL

ANNE PERRY

Ballantine Books Trade Paperbacks
New York

Weighed in the Balance is a work of fiction. Names, characters, places, and incidents are the products of the author's imagination or are used fictitiously. Any resemblance to actual events, locales, or persons, living or dead, is entirely coincidental.

2010 Ballantine Books Trade Paperback Edition

Published in the United States by Ballantine Books, an imprint of
The Random House Publishing Group, a division of
Random House, Inc., New York.

Originally published in hardcover in the United States by Ivy Books, an imprint of
The Random House Publishing Group, a division of
Random House, Inc., in 1996.

ISBN 978-0-345-51405-9

Printed in the United States of America

www.mortalis-books.com

2 4 6 8 9 7 5 3 1

Dedicated to Jane Merrow
in friendship

"Thou art weighed in the balances, and art found wanting."

—DANIEL 5:27

WEIGHED IN THE BALANCE

1

SIR OLIVER RATHBONE SAT in his chambers in Vere Street, just off Lincoln's Inn Fields, and surveyed the room with eminent satisfaction. He was at the pinnacle of his career, possibly the most highly respected barrister in England, and the Prime Minister had recently recommended him to Her Majesty, who had seen fit to honor him with a knighthood in recognition of his services to criminal justice.

The room was elegant but not ostentatious. Intellect and purpose were served before the desire to impress a client. Comfort was necessary. Beyond the door was the outer office, full of clerks writing, calculating, looking up references, being courteous to those who came and went in the course of business.

Rathbone was almost at the conclusion of a case in which he had defended a distinguished gentleman accused of misappropriating funds. He had every confidence in a satisfactory outcome. He had enjoyed an excellent luncheon in the company of a bishop, a judge and a senior member of Parliament. It was time he directed his attention towards the afternoon's work.

He had just picked up a sheaf of papers when his clerk knocked at the door and opened it. There was a look of surprise on the clerk's usually imperturbable face.

"Sir Oliver, there is a Countess Zorah Rostova desiring to

see you on a matter she says is of great importance—and some urgency."

"Then show her in, Simms," Rathbone directed. There was no need for him to be surprised that a countess should call. She was not the first titled lady to seek counsel in these chambers, nor would she be the last. He rose to his feet.

"Very good, Sir Oliver." Simms backed away, turned to speak to someone out of sight, then a moment later a woman swept in wearing a black-and-green crinoline dress, except that the hoop was so small it hardly deserved the name, and her stride was such that one might have supposed her to have only a moment since dismounted from a horse. She had no hat. Her hair was held back in a loose bun with a black chenille net over it. She did not wear her gloves but carried them absent-mindedly in one hand. She was of average height, square-shouldered and leaner than is becoming in a woman. But it was her face which startled and held attention. Her nose was a little too large and too long, her mouth was sensitive without being beautiful, her cheekbones were very high and her eyes were wide-set and heavy lidded. When she spoke, her voice was low with a slight catch in it, and her diction was remarkably beautiful.

"Good afternoon, Sir Oliver." She stood quite still in the center of the room. She did not even glance around but stared at him with a vivid, curious gaze. "I am sued for slander. I need you to defend me."

Rathbone had never been approached so boldly and so simply before. If she had spoken to Simms like that, no wonder the man was surprised.

"Indeed, ma'am," he said smoothly. "Would you care to sit down and tell me the circumstances?" He indicated the handsome green-leather-covered chair opposite his desk.

She remained where she was.

"It is quite simple. Princess Gisela . . . you are aware who she is?" Her brows rose. Rathbone could see now that her remarkable eyes were green. "Yes, of course you are. She has accused me of slandering her. I have not."

Rathbone also remained standing. "I see. What has she accused you of saying?"

"That she murdered her husband, Prince Friedrich, the crown prince of my country, who abdicated in order to marry her. He died this spring, after a riding accident, here in England."

"But of course you did not say so?"

She lifted her chin a little. "Most certainly I said so! But in English law if a thing is true it is not a slander to say so, is it?"

Rathbone stared at her. She seemed perfectly calm and in control of herself, and yet what she said was outrageous. Simms should not have allowed her in. She was obviously unbalanced.

"Madam, if . . ."

She moved over to the green chair and sat down, flicking her skirts absently to put them into a satisfactory position. She did not take her eyes from Rathbone's face.

"Is truth a defense in English law, Sir Oliver?" she repeated.

"Yes, it is," he conceded. "But one is obliged to prove truth. If you have no facts to demonstrate your case, simply to state it is to repeat the slander. Of course, it does not require the same degree of proof that a criminal case does."

"Degree of proof?" she questioned. "A thing is true or it is false. What degree of proof do I require?"

He resumed his own seat, leaning forward over the desk a trifle to explain.

"Scientific theory must be proved beyond all doubt at all, usually by demonstrating that all other theories are impossible. Criminal guilt must be proved beyond all reasonable doubt. This is a civil case, and will be judged on balance of probability. The jury will choose whichever argument it considers the most likely to be true."

"Is that good for me?" she asked bluntly.

"No. It will not require a great deal for her to convince them that you have slandered her. She must prove that you did indeed say this thing and that it has damaged her reputation. The latter will hardly be difficult."

"Neither will the former," she said with a very slight smile. "I have said it repeatedly, and in public. My defense is that it is true."

"But can you prove it?"

"Beyond reasonable doubt?" she asked, opening her eyes very wide. "That rather begs the question as to what is reasonable. I am quite convinced of it."

He sat back in his chair, crossing his legs and smiling very courteously.

"Then convince me of it, ma'am."

Quite suddenly she threw back her head and burst into laughter, a rich, throaty sound rippling with delight.

"I think I like you, Sir Oliver!" She caught her breath and composed herself with difficulty. "You are fearfully English, but I am sure that is all to the good."

"Indeed," he said guardedly.

"Of course. All Englishmen should be properly English. You want me to convince you that Gisela murdered Friedrich?"

"If you would be so good," he said a little stiffly.

"And then you will take the case?"

"Possibly." On the face of it, it was preposterous.

"How cautious of you," she said with a shadow of amusement. "Very well. I shall begin at the beginning. I presume that is what you would like? I cannot imagine you beginning anywhere else. For myself, I would rather begin at the end; it is then all so much easier to understand."

"Begin at the end, if it pleases you," he said quickly.

"Bravo!" She made a gesture of approval with her hand. "Gisela realized the necessity of murdering him, and almost immediately was presented with the opportunity, as a calling card is on a silver tray. All she had to do was pick it up. He had been injured in a riding accident. He was lying helpless." Her voice dropped; she leaned forward a little. "No one was certain how ill he was, or whether he would recover or not. She was alone with him. She killed him. There you are!" She spread her hands. "It is accomplished." She shrugged. "No one suspected because no one thought of such a thing, nor did they know how badly he was hurt anyway. He died of his injuries." She pursed her lips. "How natural. How sad." She sighed. "She is desolate. She mourns and all the world mourns with her. What could be easier?"

Rathbone regarded the extraordinary woman sitting in front of him. She was certainly not beautiful, yet there was a vitality in her, even in repose, which drew the eye to her as if she were the natural center of thought and attention. And yet what she was saying was outrageous—and almost certainly criminally slanderous.

"Why should she do such a thing?" he said aloud, his voice heavy with skepticism.

"Ah, for that I feel I should go back to the beginning," she said ruefully, leaning back and regarding him with the air of a lecturer.

"Forgive me if I tell you what you already know. Sometimes we imagine our affairs are of as much interest to others as they are to us, and of course they are not. However, most of the world is familiar with the romance of Friedrich and Gisela, and how our crown prince fell in love with a woman his family would not accept and renounced his right to the throne rather than give her up."

Rathbone nodded. Of course, it was a story that had fascinated and bewitched Europe; it was the romance of the century, which was why this woman's accusation of murder was so absurd and unbelievable. Only innate good manners prevented him from stopping her and asking her to leave.

"You must understand that our country is very small," she

continued, amusement on her lips as if she understood his skepticism completely, and yet also an urgency, as if in spite of her intellectual awareness it mattered to her passionately that he believe her. "And situated in the heart of the German states." Her eyes did not leave his face. "On all sides of us are other protectorates and principalities. We are all in upheaval. Most of Europe is. But unlike France or Britain or Austria, we are faced with the possibility of being united, whether we like it or not, and forming one great state of Germany. Some of us do like it." Her lips tightened. "Some of us do not."

"Has this really to do with Princess Gisela and the death of Friedrich?" he interrupted. "Are you saying it was a political murder?"

"No, of course not! How could you be so naive?" she said with exasperation.

Suddenly he wondered how old she was. What had happened to her in her life? Whom had she loved or hated; what extravagant dreams had she pursued and won, or lost? She moved like a young woman, with an ease and pride, as if her body were supple. Yet her voice had not the timbre of youth, and her eyes had far too much knowledge and too much wit and assurance to be immature.

The response that rose to his lips was stiff, and he knew before he spoke that he would sound offended. He changed his mind.

"The jury will be naive, madam," he pointed out, carefully keeping his face expressionless. "Explain to me—to us, the jury—why the princess for whom Prince Friedrich gave up his crown and his country should, after twelve years of marriage, suddenly murder her husband. It seems to me she would have everything to lose. What can you persuade me she has to gain?"

Outside, the dull rumble of the traffic was broken by a drayman's shout.

The amusement faded in her eyes.

"We must go back to politics, but not because this was a political murder," she said obediently. "On the contrary, it was highly personal. Gisela was a totally material woman. There are very few political women, you know? Most of us are far too immediate and too practical. Still, that is not a crime." She dismissed it. "I need to explain the politics to you so you will understand what she had to lose . . . and to gain." She rearranged herself slightly in the chair. Even the very small hoop of her skirt seemed to annoy her, as if it was an affectation she would sooner have done without.

"Would you care for tea?" he offered. "I can have Simms bring a tray."

"I should only talk too much and allow it to go cold," she responded. "I loathe cold tea. But thank you for the offer. You have beautiful manners, so very correct. Nothing ruffles you. That is the stiff upper lip you English are so famous for. I find it infuriating and charming at the same time."

To his fury, he felt himself blushing.

She ignored it, although she undoubtedly noticed.

"King Karl is not in good health," she said, resuming the story. "He never has been. And quite frankly, we all know that he will not live more than another two or three years, at the most. Since Friedrich abdicated, Karl will now be succeeded by his younger son, Crown Prince Waldo. Waldo is not against unification. He sees that it has certain advantages. Fighting against it unquestionably would have many disadvantages—such as the likelihood of a war, which we would eventually lose. The only people who would be certain to profit would be arms manufacturers and their like." Her face was heavy with contempt.

"Princess Gisela." He brought her back to the subject.

"I was coming to her. Friedrich was for independence, even at the price of fighting. There were many of us who felt as he did, most particularly in and about the court."

"But not Waldo? Surely he had most to lose?"

"People see love of their country in different ways, Sir Oliver," she said with sudden gravity. "For some it is to fight for independence, even to give our lives for it if necessary." She looked at him very directly. "For Queen Ulrike it is to live a certain kind of way, to exercise self-control, mastery of will, to spend her whole life trying to connive and coerce what she sees as right. To make sure everyone else behaves according to a code of honor she holds dear above all things." She was watching him closely, judging his reactions. "To Waldo it is that his people should have bread on their tables and be able to sleep in their beds without fear. I think he would like them to be able to read and write whatever they believe also, but that may be asking for too much." There was an unreadable sadness behind her green eyes. "No one has everything. But I think Waldo may be rather more realistic. He will not have us all drown trying to hold back a tide which he believes is bound to come in, whatever we do."

"And Gisela?" he asked yet again, as much to bring his own mind to the subject as hers.

"Gisela has no patriotism!" she spat, her face tight and hard. "If she had, she would never have tried to be queen. She wanted it for herself, not for her people—or for independence or unification or anything political or national, just for the allure."

"You dislike her," Rathbone observed mildly.

She laughed, her face seemingly transformed, but the relentless anger was only just behind the amusement. "I loathe her. But that is beside the point. It does not make what I say true or untrue. . . ."

"But it will prejudice a jury," he pointed out. "They may think you speak from envy."

She was silent for a moment.

He waited. No sound penetrated from the office beyond the door, and the traffic in the street had resumed its steady noise.

"You are right," she admitted. "How tedious to have to consider such logicalities, but I can see it is necessary."

"Gisela, if you please. Why should she wish to murder Friedrich? Not because he was for independence, even at the cost of war?"

"No, and yet indirectly, yes."

"Very clear," he said with a whisper of sarcasm. "Please explain yourself."

"I am trying to!" Impatience flared in her eyes. "There is a considerable faction which would fight for independence. They need a leader around whom to gather—"

"I see. Friedrich—the original crown prince! But he abdicated. He lives in exile."

She leaned forward, her face eager.

"But he could return."

"Could he?" Again he was doubtful. "What about Waldo? And the Queen?"

"That's it!" she said almost jubilantly. "Waldo would fight against it, not for the crown but to avoid a war with Prussia or whoever else was first to try to swallow us. But the Queen would ally with Friedrich for the cause of independence."

"Then Gisela could be queen on the King's death," Rathbone pointed out. "Didn't you say that was what she wanted?"

She looked at him with gleaming eyes, green and brilliant, but her face was filled with exaggerated patience.

"The Queen will not tolerate Gisela in the country. If Friedrich comes back, he must come alone. Rolf Lansdorff, the Queen's brother, who is extremely powerful, is also for Friedrich's return, but would never tolerate Gisela. He believes Waldo is weak and will lead us to ruin."

"And would Friedrich return without Gisela, for his country's sake?" he asked doubtfully. "He gave up the throne for her once. Would he now go back on that?"

She looked at him steadily. Her face was extraordinary; there was so much force of conviction in it, of emotion and will. When she spoke of Gisela it was ugly, the nose too large, too long, the eyes too widely spaced. When she spoke of her country, of love, of duty, she was beautiful. Compared with her, everyone else seemed ungenerous, insipid. Rathbone was quite unaware of the traffic beyond the window, the clatter of hooves, the occasional call of voices, the sunlight on the glass, or of Simms and the other clerks in the office beyond the door. He was thinking only of a small German principality and the struggle for power and survival, the loves and hates of a royal family, and the passion which fired this woman in front of him and made her more exciting and more profoundly alive than anyone else he could think of. He felt the surge of it run through his own blood.

"Would he go back on that?" he repeated.

A curious look of pain, pity, almost embarrassment, crossed her face. For the first time she did not look directly at him, as though she wished to shield her inner feelings from his perception.

"Friedrich has always believed in his heart that his country would want him back one day and that when that time came, they would accept Gisela also and see her worth—as he does, of course, not as it is. He lived on those dreams. He promised her it would be so. Every year he would say it yet again." She met Rathbone's eyes. "So to answer your question, he would not see returning to Felzburg as going back on his commitment to Gisela but as returning in triumph with her at his side, vindicating all he had ever believed. But she is not a fool. She knows it would never be so. He would return, and she would be denied entrance, publicly humiliated. He would be astounded, dismayed, distraught, but by then Rolf Lansdorff and the Queen would see to it that he did not renounce a second time."

"You believe that is what would have happened?" he asked quietly.

"We shall never know, shall we?" Zorah said with a curious, bleak smile. "He is dead."

The impact of it shook Rathbone suddenly and forcibly. Now murder did not seem so unreasonable. People had been killed for immeasurably less.

"I see," he said very soberly. "That does make a very strong argument which a jury of ordinary men from any street would grasp." He folded his hands into a steeple and leaned his elbows on the desk. "Now, why should they believe it was the unfortunate widow who committed murder, and not some follower of Prince Waldo or of any other German power who believes in unification? Surely they also have powerful motives? Countless murders have been committed for the gain or loss of a kingdom, but would Gisela really kill Friedrich rather than lose him?"

Her strong, slender fingers grasped the arms of the leather chair as she leaned forward towards him, her face intent.

"Yes!" she said unwaveringly. "She doesn't care a fig about Felzburg, or any of us. If he returns now, renouncing her—whether it was by his own will or by coercion is immaterial; the world won't know or care—then the whole dream crumbles, the great love story falls apart. She is a pathetic, even ridiculous figure, a woman abandoned after twelve years of marriage, no longer in her first youth."

Her face sharpened, her voice grew husky. "On the other hand, if she is widowed, then she is the great figure of domestic tragedy again, the center of admiration and envy. She has mystery, allure. And she is free to offer her favor to admirers or not, as long as she is discreet. She goes down in legend as one of the world's great lovers, to be remembered in song and story. Who would not in their hearts envy that? It is a kind of immortality. Above all, one remembers her with awe, with respect. No one laughs. And of course," she added, "she has his private fortune."

"I see." He was convinced in spite of himself. She had his total attention, his intellect and his emotion. He could not help imagining the passions which had moved the Prince at first, his overwhelming love for a woman, so intense he had sacrificed a country and a throne for her. What must she be like? What radiance of character, what unique charms, had she to inspire such a love?

Was she something like Zorah Rostova herself, so intensely alive she awoke in him dreams and hungers he had not even realized he possessed? Did she fill him with vitality also, and make him believe in himself, see in a wild glance all that he could be or become? What sleepless nights had he spent, struggling between duty and desire? How had he compared the thought of a life devoted to the court—the daily, endless formalities, the distance which must inevitably surround a king, the loneliness of being without the woman he loved—and the temptation of a life in exile with the constant companionship of such an extraordinary lover? They would grow old together, separated from family and country, and yet never alone. Except for the guilt. Did he feel guilt for having chosen the path of his longing, not his duty?

And the woman. What choices had she faced? Or was it for her simply a battle, win or lose? Was Zorah right, had Gisela wanted desperately to be queen—and lost? Or had she only loved the man and been prepared to be painted the villainess by her country as long as she could love him and be with him? Was she now a woman whose life was ended by grief? Or was it a circumstance brought about by her own hand, either as the only alternative to being left, the very public end of the great royal romance, not in the grand tragedy of death but in the pathetic anticlimax of being deserted?

"So you will take my case?" Zorah said after several minutes.

"Perhaps," he said cautiously, although he could feel an excitement of challenge wakening inside him, a breath of danger which he had to admit was exhilarating. "You have convinced me she may have had a reason, not yet that she did." He steadied his voice. He must appear cool. "What evidence have you that Friedrich indeed intended to return, even given Queen Ulrike's stipulation that he leave Gisela to do it?"

She bit her lip. Anger flickered across her face, then laughter.

"None," she admitted. "But Rolf Lansdorff was there that month, at the Wellboroughs' house, and he spoke frequently with Friedrich. It is reasonable to suppose he put it to him. We can never know what Friedrich would have said had he lived. He is dead—is that not enough for you?"

"To suspect, yes." He too leaned forward. "But it is not proof. Who else was there? What happened? Give me details, evidence, not emotion."

She looked at him long and levelly.

"Who was there?" She raised her eyebrows slightly. "It was late spring. It was a country house party at the home of Lord and Lady Wellborough." Her mouth twisted in a wry, amused smile. "Not a suspect. Lord Wellborough manufactures and deals in guns. A war, any war, except in England, will suit him very well."

Rathbone winced.

"You asked for realism," she pointed out. "Or does that fall into the category of emotion? You seem to feel some emotion, Sir Oliver." Now there was mocking amusement plain in her eyes.

He was not prepared to tell her the repugnance he felt. Wellborough was an Englishman. Rathbone was profoundly ashamed that any Englishman should be happy to profit from the killing of people, so long as it did not touch him. There were all manner of sophisticated arguments about necessity, inevitability, choice and liberty. He still found the profit in it repellent. But he could not tell this extraordinary woman this.

"I was playing the part of the jury," he said smoothly. "Now I am counsel again. Continue with your list of guests, if you please."

She relaxed. "Of course. There was Rolf Lansdorff, as I

have said before. He is the Queen's brother, and extremely powerful. He has considerable disdain for Prince Waldo. He considers him weak, and would prefer Friedrich to return—without Gisela, naturally. Although I am not sure if that is for reasons of his own or because Ulrike would not tolerate it, and she wears the crown, not he."

"Or the King?"

Now her smile was genuinely amused, close to laughter.

"I think it is a long time, Sir Oliver, since the King went against the Queen's wishes. She is cleverer than he, but he is clever enough to know it. And at present he is too ill to fight for or against anything. But what I meant was that Rolf is not royalty. And close as he is, there is all the difference in the world between a crowned head and an uncrowned one. When the will is there and the fight is real, Ulrike will win, and Rolf has too much pride to begin a battle he must lose."

"She hates Gisela so much?" He found it hard to imagine. Something very deep must lie between the two women that one would hate the other sufficiently to refuse her return, even if it meant the possible victory of those who favored independence.

"Yes, she does," Zorah replied. "But I think you misunderstand, at least in part. She does not believe that Gisela would add to the cause. She is not a fool, nor a woman to put personal feelings, no matter what they are, before duty. I thought I explained that. Did you doubt me?"

He shifted position slightly.

"I believe everything only provisionally, ma'am. This seemed to be a contradiction. Nevertheless, proceed. Who else was there, apart from Prince Friedrich and Princess Gisela, Count Lansdorff, and, of course, yourself?"

"Count Klaus von Seidlitz was there with his wife, Evelyn," she resumed.

"His political position?"

"He was against Friedrich's return. I think he is undecided

about unification, but he does not believe that Friedrich would resume the succession without causing great upheaval—and possibly civil division, which could only be to our enemies' advantage."

"Is he correct? Might it produce civil war?"

"More guns for Lord Wellborough?" she said quickly. "I don't know. I think internal disunity and indecision might be more likely."

"And his wife? Has she loyalties?"

"Only to the good life."

It was a harsh judgment, but he saw no softening of it in her face.

"I see. Who else?"

"The Baroness Brigitte von Arlsbach, whom the Queen originally chose for Friedrich before he renounced everything for Gisela."

"Did she love him?"

A curious look crossed her face.

"I never thought so, although she has never married since."

"And if he left Gisela, might he in time have married her, and she become queen?"

Again the idea seemed to amuse her, but it was a laughter that showed awareness of pain.

"Yes. I suppose that is what would have happened if he had lived, and gone home, and Brigitte had felt it her duty. And she might have, to strengthen the throne. Although possibly he would have found it politic to take a younger wife so that he might produce an heir. The throne must have an heir. Brigitte is now nearer forty than thirty. Old, for a first child. But she is very popular in the country, very admired."

"Friedrich has no children with Gisela?"

"No. Nor has Waldo."

"Waldo is married?"

"Oh, yes, to Princess Gertrudis. I would like to say I dislike her, but I cannot." She laughed self-mockingly. "She is everything I think I detest and find irretrievably tedious. She is domestic, obedient, pleasant-tempered, becomingly dressed and handsome to look at, and civil to everyone. She always seems to have the appropriate thing to say—and says it."

He was amused.

"And you think that tedious?"

"Incredibly. Ask any woman, Sir Oliver. If she is honest, she will tell you such a creature is an affront to ordinary nature."

He immediately thought of Hester Latterly, independent, arbitrary, opinionated, definitely short-tempered when she perceived stupidity, cruelty, cowardice or hypocrisy. He could not imagine her being obedient to anyone. She must have been a nightmare to the army when she served in its hospitals. All the same, he found himself smiling at the thought of her. She would have agreed with Zorah.

"Someone you are fond of has come to your mind," Zorah cut across his thoughts, and again he felt the color mount up his face.

"Tell me why you still find yourself liking Gertrudis," he said somewhat irritably.

She laughed with delight at his predicament.

"Because she has the most marvelous sense of humor," she replied. "It is as simple as that. And it is very difficult not to like someone who likes you and who can see the absurd in life and enjoy it."

He was obliged to agree with her, although he would rather not have. It was disturbing; it threw him off balance. He returned abruptly to his earlier question.

"What does Brigitte wish? Does she have allegiances, desires for independence or unification? Does she want to be queen? Or is that a foolish question?"

"No, it is not foolish at all. I don't think she wishes to be queen, but she would do it if she felt it her duty," Zorah replied, all laughter vanished from her face. "Publicly, she would have liked Friedrich to return and lead the fight for independence.

Personally, I think she might have preferred he remain in exile. It would then not have placed on her the burden and the humiliation of having to marry him, if that proved to be what the country wanted."

"Humiliation?" Her remark was incomprehensible. "How can marrying a king, because you are beloved of the people, be a humiliation?"

"Very easily," she said sharply, a stinging contempt at his obtuseness in her eyes. "No woman worth a sou would willingly marry a man who has publicly sacrificed a throne and a country for someone else. Would you wish to marry a woman who was half of one of the world's great love stories, when you were not the other half?"

He felt foolish. His lack of perception opened up in front of him like an abyss. A man might want power, office, public recognition. He should have known a woman wanted love, and if she could not have the reality, then at least the outer semblance of it. He did not know many women well, but he had thought he knew about them. He had tried enough cases involving women at their most wicked or vulnerable, passionate or cold-blooded, innocent or manipulative, clever or blindly, unbelievably silly. And yet Hester still confused him . . . at times.

"Can you imagine being made love to by someone who is making love to you because it is a duty?" Zorah continued mercilessly. "It would make me sick! Like going to bed with a corpse."

"Please!" he expostulated vehemently. One moment she was as delicate in her perception as the touch of a butterfly, the next she said something so coarse as to be disgusting. It made him acutely uncomfortable. "I have understood your argument, madam. There is no need for illustration." He lowered his tone and controlled it with difficulty. He must not allow her to see how she rattled him. "Are those all the people who were present at this unfortunate house party?"

She sighed. "No. Stephan von Emden was there as well. He is from one of the old families. And Florent Barberini. His mother is distantly related to the king, and his father is Venetian. There is no purpose in your asking me what they think, because I don't know. But Stephan is an excellent friend to me, and will assist you in my case. He has already promised as much."

"Good!" he said. "Because, believe me, you will need all the friends and all the assistance you can acquire!"

She saw that she had annoyed him.

"I'm sorry," she said gravely, her eyes suddenly soft and rueful. "I spoke too bluntly, didn't I? I only wanted to make you understand. No, that is not true." She gave a little grunt of anger. "I am furious over what they would do to Brigitte, and I desire you to come out of your masculine complacency and understand it too. I like you, Sir Oliver. You have a certain aplomb, an ice-cool Englishness about you which is most attractive." She smiled suddenly and radiantly.

He swore under his breath. He hated such open flattery, and he hated still more the acute state of pleasure it gave him.

"You wish to know what happened?" she went on imperturbably, settling a little back in her seat. "It was the third day after the last of us arrived. We were out riding, rather hard, I admit. We went across the fields and took several hedges at a gallop. Friedrich's horse fell and he was thrown." A shadow of distress crossed her face. "He landed badly. The horse scrambled to its feet again, and Friedrich's leg was caught in the stirrup iron. He was dragged several yards before the animal was secured so we could free him."

"Gisela was there?" he interrupted.

"No. She doesn't ride if she can avoid it, and then only at a walk in some fashionable park or parade. She is a woman for art and artifice, not for nature. Her pursuits all have a very serious purpose and are social, not physical." If she was trying to keep the contempt out of her voice she did not succeed.

"So she could not conceivably have caused the accident?"

"No. So far as I am aware, it was truly mischance, not aided by anyone."

"You took Friedrich back to the house?"

"Yes. It seemed the only thing to do."

"Was he conscious?"

"Yes. Why?"

"I can't think of any reason. He must have been in great pain."

"Yes." Now there was unmistakable admiration in her face. "Friedrich may have been a fool in some ways, but he never lacked physical courage. He bore it very well."

"You called a doctor immediately, of course?"

"Naturally. Gisela was distraught, before you ask me." A faint smile flickered across her mouth. "She never left his side. But that was not unusual. They were seldom apart at any time. That seemed to be his wish as much as hers, perhaps more. Certainly no one could fault her as the most diligent and attentive nurse."

Rathbone returned the smile. "Well, if you could not, I doubt anyone else will."

She held up one finger delicately. "Touché, Sir Oliver."

"And how did she murder him?"

"Poison, of course." Her eyebrows rose in surprise that he should have needed to ask. "What did you imagine, that I thought she took a pistol from the gun room and shot him? She wouldn't know how to load it. She would barely know which end to point." Again the contempt was there. "And Dr. Gallagher might be a fool, but not so big a one as to miss a bullet wound in a corpse that is supposed to have died of a fall from a horse."

"Doctors have been known to miss a broken bone in the neck before now," Rathbone said, justifying himself. "Or a suffocation when a person was ill anyway and they did not expect him to make an easy recovery."

She pulled a face. "I daresay. I cannot imagine Gisela suffocating him, and she certainly wouldn't know how to break a bone in his neck. That sounds like an assassin's trick."

"So you deduce that she poisoned him?" he said quietly, making no reference to how she might know anything about assassins.

She stopped, staring at him with steady, brilliant eyes.

"Too perceptive, Sir Oliver," she conceded with a sting. "Yes, I deduce it. I have no proof. If I had, I would not have accused her publicly, I would simply have gone to the police. She would have been charged, and all this would not have been necessary."

"Why is it necessary?" he said bluntly.

"The cause of justice?" She tilted her head a little to one side. It was quite definitely a question.

"No," he said.

"Oh. You don't believe I would do this for the love of justice?"

"No, I don't."

She sighed. "You are quite right; I would leave God or the devil to take care of it when it suited them."

"So why, madam?" he pressed. "You do it at very great risk to yourself. If you cannot defend your claim, you will be ruined, not only financially but socially. You may even face criminal charges. It is a very serious slander, and you have made it highly public."

"Well, there's hardly any point in doing it privately!" she retorted, wide-eyed.

"And what is the point in doing it at all?"

"To oblige her to defend herself, of course. Is that not obvious?"

"But it is you who have to defend yourself. You are the one accused."

"By the law, yes, but she is accused by me, and in order to appear innocent to the world, she will have to prove me a liar."

Her expression suggested that hers had been the most reasonable of acts, as should be plain enough to anyone.

"No, she doesn't," he contradicted. "She simply has to prove that you have said these things about her and that they have damaged her. It is you who have the burden of proof as to whether they are true. If you leave any doubt, the case is hers. She does not have to prove them untrue."

"Not in law, Sir Oliver, but before the world, of course she does. Can you see her, or anyone, leaving court with the question still open?"

"I confess it is unlikely, although it is possible. But she will almost certainly counter by attacking you, accusing you of motives of your own for having made the charge in the first place," he warned. "You must be prepared for a very ugly battle which will become as personal to you as you have made it to her. Are you prepared for that?"

She took a deep breath and straightened her thin shoulders.

"Yes, I am."

"Why are you doing this, Countess?" He had to ask. It was bizarre and dangerous. She had a unique and reckless face, but she was not foolish. She might not know the law, but she certainly knew the ways of the world.

Her face was suddenly totally serious, naked of all humor or contention.

"Because she has used a man to his destruction, and that man, for all his folly and self-indulgence, should have been our king. I will not allow the world to see her as one of the great lovers, when she is an ambitious and greedy woman who loves herself before anyone, or anything, else. I hate hypocrisy. If you cannot believe I love justice, perhaps you can believe that?"

"I can believe it, madam," he said without hesitation. "So do I. And so, I profoundly believe, does the average British jury." He meant that with a passion and total sincerity.

"Then you will take my case?" she urged. It was a challenge, defying his safety, his correctness, his years of brilliant but always appropriate behavior.

"I will." He accepted without even hesitating. There was the moral point that if the case were to be tried in an English court, then for the reputation both of Gisela, if she was innocent, and, more precious to him, of the law, both sides must be represented by the best counsel possible. Otherwise the issue would never be settled in the public mind. Its ghost would arise again and again.

There was a danger in it, certainly, but of the kind which quickened the blood and made one aware of the infinite value of life.

Zorah had left her card with him. He called upon her in her London rooms the following afternoon, having sent a note in advance to inform her of his intention.

She received him with an enthusiasm most well-bred ladies would have considered unbecoming. But he had long ago learned that people who are facing trial, civil or criminal, frequently wear their fear in ways that might lie outside their usual character. If one looked carefully, it was always a facet of something that was there, perhaps hidden in less stressful times. Fear was the most universal stripper of disguise and the self-protection of contrived attitudes.

"Sir Oliver! I am delighted you have come," she said immediately. "I took the liberty of asking Baron Stephan von Emden to join us. It will save having to send for him, and I am sure you have no time to waste. If you should wish to speak privately, I have another chamber where we may do so." And she turned and led him through a vestibule of rather formal and uninteresting character into a room of so extraordinary a decor he drew in his breath involuntarily. The farther wall was hung with a gigantic shawl woven in russets, Indian reds, bitter chocolate browns and stark black. It had a long, silk fringe which hung in complicated woven knots. There was a silver samovar on an ebony table, and on the floor a series of bearskin rugs, again of warm browns. A red leather couch was swamped in embroidered cushions, each different.

By one of the two tall windows stood a young man with fair brown hair and a charming face, at the moment filled with concern.

"Baron Stephan von Emden," Zorah said almost casually. "Sir Oliver Rathbone."

"How do you do, Sir Oliver." Stephan bowed from the waist and brought his heels together, but almost silently. "I am enormously relieved that you are going to defend the Countess Rostova." The sincerity of this remark was apparent in his face. "It is an extraordinarily difficult situation. Anything I can do to help, I will, gladly."

"Thank you," Rathbone accepted, uncertain if this was merely a show of friendship or if there could be anything whatever the young baron might achieve. Remembering Zorah's own candor, he spoke directly. It was a room in which it was impossible to be halfhearted. One would either be honest, whatever the consequences, or else be appalled and retract entirely. "Do you believe the Princess to be guilty of having murdered her husband?"

Stephan looked startled, then a flash of humor lit his eyes.

Zorah let out her breath in a sigh, possibly of approval.

"I've no idea," Stephan replied, his eyes wide. "But I have no doubt whatever that Zorah believes it, so I expect it is true. I am sure she did not say it either lightly or maliciously."

Rathbone judged he was in his early thirties, probably ten years younger than Zorah, and he wondered what their relationship might be. Why was he prepared to risk his name and reputation supporting a woman who made such a claim? Could it be that he was sure, not only that she was correct, but also that it could be proved? Or had he some more emotional, less rational motive, a love or a hate of someone in this tragedy?

"Your confidence is very assuring," Rathbone said politely.

"Your help will be greatly appreciated. What have you in mind?"

If he had expected Stephan to be thrown off balance, he was disappointed. Stephan straightened up from the rather relaxed attitude he had adopted and walked towards the chair in the center of the room. He sat sideways on it and looked at Rathbone intently.

"I thought you might wish to send someone—discreetly, of course—to the Wellboroughs' to ask questions of all the people who were there at the time. Most of them will be there again because of this furor, of course. I can tell you everything I can remember, but I imagine my evidence would be considered biased, and you'll need a great deal more than that." He shrugged his slim shoulders. "Anyway, I don't know anything useful, or I would have told Zorah already. I don't know what to look for. But I do know everyone, and I would vouch for anyone you cared to send. Go with him, if you wish."

Rathbone was surprised. It was a generous offer. He could see nothing in Stephan's hazel-gold eyes but candor and a slight concern.

"Thank you," he accepted. "That might be an excellent idea." He thought of Monk. If anyone could find and retrieve evidence of the truth, good or bad, it would be he. Nor would the magnitude of the case and its possible repercussions frighten him. "Although it may not be sufficient. This will be an extremely difficult case to prove. A great many vested interests lie against us."

Stephan frowned. "Of course." He regarded Rathbone very seriously. "I am most grateful you have the courage, Sir Oliver. Many a lesser man would have balked at trying. I am completely at your service, sir, at any time."

He was so utterly serious Rathbone could only thank him again and turn to Zorah, who was now sitting on the red sofa, leaning back against the arm of it, her body relaxed amid her billowing, tawny skirts, her face tense, her eyes on Rathbone's.

She was smiling, but there was no laughter in her, no brilliance or ease.

"We will have other friends," she said in her slightly husky voice. "But very few. People believe what they need to, or what they have committed themselves to. I have enemies, but so has Gisela. There are many old scores to settle, old injuries, old loves and hates. And there are those whose only interest will be in the politics of the future, whether we remain independent or are swallowed up in a greater Germany, and who will win the profits of that battle. You will need to be both brave and clever."

Her remarkable face softened till she looked more than beautiful. There was a radiance in her. "But, then, if I had not believed you to be both, I should not have come to you. We shall give them a great fight, shall we not? No one shall murder a man, and a prince, while we stand by and allow the world to think it an accident. God, I hate a hypocrite! We shall have honesty. It is worth living and dying for, isn't it?"

"Of course," Rathbone said with absolute conviction.

That evening in the long summer twilight he went out to see his father, who lived to the north of London in Primrose Hill. It took him some time, and he did not hurry. He traveled in an open gig, light and fast, easy to maneuver through the traffic of barouches and landaus as people took the air in the dappled sunlight of tree-lined avenues or made their way home after the heat of a day in the city. He seldom drove, he had not the time, but he enjoyed it when he did. He had a light hand, and the pleasure was well worth the price of the hire from a local stable.

Henry Rathbone had retired from his various mathematical and inventive pursuits. He still occasionally looked through his telescope at the stars, but merely for interest. On this evening, when Oliver arrived he was in his garden, standing on the long lawn looking towards the honeysuckle hedge at the bottom and the apple trees in the orchard beyond. It had been rather a dry season, and he was pondering whether the fruit would swell to an acceptable quality. The sun was still well above the horizon, blazing gold and sending long shadows across the grass. He was a tall man, taller than his son, square-shouldered and thin. He had a gentle, aquiline face and farsighted blue eyes. He was obliged to remove his spectacles to study anything closely.

"Good evening, Father." Rathbone walked down the lawn to join him. The butler had conducted him through the house and out of the open French doors.

Henry turned with slight surprise. "I wasn't expecting you. I've only got bread and cheese for dinner, and a little rather good pâté. Got a decent red wine, though, if you feel like it."

"Thank you," Oliver accepted immediately.

"Bit dry for the fruit," Henry went on, turning back to the trees. "But still got a few strawberries, I think."

"Thank you," Oliver repeated. Now that he was here, he was not quite sure how to begin. "I've taken a slander case."

"Oh. Is your client plaintiff or defendant?" Henry started to amble gently back towards the house, the sun casting long shadows in the gold-green grass and making the spires of the delphiniums almost luminous.

"Defendant," Oliver replied.

"Who did he slander?"

"She," Oliver corrected. "Princess Gisela of Felzburg."

Henry stopped and turned to face him. "You haven't taken up the Countess Zorah's defense, have you?"

Oliver stopped also. "Yes. She's convinced Gisela killed Friedrich and that it can be proved." He realized as he said it that that was rather an overstatement. It was a belief and a determination. There was still doubt.

Henry was very grave, his brow wrinkled.

"I do hope you are being wise, Oliver. Perhaps you had better tell me more about it, assuming that it is not in confidence?"

"No, not at all. I think she would like it as widely known as possible." He started to walk again up the slight slope towards the French doors and the familiar room with its easy chairs by the fireplace, the pictures and the case full of books.

Henry frowned. "Why? I assume you have some idea of her reasons for this? Insanity isn't a defense for slander, is it?"

Oliver looked at him for a moment before he was quite sure there was a dry, rather serious humor behind the remark.

"No, of course not. And she won't retract. She is convinced that Princess Gisela murdered Prince Friedrich, and she won't allow the hypocrisy and injustice of it to pass unchallenged." He took a breath. "Neither will I."

They went up the steps and inside. They did not close the doors; the evening was still warm, and the air smelled sweet from the garden.

"That is what she told you?" Henry asked, going to the hall door and opening it to tell the butler that Oliver would be staying to dinner.

"You doubt it?" Oliver asked, sitting in the second-most comfortable chair.

Henry returned. "I take it with circumspection." He sat down in the best chair and crossed his legs, but he did not relax. "What do you know of her relationship with Prince Friedrich, for example, before Gisela married him?" he asked, looking gravely at Oliver.

Oliver repeated what Zorah had told him.

"Are you sure that Zorah didn't want to marry Friedrich?"

"Of course she didn't," Oliver said. "She is the last sort of woman to wish to be restricted by the bounds of royal protocol. She has a hunger for freedom, a passion for life far too big for . . ." He hesitated, aware from the look in his father's eyes that he was betraying himself.

"Perhaps," Henry said thoughtfully. "But it is still possible to resent someone else taking something from you, even if you don't especially want it yourself."

2

MONK RECEIVED THE LETTER from Oliver Rathbone with interest. It came with the first post when he had only just finished breakfast. He read it still standing by the table.

Rathbone's cases were always serious ones, frequently involving violent crime, intense emotions, and they tested Monk's abilities to the limit. He liked finding the outer limits of his skill, his imagination, and his mental and physical endurance. He needed to learn about himself far more than most men because a carriage accident three years before had robbed him of every shred of his memory. Except for the flickers, the remnants of light and shadow which danced across his mind, elusively, without warning every now and then, there was nothing. Occasionally those memories were pleasant, like the ones from childhood of his mother, his sister, Beth, and the wild Northumberland coast with its bare sands and infinite horizon. He heard the sound of gulls and saw in his mind's eye the painted wood of fishing boats riding the gray-green water, and smelled the salt wind over the heather.

Other memories were less agreeable: his quarrels with Runcorn, his superior while he was on the police force. He had sudden moments of understanding that Runcorn's resentment of him was in large part provoked by his own arrogance. He had been impatient with Runcorn's slightly slower mind. He had mocked his boss's social ambition, and had used his knowledge of the vulnerability which Runcorn had never been able to hide. Had their roles been reversed, Monk would have hated Runcorn just as much as Runcorn hated him. That was the painful part of it: he disliked so much of what he learned of himself. Of course, there had been good things as well. No one had ever denied he had courage and intelligence, or that he was honest. Sometimes he told the truth as he saw it when it would have been kinder, and certainly wiser, to have kept silence.

He had learned a little of his other relationships, particularly with women. None of them had been very fortunate. He seemed to have fallen in love with women who were softly beautiful, whose loveliness and gentle manners complemented his own strength and, in the end, whose lack of courage and passion for life had left him feeling lonelier than before, and disillusioned. Perhaps he had expected the things he valued from the wrong people. The truth was, he knew their relationships only from the cold evidence of facts, of which there were few, and the emotions of memory stirred by the women concerned. Not many of them were kind, and none explained.

With Hester Latterly it was different. He had met her after the accident. He knew every detail of their friendship, if that was the term for it. Sometimes it was almost enmity. He had loathed her to begin with. Even now she frequently angered him with her opinionated manner and her stubborn behavior. There was nothing romantic about her, nothing feminine or appealing. She made no concession to gentleness or to the art of pleasing.

No, that was not entirely true. When there was real pain, fear, grief or guilt, then no one on earth was stronger than Hester, no one braver or more patient. Give the devil her due—there was no one as brave . . . or as willing to forgive. He valued those qualities more than he could measure. And they also infuriated him. He was so much more attracted to women who were fun, uncritical, charming; who knew when to speak, how to flatter and laugh, how to enjoy themselves; who knew how to be vulnerable in the little things it was so easy to supply, and yet not discard the great things, the sacrifices which cost too much, asked of the fabric of his nature and his dreams.

He stood in his room, which Hester had arranged so as to be more inviting to prospective clients for his services, now that he had acrimoniously departed from the police force. Investigation, so far as he knew, was his only art. He read Rathbone's letter, which was short and lacking in detail.

Dear Monk,

I have a new case in which I require some investigation which may be complicated and delicate. The case, when it comes to trial, will be hard fought and most difficult to prove. If you are willing and able to undertake it, please present yourself at my chambers at the soonest possible moment. I shall endeavour to make myself available.

Yours,
Oliver Rathbone

It was unlike Rathbone to give so little information. He sounded anxious. If the urbane and so very slightly condescending Rathbone was worried, that in itself was sufficient to intrigue Monk. Their relationship was of grudging mutual respect tempered by spasms of antipathy born of an arrogance, an ambition, and an intelligence in common, and temperaments, social background, and professional training entirely different. It was added to by the very specific thing they shared, cases they had fought together and in which they had believed passionately, disasters and triumphs; and by a deep regard for Hester Latterly, denied by each of them as anything more than a sincere friendship.

Monk smiled to himself and, collecting his jacket, went to

the door to find a hansom cab from Fitzroy Street, where he lodged, to Vere Street and Rathbone's offices.

Monk, duly engaged by Rathbone, went to the Countess's apartments off Piccadilly just before four o'clock in the afternoon. He thought it a likely time to find her at home. And if she were not there, then she would almost certainly return in time to change for dinner—if she still continued to go out for dinner after having publicly made such a startling accusation. She would hardly be on most people's guest lists anymore.

The door was opened by a maid he assumed to be French. She was small and dark and very pretty, and he remembered from somewhere that fashionable ladies who could afford it had French maids. Certainly this girl spoke with a decided accent.

"Good afternoon, sir."

"Good afternoon." Monk did not feel it necessary to try to win anyone's liking. The Countess was the person in need of help, if she had not already placed herself beyond it. "My name is William Monk. Sir Oliver Rathbone"—he recalled the "sir" only just in time to include it—"asked me to call upon the Countess Rostova to see if I could be of assistance."

The maid smiled at him. She really was very pretty indeed.

"But of course. Please come in." She opened the door wider and held it while he passed her and walked into a spacious but unremarkable vestibule. There was a large urn of daisies of some sort on a jardiniere. He could smell the rich summery aroma of them. She closed the door, then led him straight into a farther room and invited him to wait while she summoned her mistress.

He stood and stared around him. The room was utterly alien to his taste or experience, and yet he did not feel uncomfortable. He wondered what Rathbone had made of it. It obviously belonged to someone who did not give a fig for convention. He walked over to look more closely at the ebony-fronted bookcase. The books inside were in several languages: German, French, Russian and English. There were novels, poetry, accounts of travels, and some philosophy. He took out one or two and saw that they all opened quite easily, as if they had been well handled. They were not there for effect, but because someone liked to read them.

The Countess seemed in no hurry. He was disappointed. She was going to be one of those women who kept a man waiting in order to feel some kind of mastery of the situation.

He swung around towards the room and was startled to see her standing in the doorway, absolutely still, watching him. Rathbone had not said that she was beautiful, which was an extraordinary omission. Monk did not know why, but he had imagined someone plain. She had dark hair, tied very loosely. She was of roughly average height, and had no figure to speak of, but her face was extraordinary. She had long, slightly slanted eyes of golden green above wide cheekbones. It was not so much a thing of form or color which made her so arresting as the laughter and the intelligence in her—and the sheer vibrancy of her character. She made anyone else seem slow and apathetic. He did not even notice what she was wearing; it could have been anything, fashionable or not.

She was looking at him with curiosity. She still did not move from the doorway.

"So you are the man who is going to assist Sir Oliver." She was on the brink of smiling, as if he interested and amused her. "You are not what I expected."

"Which, no doubt, I should take as a compliment," he said dryly.

This time she did laugh, a rich, slightly husky sound full of pleasure. She came in and walked easily over to the chair opposite where he stood.

"You should," she agreed. "Please sit down, Mr. Monk, unless standing makes you feel more comfortable?" She sank, in a single, graceful movement, onto the chair and sat, straight-backed, her feet sideways, staring at him. She managed her skirt as if it were only the slightest hindrance to her. "What do you wish to know from me?"

He had considered this carefully on his way over. He did not wish for emotions, opinions, convictions as to other people's motives or beliefs. There might be a time for that later, as indications of which way to look for something or how to interpret ambiguous information. From what Rathbone had told him, he had expected someone far less intelligent, but all the same he would proceed with his original plan.

He sat down on the leather-covered sofa and relaxed as if he were utterly comfortable too.

"Tell me what happened from the first incident or occasion you believe relevant. I want only what you saw or heard. Anything that you suppose or deduce can wait until later. If you say you know something, I shall expect you to be able to prove it." He watched her carefully to see irritation and surprise in her face, and did not find it.

She folded her hands, like a good schoolgirl, and began.

"We all dined together. It was an excellent party. Gisela was in good spirits and regaled us with anecdotes of life in Venice, which is where they live most of the time. The exile court is there, in so much as it is anywhere at all. Klaus von Seidlitz kept turning the conversation to politics, but we all find that a bore and no one listened to him, least of all Gisela. She made one or two rather cutting remarks about him. I can't remember now what she said, but we all thought it was funny, except Klaus himself, of course. No one likes being the butt of a joke, especially a truly amusing one."

Monk was watching her with interest. He was tempted to let his imagination wander and think what kind of woman she was when not pressed by circumstances of death, anger and a lawsuit which could ruin her. Why on earth had she chosen to speak out about her suspicions? Had she no idea what it would cost her? Was she such a fanatic patriot? Or had she once loved

Friedrich herself? What consuming passion lay behind her words?

She was talking about the following day now.

"It was mid-morning." She looked at him curiously, aware he was only half listening. "We were to have a picnic luncheon. The servants were bringing everything in the pony trap. Gisela and Evelyn were coming in a gig."

"Who is Evelyn?" he interrupted.

"Klaus von Seidlitz's wife," Zorah replied. "She doesn't ride either."

"Gisela doesn't ride?"

Amusement flickered over her face. "No. Did Sir Oliver not tell you that? There is no question of the accident's being deliberate, you know. She would never do anything so bold or so extremely risky. Not many people die in riding falls. One is far more likely to break a leg, or even one's back. The last thing she wanted was a cripple!"

"It would stop him returning home to lead the resistance to unification," he argued.

"He wouldn't have to lead them physically, riding on a white horse, you know," she said with dismissive laughter. "He could have been a figurehead for them even in a Bath chair!"

"And you believe he would have gone, even in those circumstances?"

"Certainly he would have considered it," she said without hesitation. "He never abandoned the faith that one day his country would welcome him back and that Gisela would have her rightful place beside him."

"But you told Rathbone that they would not accept her," he pointed out. "You could not be mistaken about that?"

"No."

"Then how could Friedrich still believe it?"

She shrugged very slightly. "You would have to know Friedrich to understand how he grew up. He was born to be king. He spent his entire childhood and youth being groomed for it, and the Queen is a rigid taskmistress. He obeyed every rule, and the crown was his burden and his prize."

"But he gave it all up for Gisela."

"I don't think until the very last moment he believed they would make him choose between them," she said with faint surprise in her eyes. "Then, of course, it was too late. He could never understand the finality of it. He was convinced they would relent and call him back. He saw his banishment as a gesture, not something to last forever."

"And it seems he was right," Monk pointed out. "They did want him back."

"But not at the price of bringing Gisela with him. He did not understand that—but she did. She was far more of a realist."

"The accident," he prompted.

"He was taken back to Wellborough Hall," she resumed. "The doctor was called, naturally. I don't know what he said, only what I was told."

"What were you told?" Monk asked.

"That Friedrich had broken several ribs, his right leg in three places, his right collarbone, and that he was severely bruised internally."

"Prognosis?"

"I beg your pardon?"

"What did the doctor expect of his recovery?"

"Slow, but he did not believe his life to be in danger, unless there were injuries that he had not yet determined."

"How old was Friedrich?"

"Forty-two."

"And Gisela?"

"Thirty-nine. Why?"

"So he was not a young man, for such a heavy fall."

"He did not die of his injuries. He was poisoned."

"How do you know?"

For the first time she hesitated.

He waited, looking at her steadily.

After a while she gave a very slight shrug. "If I could prove it, I would have gone to the police. I know it because I know the people. I have known them for years. I have watched the whole pattern unfold. She is performing the desolated widow very well . . . too well. She is in the center of the stage, and she is loving it."

"That may be hypocritical and unattractive," he replied. "But it is not criminal. And even that is still only belief, your perception of her."

She looked down at last. "I know that, Mr. Monk. I was there in the house all the time. I saw everyone who came and went. I heard them speak and saw their looks towards one another. I have been part of the court circle since my childhood. I know what happened, but I have not a shred of proof. Gisela murdered Friedrich because she was afraid he would hear the voice of duty at last and go home to lead the fight against unification into greater Germany. Waldo would not do it, and there is no one else. He might have thought he could take her, but she knew the Queen would never permit it, even now, on the brink of dissolution or war."

"Why did she wait for days?" he asked. "Why not kill him immediately? It would have been safer and more readily accepted."

"There was no need, if he was going to die anyway," she responded. "And to begin with we all thought he would."

"Why does the Queen hate her so much?" he probed. He could not imagine a passion so virulent it would overshadow even this crisis. He wondered whether it was the character of the Queen which nurtured it or something in Gisela which fired such a fierce emotion in Friedrich and the Queen—and seemingly in this extraordinary woman in front of him in her vivid, idiosyncratic room with its burnished shawl and unlit candles.

"I don't know." There was a slight lift of surprise in her

voice, and her eyes seemed to stare far away to some vision of the mind. "I have often wondered, but I have never heard."

"Have you any idea of the poison you believe Gisela used?"

"No. He died quite suddenly. He became giddy and cold, then went into a coma, so Gisela said. The servants who were in and out said the same. And, of course, the doctor."

"That could be dozens of things," he said grimly. "It could perfectly well be bleeding to death from internal injuries."

"Naturally!" Zorah replied with some asperity. "What would you expect? Something that looked like poison? Gisela is selfish, greedy, vain and cruel, but she is not a fool." Her face was filled with deep anger and a terrible sense of loss, as if something precious had slipped away through her fingers, even as she watched it and strove desperately to cling on. Her features, which had seemed so beautiful to him when he first came in, were now too strong, her eyes too clever, her mouth pinched hard with pain.

He rose to his feet.

"Thank you for your frank answers, Countess Rostova. I will go back to Mr. Rathbone and consider the next steps to be taken."

It was only after taking his leave, when he was outside in the sun, that he remembered he had omitted Rathbone's new title.

"I can't imagine why you took the case!" he said abruptly to Rathbone when he reported to him in his office an hour later. The clerks had all gone home, and the dying light was golden in the windows. Outside in the street the traffic was teeming, carriage wheels missing each other by inches, drivers impatient, horses hot and tired and the air sharp with droppings.

Rathbone was already on edge, aware of his own misjudgment.

"Is that your way of saying you feel it is beyond your ability to investigate?" he said coldly.

"If I had meant that, I would have said it," Monk replied,

sitting down unasked. "When did you ever know me to be indirect?"

"You mean tactful?" Rathbone's eyebrows shot up. "Never. I apologize. It was an unnecessary question. Will you investigate her claim?"

That was more bluntly put than Monk had expected. It caught him a little off guard.

"How? Unless, of course, you have formed some opinion that the original fall was contrived?"

Monk went on, "Even she is quite certain it was exactly what it seemed. She thinks Gisela poisoned him, although she doesn't know how, or with what, and has only a very general idea why."

Rathbone smiled, showing his teeth only slightly. "She has you rattled, Monk, or you would not be misquoting her so badly. She knows very precisely why. Because there was a strong possibility Friedrich might return home without her, divorcing her for his country's sake. She would cease to be one of the world's most glamorous lovers, titled, rich and envied, and would instead become an abandoned ex-wife, dependent, her erstwhile friends pitying her. It doesn't take a great leap of the imagination to understand her emotions faced with those alternatives."

"You think she killed him?" Monk was surprised, not that Rathbone should believe it, that was easy enough, but that he should be prepared to defend that belief in court. At the very kindest, it was foolish; at the unkindest, he had taken leave of his wits.

"I think it is highly probable that someone did," Rathbone corrected coldly, leaning back in his chair, his face hard. "I would like you to go to Lord and Lady Wellborough's country home, where you will be introduced by Baron Stephan von Emden, a friend of the Countess who will know who you are." He pursed his lips. "You will be able to learn all that is now possible of the events after the accident. You will have to make the opportunity to question the servants and observe the people who were there at the time, with the exception, of course, of the Princess Gisela. Apparently this accusation has brought them together again, not unnaturally, I suppose.

"I hope you will be able to deduce at least who had opportunity to have poisoned the Prince, and if anything whatever was observed that could be used in evidence. You will also question the doctor who attended the Prince and wrote the death certificate."

From outside in the street the noise of the traffic drifted up through the half-open window. In the office beyond the door there was silence.

There were many reasons to accept the case: Rathbone needed help urgently, and it would give Monk considerable satisfaction to be in a position where for once Rathbone was in his debt. Monk had no other cases of any importance at the moment and would value the occupation and the income from it. But most of all, his curiosity was so sharp he could feel it as distinctly as an itching of the skin.

"Yes, of course I will," he said with a smile, perhaps more wolfish than friendly.

"Good," Rathbone accepted. "I am obliged. I shall give you Baron von Emden's address and you can introduce yourself to him. Perhaps you could go to Wellborough Hall as his manservant?"

Monk was appalled. "What?"

"Perhaps you could go as his manservant," Rathbone repeated, his eyes wide. "It would give you an excellent opening to speak with the other servants and learn what they . . ." He stopped, the ghost of a smile on his lips. "Or you could go as an acquaintance, if you would feel more at ease. I realize you may not be familiar with the duties of a valet . . ."

Monk rose to his feet, his face set. "I shall go as his acquaintance," he said stiffly. "I shall let you know what I learn, if anything. No doubt you will be somewhat concerned to know."

And with that he bade Rathbone good night and took the piece of paper on which Rathbone had written the Baron's address from the desktop and went out.

Monk arrived at Wellborough Hall six days after Zorah Rostova walked into Rathbone's offices and requested the lawyer's help. It was now early September, golden autumn, with the stubble fields stretching into the distance, the chestnuts just beginning to turn amber and the occasional strip of newly plowed land showing rich and dark where the wet earth was ready for planting.

Wellborough Hall was a huge, spreading Georgian building of classical proportions. One approached it up a drive that was over a mile long and largely lined with elms. On either side parkland spread towards woods, and beyond that were more open fields and copses. It was easy to picture the owners of such a place entertaining royalty, riding happily amid such beauty, until tragedy had halted them, reminding them of their frailty.

Monk had called upon Stephan von Emden and found him happy to offer all the assistance he could to angle for an invitation for Monk to accompany him as his "friend" on his imminent trip to the Hall. Stephan said he was fascinated by the idea of investigation and found Monk an intriguing study, his manner of life utterly different from his own. He also explained that they were all gathering at Wellborough Hall again to make sure of their stories about Friedrich's death in case there should be a trial.

Monk felt a trifle disconcerted to be watched so closely, and as their journey continued, he had realized that Stephan was neither as casual nor as uninformed as he had at first assumed. Monk had betrayed himself, at least in his own eyes, more than once by his own prejudgments that because Stephan was titled and wealthy, he was also narrow in his outlook and relatively useless in any practical sense. Now Monk was angry with himself for allowing the restrictions of his upbringing to show. He was trying to pass himself off as a gentleman. Some part of his mind knew that gentlemen were not so brittle, so quick to assume, or so defensive of their dignity. They knew they did not need to be.

He was disgusted with himself because his prejudgments were unfair. He despised unfairness, the more so when it was also stupid.

They arrived at the magnificent entrance and stepped out of the carriage to be welcomed by a liveried footman. Monk was about to look for his very carefully packed cases when he remembered just in time that to bring them in was the valet's job, and he should not even think of doing it himself. A gentleman would walk straight into the house in the total trust that servants would see that his belongings were taken to his room, unpacked and everything put in its appropriate place.

They were welcomed by Lady Wellborough, a far younger woman than Monk had expected. She looked no more than in her middle thirties, slender, fractionally above average height, with thick brown hair. She was comely enough to look at, but not beautiful. Her chief charms lay in her intelligence and vitality. The moment she saw them she sailed down the marvelous staircase with its wrought iron railing gleaming with the occasional gold. Her face was alight with enthusiasm.

"My dear Stephan!" Her gigantic skirts swirled around her, the hoops springing back as she stopped. Her gown had a separate bodice, as was now fashionable, large sleeved, tight waisted, showing off her slenderness. "How wonderful to see you," she went on. "And this must be your friend Mr. Monk." She looked at Monk with great interest, eyeing his smooth, high-boned cheeks, slightly aquiline nose and sardonic mouth. He had seen that look of surprise in women's eyes before, as if they saw in him something they had not expected, but against their judgment could not dislike.

He inclined his head.

"How do you do, Lady Wellborough. It was most generous of you to permit me to join you this weekend. Already I am more than rewarded."

She smiled widely. It was a most engaging expression and entirely unstudied.

"I hope you will find yourself much more so before you leave." She turned to Stephan. "Thank you, you have done particularly well this time, my dear. Allsop will show you upstairs, although I'm sure you know the way." She looked back at Monk. "Dinner is at nine. We shall all be in the withdrawing room by about eight, I should imagine. Count Lansdorff and Baron von Seidlitz went out walking, towards the weekend shoot, I think. See the lie of the land. Do you shoot, Mr. Monk?"

Monk had no memory of ever having shot, and his social position made it almost impossible that he would have had the opportunity.

"No, Lady Wellborough. I prefer sports of a more equal match."

"Oh, my goodness!" She laughed in high good humor. "Bare-knuckle boxing? Or horse racing? Or billiards?"

He had no idea if he had skill in any of these either. He had spoken too quickly, and now risked making a fool of himself.

"I shall attempt whatever is offered," he replied, feeling the color burn up his cheeks. "Except where I am likely to endanger the other guests by my lack of proficiency."

"How original!" she exclaimed. "I shall look forward to dinner."

Monk already dreaded it.

It turned out to be every bit as testing to his nerves as he had expected. He looked well. He knew that from the glass. As far as he was aware, he had spent much of his professional life in the police force and he had always been personally vain. His wardrobe and his tailor's, bootmaker's and shirtmaker's bills attested to that. He must have spent a great deal of his salary on his appearance. He had no need to borrow in order to present himself at this house respectably attired.

But conducting himself at table was another matter. These people all knew each other and had an entire lifestyle in common, not to mention hundreds of acquaintances. They would know within ten minutes that he was an outsider in every sense. What conceivable excuse could he find, not only to preserve his pride, but to fulfill his purpose and save Rathbone's extraordinarily stupid neck?

There were only nine of them at the dinner table, an extremely small number for a country house party, although it was early September, and therefore still the tail end of the London season, and too early for the great winter house parties where guests frequently stayed for a month or more, coming and going as they pleased.

Monk had been introduced to them all, quite casually, as if one might have expected him to be here and it needed no explanation. Opposite him at the table sat Friedrich's uncle, Queen Ulrike's brother, Count Rolf Lansdorff. He was a fairly tall man with military bearing, dark hair smoothed close to his head and receding a little at the front. His face was agreeable, but there was no mistaking the power in the thin, delicate lips or the broad nose. His diction was precise, his voice beautiful. He regarded Monk with only the very mildest interest.

Klaus von Seidlitz was utterly different. He was physically very large, several inches taller than the others, broad shouldered, rather shambling. His thick hair fell forward a little, and he had a habit of pushing it back with his hand. His eyes were blue and rather round, and his brows tilted down at the outer edges. His nose was crooked, as if it had been broken at some time. He seemed very amiable, making frequent jokes, but in repose there was a watchfulness in his face which belied his outward ease. Monk wondered if he might be a great deal cleverer than he pretended.

His wife, the Countess Evelyn, was one of the most charming women Monk had ever seen. He found it difficult not to watch her across the glittering table for longer than was seemly. He could happily have forgotten the rest of the company and simply delighted in speaking to and listening to her. She was slight, although her figure was completely feminine, but it was her face which enchanted. She had large brown eyes which seemed to be filled with laughter and intelligence. Her expression made it seem as if she knew some delightful joke about life which she would willingly share, if only she could find someone who would understand it as she did. Her mouth was always smiling and she behaved as if she wished everyone well. She was quite candid about finding Monk intriguing. The fact that he knew no one she did was a source of fascination, and had it not been unpardonably discourteous, she would have questioned him all evening as to exactly who he was and what he did.

Brigitte—according to Rathbone, the woman Prince Friedrich should have married in order to please their country—sat beside Monk. She spoke very little. She was a handsome woman, broad shouldered, deep bosomed, with exquisite skin, but Monk had the sense that there was a sadness in her for all her wealth and reputed popularity.

The remaining guest was Florent Barberini, a distant cousin to Friedrich, half Italian. He had all the dramatic dark good looks Monk would have expected from such a lineage, as well as an ease of manner and total self-confidence. His thick, wavy hair grew from his brow in a widow's peak. His eyes were dark, heavily lashed; his mouth full of humor and sensuality. He flirted with all three women as if it were a habit. Monk disliked him.

Their host, Lord Wellborough, sat at the head of the table in the magnificent French blue and rose dining room with its twenty-foot oak table, three oak sideboards, and a blazing fire. He was a man of very average height with fair hair which he wore rather short, springing up from his head as if to give him extra height. He had very good eyes, clear gray-blue, and strong bones, but an almost lipless mouth. In repose his face had a hard, closed look.

The first course was served, a choice of soups, either vermicelli or bisque. Monk took the bisque and found it delicious. It was followed by salmon, smelts or deviled whitebait. He chose the salmon, delicate, pink, falling from the fork. He saw how much was taken away untouched and wondered if the servants would be offered any of it. Every other guest would have come with the proper complement of valets, lady's maids, and possibly footmen and coachmen as well. Stephan had very smoothly explained Monk's lack of a manservant by saying that he had been taken unwell. Whatever thoughts might have crossed their minds, no one was impolite enough to ask for further enlightenment.

The fish was followed by entrées of curried eggs, sweetbreads and mushrooms, or quenelles of rabbit.

Evelyn was the center of much attention, and this gave Monk an excuse to look at her himself. She was truly enchanting. She had the wholesomeness and the innocent mischief of a child, and yet the warmth and the wit of a woman of intelligence.

Florent flattered her shamelessly, and she parried it with grace, laughing at him, but not with any displeasure.

If Klaus minded there was no reflection of it in his rather heavy features. He was apparently more interested in discussing certain mutual acquaintances with Wellborough.

The entrée plates were cleared away and the removes were served, which that night were iced asparagus. The table sparkled with crystal, the facets reflecting the myriad candles of the chandeliers. Silver cutlery, condiment sets, goblets and vases gleamed. The flowers from the conservatory scented the air and were piled around with ornamental fruit.

Monk dragged his attention from Evelyn and discreetly studied the other guests in turn. They had all been present when Friedrich fell, during his seeming convalescence, and at the time of his death. What had they seen or heard? What did they believe had happened? How much truth did they want, and at what price? He was not there to eat exquisite food and playact at being a gentleman, subtle anguish as that was, lurching from one social tightrope to another. Zorah's reputation, her whole manner of life, hung in the balance, and so very possibly did Rathbone's. In a sense Monk's honor did too. He had given his word to help. The fact that the cause was almost impossible was irrelevant. There was also the chance that Prince Friedrich had indeed been murdered, probably not by his widow but by one of the people talking and laughing around this splendid table, lifting the wine goblets to their lips, diamonds winking in the candlelight.

They finished the asparagus and the game course was brought, a choice of quails, grouse, partridge or black cocks, and of course more wine. Monk had never seen so much food in his life.

The conversation swirled around him, talk of fashion, of theater, of social functions at which they had seen this person or that, who had been in whose company, possible forthcoming betrothals or marriages. It seemed to Monk as if every major family must be related to every other in ramifications too complex to disentangle. He felt more and more excluded as the evening wore on. Perhaps he should have taken Rathbone's suggestion, repugnant as it was, and come as Stephan's valet. It would have galled his pride, but it might in the long run have been less painful than being shown to be a social inferior, pretending to be something he was not, as if being accepted mattered to him so much he would lie! He could feel the rage at such a thought tightening his stomach till he was sitting so rigidly in his carved, silk-covered chair that his back ached.

"I doubt we shall be invited," Brigitte was saying ruefully to some suggestion Klaus had made.

"Why ever not?" He looked annoyed. "I always go. Been every year since, oh, '53!"

Evelyn put her fingers up to cover her smile, her eyes wide.

"Oh, dear! Do you really think it makes that much difference? Shall we all be personae non grata now? How perfectly ridiculous. It's nothing to do with us."

"It has everything to do with us," Rolf said flatly. "It's our royal family, and we specifically were all here when it happened."

"Nobody believes the damn woman!" Klaus said, his heavy face set in lines of anger. "As usual, she has only spoken out of a desire to draw attention to herself at any price, and possibly from revenge because Friedrich threw her over twelve years ago. The woman's mad . . . always was."

Monk realized with sharpened interest that they were speaking of Zorah and the effect her accusation was having upon their social lives. It was an aspect that had not occurred to him, and it was peculiarly repugnant. But he should not lose the opportunity to make something of it.

"Surely it will all be forgotten as soon as the case is heard?" he asked, trying to affect innocence.

"That depends on what the wretched woman says," Klaus replied sourly. "There's always someone fool enough to repeat a piece of gossip, however fatuous."

Monk wondered why Klaus should care what anyone whom he held in such contempt thought, but there were more profitable questions to ask.

"What could she say that any sane person could credit?" he asked, with the same air of sympathy.

"You must have heard the gossip." Evelyn stared at him, wide-eyed. "Simply everyone is talking about it. She has virtually accused Princess Gisela of having killed poor Friedrich . . . I mean intentionally! As if she would! They adored each other. All the world knows that."

"It would have made more sense if someone had killed Gisela," Rolf said with a grimace. "That I could believe."

Monk did not have to feign interest. "Why?"

Everyone at the table turned to look at him, and he realized with anger at himself that he had been naive and too abrupt. But it was too late to retreat. If he added anything he would only make it worse.

It was not Rolf who answered but Evelyn.

"Well, she is very quick-witted, very glamorous. She does overshadow people a bit. It wouldn't be hard to imagine someone being the butt of her wit and feeling so angry, and perhaps humiliated, they could"—she shrugged her beautiful shoulders—"lose their temper and wish her ill." She smiled as she said it, robbing it of any viciousness.

It was a picture of Gisela that Monk had not seen before; not merely funny, but a cruel wit. Perhaps he should not be surprised. These people had little to fear, little need to guard what they said or whether they offended, unlike most of the people he knew. He wondered fleetingly how much of anyone's good manners was a matter of self-preservation, how much genuine desire for the comfort of mind of others. Only in those with nothing at all to fear would he know.

He looked from Evelyn's charming face to Lady Wellborough, then Klaus, and then Rolf.

"Surely, if it actually comes to a trial, it will be easy enough to prove what happened?" he asked mildly. "Everyone who was here can testify, and with you all of one accord, she will be shown up for a liar, or worse."

"We shall have to see that we do agree first," Stephan said with a twisted smile and serious eyes. "After all, we do know more or less what happened. We shall have to be clear about what we don't know so we don't contradict each other."

"What the devil do you mean?" Lord Wellborough demanded, his face pinched till his already thin lips all but disappeared. "Of course we know what happened. Prince Friedrich died of his injuries." He said it as if even the words pained him. Monk wondered uncharitably if the pain came from his affection for Friedrich or from the stain on his reputation as a host.

Monk set down his spoon and ignored his confiture of nectarines. "I imagine they will require greater detail. They will wish to know what happened in the moment-to-moment running of the house, who had access to the rooms where Prince Friedrich was, who prepared his food, who brought it up, who came or went at any time."

"Whatever for?" Evelyn asked. "They don't imagine any of us harmed him, do they? They couldn't. Why? Why should we? We were all his friends. We have been for years."

"Domestic murders are usually committed by one's family . . . or one's friends," Monk replied.

A look of profound distaste crossed Rolf's face. "Possibly. It is something of which, thank God, I have very little knowledge. I presume Gisela will employ the best barrister available, a queen's counsel at the least. And he will conduct the case in the manner best designed to avoid whatever scandal is not already inevitable." He looked at Monk coldly. "Would you be good enough to pass me the cheese, sir?"

There was already a board with seven cheeses in front of him. His meaning was perfectly clear. They ate the ices course—Neapolitan cream and raspberry water—without referring to it again, and then the fruit, pineapples, strawberries, apricots, cherries and melons.

Monk did not sleep well, in spite of the train journey, which had been tiring, the long evening's endurance test at the table and afterwards in the smoking room, and lastly the excellent four-poster bed with down pillows and quilt. When Stephan's valet came in the morning to inform him that his bath was drawn and his clothes for the morning were laid out, he awoke with an uncomfortable jolt.

Breakfast was a vast affair, but informal. People came and went as they pleased, taking from a sideboard laden with chafing dishes filled with eggs, meat, vegetables and various baked pastries and breads. On the table were frequently renewed pots of tea, dishes of preserves, butter, fresh fruit and even sweetmeats.

The only other diners present when Monk arrived were Stephan, Florent and Lord Wellborough. The conversation was unremarkable. When they had finished, Stephan offered to show Monk around the nearer parts of the estate, and Monk accepted with alacrity.

"What are you going to do to help Zorah?" Stephan asked as he conducted Monk around the orangery, pointing towards various features while saying nothing about them at all. "We were all here after Friedrich's fall, but he was confined to his rooms, and Gisela wouldn't allow anyone else to visit him except Rolf, and even he went only twice, so far as I know. But anyone at all could have visited the kitchens or waylaid a servant on the stairs who was carrying a tray."

"Is that why you think it was Gisela?" Monk asked.

Stephan seemed genuinely surprised. "No, of course not. It'll be the devil's own job to prove he was murdered at all! I believe it was Gisela because Zorah says it was. And she is absolutely right about him always believing he could return, and Gisela knowing he couldn't . . . not with her."

"Not very convincing," Monk observed.

They walked around the edge of the orangery and along a path between graceful hedges of close-clipped hornbeam. At the end of the way, about forty yards, there was a stone urn dripping scarlet with late geraniums, and behind that a dark yew hedge.

"I know," Stephan said with a sudden smile. "But if you

knew those people it would make sense to you. If you had seen Gisela . . ."

"Tell me about the day before the accident," Monk said quickly. "Or if you prefer, the day you remember most vividly, even the week before."

Stephan thought for several minutes before he began. They moved slowly down the path towards the urn and the yew hedge, then turned left along an elm avenue that stretched for half a mile.

"Breakfast was always much the same," he said, knitting his brows in concentration. "Gisela was not down. She ate in her room, and Friedrich took his with her. He usually did. It was one of the rituals of the day. I think, actually, he liked to watch her dress. No matter what time or season, she always looked superb. She had a genius for it."

Monk made no reply to that. "What did everyone else do, after?" he asked, slowing the pace a trifle.

Stephan smiled. "Florent flirted with Zorah—in the orangery, I think. Brigitte went walking alone. Wellborough and Rolf talked business in the library. Lady Wellborough did something domestic. I spent the morning playing golf with Friedrich and Klaus. Gisela and Evelyn walked roughly where we are now, and quarreled over something. They came back separately, and both in a temper."

They were moving away from the house, still under the elms. A gardener passed them pushing a wheelbarrow. He raised his cap respectfully and mumbled something. Stephan acknowledged him with a nod. Monk felt rude, but he did not wish to distinguish himself as different by speaking to the man. It was not expected.

"And the afternoon?" he pressed.

"Oh, we all had luncheon rather early and everyone disappeared to plan the evening, because we were having a party and there were to be amateur theatricals. Gisela was terribly good at it, and she was to take the lead."

"Was that unusual?"

"Not at all. She often did. One of her great gifts is the ability to enjoy herself completely, and to do it in such a way that everyone around her enjoys themselves also. She can be totally impulsive, think of the most entertaining ideas, and then simply do them. Without making a fuss or getting weighed down in preparations, which kill the fun. She is the most spontaneous person I ever have known. I think after all the rigid formality of court, when everything is planned weeks in advance and everyone follows the rules, that was what so enchanted Friedrich about her. She was like a summer wind through a house that had been closed up for centuries."

"You like her," Monk observed.

Stephan smiled. "I don't think I would say I like her, but I am fascinated by her and by the effect she has on people."

"Which is?"

Stephan glanced at him, his eyes bright. "Varied," he replied. "The only thing it never is is indifferent."

"How about Evelyn and Zorah?" Monk asked. "How did they like playing supporting roles to Gisela's lead?"

Stephan's expression was hard to read. "Evelyn can play the ingenue, or even a boy, rather well, which she did on this occasion. She was captivating. She managed to be boyish and utterly feminine at the same time."

Monk could imagine it with pleasure. Evelyn's mischievous face, with its youthful lines and wide eyes, and her completely womanly softness would make a beguiling youth full of appeal. Her slender figure would still be unmistakably female, even in masculine costume.

"I can't see Zorah in that role," he admitted, looking sideways at Stephan.

Stephan hesitated before he replied. They were several paces farther along the track when he spoke.

"No. She was cast as a loyal friend who carried the messages which furnished some of the plot."

Monk waited, but Stephan did not add anything.

"Who was the hero?"

"Florent, of course."

"And the villain?"

"Oh—I was." He laughed. "Actually, I rather enjoyed it. Other people you don't know took the minor parts. Brigitte did one of them; somebody's mother, I think."

Monk winced. Perhaps it had not been intended as cruel, but he perceived it so.

"Was it a success?"

"Enormously. Gisela was very good. She made up a bit of it as she went along. It was difficult for the others to follow, but it was so witty no one minded. The audience applauded wildly. And Florent was good as well. He seemed to know instinctively what to say or do to make it look natural."

"And Zorah?"

Stephan's expression changed; the amusement drained away, leaving unhappiness. "I'm afraid she did not enjoy it so much. She was the butt of a few of Gisela's funnier remarks, but Friedrich was amused and hardly ever took his eyes from Gisela, and Zorah had the sense not to show her feelings."

"But she was angry."

"Yes, she was. However, she had her revenge the following day." They climbed a dozen shallow stone steps to a grass walk and the shadow of the elms. "They all went riding," he went on. "Gisela came in the gig. She doesn't ride well, or care for it. Zorah is marvelous. She dared Florent to follow her over some very rough country, and they left Gisela behind in the gig and she came home alone. They arrived back an hour later, flushed and laughing, he with his arm around her. It was obvious they had had an excellent time." He laughed, his eyes bright. "Gisela was furious."

"I thought she was devoted to Friedrich?" Monk looked at him anxiously. "Why should she care if Zorah rode with Florent?"

Now Stephan was thoroughly amused.

"Don't be naive!" he exclaimed. "Certainly, she was devoted to Friedrich, but she adored other admirers. It was part of her role as the great lover that all men should admire her. She is the woman for whom a throne was lost: always gorgeous, always desirable, always utterly happy. She had to be the center of the party, the most alluring, the one who could make everyone laugh at whatever she chose. She was terribly witty at dinner that evening, but Zorah was just as quick. It was a battle royal over the dinner table."

"Unpleasant?" Monk asked, trying to visualize it and gauge the underlying emotion. Was her hatred really enough to prompt Zorah to fabricate this charge, or even to blind her to the truth and make her believe a lie because she wanted to? Was it all really stung vanity, a battle for fame and love?

Stephan stopped and stood still on the path, looking at Monk carefully for some time before answering.

"Yes," he said at last. "I think there is a sense in which it has always been unpleasant. I'm not really sure. Perhaps I don't understand people as well as I thought I did. I couldn't speak as she did to anyone whom I liked, but I don't think I really know what they felt." The wind blew in his face, lifting his hair a little. The sky was clouding over to the west. "Zorah always believed Gisela to be selfish," he went on. "A woman who married for position and then was cheated out of the ultimate glory. Most people believed she married for love and didn't care about anything else. They would have thought Zorah merely jealous, had she expressed her views, but she had enough sense not to. They could never have liked each other; they were too utterly different."

"But you believe Zorah?"

"I believe her honesty." He hesitated. "I am not absolutely certain I believe her to be correct."

"And yet you will stake so much to help me defend her?"

Stephan shrugged and flashed a sudden, brilliant smile. "I

like her . . . I like her enormously. And I do think poor Friedrich might have been murdered, and if he was, we ought to know. You can't murder princes and simply walk away. I have that much loyalty to my country."

Monk received a very different picture when he spent a delicious afternoon in the rose garden with Evelyn. The flowers were in their second blossoming. The garden was sheltered from the light breeze, and in the still air the perfume was heavy and sweet. The climbing roses had been trained up columns and over arches, and the shrub roses were four or five feet high, making dense mounds of blossom on either side of the grass paths. Evelyn's huge crinoline skirts touched the lavender at the edges of the beds, disturbing their scent. The two strollers were surrounded by color and perfume.

"It's an unspeakable thing for Zorah to do," Evelyn said, her eyes wide as if she were still amazed at it, her voice rising in indignation. "She's always been very odd, but this is incredible, even for her."

Monk offered his arm as they walked up a flight of stone steps to another level, and Evelyn took it quite naturally. Her hand was small and very beautiful. He was surprised how much pleasure it gave him to feel its feather touch on his sleeve.

"Has she?" he asked casually. "Why on earth do you think she said anything as strange as this? She cannot possibly believe it is true, can she? I mean, is the evidence not entirely against it?"

"Of course it is," she said with a laugh. "For a start, why would she? If you want to be quite brutal about it . . . married to Friedrich, Gisela had wealth, rank and extraordinary allure. As a widow she has no rank anymore, Felzburg will make her no allowance, and even the wealth will be used up pretty rapidly if she continues the life to which she has been accustomed—and believe me, enjoyed very much indeed. He spent a fortune on jewels and gowns for her, carriages, their palace in Venice, parties, travel to anywhere she wanted. Admittedly that was only within Europe, not like Zorah, who went to the oddest places." She stopped in front of a huge wine-red Bourbon rose and looked up at him. "I mean, why would any woman want to go to South America? Or to Turkey, or up the Nile, or to China, of all things? No wonder she never married. Who'd have her? She's never here." She laughed happily. "Any respectable man wants a wife who has some sense of how to behave, not one who rides astride a horse and sleeps in a tent and can and does converse with men from every walk of life."

Monk knew that what she said was true, and he would not want such a woman as a wife himself. Zorah sounded far too like Hester Latterly, who was also outspoken and opinionated. Nevertheless, she sounded brave, and extraordinarily interesting as a friend, if nothing else.

"And Gisela is quite different?" he prompted.

"Of course." Evelyn seemed to find that funny also. Her voice was rich with underlying amusement. "She loves the luxuries of civilized life, and she can entertain anyone with her wit. She has a gift of making everything seem sophisticated and immense fun. She is one of those people who, when she listens to you, makes you feel as if you are the most interesting person she has met and are the center of her entire attention. It is quite a talent."

And very flattering, Monk thought with a ripple of appreciation—and a sudden warning. It was a powerful art, and perhaps a dangerous one.

They came to an arch of late-flowering white roses, and she moved a little closer to him so they could pass through side by side.

"Did Friedrich never mind Gisela's being the center of so much attention?" Monk asked as they moved beyond the rose arch onto a path between iris beds, only green sword blades now, the flowers long over.

Evelyn smiled. "Oh, yes, sometimes. He could sulk. But she always won him around. She had only to be sweet to him and he would forget about it. He was terribly in love with her, you know, even after twelve years. He adored her. He always knew exactly where she was in a room, no matter how many other people were there." She looked across the green iris leaves back towards the rose arch, the expression in her eyes bright and far away. He had no idea what lay in it.

"She used to dress marvelously," she went on. "I loved just seeing what she would wear next. It must have cost a fortune, but he was so proud of her. Whatever she wore one week would be the vogue the week after. It always looked right on her. That's a wonderful thing, you know. So feminine."

He looked at Evelyn's own golden brown dress with its enormous skirts and delicately cut bodice with a froth of creamy lace at the bosom, fine pointed waist and full sleeves. It was a gift she had no cause to envy. He found himself smiling back at her.

Perhaps she read his appreciation in his eyes, because she blinked and looked down, then smiled a little and began to walk away. There was a grace in her step which showed her satisfaction.

He followed her and asked more about the weeks before Friedrich's accident, even the years in exile in Venice and a little of the life at court before Gisela first came. The picture she painted was full of color and variety, but also rigid formality, and for royalty itself, intense discipline to duty. There was extravagance beyond anything he had imagined, let alone seen. No one he knew in London had spent money as Evelyn described quite casually, as if it were a feature of the way everyone lived.

Monk's head swam. Half of him was dazzled and fascinated, half was bitterly conscious of the hunger and humiliation, the dependency, and the constant fear and physical discomfort of those who worked all their waking hours and were still always on the brink of debt. He was even uncomfortably aware of the servants who existed to fill any whim of the guests in this exquisite house who day and night did nothing but pass from one amusement to another.

And yet without such places as Wellborough Hall, so much beauty would be lost. He wondered who was happier, the gorgeous baroness who strolled through the gardens, flirting with him, telling stories of the parties and masques and balls she remembered in the capitals of Europe, or the gardener fifty yards away snipping the dead heads off the roses and threading the tendrils of the new growth through the bars of the trellis. Which of them saw the blooms more clearly and took more joy in them?

He did not enjoy dinner that evening either, and his discomfort was made worse when Lord Wellborough asked him quietly at the table if Monk would excuse them all that evening. They were all there to discuss the sensitive matter with which Monk was now acquainted, and as Monk was not involved, surely he wouldn't be offended by being excluded from their talk that evening. There was some decent Armagnac in the library, and some rather fine Dutch cigars . . .

Monk was furious, but forced a smile as natural and diplomatic as he could. He had hoped that he might be present when they decided to discuss the matter and had invented a pretext of being an objective and fresh mind to aid them in covering all eventualities. However, it seemed natural that they regarded Monk as an interesting guest but an outsider, and Monk didn't dare press the point. He was thankful that Stephan would be there and could convey back to him anything of use, but he would have welcomed the opportunity to question them himself.

The next day, Monk did, however, find an opportunity to

visit Gallagher, the doctor who had attended Friedrich after his fall and until his death. Everyone else went shooting for the day, but Stephan affected a slight indisposition and requested that Monk accompany him to the doctor. It was an injury to his hand, and he asked Monk to drive him in the gig.

"What was said last night?" Monk asked as soon as they were out of the drive and into the lane which led to the doctor's house. Despite his walks with Stephan in the gardens of the Hall, he had felt oppressed and was glad to be out in the clear autumn air.

"I'm going to disappoint you," Stephan said regretfully. "It turned out that I'd observed or remembered more than any of the others, and a few of them know more this morning than they did yesterday, thanks to me."

Monk frowned. "Well, you could hardly not have pooled your knowledge with them, and at least we know what they're likely to say, should it come to trial."

"But you feel you have wasted an opportunity."

Monk nodded, too angry to speak. He would not be reporting this to Rathbone.

Dr. Gallagher turned out to be a mild-mannered man of about fifty or so who was not perturbed about being summoned away from his books to attend two gentlemen from the Hall who had called for his help.

"Indeed," he said courteously. "What a shame, Baron von Emden. Let me have a look at it. Right wrist, is it?"

"Sorry for our deception, Doctor." Stephan smiled and rested his hands on his hips, demonstrating two perfectly supple wrists. "Rather a delicate matter. Didn't want to advertise it. Hope you understand. Mr. Monk"—he gestured towards Monk, beside him—"is trying to help us deal with this abysmal business of the Countess Rostova's accusations."

Gallagher looked blank.

"Oh, you haven't heard?" Stephan pulled a face expressing

chagrin. "I am afraid she has behaved quite . . . quite extraordinarily. The whole affair will have to come to trial."

"What affair?"

"Prince Friedrich's death," Monk said, stepping in. "I regret to say she has started spreading the charge around society that it was not an accident but deliberate poison."

"What?" Gallagher was aghast. He seemed almost unable to believe he had heard correctly. "What do you mean? Not . . . not that . . . that I . . ."

"No, of course not!" Monk said immediately. "No one even thought of such a thing. It is the widow, Princess Gisela, whom she is accusing."

"Oh, my God! How perfectly fearful." Gallagher stepped back and all but collapsed into the chair behind him. "How can I help?"

Stephan was about to speak, but Monk cut across him.

"You will no doubt be called to give evidence, unless we can gather sufficient proof to force her to withdraw the charge and offer the fullest apology. The greatest assistance you could give would be to answer all our questions with the utmost candor, so we know precisely where we stand, and if she has clever counsel, what is the worst we must fear."

"Of course. Of course. Anything I can do." Gallagher pressed his hand to his brow. "Poor woman! To lose the husband she loved so profoundly and then to face such a diabolical slander, and from one she must have supposed her friend. Ask me anything you wish."

Monk sat down opposite the doctor in a well-worn brown chair. "You understand I am speaking as a sort of devil's advocate? I shall probe for weaknesses, so if I find them, I shall know how to defend."

"Of course. Proceed!" Gallagher said almost eagerly.

Monk felt a tinge of conscience, but only a slight one. The truth was what mattered.

"You were the only physician to treat Prince Friedrich?"

"Yes, from the accident until he died." His face was pale at the memory. "I . . . I honestly thought the poor man was recovering. He seemed to be considerably better. Of course, he had a great deal of pain, but one does from broken bones. But he was far less feverish, and he had begun to take a little nourishment."

"The last time you saw him alive?" Monk asked. "Before the relapse?"

"He was sitting up in bed." Gallagher looked very strained. "He seemed pleased to see me. I can picture it exactly. It was spring, as you know, late spring. It was a beautiful day, sunlight streaming in through the windows, a vase of lily of the valley on the bureau in the sitting room. The perfume of them filled the room. They were a particular favorite of the Princess's. I hear she cannot abide them since that day. Poor creature. She idolized him. She never left his side from the moment he was carried in from his accident. Distraught, she was, absolutely distraught. Beside herself with distress for him."

He took a deep breath and let it out silently. "Quite different from when he died. Then it was as if the world had ended for her. She simply sat there, white-faced, neither moving nor speaking. She did not even seem to see us."

"What did he die of?" Monk asked a little more gently. He was aware of conflicting emotions tearing inside him. "Medically speaking."

Gallagher's eyes widened. "I did not do a postmortem examination, sir. He was a royal prince! He died as the result of his injuries in the fall. He had broken several bones. They had seemed to be healing, but one cannot see inside the living body to know what other damage there may be, what organs may have been crushed or pierced. He bled to death internally. That is what every symptom led me to believe. I had not expected it, because he seemed to be recovering, but that may have been the courage of his spirit, when in truth he was injured so seriously that the slightest movement may have ruptured some vessel and caused a fatal hemorrhage."

"The symptoms . . ." Monk prompted, this time quite softly. Whatever the cause of it, or whoever, he could not help feeling pity for the man whose death he was trying to examine so clinically. All he had heard of him suggested he was a man of courage and character, willing to follow his heart and pay the cost without complaint, a man capable of immense love and sacrifice, perhaps, in the last, a man torn by duty—and murdered for it.

"Coldness," Gallagher replied. "Clamminess of the skin." He swallowed; his hands tightened on his lap. "Pains in the abdomen, nausea. I believe that was the site of the bleeding. That was followed by disorientation, a sense of giddiness, numbness in the extremities, sinking into a coma, and finally death. Very precisely, heart failure. In short, sir, the symptoms of internal bleeding."

"Are there any poisons which produce the same symptoms?" Monk asked, frowning, disliking having to say it.

Gallagher stared at him.

Monk thought of the yew trees at the end of the hornbeam hedge, the stone urn pale against their dark mass. Everyone knew that the needlelike yew leaves were bitterly poisonous. Everyone in the house had access to them; one simply had to take a walk in the garden, the most natural thing in the world to do.

"Are there?" he repeated.

Stephan shifted his weight.

"Yes, of course," Gallagher said reluctantly. "There are thousands of poisons. But why in heaven's name should such a woman poison her husband? It makes no conceivable sense!"

"Would the leaves of the yew trees produce such symptoms?" Monk pressed.

Gallagher thought for so long Monk was about to ask him again.

"Yes," he said at last. "They would." He was white-faced.

"Exactly those symptoms?" Monk could not let it go.

"Well . . ." Gallagher hesitated, his face filled with misery. "Yes . . . I am not an expert in such matters, but one does occasionally find village children put the leaves in their mouths. And women have been known to—" He stopped for a moment, then continued unhappily. "To use it in an effort to procure an abortion. A young woman died in the next village about eight years ago."

Stephan shifted his weight again. "But Gisela never left Friedrich's rooms," he said quietly. "Even if he was poisoned, she is about the only one in the house who could not possibly have done it. And believe me, if you knew Gisela you would not even entertain the idea of her having someone else provide the poison for her. She would never put herself so fatally in someone else's power."

"This is monstrous," Gallagher said miserably. "I hope you will do everything in your ability to fight such a dreadful shadow and at least clear that poor woman's name."

"We will do everything we can to find the truth—and prove it," Monk promised ambiguously.

Gallagher did not doubt him for a moment. He rose to his feet and clasped Monk's hand. "Thank you, sir. I am most relieved. And if there is anything further I can do to assist you, you have but to say. And you too, of course, Baron von Emden. Good day to you, gentlemen, good day."

"That hardly helps us at all," Stephan said as they climbed into the gig and Monk took the reins. "Perhaps it was yew poison . . . but it wasn't Gisela!"

"So it would seem," Monk agreed. "I am afraid we still have rather a long way to go."

3

HESTER *LATTERLY*, about whom Monk and Rathbone had both thought so recently, was unaware of their involvement in the case of Princess Gisela and the Countess Rostova, although she had heard murmurs of the affair in general.

Since her return from nursing in the Crimea with Florence Nightingale, she had held several posts in that profession, mostly private. She had just completed the care of an elderly lady recuperating from a nasty fall, and was presently not engaged. She was delighted to receive a call from her friend and sometimes patroness Lady Callandra Daviot. Callandra was well into her fifties. Her face was full of wit and character, but even her most ardent admirer would not have said she was beautiful. There was too much strength in her, and far too much eccentricity. She had a very agreeable lady's maid who had years ago given up trying to do anything elegant with Callandra's hair. If it stayed more or less within its pins, that was victory enough.

On this day she was even untidier than usual, but she swept in with an armful of flowers and an air of excited purpose.

"For you, my dear," she announced, placing the flowers on the side table in Hester's small sitting room. There was no purpose in Hester's renting more spacious accommodation, even could she have afforded it; she was hardly ever there. "Although I hope you will not be here long enough to enjoy them. I simply brought them because they are so lovely." Callandra sat down on the nearest chair, her skirts crooked, hoops at an angle. She slapped at the skirt absently and it remained where it was.

Hester sat opposite her, listening with attention she did not have to feign. "Thank you anyway," she said, referring to the flowers.

"There is a case I should be most grateful if you would take. A young man with whom I have a very slight acquaintance. He first introduced himself to me as Robert Oliver, an Anglicism he affected, possibly because he was born in this country and feels utterly at home here. However, his name is actually Ollenheim, and his parents, the Baron and Baroness, are expatriates from Felzburg . . ."

"Felzburg?" Hester said in surprise.

Callandra's face suddenly lost all its humor and became filled with profound pity. "Young Robert contracted a very serious illness, a fever which, when the worst of it passed, left him without movement in his lower body and legs. His natural functions are unimpaired, but he is helpless to leave his bed and needs the constant care of a nurse. He has been attended so far by the doctor daily, and his mother, and the household servants, but a professional nurse is required. I took the liberty of suggesting your name for a number of reasons."

Hester listened in silence, but with growing interest.

"To begin with, and most important," Callandra enumerated earnestly, "Robert may be severely damaged. It is even conceivable he may not regain the use of his legs. If that is so, it is going to be desperately difficult for him to face. He will need all the help and the wisdom that can be offered him. You, my dear, have had much experience, as an army nurse, of caring for young men fearfully disabled. You will know, as much as anyone can, how best to help him.

"My second reason is that some time ago, during the time we were investigating the murder of poor Prudence Barrymore"—again Callandra's face darkened with memory of pain, and of love—"I spent a little time with Victoria Stanhope and learned that the child was a victim of incest, and then of a badly performed abortion, as a result of which she is internally damaged for life. She is in almost continuous pain, at times greater than others, and has no prospects of marriage because she will be unable to fulfill its physical obligations." She held up her hand to prevent Hester from interrupting. "I was with her when she and young Robert met, and they were instantly attracted. Of course, at that time I hastened her away before further tragedy could ensue. Now matters are different. Robert is also damaged. Her courage and innocence may be the thing which will best help him to come to terms with his altered situation."

"And if he recovers?" Hester said quickly. "But she falls in love with him? And she will never be whole! What then?"

"I don't know," Callandra admitted. "But if he does not, and she is the person who could lift him from despair, and by so doing, believe in her own value and purpose, how terrible that we should have allowed our fear to have prevented it."

Hester hesitated, torn between the two dangers.

Callandra had had far longer to weigh the issues. There was no indecision in her eyes.

"I truly believe there is more regret over what we fail to do than over decisions made which turned out badly," she said with conviction. "Are you willing to try, at least?"

Hester smiled. "And your third reason?"

"You need a position!" Callandra said simply.

It was true. Since her father's ruin and death Hester had no means of her own, and she refused to be dependent upon her brother; therefore, she must earn her own living as her skills allowed. Not that it was an issue she resented. It gave her both independence and interest, both of which she prized highly.

The financial urgency of it was less pleasant, but common to most people.

"I should be happy to do what I can," she said sincerely. "If you feel that Baron and Baroness Ollenheim would find me acceptable."

"I have already seen to that," Callandra replied decisively. "The sooner you can take up the position, the better."

Hester rose to her feet.

"Oh," Callandra added with bright eyes. "By the way, Oliver Rathbone has taken up the case of the Countess Rostova."

"What?" Hester stopped abruptly and stood motionless. "I beg your pardon. What did you say?"

Callandra repeated herself.

Hester swung around to stare at her.

"Then I can only believe there must be more to the case than there seems. And pray so!"

"And William is investigating it for him," Callandra added. "Which, of course, is how I know about it." Callandra was also William Monk's patroness, tiding him through his leaner times.

Hester merely said "I see." But she did not see at all. "Then, if you are sure the Baron and Baroness Ollenheim are expecting me, I had better pack a case and make myself available."

"I shall be happy to take you," Callandra said generously. "The house is on Hill Street, near Berkeley Square."

"Thank you."

Callandra had prepared the way well, and Baron and Baroness Ollenheim welcomed Hester's professional services. The burden of caring for their son had fallen heavily upon them, as their emotions were so deeply involved. Hester found the Baroness Dagmar a charming woman who in times less stressful, when not exhausted and strained with grief and anxiety, would have been beautiful. Now she was pale with fatigue, sleepless nights had left deep shadows under her eyes, and she had no time or interest to dress more than simply.

Baron Bernd was also disturbed by feelings which harrowed him profoundly, but he made a greater effort to conceal them, as was expected of a man and an aristocrat. Nevertheless, he was more than courteous to Hester and permitted her to see his relief at her presence.

Robert Ollenheim himself was a young man of perhaps twenty, with a fair face and thick, light brown hair which fell forward over the left side of his brow. In normal health he would have been most handsome; lying wasted by the recent fever, weak and still aching, he nevertheless managed a certain grace in greeting Hester when she made herself known to him and began her duties. He must have been aware of the seriousness of his situation, and the possibility of permanent disability had to have crossed his mind, but no mention was made of it.

She found caring for him easy in its physical work. It was simply a matter of nursing, keeping him as comfortable as possible, trying to reduce his distress and discomfort, seeing that he drank broth and beef tea frequently and gradually began to take greater nourishment. The doctor called very regularly, and she was left no important decisions to make. The difficulty lay in the concern for him and the fear that lay at the back of all their minds as to how complete his recovery would be. No one spoke of paralysis, but as each day went by, and still he felt no sensation and gained no power of movement below the waist, the fear grew.

She did not forget the extraordinary case with which Monk and Rathbone were involved, and once or twice she overheard Bernd and Dagmar discussing it when they were not aware she was close by.

"Will Prince Friedrich's death make a great deal of political difference?" she asked one day about a week after her arrival. She and Dagmar were putting away clean linen the laundry maid had brought up. Ever since she first met Monk and became involved in the murder of Joscelin Gray, she had asked questions almost as of second nature.

"I think so," Dagmar replied, examining the embroidered corner of a pillow slip. "There is considerable talk of uniting all the German states under one crown, which would naturally mean our being swallowed up. We are far too small to become the center of such a new nation. The King of Prussia has ambitions in that direction, and, of course, Prussia is very military. And then there are Bavaria, Moravia, Hannover, Bohemia, Holstein, Westphalia, Würtemberg, Saxony, Silesia, Pomerania, Nassau, Mecklenburg and Schwerin, not to mention the Thuringian states, the Electorate of Hesse, and above all Brandenburg. Berlin is an immensely tedious city, but it is very well placed to become the capital for all of us."

"You mean all the German states as one country?" Hester had never really thought of such a thing.

"There is much talk of it. I don't know if it will ever happen." Dagmar picked out another of the slips. "This needs mending. If one caught a finger in this it would ruin it. Some of us are for unification, others against. The King is very frail now, and possibly will not live more than another year or two. Then Waldo will be king, and he is in favor of unification."

"Are you?" Perhaps it was an intrusive question, but she asked it before thinking. It seemed to spring naturally from the statement.

Dagmar hesitated several moments before replying, her hands motionless on the linen, her brow furrowed.

"I don't know," she said finally. "I've thought about it. One has to be reasonable about these things. To begin with, I was utterly against it. I wanted to keep my identity." She bit her lip, as if laughing at her own foolishness, looking directly at Hester. "I know that may seem silly to you, since you are British and at the heart of the largest empire in the world, but it mattered to me."

"It's not foolish at all," Hester said sincerely. "Knowing

who you are is part of happiness." Unexpectedly, a sharp thought of Monk came to her mind, because he had been injured three years before in an accident and had lost every shred of his memory. Even his own face in the glass woke no familiarity in him at all. She had watched him struggle with remnants of his past as they flashed to his mind, or some event forced upon him evidence of who and what he had been. Not all of it was pleasant or easy to accept. Even now it was only fragments, pieces here and there. The vast bulk of it was closed within recesses of his mind he could not reach. He felt too vulnerable to ask questions of those few who knew anything. Too many of them were enemies, rivals, or simply people he had worked with and ignored. "To know your own roots is a great gift," she said aloud. "To tear them up, willingly, is an injury one might not survive."

"It is also an injury to refuse to acknowledge change," Dagmar answered thoughtfully. "And to hold out against unification, if the other states seem to want it, could leave us very isolated. Or far worse than that, it could provoke war. We could be swallowed whether we want it or not."

"Could you?" Hester took the slip from Dagmar and placed it in a separate pile.

"Oh, yes." The Baroness picked up the last sheet. "And far better to be allied as part of a larger Germany in general than to be taken over in war as a subject province of Prussia. If you know anything of Prussian politics, you'd think the same, believe me. The King of Prussia isn't bad at heart, but even he can't keep the army under control—or the bureaucrats or the landowners. That is a lot of what the revolutions of '48 were all about, a sort of middle class trying to obtain some rights, some freedom for the press and literature, and a wider franchise."

"In Prussia or in your country?"

"Everywhere, really." Dagmar shrugged. "There were revolutions in just about every part of Europe that year. Only France seemed to have succeeded in winning anything. Certainly Prussia didn't."

"And you think that if you try to remain independent there could be war?" Hester was horrified. She had seen too much of the reality of war, the broken bodies on the battlefield, the physical agony, the maiming and the death. For her, war was not a political idea but an endless unfolding and living of pain, exhaustion, fear, hunger, and heat in the summer and cold even to death in the winter. No sane person would enter into it unless occupation and slavery were the only alternatives.

"There might." Dagmar's voice came from far away, although she was standing only a yard from Hester in the corridor with the sunlit landing beyond. But Hester's mind had been in the rat-infested, disease-ridden hospital in Scutari, and in the carnage of Balaclava and Sebastopol. "There are many people who make money from war," Dagmar went on somberly, the sheet forgotten. "They see it primarily as an opportunity to profit from the sale of guns and munitions, horses, rations, uniforms, all kinds of things."

Unconsciously, Hester winced. To wish such a horror upon any people in order to make money from it seemed like the ultimate wickedness.

Dagmar's fingers examined the hem of the sheet absentmindedly, tracing the embroidered flowers and monogram.

"Please God it won't come to that. Friedrich was for independence, even if he had to fight for it, but I don't know who else is who could lead us. Anyway, it doesn't matter anymore. Friedrich is dead, and he wouldn't have returned without Gisela. And it seems as if the Queen would not have allowed him back with her, no matter what the cost or the alternative."

Hester had to ask.

"Would he ever have gone without her—if it were to save his country, to keep Felzburg independent?"

Dagmar looked at her steadily, her face suddenly tense, her eyes very level.

"I don't know. I used to think not . . . but I don't know."

A day went by, and another, and another. Robert's fever was gone now. He was beginning to eat proper meals, and to enjoy them. But he still had no sensation or power of movement below the waist.

Bernd came every evening to sit and talk with his son. Hester naturally did not remain in the room, but she knew from the remarks she overheard, and from Robert's own attitude after his father had left, that Bernd was still, at least outwardly, convinced that complete healing was only a matter of waiting.

Dagmar kept up the same manner on the surface, but when she left Robert's room and was alone with Hester on the landing, or downstairs, she allowed her anxiety to show through.

"It seems as if he is not getting any better," she said tensely on the fourth day after their discussion of German reunification politics. Her eyes were dark with anxiety, her shoulders stiff under her fine woolen day bodice with its white lawn collar. "Am I expecting too much too quickly? I thought he would have been able to move his feet now. He just lies there. I dare not even ask what he is thinking." She was desperate for Hester to reassure her, waiting for the word that would ease her fears, at least for a while.

Was it kinder, or crueler, to say something that was not true? Surely trust also mattered? In the future it might matter even more.

"Perhaps you shouldn't ask," Hester replied. She had seen many men face maiming and loss of limbs, disfigurement of face or body. There were things for which no one could offer help. There was nothing to do but stand and wait for the time or the depth of pain when another person was needed. It might come sooner or later. "He will talk about it when he is ready.

Perhaps a visitor would take his mind from thinking of it. I believe Lady Callandra mentioned a Miss Victoria Stanhope, who has suffered some misfortune herself and might be of encouragement . . ." She did not know how to finish.

Dagmar looked startled and seemed about to dismiss the idea.

"Someone who is less close, less obviously anxious, may be helpful," Hester urged.

"Yes . . ." Dagmar agreed hopefully. "Yes, perhaps she may. I shall ask him."

The following day, Victoria Stanhope, still thin, still pale and moving with slight awkwardness, paid a call upon Hester, who conducted her to Robert.

Dagmar had remained uncertain about the suitability of a young, single woman's visiting in such circumstances, but when she saw Victoria, her shyness and her obvious disability, she changed her mind. And apart from that, the girl's dress immediately proclaimed her lack of means or social position. The fact that she spoke with dignity and intelligence made her otherwise most agreeable. The name Stanhope was familiar to Dagmar, but she did not immediately place it.

Victoria stood on the landing beside Hester. Now that the moment had come, her courage failed her.

"I can't go in," she whispered. "What can I say to him? He won't remember me, and if he does, it will only be that I rebuffed him. Anyway"—she gulped and turned, white-faced, to Hester—"what about my family? He'll remember that, and he won't want to have anything to do with me. I can't—"

"Your family's situation is nothing to do with you," Hester said gently, putting her hand on Victoria's arm. "Robert is far too fair to make such a judgment. Go in there thinking of his need, not your own, and I promise you, you will have nothing at the end which you can look back on with regret." The moment she had said it, she realized how bold she had been, but Victoria's smile prevented her from withdrawing it.

Victoria took a deep breath and let it out in a sigh, then knocked on the door again.

"May I come in?"

Robert looked at her with curiosity. Hester had prepared him for the visit, naturally, and had been surprised how clearly he had recalled their one brief encounter over a year before.

"Please do, Miss Stanhope," he said with a slight smile. "I apologize for the hospitality I can offer, but I am at a slight disadvantage right at the moment. Please sit down. That chair"—he pointed to the one beside the bed—"is quite comfortable."

She walked in and sat down. For a moment her fingers moved as if to rearrange her skirts. The new concertina-type steel hoops could be quite awkward, even if they were better than the old bone ones. Then, with an effort of will, she ignored them and let them fall as they would.

Hester waited for the inevitable "How are you feeling?" Even Robert looked prepared for the traditional answer.

"I imagine now you are over the fever and most of the pain, you are thoroughly bored," Victoria said with a little shake of her head.

Robert was startled, then his face broke into a wide smile.

"I didn't expect you to say that," he admitted. "Yes, I am. And terribly tired of assuring everyone that I feel all right—far, far better than I did a week ago. I read, of course, but sometimes I can hear the silence prickling in my ears, and I find my attention wandering. I want a sound of some sort, and something that responds to me. I am weary of being done to, and not doing." He blushed suddenly, realizing how forthright he had been to a young woman who was almost a complete stranger. "I'm sorry! You didn't come here out of kindness just to hear me complain. Everyone has been very good, really."

"Of course they have," she agreed, smiling back, tentatively at first. "But this is something they cannot alter. What have you been reading?"

"Dickens's *Hard Times*," he replied with a grimace. "I admit, it doesn't cheer me much. I care about its people," he added quickly, "but I'm not happy for them. I go to sleep and dream I live in Coketown."

"May I bring you something different?" she offered. "Perhaps something happy? Are you"—she drew a deep breath—"are you familiar with Edward Lear's *Book of Nonsense*?"

His eyebrows rose. "No. But I think I might like it. It sounds like an excellent refuge from the world of Coketown."

"It is," she promised. "You'll find in it the Dong with the Luminous Nose, and Jumblies, who went to sea in a sieve, and all sorts of other oddities, like Mr. Daddy Longlegs and Mr. Floppy Fly, who played at battlecock and shuttledore in the sand."

"Please do bring it."

"And there are drawings, of course," she added.

Hester was satisfied. She turned and tiptoed away and went down the stairs to where Dagmar was waiting in the hall.

Victoria Stanhope visited again, on two more occasions, staying longer each time.

"I think she does him good," Dagmar said when the maid had shown Victoria upstairs on the fourth time she called. "He seems very pleased to see her, and she is a most agreeable child. She would be quite pretty, if she were—" She stopped. "Oh, dear. That is very uncharitable of me, isn't it?" They were standing in the conservatory in the early autumn sun. It was a charming room, full of white-painted wrought iron furniture and shaded by a mixture of potted palms and large-leafed tropical plants. The air was filled with the sweetness of several late, heavily scented lilies. "That was a terrible business about her family," she added sadly. "I expect it has ruined her chances, poor thing."

Naturally, she was referring to Victoria's chances of marriage. There was no other desirable life open to a young woman of breeding, unless she had a great deal of money, or some remarkable talent, or excellent health and a burning desire for good works. Hester did not tell her that Victoria's chances for any of these things had been ruined long before her family's disgrace. That was Victoria's secret to keep or to tell as she wished. Were Hester in her place, she felt she would never tell anyone at all. It was about as private a tragedy as could be imagined.

"Yes," she said bluntly. "I expect it has."

"How very unfair." Dagmar shook her head slightly. "You never know what is going to happen, do you? Six weeks ago I could not have imagined Robert's illness. Now I don't know how much it will change our lives." She was not looking at Hester, perhaps deliberately. After only a moment's hesitation, as though she did not want to allow time for an answer, she hurried on. "Poor Princess Gisela must feel the same. This time last year she had all she cared about. I think every woman in the world envied her, at least a little." She smiled. "I know I did. Don't we all dream of having a handsome and charming man love us so passionately he would give up a kingdom and a throne simply to be with us?"

Hester thought back to being eighteen, and the dreams she had had then.

"Yes, I suppose so," she said reluctantly, oddly defensive of the girl she had been. She had felt so wise and invulnerable, and she had been so naive.

"Most of us settle for reality," Dagmar went on. "And find it really quite good in the end. Or we make it good. But it is still natural to dream sometimes. Gisela made her dreams come true . . . until this spring, that is. Then Friedrich died, which left her desolated. To have had such a . . . a unity!" She turned to Hester. "You know they were never apart? He loved her so much he never grew tired of watching her, listening to her, hearing her laugh. He still found her just as fascinating, after twelve years."

"It would be natural to envy that," Hester said honestly. She would not have found it easy to watch such happiness and not wish it for herself. And if she had at one time been in love with the Prince, it would never really stop hurting. She would wonder why she had not been able to awake that love in him, what was lacking in her. What gaiety or charm, what tenderness or quickness to understand, what generosity or honor did she fail to have? Or was it simply that she was physically not pleasing enough, either to look at or in those areas of intimacy of love in which her only experience lay in the imagination and the longing of dreams? Was all that the wound which had festered in Zorah Rostova all these years, and perhaps driven her a little mad?

Dagmar was absentmindedly picking off the occasional dead leaf and fiddling with the bark around the palms.

"What was the Prince like?" Hester asked, trying to picture the romance.

"To look at?" Dagmar asked with a smile.

"No, I meant as a person. What did he like to do? If I were to spend an evening in his company—at dinner, for example—what would I remember most about him?"

"Before he met Gisela, or afterwards?"

"Both! Yes, tell me both."

Dagmar concentrated her memory, forgetting the plants. "Well, before Gisela, you would think first how utterly charming he was." She smiled as she recollected. "He had the most beautiful smile. He would look at you as if he were really interested in all you said. He never seemed to be merely polite. It was almost as if he were half expecting you to turn out to be special, and he did not want to miss any opportunity to find out. I think what you might remember afterwards was the certainty that he liked you."

Hester found herself smiling too. The warmth rippled

through her at the idea of meeting someone who gave so much of himself. No wonder Gisela had loved him, and how devastated she must feel now. And on top of the loneliness and the loss which darkened everything had come this nightmare accusation. What on earth had possessed Rathbone to take up Zorah's case? His knighthood had gone to his wits. When the Queen touched him on the shoulder with the sword she must have pricked his brain.

"And after he met Gisela . . ." Dagmar went on.

Hester jerked her attention back. She had forgotten she had asked that question also.

"Yes?" she said, trying to sound attentive.

"I suppose he was different," Dagmar responded thoughtfully. "He was hurt that people wouldn't accept Gisela, because he loved her so much. But he was never so very close to his family, especially his mother. He was sad going into exile. But I think he believed in his heart that one day they would want him back and then they would see Gisela's worth and accept her." She looked along the passage between the leaves and fronds towards the windows. "I remember the day he left. People were lining the streets. A lot of women were weeping, and they all wished him well, and cried 'God bless you!' and waved kerchiefs and threw flowers."

"And Gisela?" Hester asked curiously. "What did they feel about her?"

"They resented her," Dagmar replied. "In a way, it was as if she had stolen him from us."

"What is his brother like?"

"Waldo? Oh!" Dagmar laughed as if some memory amused her. "Much plainer, much duller, at first. He hasn't any of Friedrich's charm. But we grew to appreciate him. And, of course, his wife was always popular. It makes such a difference, you know. Perhaps in a way Ulrike was right. Whom we marry does alter us more than I used to think. In fact, only when you ask me do I realize how both brothers changed over the years. Waldo became stronger and wiser, and he learned how to win people's affection. I think he's happy, and that makes people kinder, don't you think?"

"Yes," Hester said with sudden feeling. "Yes, it does. What happened to Countess Rostova after Friedrich and Gisela left? Did she miss him terribly?"

Dagmar seemed surprised by the question.

"I don't know. She did some very strange things. She went to Cairo and took a boat up the Nile to Karnak. But I don't know if that had anything to do with Friedrich or if she would have gone anyway. I liked Zorah, but I can't say I ever understood her. She had some most peculiar ideas."

"For example?" Hester asked.

"Oh, about what women could achieve." Dagmar shook her head, laughing a little. "She even wanted us all to band together and refuse to have relations with our husbands unless they gave us some sort of political power. I mean . . . she was quite mad! Of course, that was when she was very young."

Something stirred in Hester's memory. "Wasn't there a Greek play about something like that?"

"Greek?" Dagmar was amazed.

"Yes, ancient Greek. All the women wanted to stop a war between two city-states . . . or something of the sort."

"Oh. I don't know. Anyway, it's absurd."

Hester did not argue, but she thought perhaps Zorah was not as alien to her own thoughts as she had supposed. She could imagine Rathbone's reaction if she were to tell him of such an idea. It made her laugh even to contemplate it.

Dagmar mistook her reaction, and relaxed, smiling as well, forgetting old tragedies and present threats for a while as they walked the length of the conservatory and smelled the flowers and the damp earth, before Hester went to see how Robert was.

As usual, she climbed the stairs and walked across the landing almost silently. She stood outside Robert's door, which was open about a foot, as was appropriate while he had a female visitor. She looked in, not wishing to interrupt should they be in conversation.

The room was full of sunlight.

Robert was lying back against his pillows, smiling, his attention entirely upon Victoria. She was reading to him from Malory's *Morte d'Arthur*, the love story of Tristram and Isolde. Her voice was gentle and urgent, filled with tragedy, and yet there was a music in it which transcended the immediacy of the quiet sickroom in an elegant London house and became all magic and doomed love, a universal longing.

Hester crept away and went into the dressing room where she had a cot bed made up so she could be close to Robert and respond instantly if he called her. She busied herself with a few duties of tidying up, folding and putting away clothes the laundry maid had brought back.

It was fifteen minutes later when she tapped on the door between her room and Robert's, and then gently pushed it open to see if perhaps he would like something to eat or a cup of tea.

"Next time I'll read about the Siege Perilous and the coming of Sir Galahad," Victoria said eagerly. "It is so full of courage and honor."

Robert sighed. Hester could see his face, pale and pinched with a kind of sadness at the corners of his mouth. Or perhaps it was fear. Surely he must have realized that he might never recover. He had said nothing to her, but he must have lain alone in that silent, tidy room with everything placed there by his parents' love. They were always just beyond the door watching, aching to help him, and knowing that nothing they could do did more than touch the surface. Underneath, the consuming fear, the darkness of dread, was beyond their ability to reach. It must never be out of their minds, and yet they dare not speak it.

Looking at Robert's eyes with the shadowed skin around them, thin and bruised, Hester knew it was just under the surface of all he said.

"Good," he replied politely to Victoria. "That's very kind of you."

She looked at him steadily.

"Would you rather that I didn't?" she asked.

"No!" he responded quickly. "It sounds an excellent story. I think I probably know much of it already. It will be good to hear it again, as it should be told. You read so well." His voice dropped on the last word, in spite of his effort to be courteous and appreciative.

"But you don't want to listen to stories about heroes who can fight, and wield swords, and ride horses, when you are lying in bed and cannot move," Victoria said with shattering bluntness.

Hester felt a chill run through her as if she had swallowed ice.

Robert's face went white. He was still for so long she was afraid that when he did speak he would say something so violent it would be irretrievable.

If Victoria was afraid, she hid it superbly. Her back was ramrod stiff, her thin shoulders straight, her head high.

"There were times when I didn't want to either," she said quite calmly, but there was a tremor in her voice. The memory hurt.

"You can walk!" The words tore out of Robert as if speaking them caused him a physical pain.

"I couldn't for a long time," she replied, now almost matter-of-factly. "And now, when I do, it still hurts." Her voice was trembling, and there was a flush of shame and misery on her cheeks, the delicate bones showing under the too-thin flesh. "I walk badly. I'm clumsy. I knock things. You don't hurt."

"I . . ." He started to retaliate, then realized he had no grounds. His pain of the body was almost gone. Now it was all the desperate, aching, helpless pain of the mind, the knowledge of imprisonment with his lifeless legs.

Again Victoria said nothing.

"I'm sorry for your pain," he said at last. "But I would rather hurt, and be able to move, even awkwardly, than spend the rest of my life lying here like a cabbage."

"And I would rather be able to lie beautifully on a chaise longue." Her voice was thick with emotion. "I'd like to be loved by an honorable family, knowing I would always be cared for, never cold or hungry or alone. And I would love not to dread the pain coming back. But we can neither of us choose. And perhaps you will walk again. You don't know."

Again he was silent for a long time.

Behind the door, Hester dared not make the slightest movement.

"Will your pain get better?" he said at last.

"No. I have been told not," she replied.

He drew a breath as if to ask her more, perhaps about her means and why she feared cold and hunger, but even in his distress he pulled back from such indelicacy.

"I'm sorry."

"Of course you are," she agreed. "And it doesn't help in the slightest, knowing that you are not the only one to suffer. I know that. It doesn't help me either."

He leaned back on the pillows, turning away from her. The soft brown hair flopped over his brow and he ignored it. The sunlight made bright patterns on the floor.

"I suppose you are going to tell me it will get better with time," he said bitterly.

"No, I'm not," she contradicted him. "There are days when it's better and days when it's worse. But when you can't live in your body, then you must make the best of living in your mind."

This time he did not reply, and eventually Victoria stood up. She half turned, and Hester could see in the light the tears on her face.

"I'm sorry," the girl said gently. "I think perhaps I spoke when I should not have. It was too soon. I should have waited longer. Or perhaps I should not have been the one to say it at all. I did because it is too hard for those who love you so much and have never lain where you lie." She shook her head a little. "They don't know whether to be honest or not, or how to say it. They lie awake and hurt, helplessly, and weigh one choice against another, and cannot decide."

"But you can?" He turned back to her, his face twisted with anger. "You have been hurt, so you know everything! You have the right to decide what to tell me, and how, and when?"

Victoria looked as if she had been slapped, but she did not retract.

"Will it be any different tomorrow or next week?" she asked, trying to steady her voice and not quite succeeding. She was standing awkwardly, and from the doorway Hester could see she was adjusting her weight to try to ease the pain. "You lie alone and wonder," she went on. "Not daring to say the words, even in your mind, as if they could make it more real. Part of you has already faced it, another part is still screaming out that it is not true. And for you perhaps it won't be. How much longer do you want to fight with yourself?"

He had no answer. He stared at her while the seconds ticked away.

She took a deep breath and straightened her shoulders, then limped to the door, bumping against the chair. She turned back to him.

"Thank you for sharing Tristram and Isolde with me. I enjoyed your company and your voyage of the mind with me. Good night." And without waiting for him to respond, she pulled the door wider and went out into the landing and down the stairs.

Hester left Robert alone until it was time to take him his supper. He was lying exactly as Victoria had left him, and he looked wretched.

"I don't want to eat," he said as soon as he realized Hester was there. "And don't tell me it would be good for me. It wouldn't. I should choke."

“I wasn’t going to,” she answered quietly. “I agree with you. I think perhaps you need to be alone. Shall I close the door and ask that no one disturb you?”

He looked at her with slight surprise.

“Yes. Yes, please do that.”

She nodded, closing one door and then the other, leaving only one small lamp burning. If he wept himself to sleep, he should at least have privacy to do it, and no one to know or remember it afterwards.

4

HESTER WAS AWARE of Robert's restlessness all night, but she knew she could not help, and to intrude would be inexcusable.

The following morning she found him still asleep, his face pale. He looked very young and very tired. He was just over twenty, but she could see the boy in his features too easily, and feel the isolation and the pain. She did not disturb him. Breakfast hardly mattered.

"Is he all right?" Dagmar said anxiously, meeting Hester on the stairs. "His door was closed last night. I did not like to go in." She blushed faintly, and Hester knew she must have opened the door and heard him weeping. She could only imagine Dagmar's distress. It must ache inside her beyond bearing that there was nothing to do except bear it. For his sake, she would also try to hide it.

Hester did not know what to say. Perhaps she should not mask the truth any longer. It would need a deliberate lie to do it.

"I think he may be facing the possibility that the paralysis may not go away," she said haltingly. "Of course, it may . . ."

Dagmar started to speak, but her voice weakened and would not come. Her mind could find hundreds of words, and none that helped. Hester could see it all in her eyes. Dagmar stood still for a moment, then, unable to maintain her composure, she turned and ran down the stairs again and blindly across the hall to the morning room, where she could be alone.

Hester went back upstairs feeling sick.

In the middle of the morning Robert woke up saying that his head was throbbing and his mouth was dry. Hester helped him into the nearby chair. In the hospital in Scutari, she had learned how to lift people who did not have the strength or the feeling to lift themselves, even men larger and heavier than Robert. She gave him the bowl of water so he could wash and shave himself while she changed the bed, put on clean sheets and pillow slips, plumped them up and smoothed the coverlet. She was not finished when Dagmar knocked and came in.

Robert was composed and very grave, but he looked in command of himself. He refused his mother's help back into bed, but, of course, he could not manage without Hester.

"If Miss Stanhope upset you yesterday," Dagmar began, "I shall send a polite note thanking her and asking her not to come again. It can all be managed without distressing you."

"She probably won't come anyway," Robert said miserably. "I was very rude to her."

"I'm sure it wasn't your fault—" Dagmar began.

"Yes it was! Don't defend me as if I were a child, or an idiot, and not responsible for my actions! I've lost the use of my legs, not my mind!"

Dagmar winced and her eyes filled with tears.

"I'm sorry," Robert said immediately. "You'd better leave me alone. I don't seem to be able to be civil to anyone, except Miss Latterly. At least she's paid to look after me, and I daresay she's used to people like me, who behave wretchedly to all those we should be most grateful to."

"Are you saying you want me to go?" Dagmar tried to master her hurt, but it was naked in her face.

"No, of course not. Yes, I am. I hate hurting you! I hate myself!" He turned away, refusing to look at her.

Hester could not make up her mind whether to step in or not. Maybe this needed to run to its conclusion so all the things unsaid would not be hurting in the mind. Or maybe they were better not spoken? Then they would not have to be taken back and apologized for. And there would be no doubt afterwards whether they were forgiven or not.

"I'll write to Miss Stanhope," Dagmar said hesitantly.

Robert turned back quickly. "No! Please don't. I'd . . . I'd like to write to her myself. I want to apologize. I need to." He bit his lip. "Don't do everything for me, Mama. Don't take that much dignity from me. I can at least make my own apologies."

"Yes . . ." She swallowed as if there were something stuck in her throat. "Yes, of course. Will you ask her to come again, or not to?"

"I'll ask her to come again. She was going to read to me about Sir Galahad and the search for the Holy Grail. He found it, you know."

"Did he?" She forced herself to smile, though tears spilled over her cheeks. "I'll . . . I'll fetch you some paper. And I'll bring you a tray. Will you be all right with ink in bed?"

He smiled twistedly. "I had better learn, hadn't I?"

The doctor called in the afternoon, as he did almost every day. He was quite a young man and had not the professional manner which usually distances a doctor from his patients. There was no air of authority, which to some gave great comfort and to others seemed like condescension. He examined Robert and asked him questions, always addressing him directly and without any false optimism.

Robert said very little. Hester felt certain he was trying to call up the courage to ask if he was going to walk again. He asked no other questions, and that one still seemed too enormous to grasp.

"You are progressing very satisfactorily," the doctor said at length, closing up his bag, still speaking to Robert, not to

Hester or Dagmar, who stood by. "Lying still seems to have had no adverse effect upon your circulation."

Dagmar made as if to speak and then changed her mind.

"I will have a word with Nurse Latterly about your treatment," the doctor went on. "You must keep from getting sores when you lie in one position."

Robert drew in his breath and let it out again in a sigh.

"I don't know," the doctor said softly, answering the question his patient had not asked. "That is the truth, Mr. Ollenheim. I am not saying that if I did know I should necessarily tell you, but I should not lie, that I swear to you. It is not impossible that the nerves have been so badly damaged that it will take a long time to regain their use. I don't know."

"Thank you," Robert said uncertainly. "I was not sure if I wanted to ask."

The doctor smiled.

But downstairs in the withdrawing room, to which Hester had followed Dagmar so that the doctor might speak to them and to Bernd at once, his manner was very grave.

"Well?" Bernd demanded, his eyes dark with fear.

"It does not look promising," the doctor replied, letting his bag rest on the seat of one of the armchairs. "He has no feeling whatever in his legs."

"But it will come back!" Bernd said urgently. "You told us at the time that it could take weeks, even months. We must be patient."

"I said it may come back," the doctor corrected. "I am deeply sorry, Baron Ollenheim, but you must be prepared for the possibility that it may not. I think it would be unfair to your son to keep that knowledge from him. There is still hope, of course, but it is by no means a certainty. The other possibility must also be considered and, as much as lies in your power, prepared for."

"Prepared for!" Bernd was horrified; his face went slack, as if he had been struck. "How can we prepare for it?" His voice rose angrily. "Do what?" he demanded, waving his arms. "Purchase a chair with wheels? Tell him he may never stand again, let alone walk? That . . . that . . ." He stopped, unable to continue.

"Keep courage," the doctor said painfully. "But do not pretend that the worst cannot happen. That is no kindness to him. He may have to face it."

"Isn't there something that can be done? I will pay anything I have . . . anything . . ."

The doctor shook his head. "If there were anything, I would have told you."

"What can we say or do that will make it easier for him," Dagmar asked softly, "if . . . if that should happen? Sometimes I don't know whether it would be easier for him if I said something or if I didn't."

"I don't know either," the doctor admitted. "I've never known. There are no certain answers. Just try not to let him see too much of your own distress. And don't deny it once he has accepted it himself. He will have sufficient battles of his own without having to fight yours as well."

Dagmar nodded. Bernd stood silently, staring past the doctor towards a magnificent painting on the wall of a group of horsemen riding at a gallop, bodies strong, lithe, molded to the movement in perfect grace.

Hester was taking a brief walk in the garden early the following morning when she came upon Bernd standing alone beside a fading flower bed. It was now near the end of September, and the early asters and Michaelmas daisies were in bloom over in the farther bed, a glory of purples, mauves and magentas. Closer to, the gardener had already cut back the dead lupines and delphiniums gone to seed. Other summer flowers were all long over. There was a smell of damp earth, and the rose hips were bright on the rugosa. October was not far away.

Actually, she had come to pick some marigolds. She needed to make more lotion from the flowers. It was most healing to the skin for wounds and for the painful areas of someone lying long in one position. When she saw Bernd she stopped and was about to turn back, not wishing to intrude, but he saw her.

"Miss Latterly!"

"Good morning, Baron." She smiled slightly, a little uncertain.

"How is Robert this morning?" His face was puckered with concern.

"Better," she answered honestly. "I think he was so tired he slept very well and is anxious that Miss Stanhope will consent to return."

"Was he very rude to her?"

"No, not very; simply hurtful."

"I would not like to think he was . . . offensive. One's own pain is not an excuse for the abuse or embarrassment of those not in a position to retaliate!"

In one sentence he had stated all that his status meant, both the innate conviction of superiority and the unbreakable duty of self-discipline and honor that went with it. She looked at his grave profile with its strong, well-shaped bones, a much older, heavier edition of Robert's. His mouth was half obscured by his dark mustache, but the lines were so alike.

"He was not offensive," she assured him, perhaps less than truthfully. "And Miss Stanhope understood precisely why he was abrupt. She has suffered a great deal herself. She knows the stages one passes through."

"Yes, she is obviously"—he hesitated, not sure how to phrase it delicately—"damaged in some way. Was it a disease or an accident, do you know? Of course, she is more fortunate than Robert. She can walk, even if somewhat awkwardly."

She watched his expression of certainty, closed in his own world of assumptions he held as to the lives of others. She could not tell him about Victoria's tragedies or those of her family. He might understand, but if he did not, the damage would be irretrievable. Victoria's privacy would be shattered, and with it the frail confidence she had struggled so hard to achieve.

"An accident," Hester replied. "And then a clumsy piece of surgery. I am afraid it has left her with almost constant pain, sometimes less, sometimes more."

"I'm sorry," he said gravely. "Poor child." That was the end of the subject for him. Courtesy had been satisfied. It had not entered his thinking that Victoria could in any permanent sense be part of Robert's life. She was merely an unfortunate person who had been kind at a time of need, and when that period was over she would disappear, possibly to be remembered with regard, but no more.

He stared beyond the faded bed of flowers towards the brave show of daisies and asters beyond and the bright, rather straggling marigolds, a sudden flare of color against the wet earth and darkening leaves.

"Miss Latterly, if you should happen to become aware of any of the details of this miserable business of Countess Rostova and the Princess Gisela, I would appreciate it if you did not mention it to Robert. I fear it may become extremely unpleasant by the time it reaches trial, if that cannot be prevented. I don't wish him to be unnecessarily distressed. My wife has a somewhat romantic view of things. That would be a pleasanter one for him to accept."

"I know very little of it," Hester said honestly. "The Baroness told me how the Prince and Gisela met, which I suppose I should already have known, and I believe Robert knew that too. But I have no idea why the Countess Rostova should make such an accusation. I don't even know if it is personal or political. It seems extraordinary, when she obviously cannot prove it."

Bernd pushed his hands into his pockets and swayed very slightly on his feet.

Hester was fascinated by the passion which must have driven Countess Rostova, but more urgently than that, she was deeply concerned for Rathbone. It would not matter greatly that he should lose a case. In fact, she thought privately that it might do him good. He had become very pleased with himself since his knighthood. But she did not want to see him humiliated by having taken up a case which was absurd, or alienate himself from his colleagues and from society, even from the ordinary people in the street who identified with the romance of Gisela's story and wished to believe well of her. People do not like their dreams trampled upon.

"Why should she do such a thing?" she asked aloud, aware that he might consider her impertinent. "Is it possible someone else prompted her?"

A slight wind stirred in the trees, sending a drift of leaves down.

He turned around slowly and looked at her, a furrow across his brow.

"I had not thought of that. Zorah is a strange and willful woman, but I have never known her to act in so self-destructive a manner before. I can think of no sane reason why she should make such a charge. She never liked Gisela, but then neither did a great many people. Gisela is a woman with a talent for making both friends and enemies."

"Could Zorah be acting for one of her enemies?"

"In such a suicidal manner?" He shook his head fractionally. "I wouldn't do that for anyone else. Would you?"

"That depends upon who it was and why I thought they wanted me to," she replied, hoping he would tell her more about Zorah. "Do you think she really believes it is true?"

He considered the question for several moments.

"I would find it difficult," he said at last. "Gisela could have nothing to gain personally or politically by Friedrich's death, and everything to lose. I don't see how Zorah could fail to know that."

"Do they know each other well?" It piqued her curiosity sharply. What would the relationship be between those two so different women?

"In a sense, as I think all women know each other when they have lived many years in such circumstances, amid the same circle of people. Their characters are quite different, but there are ways in which their lives are not. Zorah could very easily have been where Gisela was, had Friedrich been of a different personality, had he fallen in love with Zorah's type of unsuitable woman instead of Gisela's." A sudden distaste marred his expression, and she realized with intense sharpness the degree of his anger against the woman who had disrupted the royal house and caused a prince to abandon his people and his duty.

"They couldn't have quarreled over another man, could they?" she said aloud, still searching for reasons.

"Gisela?" Bernd seemed surprised. "I doubt it. She flirted, but it was only a sort of . . . a sort of exercise of her power. She never encouraged anyone. Certainly, I would swear she had no interest."

"But Zorah could have, and if the man was in love with Gisela . . . Gisela must have had the most amazing charm, a magnetic allure." She realized she was speaking of her as if she were dead. "I mean she must have still, I imagine."

Bernd's lips tightened a little, and he turned away, the sharp autumn sun on his face. "Oh, yes. One does not lightly forget Gisela." His expression softened, the contempt fading. "But then you would not forget Zorah either. I think a political answer more probable. We are on the verge of a most dangerous time in our history. We may cease to exist as a country if we are swallowed up into a greater Germany by unification. On the other hand, if we remain independent, we may be ravaged by war, possibly even overrun and obliterated."

"Then surely it seems most likely that if Friedrich was killed, it was to prevent him from returning and leading the fight to retain independence," she said with growing conviction.

"Yes . . ." he agreed. "If, in fact, he really was considering going home. We don't know that he was. But it is possible that that is why Rolf was in England that month, in order to persuade him. Perhaps Rolf was closer to victory than any of us thought."

"Then Gisela might have killed him rather than have him leave her!" Hester said with more triumph than was becoming. "Isn't that what Zorah will say?"

"She may, but I find it hard to believe." He looked back at her, a curious expression on his face which she could not read. "You didn't know Friedrich, Miss Latterly. I cannot imagine the man I knew leaving Gisela behind. He would have made it the price of his return that he should take her with him. That I could believe easily. Or else he would have refused the call."

"Then one of Gisela's enemies may have killed him to prevent that," she reasoned. "And at the same time perhaps they were passionately for unification and saw it as an act of patriotism to stop him from leading the fight for independence. Or could it be someone who was secretly allied with one of the other principalities, who hopes to become the leading power in a new Germany?"

He looked at her with sharpened interest, as if in some aspect he were seeing her for the first time.

"You have a very keen interest in politics, Miss Latterly."

"In people, Baron Ollenheim. And I have seen enough of war to dread it anywhere, for any country."

"Do you not think there are some things worth fighting for, even if it means dying?" he said slowly.

"Yes. But it is one thing to judge the prize worth someone else's life, and another judging it worth your own."

He looked at her thoughtfully, but he did not add anything further to the subject. She collected the marigolds, and he walked back towards the house with her.

* * *

Victoria accepted Robert's apology and was quick to return only two days later. Hester had expected her to be uncertain in her manner, afraid of another attack sprung from a fear Robert could not help, or from anger which was only fear in disguise, and directed at her, because in his eyes she was less vulnerable than his parents.

Hester was in the dressing room next door, and she heard the maid showing Victoria in, and then her retreating footsteps as she left them alone.

Robert's voice came clear and a little abashed. "Thank you for coming back."

"I wanted to," Victoria replied with certain shyness, and Hester could glimpse her back through the open crack of the door. "I enjoy sharing things with you."

Hester could see Robert's face. He was smiling.

"What have you brought?" he asked. "Sir Galahad? Please sit down. I'm sorry for not asking you to. You look chilly. Is it cold outside? Would you like me to send for tea?"

"Thank you, yes it is, and no, I'd like tea later, if I may, whenever you are ready." She sat carefully, trying not to twist her back as she arranged her skirts. "And I didn't bring Galahad. I thought perhaps not yet. I brought one or two different things. Would you like something funny?"

"More Edward Lear?"

"I thought something much older. Would you like some Aristophanes?"

"I have no idea," he said, making himself smile. "It sounds very heavy. Are you sure it's funny? Does it make you laugh?"

"Oh, yes," she said quickly. "It shows up some of the ridiculousness of people who take themselves terribly seriously. I think when you can no longer laugh at yourself, you are beginning to lose your balance."

"Do you?" He sounded surprised. "I always thought of

laughter as a little frivolous, not the stuff of real life so much as an escape."

"Oh, not at all." Her voice was full of feeling. "Sometimes that is when the most real things of all are said."

"You think the absurd is the most real?" He sounded puzzled, but not critical.

"No, that is not what I mean," she explained. "I do not mean the laughter of mockery, which devalues, but the laughter of the comic, which helps us to realize we are no more or less important than anyone else. What is funny is when things are unexpected, disproportionate. It makes us laugh because it is not as we thought, and suddenly we see the silliness of it. Isn't that a kind of sanity?"

"I never thought of it like that." He was turned towards her, his face absorbed in concentration. "Yes, I suppose that is the best kind of laughter. How did you discover that? Or did someone tell you?"

"I thought about it a lot. I had much time to read and to think. That is the magical thing about books. You can listen to all the greatest people who have ever lived, anywhere in the world, in any civilization. You can see what is completely different about them, things you never imagined." Her voice gathered urgency and excitement, and Hester could see through the crack in the door that she was leaning forward towards the bed, and Robert was smiling as he watched her.

"Read me your Aristophanes," he said softly. "Take me to Greece for a little while, and make me laugh."

She settled back in her chair and opened her book.

Hester returned to the sewing she was doing, and a little while later she heard Robert's voice in a loud guffaw, and then a moment after, another.

As Robert grew stronger and needed less constant care, Hester was able to leave Hill Street on occasion. At the first opportunity she wrote to Oliver Rathbone and asked if she might call upon him at his chambers in Vere Street.

He answered that he would be pleased to see her, but it would be necessary to restrict the meeting to a luncheon because of the pressure of the case he was preparing.

Accordingly, she presented herself at midday and found him pacing the floor of his chamber, his face showing the marks of tiredness and unaccustomed anxiety.

"How very nice to see you," he said, smiling as she was shown in and the door closed behind her. "You look well."

It was a meaningless comment, a politeness, and one that could not be returned with any honesty.

"You don't," she said with a shake of her head.

He stopped abruptly. It was not the reply he had expected. It was tactless, even for Hester.

"The Countess Rostova's case is causing you concern," she said with a faint smile.

"It is complex," he said guardedly. "How did you know about it?" Then instantly he knew the answer. "Monk, I suppose."

"No," she replied a trifle stiffly. She had not seen Monk in some time. Their relationship was always difficult, except in moments of crisis, when the mutual antipathy between them dissolved in the bonds of a friendship founded in instinctive trust deeper than reason. "No, I heard from Callandra."

"Oh." He looked pleased. "Would you accompany me to luncheon? I am sorry I can spare so little time, but I am having to deal with other matters rather hastily in order to try to gather some of the defense in what I am sure will prove a very public affair."

"Of course," she accepted. "I should be delighted."

"Good." He led the way out of his office; through the outer room, past the clerks in their neat, high-buttoned suits, pens in hand, ledgers open in front of them; and out onto the street. They spoke of trivial matters until they were seated in a quiet corner of a public hostelry and had ordered a meal of cold game pie, vegetables and pickle.

"I am presently nursing Robert Ollenheim," Hester said after the first mouthful of pie.

"Indeed." Rathbone showed no particular interest, and she realized he had not heard the name before and it had no meaning for him.

"The Ollenheims knew Prince Friedrich quite well," she explained, taking a little more pickle. "And, of course, Gisela—and the Countess Rostova too."

"Oh. Oh, I see." Now she had his attention. The color deepened in his cheeks as he realized how easily she had read him. He bent his head and concentrated on eating his pie, avoiding her eyes. "I'm sorry. Perhaps I am a trifle preoccupied. Proof for this case may be harder to find than I had anticipated." He looked up at her quickly with a slightly rueful smile.

A buxom woman passed by, her skirts brushing their chairs.

"Have you learned anything yet from Monk?" she asked.

He shook his head. "He hasn't reported back to me so far."

"Where is he? In Germany?"

"No, Berkshire."

"Why Berkshire? Is that where Friedrich died . . . or was killed?"

His mouth was full. He glanced up at her without bothering to reply.

"Do you think it might be political?" she said, trying to sound casual, as if the idea had just occurred to her. "To do with German unification rather than a personal crime . . . if indeed there was a crime?"

"Quite possibly," he answered, still concentrating on the pie. "If he returned to his own country to lead the fight against forced unification, he would almost certainly have been obliged to leave Gisela, in spite of the fact that he did not apparently believe so, and that was what she dreaded."

"But Gisela loved him so much, and always has done. No

one at all, except Zorah, has ever questioned that," she pointed out, trying not to sound like a governess with a slow child, but she heard her own voice sounding impatient and a little too distinct. "Even if he returned for a short while without her, if he succeeded in the fight for independence, then he could demand she return also as his queen, and they could not deny him. Does it not seem at least equally possible that someone else would have killed him to prevent him returning, perhaps someone who wanted unification?"

"Do you mean someone in the pay of one of the other German states?" he asked, considering the question.

"Possibly. Could the Countess Rostova have made the charge at someone else's instigation, trusting that they know something they have not yet told her but will reveal when the matter comes to trial?"

He thought about it for a few moments, reaching for his glass of wine.

"I doubt it," he said at last. "Simply because she does not seem like a person who would follow someone else's lead."

"What do you know about the other people who were at the house?"

He poured her a little more wine. "Very little, as yet. Monk is presently learning what he can. Most of them have gathered together there again, I presume to defend themselves against the charge. It is hardly the sort of thing an ambitious hostess wishes said about her country house party." A very brief flicker of sardonic amusement crossed his face and was gone almost instantly. "But that is no defense for the Countess Rostova."

She studied his features carefully, trying to read in them the complexity of his feelings. She saw the quick intelligence that had always been there, the wit, and a flash of the self-assurance which made him at once attractive and irritating. She also caught a glimmer that it was not only this case itself which caused him concern, but the flicker of doubt as to whether he had been entirely wise to take it in the first place.

"Perhaps she knows it is murder but has accused the wrong person?" she said aloud, watching him with gentleness which surprised her. "She may not be guilty of either mischief or spite, simply of not having understood the complications of the situation. Or is it possible Gisela was the one who gave him the poison without realizing what it was? She may be technically guilty and morally innocent." She had forgotten the almost finished pie on her plate. "And when it is proved, she will withdraw her charge and apologize. And then perhaps Gisela will be sufficiently glad that the truth is known and she will accept it without seeking recompense or punishment."

Rathbone was silent for some time.

Hester started to eat again. She was actually hungry.

"Of course it is possible," he said after a while. "If you had met her you would not doubt either her perception or her integrity."

Hester would question that, but realized with a jolt of surprise, and amusement, that Rathbone had been profoundly impressed by the Countess, so much so that he suspended his usual caution. It made her extremely curious about Zorah Rostova, and perhaps just a little piqued. There was rather a lot of enthusiasm in his tone.

It also showed a human vulnerability in Rathbone she had not seen before, a gap in his usual armor. It made her angry with him for being too naive, frightened that he should prove more fallible than she had imagined. She was surprised at herself, and at him, and aware every moment that passed of an increasing protectiveness.

He did not seem to have realized the heat of the emotions which were aroused by such a great public romance, the dreams quite unconnected people invested in it. In some ways he had lived a curiously protected life, from comfortable home, excellent education, exclusive university, and then training in the best solicitor's office before being called to the bar. He knew the law, few better, and he had certainly seen crimes of passion and even depravity. But had he really tasted any breadth of ordinary human life, with its frailty, complexity and seeming contradictions?

She thought not, and the lack frightened her for him.

"You will need to learn as much as you can about the politics of the situation," she said earnestly.

"Thank you!" There was a flicker of sarcasm in his eyes. "I had thought of that."

"What are the Countess's political views?" she persisted. "Is she for unification or independence? What about her family connections? Where does her money come from? Is she in love with anybody?"

She could see by his face that he had not thought of at least the last question. A moment of surprise lit in his eyes, and then he masked it.

"I suppose there is no chance she will withdraw the allegation before the trial?" she said without hope. He must already have tried everything he knew to persuade her.

"None," he said ruefully. "She is determined to see justice done, whatever the cost to herself, and I have warned her it may be very high."

"Then you cannot do more," she said with an attempt at a smile. "I have talked with Baron and Baroness Ollenheim about it when I have the opportunity. She sees it all very romantically. He is a little more practical about it, and I gathered the impression that he did not greatly like Gisela. Both of them seem convinced that she and Friedrich adored each other and he would never have considered going home without her, even if the country were swallowed up in unification." She sipped her wine, looking at him over the top of the glass. "If you can prove murder, I think it will be someone else who is guilty."

"I am already aware of the ramifications." He kept his voice steady, even trying to make it buoyant, and failing. "And that the Countess will be extremely unpopular for leveling such a charge. Breaking dreams never makes one liked, but sometimes it is necessary in pursuing any kind of justice."

It was a brave speech, and the fact that he made it showed the level of his anxiety. He seemed to wish to confide in her, and yet to take the discussion only to a certain point, as if perhaps he had not yet thought beyond that point himself.

She also felt a trifle defensive against this woman who had disturbed Rathbone so uncharacteristically.

"She seems a woman of great courage," she remarked. "I hope we shall be able to find enough evidence to open up a proper investigation. After all, it is in a sense our responsibility, since it happened in England."

"Quite!" he agreed vehemently. "We cannot simply allow it to slip into a legend that is untrue without at least a struggle. Maybe Monk will uncover some facts which will be helpful—I mean simple things, like who had opportunity . . ."

"How does she believe he was killed?" she inquired.

"Poison."

"I see. Everybody thinks that is what women use. But that doesn't mean to say it was a woman. And everyone may not want what they say they do regarding unification or independence."

"Of course not," he conceded. "I shall see what Monk has learned and what new light it throws on the situation." He tried to sound hopeful.

She smiled at him. "Don't worry yet. This is only the beginning. After all, no one even thought of murder until the Countess said so. Everyone was happy to accept that it was natural. This may waken all sorts of memories, if we work hard enough. And there will be friends of independence who will want to know the truth, whatever it was. Perhaps even the Queen? She may be of some assistance, even if only by lending her name and her support to learning what really happened."

He pulled a rueful face. "To prove that one of the royal

family committed murder? I doubt it. It is a terrible stain, no matter how she may have disliked Gisela."

"Oh, Oliver!" She leaned a little farther across the table and, without thinking, touched his fingers with hers. "Kings have been murdered by their relations since time immemorial! In fact, long before that. I think time immemorial is quite recent in the history of kings and ambition, love, hate and murder. No one who has ever read the Bible is going to find it so difficult to believe."

"I suppose you are right." He relaxed and picked up his wine again. "Thank you for your spirit, Hester." He tipped the glass a fraction towards her.

She lifted her own, and they touched rims with a faint chink, his eyes gentle over the top of his glass.

She learned in a brief note from Rathbone when Monk returned from Berkshire, and the day after she went to see him in his rooms in Fitzroy Street. Their relationship had always been volatile, often critical, poised on the edge of quarrel, a curious mixture of anger and trust underneath. He infuriated her. She deplored many of his attitudes, and she knew his weaknesses. Yet she also was absolutely certain that there were dishonesties he would never commit, cruelties or acts of cowardice he would give his life rather than allow. There was a darkness in him, the voids in his memory, which frightened him more than they did her.

There had been moments, one in particular, when she had thought he might love her. Now she did not know, and she refused to think of it. But the bonds of friendship were unbreakable, and strong beyond any nature of question. She was only just in time to catch him. He was already packing to travel again.

"You can't leave this case," she said indignantly, standing in the middle of his reception room, which she had designed, over much objection from him, in order that his clients, and prospective clients, might feel more at ease to confide in him their problems. She had finally succeeded in persuading him that people who were not physically comfortable would be far less likely to remain and to find the words to tell him the difficult and perhaps painful details he would need to know about in order to help. Now he stood by the fire, his eyebrows raised, his expression slightly contemptuous.

"Rathbone needs you!" she said, angry that he should need to be told. He should have understood it for himself. "He's fighting against far greater odds than he realizes. Perhaps he should not have taken the case, but he has, and there is no purpose now in wishing otherwise."

"And I imagine, in your usual governess fashion, you told him so?" he inquired, responding to her criticism as usual.

"Didn't you?" she challenged back.

"I told him it would be difficult . . ."

"And you are leaving us to fight alone?" She was so incredulous she was almost fumbling her words. She had thought many ill things of Monk at one time or another, but she could still hardly believe he would go away during a crisis. It was not his nature, not what she knew him to be. He had fought desperately and brilliantly to help her when she had needed it, as she and Rathbone had fought for him. Could he forget so easily?

He looked both angry and satisfied. There was a smile on his face very like a sneer.

"And what do you believe I should investigate next?" he said sarcastically. "Please, make some suggestions . . ."

"Well, you might find out a great deal more about the political situation," she began. "Was there really a plan to have Friedrich go back home, or not? Did Gisela believe he would go without her, or did she know he would never leave her? Did he actually insist that accepting her also was the price of his return? Did he say so, and what was the answer? Did Gisela know it? Why does the Queen hate her so much? Did Friedrich know about it, whatever it is? Did the Queen's brother Count Lansdorff know?" She drew in her breath, then went on. "Of all the people who were there that weekend, which of them have interests or relatives in other German states who might be affected by unification? Who had ambitions towards war or political power? Who has alliances anywhere else? What about the Countess herself? Who are her closest friends? There are dozens of things you could find out. Even if they only raised other questions, it would be a beginning."

"Bravo!" He clapped his hands. "And who should I speak to in order to learn all these things?"

"I don't know! Can't you think of anything for yourself? Go and speak to the people of the court in exile!"

His eyes opened even wider. "You mean the court in Venice?"

"Why not?"

"You think that is a good idea?"

"Of course! If you had any loyalty to Rathbone, you wouldn't need to ask me, you'd just go!"

Her concern for Rathbone must have cut sharply through her voice. He saw it, and a curious softness filled his face, and then something which might have been surprise or hurt. It was all there, and then gone in an instant before she was sure.

"I was just going!" he said tartly. "What do you imagine I am packing for? Or do you want me to go to Venice just as I stand? Don't you think it would be a little more intelligent, if I am to mix with the exile court, for me to take a few changes of suitable clothes?"

She should have known. Of course, she should have. She had misjudged him. Relief welled up inside her, filling her with warmth, untying all the knots of anger and calming her fear. She found herself smiling. She should never have doubted.

"Yes, I'm so glad." It was not quite an apology, but almost. "Yes, naturally you'll need the appropriate clothes. Are you going by boat or train?"

"Both," he replied. He hesitated. "You don't need to worry so much about Rathbone," he said grudgingly. "He isn't a fool. And I'll find enough evidence either to make a decent case or else persuade the Countess Rostova to withdraw before it comes to court."

She realized with a tingle of amazement that Monk was annoyed because she was afraid for Rathbone. He was jealous, and it infuriated him. She wanted to laugh, but it would sound hysterical, and he would be quite capable of shaking her till she stopped. And she would not stop, because it was so unbelievably funny. He would misunderstand entirely, and then she would only laugh the more. They would end, closer than ever, touching, the fears and barriers forgotten for a moment. Or they would quarrel and say things which might not be meant but could not be taken back or forgotten.

He stood motionless.

She did not dare put it to the test. It mattered too much.

"I doubt she'll apologize or withdraw," she said quietly, her voice breaking a little. "But at least you may be able to find out whether or not he was murdered. Was he?"

"I don't know," he replied soberly. "It could have been poison. There are yew trees in the garden there, and anyone could pick the leaves without being noticed."

"How would they get them to Prince Friedrich?" she asked. "You can hardly walk into a sickroom and ask the patient to eat a few leaves. Anyway, most people know what yew leaves look like; they're sort of needles, and everyone knows they're poisonous. It's the sort of thing your parents tell you not to eat when you're a child. I can remember being frightened of yew trees in graveyards when I was very young."

"Obviously, someone made an infusion and added it to his food or drink," he said dourly. "They could either have done that in his room or, far more likely, gone to the kitchen or distracted a servant carrying a tray upstairs. It would be easy enough. The only thing is, Gisela never left their suite of rooms. She is about the only person who didn't go into the garden at all. All the servants will testify to that. Even at night, she remained with him all the time."

"Someone helped her?" she said, knowing even as she did so that Gisela would never trust anyone else with such a secret.

Monk did not bother to answer.

"If he was murdered at all, it wasn't Gisela," she said quietly. "What are you going to do? How can we help Rathbone?"

"I don't know." He was unhappy and annoyed. "If we can prove it was murder, that may be all Zorah really wants. Perhaps she accused Gisela because the Princess is the one person who would have to fight to clear her name. Maybe that was the only way to force a trial and a public investigation."

"But what about Rathbone?" she insisted. "He is the one who has undertaken to defend her. How will finding someone else guilty help him?"

"I don't suppose it will," he said testily, moving away from the mantelpiece. "But if that's the truth, then that is all I can do. I assume you don't want me to manufacture evidence to convict Gisela simply to assist Rathbone out of a predicament he's dug himself into because he was fascinated by a German countess with outrageous opinions and listened to his heart, not his head? Or do you?"

She should have been furious with him for his vitriolic remarks and for deliberately trying to make her jealous by mentioning Zorah in these terms, the more so because he had succeeded. But for once she could read him too easily, and his motive at least was flattering. She smiled. "Find as much of the truth as you can," she said quite lightly. "I expect he will make something worth having of it, even if it is only the dignity of saving a reputation and making a decent apology for a misplaced belief. The truth may be hard to take, but lies are always worse, in the end. Perhaps silence would have been best, but it's too late for that now."

"Silence?" he said with a sharp laugh. "Between two

women like that? And I can't even speak to Gisela, because she is receiving nobody." He took another step forward. "Tell Rathbone I'll write to him from Venice . . . if there's anything to say."

"Of course. I'll see you when you return." She was about to add something about doing all he could, then caught his eye and kept the silence he had referred to so scathingly. She would miss him, knowing he was not even in London, but she certainly did not say that.

5

AS *MONK HAD TOLD HESTER,* his journey was first to Dover, then across the Channel to Calais, then to Paris, and then the final, large and very gracious train which took him for a long journey south and east to Venice. Stephan von Emden had gone two days before and was to meet him when he arrived, so he was traveling alone.

The trip was both fascinating and exhausting, particularly since, apart from one journey up to Scotland, he was unfamiliar with travel of any distance. If he had ever been out of Great Britain before, it was lost in that part of his memory which he could not retrieve. Snatches came back when some experience echoed something from the past and produced a fragment, sharp and unrelated, puzzling him more than it enlightened. Usually it was no more than an impression, a face seen for a moment, perhaps a powerful emotion connected with it, sometimes pleasant, more often one of anxiety or regret. Why was it that pain seemed to return more easily? Was that something about his life or his nature? Or do the darker things simply mark themselves on the mind in a different way?

He spent much of the time, as the train rattled and swayed through the countryside, thinking of the case he was pursuing, perhaps fruitlessly. Hester's attitude rankled with him. He had not appreciated that she was so fond of Rathbone. Perhaps he had never thought about it, but now he could see from the tension and the anxiety in her that she was concerned. She had seemed hardly able to think of anything else.

Possibly, her anxiety was well founded. Rathbone had been uncharacteristically rash in taking Zorah Rostova's case before looking into it more thoroughly. It would be extremely difficult to defend. The more Monk learned, the more apparent did that become. The very best they could hope for would be some limitation of the damage.

He felt guilt at traveling in a manner he could not possibly have afforded on his own means. He was going to a country he had never been to before, so far as he knew, and on what he sincerely believed would be a hopeless quest, and doing it at Zorah's expense. Perhaps honor should have dictated that he tell her directly that he did not know what he was looking for and thought there was only the slightest chance he could learn anything that would help her cause. In her interest, the best advice would be to apologize quickly and withdraw the allegation. Surely Rathbone must have said that to her?

The rhythmic rattle of the wheels over the rails and the slight sway of the carriage were almost mesmeric. The seat was most comfortable.

What if Rathbone withdrew his services? Then the Countess would have to find someone else to represent her, and that might be extremely difficult to do, perhaps sufficiently so to deter her altogether.

But Rathbone was too stubborn for that. He had given his word, and his pride would not let him admit he had made a mistake, and he could not accomplish the task—because it was not possible. The man was a fool!

But he was also, in some respects, Monk's friend as well as his employer, so there was no alternative but to continue on this excellent train journey all the way to Venice, pretending to be a gentleman, and play the courtier to what was left of the exiled royalty and learn what he could.

He approached Venice by the new land bridge, arriving late in the afternoon as the light was fading. Stephan met him at the station, which teemed with people of extraordinary variety, fair skins and dark, Persians, Egyptians, Levantines and Jews as well as emperors of a dozen countries. A Babel of languages he did not begin to recognize sounded around him, and costumes of all manner of cut and color surged past him. Alien smells of spice, garlic and aromatic oils mixed with steam, coal smuts and salt wind and sewage. He remembered with a jolt how far east Venice was; it was the place where the trade of Europe met the silk roads and spice trails of the Orient. To the west lay Europe, to the south Egypt and Africa beyond, to the east Byzantium and the ancient world, and beyond that, India and even China.

Stephan welcomed him enthusiastically. A servant a couple of steps behind him took Monk's cases and, shouldering them easily, forced a way through the crowd.

Within twenty minutes they were in a gondola moving gently along a narrow canal. High above them, the sun lit the marble faces of the buildings close in on either side, but down where they were, the shadows were dark across the water. Everything seemed to shift or waver, reflecting wave patterns on walls. The sounds of slurping and whispering came from every side, and the smells of damp, of salt, of effluent and wet stone were thick in the nose.

Monk stared to one side and then the other, fascinated. This place was unlike anything he had even dreamed. A flight of stone steps rose from the water and disappeared between buildings. Another mounted to a landing and an archway beyond which glimmered a door. Torches were reflected in shivered fire on the broken surface of the water. Other boats jostled up and down, bumping together gently where they were moored at long poles.

Monk was enthralled. He had not known what to expect. He had been too occupied with what he hoped to learn, and how he was going to go about it, to think of the city itself. He had heard tales of Venice's glory—and its ruin. He knew it was an ancient and corrupt republic which was the seafaring gateway east and west of European trade, an immense power at its height, before the decadence which had brought about its fall. This was the Pearl of the Adriatic, the Bride of the Sea, where the Doge ceremonially cast a wedding ring into the lagoon as a symbol of their union.

He had also heard of its evil, its perversions, its stagnant beauty sliding inevitably into the waters, waiting for destruction. He also knew that it had been conquered and occupied by the Austro-Hungarian Empire and he would find Austrian officials in government and Austrian soldiers on such streets as there were.

But as the sun set in a flaming sky, daubing the fretted roofs of the palaces in fire, and he heard the calls of the boatmen echoing across the water and the hollow sound of the tide sucking under the stone foundations, all he could think of was the eerie beauty of the place and its utter and total uniqueness.

Without having spoken of more than necessities, they reached a small private landing and stepped ashore. The landing was the rear entrance of a small palace whose principal facade faced a main canal to the south. A liveried attendant emerged almost immediately carrying a torch which shed an orange light on the damp stones and for a moment showed the dark surface of the water almost green. He recognized Stephan and held the torch aloft to show them the way over the flagged stones to the steps up to a narrow wooden door which was half open.

Monk was cold only because he was tired, but he was glad to go up into the warmth and brightness of a wide entrance hall, marble floored but with thick Eastern carpets giving it a luxury and sense of immediate comfort.

Stephan followed him up, and the servant could be heard calling for a footman to fetch the cases.

Monk was shown his room in Stephan's house, which was palatial, high-ceilinged, hung with dramatic tapestries now faded to earth tones of great beauty. Deep windows looked south onto the larger canal, where the light still played on the water, sending reflected waves rippling across the ceiling.

He walked straight over, ignoring the bed and the chairs, and leaned out as far as he could through the stone embrasure, staring down. There were still at least a score of barges and gondolas plying their slow way up and down the canal. On the far side, the carved and pillared facades were lit by torchflare, making the marble look rose and rust and the windows black sockets through which someone else might be staring, just as he was, from a darkened room, utterly enthralled.

Over dinner in a larger chamber, looking onto the Ca' Grande, he forced his mind to the purpose for which he was there.

"I need to know a great deal more about the political alliances and interests of the people who were at the Wellboroughs' when Friedrich died," he said to Stephan.

"Of course," Stephan agreed. "I can tell you, but I imagine you need to observe for yourself. My word is hardly evidence, and certainly not my opinion." He leaned back and touched his napkin to his lips after the shellfish of the first course. "Fortunately, there are all sorts of occasions within the next few days to which I can take you and where you will meet the sort of people you need to." His voice was full of optimism, but there was anxiety shadowing his eyes.

Again Monk wondered why he was so loyal to Zorah and what he knew of Friedrich's death that moved him to take so much trouble trying to prove it had been murder. Was he part of the story or only an onlooker? What were his own loyalties? What would he lose or gain if Gisela were proved guilty—or if Zorah were? Perhaps Monk had been rash to have taken Stephan so completely at his word. It was a mistake he did not often make.

"Thank you," he accepted. "I should be grateful for your advice and your opinion. You know these people far better than I ever will. And while certainly your view is not evidence, it may be the wisest counsel I shall have and the best guide towards finding proof other people will be obliged to believe, however much they may prefer not to."

Stephan said nothing for quite some time. He looked at Monk at first with surprise, and then curiosity, and finally with a certain amusement, as if at last he had some measure of him in his mind.

"Of course," he conceded.

"What do you believe happened?" Monk said bluntly.

The light was almost gone from the sky outside. There was only the occasional reflection of a drifting torch on the windows, and then more dimly on the water and back again on the glass. The air smelled of damp and salt, and in the background to everything there was always the constant murmur of the tide.

"I believe the atmosphere was right for murder," Stephan said guardedly, watching Monk's face as he spoke. "There was much to win or lose. People can convince themselves of all sorts of moralities where patriotism is concerned."

A servant brought a dish of baked fish and vegetables, and Monk accepted a generous portion.

"Ordinary values of life or death can be set aside," Stephan went on. "Almost as they can in war. You say to yourself, 'This is for my country, for my people. I commit a lesser evil that a greater good may be obtained.' " He was still watching Monk closely. "All through history people have done that, and depending on the outcome, they are either crowned or hanged. And history afterwards will call them hero one day and traitor another. Success is the common judge. It takes a rare man to set his values on other standards."

Monk was caught by surprise. He had thought Stephan shallower, less thoughtful of the motives of those he seemed to treat with such casual friendship. His eye was keener than Monk had supposed. Again, he should not have been so quick to judge.

"Then I had better learn a great deal more," Monk replied. "But a political murder does not help the Countess Rostova's case. Or is her motive more subtly political than I imagined?"

Stephan drew in his breath to make an instant reply, then changed his mind. He laughed slightly, spearing a piece of fish and putting it into his mouth. "I was going to answer that with absolute certainty," he replied. "Then the fact that you asked the question made me think about it. Perhaps I was mistaken. I would have denied it. She hated Gisela for entirely personal reasons and thought the Princess behaved from immediate, personal motives: pride, ambition, love of glamour, attention, luxury, status among her peers, envy, revenge for love wasted or betrayed, all the things that have nothing to do with patriotism or matters of state, simply humanity. But perhaps I was wrong. I don't think I knew Zorah as well as I had assumed."

His face became very serious, his eyes steady on Monk's. "But I would lay my life that she is no hypocrite. Whatever her cause, there is no lie in it."

Monk believed him. He was less sure that Zorah had not been used, but he had as yet no idea by whom. It was one of the things he might learn in Venice.

The next day Stephan took him to explore a little of the city, drifting gently down one waterway after another until they found themselves on the Grand Canal, and Stephan pointed out the palaces one after another, telling Monk of their history and sometimes of the present occupants. He pointed to the magnificent Gothic Palazzo Cavalli.

"Henry the Fifth of France lives there," Stephan said with a smile.

Monk was lost. "Henry the Fifth of France?" He thought he knew there was no king of France, never had been for well over half a century.

"Monsieur le Comte de Chambord," Stephan said with a laugh, leaning back on one elbow in an oddly graceful gesture of comfort. "Grandson of Charles the Tenth, and king if there were a throne in France, a fact many people here prefer to overlook. His mother, the Duchesse de Berry, married a penniless Italian nobleman and lives in good style in the Palazzo Vendramin-Calergi. She bought it in 1844, practically for a song: pictures, furniture and everything. Venice used to be terribly cheap then. You know, in '51 John Ruskin paid only twenty-six pounds a year for an apartment here on the Grand Canal, and for years before that Robert and Elizabeth Browning paid only twenty-six pounds a year for a suite at the Casa Guidi in Florence. But Mr. James, the British consul here, is paying one hundred sixty pounds a year for one floor in the Palazzo Foscolo. Everything is terribly expensive now."

They rocked slightly in the wake of a larger barge, and the sound of laughter drifted across the water from a closed gondola a hundred feet away.

"The Comte de Montmoulin lives here too," Stephan went on. "In the Palazzo Loredan, at San Vio."

"And what is he king of?" Monk asked, catching the flavor but far more interested in the mention of poets and critics such as Ruskin.

"Spain," Stephan replied. "Or so he would believe. There are all sorts of artists and poets and invalids, social and political exiles, some of marvelous color, others of utter tediousness."

It seemed eminently the right place for Friedrich and Gisela, and those who chose to follow them, for whatever reason.

An hour later they sat in a small piazza eating luncheon. Passersby strolled across the square, talking idly. Monk heard the chatter of half a dozen different languages. Here and there soldiers in Austrian uniform lounged around, guns hanging, half ready if there should be any resistance or unpleasantness. It was a startling reminder that this was an occupied city. The native Venetians were not in control. They must obey or suffer the consequences.

The streets and canals were quieter than he had expected. He was used to the noise and ebullience of London, the constant bustle of life. The contrast between the teeming capital of an empire, with its opulence and squalor, the bursting confidence of its trade and the tide of wealth and expansion, its poor and its oppressed in ever-growing slums, had an utterly different air from this glorious ruin sinking into a gentle despair under foreign domination. The past was all around as an aching memory filled with beauty that crumbled. Visitors like Monk and Stephan sat in the autumn sunlight on marble pavements and watched over wanderers and expatriates talking in hushed tones, while Venetians went about their daily business, outwardly docile, seemingly apathetic. Austrians strolled with casual arrogance around the streets and squares of a city they did not love.

"Did Zorah come here often?" Monk asked. He needed to know more of the accuser in order to understand the charge. He had neglected her until now.

"Yes, at least once a year," Stephan answered, stabbing his fork into a stuffed tomato. "Why do you ask? She did know Friedrich and Gisela well, over many years, if that is what you are wondering."

"Why? She was not in exile, was she?"

"No, of course not."

"Was it because of Friedrich?" Had he asked too bluntly to get an honest answer?

A Greek and a Levantine strolled past, and the breeze carried a perfume of spikenard and bay leaves. They were engaged in heated conversation in some language Monk did not recognize.

Stephan laughed. "Was she in love with him? You don't know much about Zorah if you can even ask that. She might have been, a long time ago, but she would never waste her passion or her pride on a man whom she couldn't win." He leaned back a little in his chair, the sunlight on his face.

"She's had many lovers over the years. I think Friedrich was probably one of them, before Gisela, but there have been several since, I assure you. There was a Turkish brigand, whom she loved for over two years, and there was a musician in Paris, but I don't think that lasted long. He was too devoted to his music to be much fun. There was someone in Rome, but I don't know who, and there was an American. He lasted quite a while, but she wouldn't marry him." He was still smiling. He had to raise his voice a little to be heard above the rising sound of chatter around him. "She loved to explore frontiers, but she didn't want to live on one. And there was an Englishman. He entertained her hugely, and I think she really cared for him a great deal. And, of course, there was a Venetian, hence many of her visits here. I think he lasted rather a long time, and perhaps she returned here to see him."

"Is he still here?"

"No, I'm afraid he died. I think he was older than she."

"Who is it at the moment?"

"I don't know. I rather think it may be Florent Barberini, but then again, it may not."

"He spoke warmly of Gisela."

Stephan's face tightened. "I know. Perhaps I am anticipating or even simply wrong." He sipped his white wine. "Shall I tell you something about the party tonight?"

"Yes, please." Monk's stomach knotted with apprehension. Would Venetian society be as formal as English society, and would he feel as monstrously out of place, as obviously not one of the small, closed elite?

"There will be about eighty of us," Stephan said thoughtfully. "I chose this number because I thought you could meet a lot of the people who knew both Zorah and Gisela—and, of course, Friedrich. And there will be many Venetians as well. Perhaps you will understand a little of exile life. It is very gay on the surface, extravagant and sophisticated. But underneath there is a lack of purpose." His face was soft with a weary compassion. "Many dream of returning home, even talk about it as if it were imminent, but they all know in the morning that it will never happen. Their own people do not want them. The places they were born for are filled by others."

Monk had a sharp vision of alienation, the same sense of being apart that he had experienced with such loneliness in the earliest months after his accident. He had known no one, not even himself. He had been a man who belonged nowhere, without purpose or identity, a man divorced from his roots.

"Did Friedrich regret his choice?" he said suddenly.

Stephan's eyes narrowed a little. "I don't think so. He didn't seem to miss Felzburg. Wherever Gisela was was home for him. She was everything he really needed or relied on." A gust of wind blew across the pavement, something of salt and effluent.

"I am not sure how much he even really wished to be king," Stephan went on. "The glamour was wonderful, the adulation, and he could do all that very well. People loved him. But he didn't like the discipline."

Monk was surprised. "Discipline?" It was the last thing he had thought of.

Stephan sipped his wine again. Behind him, Monk saw two women walk by, their heads close together, talking in French and laughing, skirts billowing around them.

"You think kings do whatever they want?" Stephan said, shaking his head. "Did you notice the Austrian soldiers in the piazza?"

"Of course."

"Believe me, they are an undisciplined rabble compared with Queen Ulrike. I've seen her rise at half past six in the morning, order her household for the parties and the banquets of the day, write letters, receive visitors. Then she'll spend time with the King, encouraging him, advising him, persuading him. She'll spend all afternoon entertaining the ladies she wishes to influence. She'll dress magnificently for dinner and outshine every other woman in the room, and be present at a banquet until midnight, never once allowing herself to appear tired or bored. And then do the same again the following day."

He looked at Monk over the top of his glass, his eyes wry and amused. "I have a cousin who is one of her ladies in waiting. She loves her and is terrified of her. She says there is nothing Ulrike could not and would not do if she believed it was for the crown."

"It must have grieved her to the core when Friedrich abdicated," Monk thought aloud. "But it seems there is one thing she would not do, and that was allow Friedrich back if he insisted on bringing Gisela with him. She could not swallow her hatred enough for that, even if it meant losing the chance to fight for independence."

Stephan stared into his wine. All around them the soft sunlight bathed the stones of the piazza in warmth. The light was different here, away from the shifting glitter of the water. The breeze died down again.

"That surprises me," Stephan said at last. "It seems out of the character I know of her. Ulrike doesn't forgive, but she would have swallowed gall if she knew it would serve the crown and the dynasty." He laughed sharply. "I've seen her do it!"

The party was splendid, a lavish, beautiful echo of high Renaissance glory. They arrived by sea along the Grand Canal just as dusk was falling. The barges and piers were all lit by torches, their flames reflecting in the water, fragmented into sparks of fire by the wakes of passing boats. The night wind was soft on the face.

The western arc of heaven was still apricot and a tender, faint blue above. The carved and fretted facades of the palaces facing west were bathed in gold. In the shadows against the light through windows shone the flickering of thousands of candles in salons and ballrooms.

The gondolas floated up and down gently, their boatmen dark silhouettes swaying to keep their balance. They called out to each other, sometimes a greeting, more often a colorful insult. Monk did not know the language, but he caught the inflection.

They arrived at the water entrance and stepped out onto a landing blazing with torches, the smell of their smoke in the wind. Monk was reluctant to go inside; the Canal was so full of vibrant, wonderful life—unlike anything he had seen before. Even in this sad, foreign-occupied decadence, Venice was a city of unique glory, and history was steeped in its stones. It was one of the great crossroads of the world; the romance of it burned like fire in his brain. He imagined Helen of Troy might have had such a beauty in her old age. The blush and the firm flesh would be gone, but the bones were there, the eyes; the knowledge of who she had been would be there forever.

Stephan had to take him by the arm and almost lead him inside through the great arched doorway, up a flight of steps and onto the main floor, which was so large it stretched from one side of the building to the other. It was filled with people laughing and talking. It blazed with light; reflections glittered on crystal, gleaming tablecloths, white shoulders and a king's ransom in jewels. The clothes were gorgeous. Every woman in the room wore something which would have cost more than Monk earned in a decade. Silks were everywhere, as were velvets, laces, beading and embroidery.

He found himself smiling, wondering if perhaps he might even meet some of the great figures of legend who had come here, someone whose thoughts and passions had inspired the world. Unconsciously, he straightened his shoulders. He cut a very good figure himself. Black became him. He was of a good height and had a curious lean grace which he knew men envied and women found more attractive than they entirely wished.

He did not know how he might have used or abused that in the past, but tonight he felt only a kind of excitement.

Of course, he knew no one except Stephan—until he heard laughter to his right and, turning, saw the dainty, elfin-faced Evelyn. He felt a surge of pleasure, almost a physical warmth. He remembered the rose garden and the touch of her fingers on his arm. He must see her again and spend more time talking with her. It would be an opportunity to learn more of Gisela. He must make it so.

It took him nearly two hours of polite introductions, trivial conversation and the most exquisite wine and food before he contrived to be alone with Evelyn at the top of a flight of stairs that led towards a balcony overlooking the Canal. He had stood there with her for several minutes, watching the light on her face, the laughter in her eyes and the curve of her lips, before he remembered with an unpleasant jolt that he would not be there at all were Zorah Rostova not paying for it. Stephan, as her friend, believing her innocence of motive, had brought him there and introduced him for a purpose. He could never have come as himself, William Monk, a private investigator of other people's sins and troubles, born in a fishing village in Northumberland, whose father worked on boats for his living, read no book but the Bible.

He dragged his mind away from Evelyn, the laughter and the music and the swirl of color.

"How terrible to lose all this suddenly, in a few hours," he said, gazing over her head at the ballroom.

"Lose it all?" Her brows puckered in confusion. "Venice may be crumbling, and there are Austrian soldiers on every corner—do you know, a friend of mine was strolling along the Lido and was actually driven away at gunpoint! Can you imagine that?" Her voice was sharp with indignation. "But Venice can't sink under the waves in an hour, I promise you!" She giggled. "Do you think we are another lost Atlantis? A Sodom and Gomorrah—about to be overwhelmed by the wrath of God?" She swiveled around, her skirts frothing against his legs, the lace catching on the cloth of his trousers. He could smell the perfume of her hair and feel the faint warmth of her, even a yard away as she was.

"I don't see the writing on the wall," she said happily, staring across the sea of color. "Don't you think it would be fair to give us some sort of a sign?"

"I was thinking of Princess Gisela." With difficulty he forced his attention back to the past. The present was too urgent, too giddy to his senses. He was desperately aware of her. "One moment she must have believed Friedrich was recovering," he said quickly. "You all did, didn't you?"

"Oh, yes!" She looked at him with wide brown eyes. "He seemed to be doing so well."

"You saw him?"

"No, I didn't. But Rolf did. He said he was a lot better. He couldn't move much, but he was sitting up and talking, and said he felt much better."

"Well enough to think of returning home?"

"Oh!" She dragged out the syllable with understanding. "You think Rolf was there to persuade him, and Gisela overheard it and thought Friedrich would go? I'm quite certain you are wrong." She leaned back a little against the railing. It was a gently provocative pose showing the curves of her body. "No one who knew them really thought he would go without her." The laughter died and there was a faintly wistful look in her face. "People who love like that cannot ever be parted. He wouldn't have survived without her, nor she without him." She was half profile to Monk. He could see her delicate nose, a little turned up, and the shadow of her lashes on the smoothness of her cheek. She stared over the hubbub of noise from scores of people chattering, the music of violins and woodwind instruments.

"I remember when one of Giuseppe Verdi's new operas was performed at the Fenice here," she said with a rueful smile. "It was about politics in Genoa. The scenery was all rather like this. Lots of water. That was ten years ago." She shrugged. "Of course, the theater is closed now. I don't suppose you have noticed it yet, but there are no carnivals anymore, and Venetian aristocracy has all moved to the mainland. They don't attend the official parties the Austrian government gives. I don't know whether that's because they hate the Austrians so much or because they are afraid of nationalist reprisals if they do."

"Nationalist reprisals?" he said curiously, still watching the light on her face. "You mean there is a nationalist movement here so strong they would actually victimize people who openly accept the occupation?"

"Oh, yes!" She shook her head in a gesture of resignation. "Of course, it doesn't matter to us, who are expatriates anyway, but to the Venetians it's terribly important. Marshal Radetzky, he's the governor, said that he would give balls and masques and dinners, and if the ladies would not come, then his officers would waltz with each other." She gave a rueful little laugh and glanced at him quickly, then away again. "When the Austrian royal family came here, they went in procession down the Grand Canal, and no one even came to the windows or balconies to look! Can you imagine that?"

He tried, visualizing the sadness, the oppression and resentment, the dignified, rather pathetic figures of the royalty in exile keeping up their pretense of ceremony, and the real royalty, carrying all its power of empire, sailing down those glittering waters in silence as they were totally ignored. And all the while the real Venetians busy elsewhere, planning and fighting and dreaming. No wonder the city had an air of desolation unlike any other.

But he was here to learn about Friedrich and Gisela, and why Zorah had made her charge. He was standing very close to Evelyn. He could feel the warmth of her body. Her soft hair was faintly tickling his face, and the perfume of her seemed to be everywhere. The noise and the glitter swirled around him, but he was islanded alone with her in the shadows. It was hard to focus his attention back to the issue.

"You were going to tell me something about Friedrich," he prompted her.

"Oh, yes!" she agreed, glancing at him for a moment. "It was the opera. Gisela wanted to go. It was to be a special performance. All sorts of old Venetian nobility were to be there. As it turned out, they were not. It wasn't really a success. Poor Verdi! Gisela was determined, and Friedrich refused. He felt he owed it to some Venetian prince or other not to go, because of the Austrian occupation. After all, Venice was his home after so many years here. A sort of loyalty, I suppose."

"But Gisela didn't care?" he questioned.

"She wasn't very political . . ."

Or very loyal either, he thought, or grateful to a people who had made her welcome. It was suddenly an ugly tone in a picture up to then in totally romantic colors. But he did not interrupt.

From the ballroom the music floated up to them, and a woman's sudden laughter. He glimpsed Klaus in conversation with a white-bearded man in military uniform.

"She dressed in a new gown," Evelyn went on. "I remember because it was one of the best I had ever seen, even on her. It was the shade of crushed mulberries, with gold braid and beaded embroidery, and the skirt was absolutely enormous. She was always slender, and she walked with her head very high. She wore a gold ornament in her hair, and a necklace with amethysts and pearls."

"And Friedrich didn't go? Who escorted her?" he asked, trying to picture it but seeing in his mind's eye only Evelyn.

"Yes, he did go," she said quickly. "That is, she went with Count Baldassare, but they had barely sat down when Friedrich arrived. To anyone else it could have looked merely as if he was late. It was only by chance I knew the truth. I don't think Friedrich even knew what the opera was about. He couldn't have told you whether the soprano was dark or fair. He watched Gisela all night."

"And she was pleased to have won?" He tried to understand whether it had been a battle of wills, a jealousy, or simply a domestic tiff. And why had Evelyn elected to tell him this?

"She didn't seem so. And yet I know perfectly well she had no interest in Count Baldassare, nor he in her. He was merely being courteous."

"He was one of the Venetian aristocracy who remained?" he assumed.

"No. Actually, he's gone too now." She sounded curious and surprised. "The fight for independence has cost a lot of people far more than I used to think. Count Baldassare's son was killed by the Austrians. His wife has become an invalid. She lost a brother too, I think. He died in prison." She looked rueful and puzzled. "I'm not sure how much it is all worth. The Austrians aren't bad, you know. They are very efficient, and they are one of the few governments in Europe who are not corrupt. At least that is what Florent says, and he's half Venetian, so he wouldn't say it if it were not true. He loathes them."

Monk did not reply. He was thinking of Gisela. She was an unclear picture in his mind. He had never seen her face. He had been told she was not beautiful, but his vision always saw her with wide eyes and a turbulent, passionate kind of loveliness. Evelyn had marred it with the story of the opera. It was a very slight thing, only an ungraciousness in insisting on attending a function her husband had considered dishonor to their hosts, a form of ingratitude he had forbidden, and she had defied him for the pleasure of an evening's entertainment.

But in the end Friedrich had gone too, rather than endure her displeasure. Monk did not admire that either.

Evelyn held out her hand, smiling again.

He took it immediately; it was warm and delicately boned, almost like a child's.

"Come," she urged. "May I call you William? Such a very proper English name. I adore it. It suits you perfectly. You look so dark and brooding, and you behave with such gravity, you are quite delightful." He felt himself blush, but it was with pleasure. "I shall make it my task to teach you to unbend a little and enjoy yourself like a Venetian," she went on happily. "Do you dance? I don't care whether you do or not. If you don't, then I shall teach you. First you must have some wine." She started to lead him towards the steps down into the ballroom again. "It will warm your stomach and your heart . . . then you will forget London and think only of me!"

Her effort was unnecessary; he was already thinking only of her anyway.

He spent much of the rest of the night with her, and of the following night as well, and of the afternoon of his fourth day in Venice. He did learn much of the life of the exile court, if it could be called such when there was still a king on the throne at home, and a new crown prince.

But he was also enjoying himself enormously. Stephan was a good companion for the mornings, showing him the byways and back alleys and canals as well as the obvious beauties of Venice, and telling him something of the republic's history, showing him its glory and its art.

Monk kept on asking occasional questions about Friedrich and Gisela, the Queen, Prince Waldo, and the politics of money and unification. He learned more than he had imagined he ever could about the great European revolutions of 1848. They had touched almost every country as desire for freedom, undreamed before, swept from Spain to Prussia. There had been barricades in the streets, gunfire, soldiers billeted in every city, a wild resurgence of hope and then a closing in of despair. Only France seemed to have gained anything specific. In Austria, Spain, Italy, Prussia and the Low Countries, the moment's freedom had been illusory. Everything returned to the oppressions of before, or worse.

In the afternoons he continued to see Evelyn, except once when she arranged it before he had the opportunity, and that knowledge gave him a lift of pleasure like a bursting of wings inside him. She was beautiful, exciting, funny, and she had a gift for enjoyment unlike anyone he had known before. She was unique and wonderful. In company with others, they attended soirees and parties, they rode in barges down the Grand Canal, calling out to acquaintances, laughing at jokes, bathed in the brilliant, shifting light of a blue-and-golden autumn. Although the Fenice was closed, they attended small theaters and saw masques and dramas and musical plays.

Monk usually got to bed by about two or three in the morning, so he was delighted to remain there until ten, be served breakfast, and then choose which suit to wear for the day and begin the new adventure of discovery and entertainment. It was a way of life to which he could very easily become accustomed. It surprised him how very comfortable it was to slide into.

It was over a week through his stay when he met Florent Barberini again. It was during an intermission in a performance of a play of which Monk understood very little, since it was in Italian. He had excused himself and gone outside onto the landing to watch the boats move up and down the canal and to try to arrange his thoughts, and think about his mission there, which he was neglecting, and about his feelings for Evelyn.

He could not honestly say he loved her. He was not sure how much he even knew her. But he loved the excitement he felt in her company, the quickening of the pulse, the delicious sense of heightened enjoyment in everything from good food and good music to the humor and grace of her conversation, the envy he saw in other men's eyes when they looked at him.

He was aware of the large, oddly perverse figure of Klaus in the background. Perhaps the risk of it, the necessity for some semblance of discretion, added a certain sharpness to the pleasure. Now and again there was a prickle of danger. Klaus was a powerful man. There was something in his face, especially caught in repose, which suggested he would be an ugly enemy.

But Monk had never been a coward.

"You seem to have taken to Venice with a will," Florent said out of the shadows where the torchlight cast only a faint glow.

Monk had not seen him, he had been lost in his own thoughts and in the sights and sounds of night on the canal.

"Yes," he said with a start. He found himself smiling. "There cannot be another city like it in the world."

Florent did not answer.

Monk was suddenly aware of a sense of grief. He looked across at Florent's dark face and saw in it not only the easy sensuality that made it so attractive to women, the dramatic widow's peak and the fine eyes, but the loneliness of a man who played the dilettante but whose mind was unfashionably aware of the rape of his culture and the slow dying of the aching splendor of his city, as decay and despair eroded its fabric and its heart. He might have followed Friedrich's court for whatever reason, but he was more Italian than German, and under his facile manner there lay a depth which Monk, in his prejudice, had chosen not to see.

He wondered now if Florent were, in his own way, fighting for the independence again of Venice, and what part Friedrich's life or death might play in that. In the last few days he had heard whispers, jokes from the ignorant, of Italian unification also, a drawing together of all the different city-states, the brilliant, individual republics and dukedoms of the Renaissance, under one crown. Perhaps that also was true? How insular one could be, wrapped in the safety of Britain and its empire—an island world, forgetful of changing borders, the shifting tides of nations in turmoil, revolution and foreign occupation. Britain had been secure for nearly eight hundred years. An arrogance had developed unlike any other, and with it a lack of imagination.

He was there as Zorah's guest. It was long past time he did

all he could to serve her interests—or, at the very least, the interests of her country. Perhaps that was why she had made this absurd, self-sacrificing accusation—to expose the murder of a prince and awaken her countrymen to some sense of loyalty before it was too late.

"I could fall in love with Venice very easily," he said aloud. "But it is a hedonistic love, not a generous one. I have nothing to give it."

Florent turned to look at him, his dark brows raised in surprise, his lips in the torchlight twitched with humor.

"So does almost everyone else," he said softly. "You don't think all those people are here, the dreamers and the would-be princes of Europe, except to live out their own personal charades, do you?"

"Did you know Friedrich well?" It was not an answer, but Florent could not have expected one.

"Yes. Why?" he asked.

Out on the water, someone was singing. The sound of it echoed against the high walls and back again.

"Would he have gone back if Rolf, or someone else, had asked him?" Monk said. "His mother, perhaps?"

"Not if it meant leaving Gisela." Florent leaned over the stone parapet and stared into the darkness. "And it would have. I don't know why, but the Queen would never have allowed Gisela back. Her hatred was boundless."

"I thought she would have done anything for the crown."

"So did I. She's a remarkable woman."

"What about the King? Wouldn't he allow Gisela back if it was the only way to persuade Friedrich?"

"Override Ulrike?" There was laughter in Florent's voice, and the tone of it was answer in itself. "He's dying. She is the strength now. Perhaps she always was."

"What about Waldo, the Crown Prince?" Monk pressed. "He can't want Friedrich home!"

"No, but if you are thinking he had him killed, I doubt it. I don't think he ever wanted to be king. He stepped into his brother's place only reluctantly, because there was no one else. And that was not affected. I know him."

"But he will not lead the battle to keep independence!"

"He thinks it will mean war, and they will still be swallowed up in Germany anyway, sooner or later," Florent explained.

"Is he right?" Monk shifted his weight to turn and look more directly at him.

On the canal, a barge went by with pennons flying, music floating behind it, and torchlight glittering on the dark water. Its wake surged and lapped over the steps of the landing with a soft sound, whispering like an incoming tide.

"I think so," Florent answered.

"But you want Venetian independence."

Florent smiled. "From Austria, not from Italy."

Someone called out, his voice echoing over the water. A woman answered.

"Waldo is a realist," Florent went on. "Friedrich was always a romantic. But I suppose that is rather obvious, isn't it?"

"You think a fight to retain independence is doomed?"

"I meant Gisela, actually. He threw duty aside and followed his heart where she was concerned. The whole affair had an air of high romance about it. 'All for love, and the world well lost.' " His voice dropped, and his banter died. "I am not sure if you can really love the world and keep love."

"Friedrich did," Monk said quietly, but he thought even as he spoke that perhaps he meant it as a question.

"Did he?" Florent replied. "Friedrich is dead—perhaps murdered."

"Because of his love for Gisela?"

"I don't know." Florent was staring over the water again, his face dramatic in the torchlight, the planes of it thrown into high relief, the shadows black. "If he had stayed at home, instead of abdicating, he could now lead the struggle for independence without question. There would be no need to plot and counterplot to bring him back. The Queen would not be making stipulations about whether his wife could come, or if he must leave her, set her aside and marry again."

"But you said he wouldn't do that."

"No, he wouldn't, not even to save his country." Florent's voice was flat, as if he were trying to be objective, but there was condemnation in it, and looking at him, Monk saw anger in his face.

"That would be a very romantic thing to do," he pointed out. "Both personally and politically."

"And also very lonely," Florent added. "And Friedrich was never one to bear loneliness."

Monk thought about that for several minutes, hearing the hum of laughter and conversation behind them as a group of people came out of the theater and hailed a gondola, and the splash of water as its wake slurped over the steps.

"What are Zorah's feelings?" Monk asked when they had moved away. "For independence or unification? Could this charge she has made be political?"

Florent considered before he replied, and then his voice was thoughtful.

"How? What could it serve now? Unless you think she is trying to suggest someone else is behind Gisela. I can't see that as likely. She never kept any affiliations to anyone at home."

"I meant if Zorah knew Friedrich was murdered, not necessarily by Gisela at all, but felt accusing her would be the best way of bringing the whole issue out into the open," Monk explained.

Florent stared at him. "That is possible," he said very slowly, as if still mulling it over in his mind. "That hadn't occurred to me, but Zorah would do something like that—especially if she thought it was Klaus."

"Would Klaus kill Friedrich?"

"Oh, certainly, if he thought it was the only way to prevent him from going home and leading a resistance which could inevitably result in a war of independence which we would lose, sooner or later."

"So Klaus is for Waldo?"

"Klaus is for himself," Florent said with a smile. "He has very considerable properties on the borders which would be among the first to be sacked if we were invaded."

Monk said nothing. The dark waters of the canal lapped at the marble behind him, and from inside came the sound of laughter.

The autumn days continued warm and mellow. Monk pursued Evelyn because he enjoyed it. Her company was delightful, making every event exciting. And he was flattered because she obviously found him interesting, different from the men she was used to. She asked him probing questions about himself, about London and the darker side of it he knew so well. He told her enough to tantalize her, not enough to bore. Poverty would have repelled her. He mentioned it once and saw the withdrawal in her eyes. The subject required an answering compassion, even a sense of guilt, and she did not wish either of those emotions to cloud her pleasure.

Also, since she was Klaus's wife, he was able to ask just as many questions of her. In the pursuit of truth he needed to know as much as possible about Klaus and his alliances with either Waldo or any other German power.

He saw her at dinners, theaters and a magnificent ball thrown by one of the expatriate Spanish aristocrats. He danced till he was dizzy and slept until noon the following day.

He drifted in the lazy afternoon along quiet backwaters, hearing little but the lapping of the tide against the walls, lying on his back and seeing the skyline slip past, exquisite towers and facades, lace carved in stone against the blue air, holding Evelyn in his arms.

He saw the Doge's palace, and the Bridge of Sighs, leading to the dungeons from which few returned. He thought of going back to the winter in London, to his own small rooms. They were quite agreeable by most standards, warm and clean and comfortably furnished. His landlady was a good cook and seemed to like him well enough, even if she was not at all certain if she approved of his occupation. But it was hardly Venice. And inquiring into the tragedies of people's lives which led to crime was a very different thing from laughter and dancing and endless charming conversation with beautiful women.

Then, when walking up a flight of stairs, he had a jolt of memory, one of those flashes that came to him now and again, a sense of familiarity without reason. For an instant he had been, not in Venice, but going up the stairs in a great house in London. The laughing voices had been English, and there was someone he knew very well standing near the newel post at the bottom, a man to whom he was immeasurably grateful. It was a feeling of warmth, a comfortable sort of certainty that the friendship required no questioning, no constant effort to keep it alive.

It was so sharp he actually turned and looked behind him, expecting to see . . . and there the image broke. He could bring no face into focus. All that remained was the knowledge of trust.

He saw the large, rather shambling figure of Klaus von Seidlitz, his face lit by the massed candles of the chandeliers, its broken nose more accentuated in the artificial light. The people beyond him were all speaking a medley of languages: German, Italian and French. There was no English anymore.

Monk knew who it was he had expected to see, the man who had been his mentor and friend, and who had since been cheated out of his good name and all his possessions, even his freedom. Monk could not remember what had happened, only the weight of tragedy and his own burning helplessness. It was that injustice which had caused him to leave the world of investment and banking and turn instead to the police.

Had he been good at banking? If he had remained with it, would he now be a wealthy man, able to live like this all the time, instead of only on Zorah's money and on Zorah's business?

What had caused the overwhelming gratitude he felt towards the man who had taught him finance and banking? Why, in the moment when he turned on the stairs, had he felt such a knowledge that he was trusted and that there was an unbreakable bond between himself and this man? It was more than the general relationship he already recalled. This was something specific, an individual act.

It was broken now. He could not even remember what it had been, except the sense of debt. Had their relationship been so unequal? Had he been given, in money, friendship, faith, so much more than he was worth?

Evelyn was talking to him, telling him some story of Venetian history, a doge who had risen to power in a spectacular way, over the ruin of his enemies.

He made an appropriate remark indicating his interest.

She laughed, knowing he had not heard.

But the feeling remained with him all evening, and would not be shaken, that he had owed something profound. The harder he tried to recapture it, the more elusive it was. And when he turned away to think of something else, it was there, touching everything.

The following day, as he drifted along a canal with Evelyn warm beside him, it still crowded his mind.

"Tell me about Zorah," he said abruptly, sitting upright as they moved out of a byway into another of the main canals. A barge with streamers rippling in the breeze moved across their bow, and they were obliged to wait. Their gondolier rested his weight, balancing with unconscious grace. He made it look as if it were quite natural to stand with the shifting boat beneath him, but Monk knew it must be difficult. He had nearly lost his own footing and pitched into the water more than once.

"Why are you so interested in Zorah?" Evelyn was equally blunt. There was a sharp light in her eye.

Monk lied perfectly easily. "Because she is going to make an extremely unpleasant scene, but it might bring you back to London, and I shall like that, but not if she has the power to hurt you."

"She cannot hurt me," Evelyn said with conviction, smiling at him now. "But you are very charming to worry. People at home don't take her as seriously as you imagine, you know."

"Why not?" He was genuinely curious.

She shrugged, sliding a little closer to him. "Oh, she's always been outrageous. People with any sense will simply think she is trying to draw attention to herself again. She's probably had an affair die on her, and she wants to do something dramatic. She gets bored very easily, you know. And she hates to be ignored."

Thinking of Zorah as he had seen her, he could not readily imagine anyone ignoring her. He could understand finding her intimidating, or embarrassing, but never boring. But perhaps even eccentricity could become tedious in time, if it were contrived for effect rather than springing from genuine character. Was Zorah a poseur after all? He would be surprisingly disappointed if it should prove to be true.

"Do you think so?" he said skeptically, touching her hair, feeling its softness slide through his fingers.

"I have no doubt. Look across the lagoon, William. Do you see the Santa Maria Maggiore over there? Isn't that marvelous?" She pointed across the great stretch of blue-green tide to the distant marble of the domed church which seemed to be floating on the water's face.

He saw it with a sense of unreality. Only the breeze on his skin and the slight movement of the boat made him realize it was not a painted scene.

"Last time Zorah had an affair which went wrong, she shot him," Evelyn said casually.

He stiffened. "What?"

"Last time Zorah had an affair and the man left her, she shot him," Evelyn repeated, twisting around to look up at Monk with wide, pansy-brown eyes.

"And she got away with it?" Monk was incredulous.

"Oh, yes. It was all quite fair. Dueling is accepted in our country." She regarded his amazement with satisfaction. Then she started to laugh. "Of course, it is normally men who duel, and then with swords. I think Zorah chose a pistol deliberately. She used to be quite good with a sword, but she's getting slower as she gets older. And he was quite young, and very good."

"So she shot him!"

"Oh, not dead!" she said happily. "Just in the shoulder. It was all very silly. She was furious because he appeared at a ball and made much play with this other woman, who was very pretty and very young. It all degenerated into a quarrel a few days later. Zorah behaved appallingly, striding into his club wearing boots and smoking a cigar. She challenged him to a duel, and without looking a complete coward, he had to accept, which made him seem a fool when she won." She nestled a little closer to him. "He never really got over it. I'm afraid people laughed. And, of course, the story grew in the telling."

Monk had some sympathy with the man. He had had his fill of overbearing women. It was an extremely unattractive trait. And it required more courage than many have, especially the young, to withstand mockery.

"And you thought she might have made this accusation simply to become the center of attraction again?" he asked, smiling down at her and tracing his finger over the curve of her cheek and neck.

"Not entirely." She was smiling. "But she has little compunction where she feels strongly."

"Against Gisela?"

"And against unification," she agreed. "She spends very

little time at home, but she is a patriot at heart. She loves individuality, character, extremes, and the right to choose. I doubt she will see the benefits of trade and protection of a larger state. It is unromantic, but then most people lead very unromantic lives."

"And you?" he asked, kissing her cheek and her throat. Her skin was soft and warm in the sunlight.

"I am very practical," she said seriously. "I know that beauty costs money; you cannot have great parties, lovely works of art or theater, horse races, operas and balls if all your money is going into arms and munitions to fight a war." She pushed her fingers gently through his hair. "I know land gets trampled, villages destroyed, crops burned and men killed when a country is invaded. There is no point whatever in fighting against the inevitable. I would rather pretend it was what I wanted all along and give in to it gracefully."

"Is it inevitable?" he asked.

"Probably. I don't know a great deal about politics. Only what I overhear." She pulled back a little and stared up at him. "If you want to know more, you'll have to come home with me when we go, next week. Perhaps you should?" There was laughter in her face. "Discover if there was really a plot to bring Friedrich back to the throne and someone murdered him to prevent it!"

"What a good idea." He kissed her again. "I think that will be absolutely necessary."

6

RATHBONE SEIZED THE LETTER Simms was holding and tore it open. It was from Venice, and that had to mean Monk. It was not as long as he had hoped.

Dear Rathbone,

I believe I have exhausted the opportunity to gain information here in Italy. Everyone speaks well of the devotion between Friedrich and Gisela, even those who did not care for them, or specifically for her. The further I examine the evidence, the less does there appear to be any motive for her to have killed him. She had everything to lose. No one believes he would have left her, even to go home and lead the fight for independence.

However, it does seem possible that others may have wished him dead for political reasons. Klaus von Seidlitz is an obvious choice, since apparently he had personal and financial interests in unification, which Friedrich's return might have jeopardized. Although no one seems to think Friedrich would have gone without Gisela, and the Queen would not have had Gisela back even if it were to save the country's independence. I should like to know why the Queen nurtures such a passionate hatred after more than a decade. I am told it is out of her character to allow any personal emotion to stand in the way of her devotion to duty and patriotism.

I am going to Felzburg to see if I can learn more there. It may all hang on whether there actually was a plot to bring Friedrich back or not. Naturally, I shall let you know anything I discover, whether it is to Zorah's benefit or not. At present I fear it may well be of no service to her at all.

What I hear of her is only partially to her credit. If you can persuade her to withdraw her accusation, that may be the greatest service you can do for her, as her legal adviser. If Friedrich was murdered, and that does seem possible, it may have been by one of a number of people, but they do not include Gisela.

I wish you luck.

Monk

Rathbone swore and threw the letter down on his desk. Perhaps it was foolish, but he had hoped Monk would discover something which would show a new aspect of Gisela, perhaps a lover, a younger man, a brief obsession which had led her to long for her freedom. Or perhaps Friedrich had discovered her indiscretion and threatened to make it public, and leave her.

But Monk was right. It was almost certainly a political crime, if there were a crime at all, and Zorah's accusation was motivated more by jealousy than any basis in fact. The only legal advice he could honestly give her was to withdraw her charge and apologize unreservedly. Perhaps if she pleaded distress at Friedrich's death, and deep disappointment that he could not lead the battle for independence, there might be some compassion towards her. Damages might be moderated. Even so, she would almost certainly have ruined herself.

"Apologize?" she said incredulously when Rathbone was shown into her room with its exotic shawl and red leather sofa. "I will not!" The weather was considerably colder than when he had first come, and there was a huge fire roaring in the grate, flames leaping, throwing a red light into the bearskins on the floor and giving the room a barbaric look, curiously warming.

"You have no other reasonable choice," he said vehemently. "We have found no proof whatever of your charge. We are left with suppositions, which may well be true, but we cannot demonstrate them, and even if we could, they are no defense."

"Then I shall have to make an unreasonable choice," she said flatly. "Do I assume this is your very proper way of retreating from my case?" Her eyes were level and cold, a flare of challenge in them, and acute disappointment.

Rathbone was irritated, and if he were honest, a little stung. "If you do assume it, madam, you do so wrongly," he snapped. "It is my duty to advise you as to facts and my considered opinion as to what they may mean. Then I shall take your instructions, providing they do not require me to say or do anything that is contrary to the law."

"How terribly English." There was both laughter and contempt in her face. "It must make you feel impossibly safe—and comfortable. You live in the heart of an empire which stretches all 'round the world." She was angry now. "Name a continent and your British redcoats have fought there, carried by your British navy, subdued the natives and taught them Christianity, whether they wished to learn it or not, and instructed their princes how to behave like Englishmen."

What she said was true, and it startled him and made him feel suddenly artificial, violated and rather pompous.

Her voice was charged with emotion, deep and husky in her throat.

"You've forgotten what it is like to be frightened," she went on. "To look at your neighbors and wonder when they are going to swallow you. Oh, I know you read about it in your history books! You learn about Napoleon and King Philip of Spain—and how you were on the brink of invasion, with your backs against the wall. But you beat them, didn't you! You always won." Her body was tight under its silk gown, and her face twisted with anger. "Well, we won't win, Sir Oliver. We shall lose. It may be immediately, it may be in ten years, or even twenty, but in the end we shall lose. It is the manner of our losing that we may be able to control, that's all. Have you the faintest idea what that feels like? I think not!"

"On the contrary," Rathbone said sardonically, although his words were only a defense against his own misjudgment and vulnerability. "I am imagining losing very vividly, and I am about to experience it in the courtroom." He knew as he said it that his own small personal defeat did not compare with the defeat of nations, the loss of centuries-old identity and concepts of freedom, however illusionary.

"You've given up!" she said with a lift of surprise which was contempt rather than question.

In spite of determining not to be, he was provoked. He would not let her see it. "I have faced reality," he contradicted. "That is a different side of the same coin. We have no alternative. It lies with me to tell you the facts and give you the best chance I can; and with you to choose."

Her eyebrows rose sharply. "Whether I surrender before the battle or fight until I may be beaten? What a nice irony. That is exactly the dilemma my country faces. For my country I think I do not choose assimilation, even though we cannot win. For myself I choose war."

"You cannot win either, madam," he said reluctantly. He hated having to tell her. She was stubborn, foolish, arrogant and self-indulgent, but she had courage and, after her own fashion, a kind of honor. Above all, she cared passionately. She would be hurt, and that knowledge pained him.

"Are you saying I should withdraw my charge, say that I lied, and ask that creature's pardon for it?" she demanded.

"You will have to eventually. Do you want to do it privately now, or publicly, when she proves you incapable of supporting your charge?"

"It would not be private," she pointed out. "Gisela would make sure everyone knew or there would be no purpose. Not that it matters. I will not withdraw. She murdered him. The fact that you cannot find the proof of it alters nothing."

He was galled that she should place the responsibility upon him.

"It alters everything in the law!" he retorted. "What can I say to make you understand?" He heard desperation rising in his voice. "It seems very likely that we may be able to give serious evidence to the theory that Friedrich was murdered. His symptoms are closer to yew poison than internal bleeding. We may even be able to force an exhumation of his body and an autopsy." He saw her wince of distaste with satisfaction. "But even if that proves us correct, Gisela was the one person who had no access to yew leaves. She never left his side. For heaven's sake, ma'am, if you believe he was assassinated for some political reason, say so! Don't sacrifice your own reputation by making a charge against the one person who cannot be guilty, simply in order to force the matter to justice!"

"What do you suggest?" she asked, her voice tense, cracking a little under the strain of effort to be light. "That I accuse Klaus von Seidlitz? But he is not guilty!"

She was still standing, the firelight reflecting red on her skirt. It was growing dark outside.

"You know it was not Klaus. You have no proof it was Gisela." Hope suddenly lifted inside him. "Then withdraw the charge, and we will investigate until we have enough evidence, then we'll take it to the police! Tell the truth! Say you believe he was murdered but you don't know by whom. You named Gisela simply to make someone listen to you and investigate. Apologize to her. Say you now realize you were wrong to suspect her, and you hope she will forgive your error of judgment and join with everyone to discover the truth. She can hardly refuse to do that. Or she will indeed look as if she may have colluded. I will draw up a statement for you."

"You will not!" she said fiercely, her eyes hot and stubborn. "We shall go to trial."

"But we don't have to!" Why was the woman so obtuse? She was going to cause such unnecessary pain to herself! "Monk will learn everything he can—"

"Good!" She swung around and stared towards the window. "Then let him do it by the time we meet in court, and he can testify for me."

"That may not be in time . . ."

"Then tell him to hurry!"

"Withdraw the charge against Gisela. Then the trial will not take place. She may ask damages, but I can plead on your behalf so that—"

She jerked back to glare at him. "Are you refusing to take my instructions, Sir Oliver? That is the right term, is it not? Instructions."

"I am trying to advise you—" he said desperately.

"And I have heard your advice and declined it," she cut across him. "I do not seem able to make you understand that I believe Gisela killed Friedrich and I am not going to accuse someone else as a device. A device, I may add, which I do not believe would work."

"But she did not kill him." His voice was getting louder and more strident than he wished, but she was trying him to exasperation. "You cannot prove something which is not true! And I will not be party to trying."

"I believe it is true," she said inflexibly, her face set, body rigid. "And it is not your calling to be judge as well as counsel, is it?"

He took a deep breath. "It is my obligation to tell you the truth . . . which is that if Friedrich was indeed murdered, by the use of yew leaves, then Gisela is the one person whose actions and whereabouts are accounted for at all times, and she could not have killed him."

She stared at him defiantly, her chin high, her eyes wide. But she had no answer to his logic. It beat her, and she had to acknowledge it.

"If you wish to be excused, Sir Oliver, then I excuse you. You need not consider your honor stained. I seem to have asked of you more than is just."

He felt an overwhelming relief, and was ashamed of it.

"What will you do?" he asked gently, the tension and the sense of doom skipping away from him, but in their place was a whisper of failure, as if some opportunity had been lost, and even a sort of loneliness.

"If you see the situation as you have said, no doubt any other barrister of like skill and honor will see it the same way," she answered. "They will advise me as you have. And then I shall have to reply to them as I have to you, so I shall have gained nothing. There is only one person who believes in the necessity of pursuing the case."

"Who is that?" He was surprised. He could imagine no one.

"I, of course."

"You cannot represent yourself!" he protested.

"There is no alternative that I am prepared to accept." She stared at him with a very slight smile, irony and amusement mixed in it—and behind it, fear.

"Then I shall continue to represent you, unless you prefer me not to." He was horrified as he heard his own voice. It was rash to a degree. But he could hardly abandon her to her fate, even if she had brought it upon herself.

She smiled ruefully, full of gratitude.

"Thank you, Sir Oliver."

"That was most unwise," Henry Rathbone said gravely. He was leaning against the mantelshelf in his sitting room. The French doors were no longer open onto the garden, and there was a brisk fire burning in the hearth. He looked unhappy. Oliver had just told him of his decision to defend Zorah in spite of the fact that she refused absolutely to withdraw her accusation or to make any sort of accommodation to sense, or even to her own social survival, possibly to her financial survival also.

Oliver did not want to repeat the details of the discussion. It sounded, in retrospect, as if he had been precipitate, governed far more by emotion than intelligence, a fault he deplored in others.

"I don't see any honorable alternative," he said stubbornly. "I cannot simply leave her. She has put herself in a completely vulnerable position."

"And you with her," Henry added. He sighed and moved away from the front of the fire, where he was beginning to be uncomfortable. He sat down and fished his pipe out of his jacket pocket. He knocked the pipe against the fireplace, cleaned out the bowl, then filled it with tobacco again. He put it in his mouth and lit it. It went out almost immediately, but he did not seem to care.

"We must see what can be salvaged out of the situation." He looked steadily at Oliver. "I don't think you appreciate how deeply people's feelings run in this sort of issue."

"Slander?" Oliver asked with surprise. "I doubt it. And if murder is proved, then she will to some extent be justified." He was comfortable in his usual chair at the other side of the fire. He slid down a little farther in it. "I think that is the thrust I must take, prove that there is sufficient evidence to believe that a crime has been committed. Possibly in the emotion, the shock and outrage of learning that Friedrich was murdered, albeit for political reasons, they will overlook Zorah's charge against Gisela." His spirits lifted a little as he said it. It was the beginning of a sensible approach instead of the blank wall he had faced even a few minutes ago.

"No, I did not mean slander," Henry replied, taking his pipe out of his mouth but not bothering to relight it. He held it by the bowl, pointing with it as he spoke. "I meant the challenging of people's preconceptions of certain events and characters, their beliefs, which have become part of how they see the world and their own value in it. If you force people to change their minds too quickly, they cannot readjust everything, and they will blame you for their discomfort, the sense of confusion and loss of balance."

"I think you are overstating the case," Oliver said firmly. "There are very few people so unsophisticated as to imagine women never kill their husbands, or that minor European royal families are so very different from the rest of us very fallible human beings. Certainly I will not have many on my jury. They will be men of the world, by definition." He found himself smiling. "The average juror is a man of property and experience, Father. He may be very sober in his appearance, even pompous in his manner, but he has few illusions about the realities of life, of passion and greed and occasionally of violence."

Henry sighed. "He is also a man with a vested interest in the social order as it is, Oliver. He respects his betters and aspires to be like them, even to become one of them, should fortune allow. He does not like the challenging of the good and the decent, which form the framework of the order he knows and give him his place and his value, which makes sure his inferiors respect him in the same way."

"Therefore, he will not like murder," Oliver said reasonably. "Most particularly, he will not accept the murder of a prince. He will want to see it exposed and avenged."

Henry relit his pipe absentmindedly. His brow was furrowed with anxiety. "He will not like lawyers who defend people who make such charges against a great romantic heroine," he corrected. "He will not like women, such as Zorah Rostova, who defy convention by not marrying, by traveling alone in all sorts of foreign lands; who dress inappropriately and ride astride a horse and smoke cigars."

"How do you know she does those things?" Oliver was startled.

"Because people are already beginning to talk about it." Henry leaned forward, the pipe going out again. "For heaven's sake, don't you suppose the gossip is running around London like smuts from a chimney in a high wind? People have believed in the love story of Friedrich and Gisela for over a decade. They don't want to think they have been deluded, and they will resent anyone who tries to tell them so."

Oliver felt the warmth of his earlier optimism begin to drain out of him.

"Attacking royalty is a very dangerous thing," Henry went on. "I know a great many people do it, especially in newspapers and broadsheets, and always have, but it has seldom made them liked among the sort of people you care about. Her Majesty has just recognized your services to justice. You are a knight, and a Queen's Counsel, not a political pamphleteer."

"That is all the more reason why I cannot allow a murder to go unquestioned," Oliver said grimly, "simply because I shall not be popular for drawing everyone's attention to it." He had placed himself in a position from which it was impossible to withdraw with any grace at all. And his father was only making it worse. He looked across at the older man's earnest face and knew that his father was afraid for him, struggling to see an escape and unable to.

Oliver sighed. His anger evaporated, leaving only fear.

"Monk is going to Felzburg. He thinks it was probably a political assassination, perhaps by Klaus von Seidlitz, in order to prevent Friedrich from returning to lead the struggle for independence, which could very easily end in war."

"Then let's hope he brings proof of it," Henry replied. "And that Zorah will then apologize, and you can persuade a jury to be lenient with the damages they award."

Oliver said nothing. The fire settled in a shower of sparks, and he found he was cold.

Hester was now sure beyond all but the slimmest hope that Robert Ollenheim would not walk again. The doctor had not said so to Bernd or Dagmar, but he had not argued when Hester had challenged him in the brief moment they had alone.

She wanted to escape from the house for a while to compose her thoughts before she faced their recognition of the truth. She knew their pain would be profound, and she felt inadequate to help. All the words she thought of sounded condescending, because in the end she could not share the hurt. What is there to say to a mother whose son will not stand or walk or run again, who will never dance or ride a horse, who will never even leave his bedroom unaided? What do you say to a man whose son will not follow in his footsteps, who will never be independent, who will never have sons of his own to carry on the name and the line?

She asked permission to leave on a personal errand, and when willingly granted it, she took a hansom east across the city to Vere Street and asked Simms if she might see Sir Oliver, if he had a few moments to spare.

She did not have long to wait; within twenty minutes she was shown in. Rathbone was standing in the middle of the room. There were several large books open on the desk, as if he had been searching for some reference. He looked tired. There were lines of stress around his eyes and mouth, and his fair hair was combed a little crookedly, a most unusual occurrence for him. His clothes were as immaculate as always, and as perfectly tailored, but he did not stand as straight.

"My dear Hester, how delightful to see you," he said with a pleasure which caught her with a sudden warmth. He closed the book in his hand and set it on the desk with the others. "How is your patient?"

"Much recovered in his health," she replied truthfully enough. "But I fear he will not walk again. How is your case?"

His face was filled with concern. "Not walk again! Then his recovery is only very partial?"

"I am afraid that is almost certainly so. But please, I should prefer not to speak of it. We cannot help. How is your case going? Have you heard from Venice? Is Monk learning anything useful?"

"If he has, I am afraid he is so far keeping it to himself." He indicated the chair opposite, and then sat at the corner of the desk himself, swinging his leg a trifle, as if he were too restless to sit properly.

"But he has written?" she urged.

"Three times, in none of them telling me anything I could use in court. Now he is off to Felzburg to see what he can learn there."

It was not only the total lack of any helpful news which worried her, but the anxiety in Rathbone's eyes, the way his fingers played with the corner of a sheaf of papers. It was not like him to fiddle pointlessly with things. He was probably not even aware he was doing it. She was unexpectedly angry with Monk for not having found anything helpful, for not being there to share the worry and the mounting sense of helplessness. But panic would not serve anyone. She must keep a calm head and think rationally.

"Do you believe Countess Rostova is honest in her charge?" she asked.

He hesitated only a moment. "Yes, I do."

"Could she be correct that Gisela murdered her husband?"

"No." He shook his head. "She is the one person who did not have the opportunity. She never left his side after his accident."

"Never?" she said with surprise.

"Apparently not. She nursed him herself. I imagine one does not leave a seriously ill patient alone?"

"As ill as he was, I would have someone in to be with him while I slept," she replied. "And I might well go to the kitchens to prepare his food myself or to make distillations of herbs to ease him. There are many things one can do to help certain kinds of distress once a patient is conscious."

He still looked slightly dubious.

"Meadowsweet," she elaborated. "Compresses are excellent for both pain and swelling. Cowslip is also good. Rosemary will lift the spirits. Cinnamon and ginger will help a sick headache. Marigold rinse will assist healing of the skin. Chamomile tea is good for digestive troubles and aids sleeping. A little vervain tea for stress and anxiety, which she might well have benefited from herself." She smiled, watching his face. "And there is always Four Thieves' Vinegar against general infection, which is the great danger after injury."

A ghost of a smile crossed his face. "I have to ask," he admitted. "What is Four Thieves' Vinegar?"

"Four healthy thieves were caught during a plague," she replied. "They were offered their freedom in return for their recipe for their remedy."

"Vinegar?" he said with surprise.

"Garlic, lavender, rosemary, sage, mint with a specific amount of mugwort and rue," she answered. "It has to be measured very exactly and made in a precise way, with cider vinegar. A few drops are sufficient, taken in water."

"Thank you," he said gravely. "But according to Monk's information, Gisela did not leave their rooms at all . . . for anything. Whatever preparations there were came up from the kitchen or were brought by the doctor. And it is stretching the bounds of belief too far to suppose she kept a distillation of yew with her beforehand just in case she might have a need for it!"

"Obviously, you have told the Countess this—and advised her to withdraw and apologize." She did not make it a question; it would have been insulting. For all his present vulnerability, she would not have dared imply she knew something of his skill that he had omitted. The balance between them was delicate, the slightest clumsiness might damage it.

"I have." He looked at his fingers, not at her. "She refuses," he went on before she could ask. "I cannot abandon her, in spite of her foolishness. I have given my undertaking that I will do what I can to protect her interests."

She hesitated a moment, afraid to ask in case he had no answer. But then the omission would have made it obvious that that was what she thought. She saw it in his eyes, steady and gentle on hers, waiting.

"What can you do?" she said deliberately.

"Not enough," he replied with the ghost of a smile, self-mockery in it.

"Anything?" She had to pursue it. He expected her to. Perhaps he needed to share the sense of defeat. Sometimes fear put into words become manageable. She had found it with men on the battlefield. The longer it remained unsaid, the larger it grew. Turned and faced, the proportions defined, one could muster forces to fight it. The nightmare quality was contained. And this could not be as bad as battle. She still remembered the bloody fields afterwards with sick horror and a pity which she needed to forget if she were to live and be useful now. Nothing in this case could compare with the past. But she could not say that to Rathbone. For him this was the struggle, and the disaster.

He was collecting his thoughts. He still sat sideways on the edge of the desk, but he had stopped fiddling with the papers.

"If we can prove it was murder, perhaps we can divert people's attention from the fact that she accused the wrong person," he said slowly. "I don't know a great deal about the Princess Gisela. I think perhaps I need to know their relationship in the past, and her present financial arrangements, in order to estimate what reparations she is likely to seek." He bit his lip. "If she hates Zorah as much as Zorah hates her, then she is very likely to want to ruin her."

"I will see if I can learn anything," Hester said quickly, glad of the chance to do something herself. "Baron and Baroness Ollenheim knew them both quite well. If I ask the right way, she may tell me quite a lot about Gisela. After all, it is possible she has no great feelings about Zorah. She won, and apparently easily."

"Won?" He frowned.

"The battle between them," she said impatiently. "Zorah was his mistress before Gisela came—at least, she was one of them. Afterwards he never looked at anyone else. Zorah has plenty of reason to hate Gisela. Gisela has none to hate her. Probably she is so devastated by Friedrich's death she has no interest in revenge for the slander. Once she is proved innocent, she may be quite happy simply to retire from the public scene as a heroine again—even a merciful one. She will be even more admired for it. People will adore her . . ."

Suddenly his expression quickened. The light returned to his eyes as he grasped an idea.

"Hester, you are remarkably perceptive! If I could persuade Gisela that mercy would be in her own best interest, that it would paint her the greater heroine even than before, that may be our only answer!" He slipped down off the desk and started to pace back and forth across the floor, but this time it was not from tension but nervous energy as his brain raced. "Of course, I shall have no direct communication with her. It will all have to be implied in open court. I must make it double-pronged."

He waved his hands, held apart to illustrate his idea. "On the one side, make mercy seem so appealing she will be drawn to it. Show how she will be remembered always for her grace and dignity, her compassion, the great qualities of womanhood that will make the whole world understand why Friedrich gave up a crown for her. And on the other, show how ugly revenge would be upon a woman who has already lost once to her and who has been shown to be mistaken—but a loyal patriot in that she was willing to risk everything to bring to light the fact that Friedrich really was indeed murdered and did not die a natural death, as everyone had supposed."

He increased his pace as his mind grasped more ideas. "And I can very subtly show that not to be grateful to her for that, at least, would suggest to some that possibly she would rather his murderer escape. She cannot allow anyone to think that." His fist clenched. "Yes! I believe at last we have the beginning of some kind of strategy." He stopped in front of her. "Thank you, my dear." His eyes were bright and gentle. "I am most grateful. You have helped immensely."

She found herself blushing under his gaze, suddenly unsure how to respond. She must remember this was only gratitude. Nothing had really changed.

"Hester . . . I . . ."

There was a knock on the door.

Simms put his head in. "Major Bartlett is here to see you, Sir Oliver. He has been waiting some ten minutes. What shall I tell him?"

"Tell him I want another ten," Rathbone said. Then he looked at Simms's startled face and sighed. "No, don't tell him that. Miss Latterly is leaving. Tell Major Bartlett I apologize for keeping him waiting. I have just received urgent information on another case, but I am now ready to see him."

"Yes, Sir Oliver." Simms withdrew with a look of restored confidence. He was a man with a profound respect for the proprieties.

Hester smiled in spite of a sense of both relief and disappointment.

"Thank you for seeing me without notice," she said gravely. "I shall let you know of anything I am able to learn." And she turned to leave.

He moved past her to open the door, standing so close to her she could smell the faint aromas of wool and clean linen—and sense the warmth of his skin. She walked out into the open office, and he turned to speak to Major Bartlett.

Hester returned to Hill Street determined to face the truth regarding Robert as soon as an opportunity arose, and if it did not, she would have to create one.

As it happened, she had very little time to wait. The doctor called again early that evening, and after he had seen Robert, he asked to speak to Hester alone. There was a boudoir on the second floor which was readily available. She closed the door.

He looked grave, but he did not avoid her eyes, nor did he try to smooth over with false optimism the bitterness of what he had to say.

"I am afraid I can do no more for him," he said quietly. "It would be unjustified, and I think cruel, to hold out any real hope that he will walk again, or . . ." This time he did hesitate, trying to find a delicate way of phrasing what he needed to explain.

She helped him. "I understand. He will be able to use no part of his lower body. Only the automatic muscles of digestion will work."

"I am afraid that is true. I'm sorry."

Even though she had known it, to have it spoken made her aware that some foolish part of her had hoped she was wrong, and that hope was now dead. She felt a profound weight settle, hard and painful, inside her. It was as if a final light had gone out.

The doctor was looking at her with great gentleness. He must hate this as much as she did.

She forced herself to lift her head a fraction and keep her voice steady.

"I shall do all I can to help them accept it," she promised. "Have you told the Baroness, or do you wish me to?"

"I have not told anyone else yet. I would like you to be there when I do. She may find it very difficult."

"And Robert?"

"I have not told him, but I believe he knows. This young woman he mentions, Miss Stanhope, seems to have prepared him to some extent. Even so, hearing it from me will be different from merely thinking of it. You know him better than I do. From whom will it be least difficult for him?"

"That depends upon how his parents react," she replied, not knowing how real their hope may have been. She feared

Bernd would fight against it, and that would make it far more difficult. Dagmar would have to face reality for both of them. "Perhaps we should allow them to choose, unless that proves impossible."

"Very well. Shall we go downstairs?"

Bernd and Dagmar were waiting for them in the huge, high-ceilinged withdrawing room, standing close together in front of the fire. They were not touching each other, but Bernd put his arm around his wife as Hester and the doctor came in. He faced them squarely, hope and fear struggling in his eyes.

Dagmar looked at them and read it in their expressions. She gulped.

"It is bad . . . isn't it?" she said with a catch in her voice.

Hester started to say that it was not as bad as it might have been, there would be no pain, then realized that was not what they would be able to hear. For them this was as bad as they could conceive.

"Yes," the doctor answered for her. "I am afraid it is unrealistic to believe now that he will walk again. I . . . I am very sorry." His nerve failed him, and he did not add the other facts Hester had deduced. Perhaps he saw in Bernd's face that they would be too much to bear.

"Can't you do . . . anything?" Bernd demanded. "Perhaps a colleague? I don't mean to insult you, but if we were to try another opinion? A surgeon? Now that you can anesthetize a person while you operate, surely you can . . . can mend what is broken? I—" He stopped.

Dagmar had moved closer to him, was holding on to his arm more tightly.

"It is not broken bones," the doctor said as calmly as he was able. "It is the nerves which give feeling."

"Then can't he walk without feeling?" Bernd demanded. "He can learn! I've known men with dead legs who managed to walk!" His face was growing dark with pain and anger at his own helplessness. He could not bear to believe what was being said. "It will take time, but we shall accomplish it!"

"No." Hester spoke for the first time.

He glared at her. "Thank you for your opinion, Miss Latterly, but at this time it is not appropriate. I will not give up hope for my son!" His voice broke, and he took refuge in anger. "Your place is to nurse him. You are not a doctor! You will please not venture medical opinions which are beyond your knowledge."

Dagmar winced as if she had been hit.

The doctor opened his mouth and then did not know what to say.

"It is not a medical opinion," Hester said gravely. "I have watched many men come to terms with the fact that an injury will not heal. Once they have accepted the truth, it is not a kindness to hold out a hope which cannot be realized. It is, in fact, making them carry your burden as well as their own."

"How dare you!" he said. "Your impertinence is intolerable! I shall—"

"It is not impertinence, Bernd," Dagmar interrupted him, touching his hand with hers even as she clung to him. "She is trying to help us to do what is best for Robert. If he will not walk again, it is kinder for us not to pretend that somehow he will."

He moved away, taking his arm from her grasp. In rejecting her he was also rejecting what she had said.

"Are you prepared to give up so easily? Well, I shall never give up! He is my son . . . I cannot give up!" He turned away to hide the emotion twisting his features.

Dagmar turned to Hester, her face bruised with pain.

"I'm sorry," she whispered, trying to control herself. "He doesn't mean it. I know you are saying what is best for Robert. We must face the truth, if that is what it is. Will you help me to tell him, please?"

"Of course." Hester nearly offered to do it for her, if she

wished, then realized that if she did, afterwards Dagmar would feel as if she had let her son down out of her own weakness. It was necessary for Dagmar, whether it was for Robert or for her own peace of mind, to tell him herself.

Together they moved towards the door, and the doctor turned to follow them.

Bernd swung around as though to speak, then changed his mind. He knew his own emotions would only make it harder.

Upstairs, Dagmar knocked at Robert's door, and when she heard his voice, pushed the door open and went in, Hester behind her.

Robert was sitting up as usual, but his face was very white.

Dagmar stopped.

Hester ached to say it for her. She choked back the impulse, her throat tight.

Robert stared at Dagmar. For a moment there was hope in his eyes, then only fear.

"I'm sorry, my darling," Dagmar began, her words husky with tears. "It will not get better. We must plan what we can do as it is."

Robert opened his mouth, then clenched his hands and gazed at her in silence. For a moment it was beyond him to speak.

Dagmar took a step forward, then changed her mind.

Hester knew that nothing she could say would help. For the moment the pain was all-consuming. It would have to change, almost certainly be in part replaced by anger, at least for a while, then perhaps despair, self-pity, and finally acceptance, before the beginning of adjustment.

Dagmar moved forward again and sat down on the edge of the bed. She took Robert's hand in hers and held it. He tightened his grip, as if all his mind and his will were in that one part of him. His eyes stared straight ahead, seeing nothing.

Hester stepped back and pulled the door closed.

* * *

It was the middle of the next morning when Hester saw Bernd again. She was sitting in the green morning room in front of the fire writing letters, one or two of her own, but mostly to assist Dagmar in conveying apologies and explanations to friends, when Bernd came in.

"Good morning, Miss Latterly," he said stiffly. "I believe I owe you an apology for my words yesterday. They were not intended as any personal discourtesy. I am most . . . grateful . . . for the care you have shown my son."

She smiled, putting down her pen. "I did not doubt that, sir. Your distress is natural. Anyone would have felt as you did. Please do not consider it necessary to think of it again."

"My wife tells me I was . . . rude . . ."

"I have forgotten it."

"Thank you. I . . . I hope you will remain to look after Robert? He is going to need a great deal of assistance. Of course, in time we shall obtain an appropriate manservant, but until then . . ."

"He will learn to do far more than you think now," she assured him. "He is disabled; he is not ill. The greatest help would be a comfortable chair with wheels so that he can move around . . ."

Bernd winced. "He will hate it! People will be . . . sorry for him. He will feel—" He stopped, unable to continue.

"He will feel some degree of independence," she finished for him. "The alternative is to remain in bed. There is no need for that. He is not an invalid. He has his hands, his brain and his senses."

"He will be a cripple!" He spoke of it in the future, as if to acknowledge it in the present made it more of a fact and he still could not bear that.

"He cannot use his legs," she said carefully. "You must help him to make all the use he can of everything else. And people may begin by being sorry for him, but they will only remain so if he is sorry for himself."

He stared at her. He looked exhausted; there were dark smudges around his eyes and his skin had a thin, papery quality.

"I would like to think you are correct, Miss Latterly," he said after a moment or two. "But you speak so easily. I know you have seen a great many young men disabled by war and injuries perhaps far worse than Robert's. But you see only the first terrible shock, then you move on to another patient. You do not see the slow years that follow afterwards, the disappointed hopes, the imprisonment that closes in, that ruins the . . . the pleasures, the achievements of life."

"I haven't nursed only soldiers, Baron Ollenheim," she said gently. "But please don't ever allow Robert to know that you believe life is so blighted for him, or you will crush him completely. You may even make your fears come true by your belief in them."

He stared at her, doubt, anger, amazement, and then comprehension passing across his face.

"Who are you writing to?" He glanced at the paper and pen in front of her. "My wife said you had agreed to assist her with some of the letters which have become necessary. Perhaps you would be good enough to thank Miss Stanhope and say that she will no longer be needed. Do you think it would be appropriate to offer her some recompense for her kindness? I understand she is of very restricted means."

"No, I do not think it would be appropriate," she said sharply. "Furthermore, I think it would be a serious mistake to tell her she is no longer needed. Someone must encourage Robert to go out, to learn new pastimes."

"Go out?" He was startled, and two spots of color stained his pale cheeks. "I hardly think he will wish to go out, Miss Latterly. That is a most insensitive remark."

"He is disabled, Baron Ollenheim, not disfigured," she pointed out. "He has nothing whatever of which to be ashamed—"

"Of course not." He was thoroughly angry now, perhaps because shame was precisely what he had felt that any member of his family should be less than whole, less than manly, and now dependent upon the help of others.

"I think it would be wise to encourage him to have Miss Stanhope visit," Hester repeated steadily. "She is already aware of his situation, and it would be easier for him than trusting someone new, at least to begin with."

He thought for several moments before replying. He looked appallingly tired.

"I do not want to be unfair to the girl," he said finally. "She has sufficient misfortune already, by her appearance and by what my wife tells me of her circumstances. We can offer her no permanent post. Robert will need a trained manservant, and naturally, in time, if he resumes his old friendships, those who are willing to make adjustments to his new state . . ." His face pinched as he spoke. "Then she would find herself excluded. We must not take advantage of either her generosity or her vulnerable position."

His choice of words was not meant to hurt, but Hester saw reflected in them her own situation: hired to help in a time of pain and despair, leaned on, trusted, at the heart of things for a brief while; then, when the crisis was past, paid, thanked and dismissed. Neither she nor Victoria was part of permanent life; they were not socially equal, and were friends only in a very narrow and closely defined sense.

Except that Victoria was not to be paid, because her situation was so less well understood.

"Perhaps we should allow Robert to make the decision," she said with less dignity or control than she had wished. She felt angry for Victoria, and for herself, and very pointedly alone.

"Very well," he agreed reluctantly, totally unaware of her emotions. It had not even occurred to him that she might have any. "At least for the time being."

* * *

In fact, Victoria came the very next morning. Hester saw her before she went upstairs. She beckoned her to the landing, close to a huge Chinese vase planted with a potted palm. The sunlight streamed in through the windows, making bright squares on the polished wood of the floor.

Victoria was dressed in a dark plum-colored wool. The dress must be one left over from more fortunate days. It became her very well, lending a little color to her cheeks, and the white collar lightened her eyes, but it could not remove the anxiety or the quick flash of understanding.

"He knows, doesn't he?" she said before Hester had time to speak.

There was no point in evasion. "Yes."

"How about the Baron and Baroness? They must be very hurt."

"Yes. I . . . I think you may be able to help. You will be less closely caught up. In a sense, you have been there already. The shock and the anger have passed."

"Sometimes." Victoria smiled, but there was bleakness in her eyes. "There are mornings when I wake up, and for the first few minutes I've forgotten, and then it all comes back just as if it were new."

"I'm sorry." Hester felt ashamed. She thought of all the hopes and dreams any young girl would have—for parties and balls, romance, love and marriage, children of her own one day. To realize in one blow that that was never possible must be as bad as everything Robert could face. "That was a stupid thing for me to say," she apologized profoundly. "I meant that you have learned to control it, instead of it controlling you."

Victoria's smile became real for a moment, before it faded and the trouble came back to her eyes. "Will he see me, do you think?"

"Yes, although I am not sure what mood he will be in or what you should hope for, or say."

Victoria did not reply, but started across the landing, her

back straight, swishing her skirts a little, the color rich where it caught the sunlight. She wanted to look pretty, graceful, and she moved awkwardly. Behind her, Hester could tell that it was a bad day for pain. Suddenly she almost hated Bernd for his dismissal of the girl as not a lasting friend for Robert, not someone who could have a place in his life once he was resigned to his dependence and had learned to live within it.

Victoria knocked, and when she heard Robert's voice, opened the door and went in. She left the door open, as propriety demanded.

"You look better," she said as soon as she was inside. "I was afraid you might feel ill again."

"Why?" he asked. "The disease is over."

She did not evade the issue. "Because you know you will not get better. Sometimes shock or grief can make you feel ill. It can certainly give you a headache or make you sick."

"I feel terrible," he said flatly. "If I knew how to die, as an act of will, I probably would . . . except that Mama would be bound to feel as if it were her fault. So I'm caught."

"It's a beautiful day." Her voice was quite clear and matter-of-fact. "I think you should come downstairs and go out into the garden."

"In my imagination?" he asked with a hard edge of sarcasm. "Are you going to describe the garden for me? You don't need to. I know what it looks like, and I'd rather you didn't. That's like pouring vinegar in the wound."

"I can't tell you about it," she replied honestly. "I've never been in your garden. I've always come straight up here. I meant that you should get someone to carry you down. As you say, you are not ill. And it isn't cold. You could sit out there perfectly well and see for yourself. I should like to see the garden. You could show me."

"What, and have the butler carry me around while I tell you 'This is the rose bed, these are the Michaelmas daisies, there are the chrysanthemums!' " he said bitterly. "I don't think the butler is strong enough! Or do you envisage a couple of footmen, one on either side?"

"The footman could bring you down, and you could sit on a chair on the lawn," she replied, still refusing to respond emotionally, whatever hurt or anger was inside her. "From there you could point out the beds to me. I don't feel like walking very far today myself."

There was a minute's silence.

"Oh," he said at last, his tone different, subdued. "You have pain?"

"Yes."

"I'm sorry. I didn't think."

"Will you show me the garden, please?"

"I should feel—" He stopped.

"Then stop thinking how you feel," she replied. "Just do it! Or are you going to spend the rest of your life here in bed?"

"Don't you dare speak . . ." His voice trailed off.

There was a long silence.

"Are you coming?" Victoria said at last.

The bell by Robert's bed rang, and Hester straightened her apron and knocked on the door.

"Come in," Robert replied.

She pushed the door wide.

"Would you be good enough to ask the footman to assist me downstairs, Hester?" Robert said, biting his lip and looking at her self-consciously, fear and self-mockery in his eyes. "Miss Stanhope wishes me to show her the garden."

Hester had promised Rathbone she would learn everything she could about Zorah and Gisela, or anything else which might help him. She was moved by curiosity to know what truth lay behind such wild charges, what emotions drove those two so different women and the prince who was between them. But far more urgently than that, she was afraid for Rathbone. He had undertaken the case in good conscience, only later to discover that the physical facts made it impossible Gisela could be guilty. There was no other possible defense for Zorah's behavior. Now the height of his career, which he had so recently achieved, looked like being short-lived and ending in disaster. Regardless of public opinion, his peers would not excuse him for such a breaking of ranks as to attack a foreign royal family with a charge he could not substantiate.

Zorah Rostova was a woman they would not ever forgive. She had defied all the rules. There was no way back for her, or for those who allied themselves with her . . . unless she could be proved innocent—in intent, if not in fact.

It was not easy to choose a time when anyone would be receptive to a conversation about Zorah. Robert's tragedy overshadowed anything else. Hester found herself growing desperate. Rathbone was almost always on her mind, and the urgency of the case became greater with every day that passed. The trial was set for late October, less than two weeks away.

She was obliged to contrive a discussion, feeling awkward and sinkingly aware that she might, by clumsiness, make future questions impossible. Dagmar was sitting by the open window in the afternoon light, idly mending a piece of lace on the neck of a blouse. She did so only to keep her fingers busy. Hester sat a little distance from her, sewing in her hand also, one of Robert's nightshirts that needed repair where the sleeve was coming away from the armhole. She threaded a needle and put on her thimble and began to stitch.

She could not afford to hesitate any longer. "Will you go to the trial?"

Dagmar looked up, surprised.

"Trial? Oh, you mean Zorah Rostova? I hadn't thought of it." She glanced out of the window to where Robert was sitting in the garden in a wheelchair Bernd had purchased. He was reading. Victoria had not come, so he was alone. "I wonder if he's cold," she said anxiously.

"If he is, he has a rug," Hester replied, biting back her

irritation. "And the chair moves really quite well. Please forgive me for saying so, but he will be better if you allow him to do things for himself. If you treat him as if he were helpless, then he will become helpless."

Dagmar smiled ruefully. "Yes. I'm sorry. Of course he will. You must think me very foolish."

"Not at all," Hester replied honestly. "Just hurt and not sure how best to help. I imagine the Baron will go?"

"Go?"

"To the trial." She could not give up. Rathbone's long, meticulous face, with its humorous eyes and precise mouth, was very sharp in her mind. She had never seen him doubting himself before. He had confronted defeat for others with resolution and skill and unflagging strength. But for himself it was different. She did not doubt his courage, but she knew that underneath the habitual composure he was profoundly disconcerted. He had discovered qualities in himself he did not care for, vulnerabilities, a certain complacency which had been shattered.

"Will he not?" she went on. "After all, it concerns not only the life and death of people you knew quite well but perhaps the murder of a man who could once have been your king."

Dagmar stopped even pretending to sew. The fabric slipped out of her hands.

"If anyone had told me three months ago that this could happen, I would have said they were ridiculous. It is so completely absurd!"

"Of course, you must have known Gisela," Hester prompted. "What was she like? Did you care for her?"

Dagmar thought for a moment. "I don't suppose I did know her, really," she said at length. "She was not the sort of woman one knows."

"I don't understand . . ." Hester said desperately.

Dagmar frowned. "She had admirers, people who enjoyed her company, but she did not seem to have close friends. If

Friedrich liked someone, then she did; if he did not, then for her that person barely existed."

"But Friedrich did not dislike you," Hester said, hoping profoundly that was true.

"Oh, no," Dagmar agreed. "I think in a slight way we were friends, at least better than mere acquaintances, before Gisela came. But she could make him laugh, even when he had thought he was tired, or bored, or weary with duty. I could never do that. I have seen him at the kind of long banquets where politicians make endless speeches, and he was growing glassy-eyed pretending to listen." She smiled as she remembered, for once forgetting Robert in the garden below, or the slight breeze stirring the curtains.

"Then she would lean across and whisper something to him," she continued. "And his eyes would brighten; it would all matter again. It was as if she could touch his mind with just a word, or even a glance, and give him of her vitality and laughter. She believed in him. She saw everything that was good in him. She loved him so very much." She stared into the distance, her face soft with memory, and perhaps a touch of envy for such a perfect closeness of heart and mind.

"And he must have loved her," Hester prompted. She tried to imagine it. With the people she cared about most, she seemed to be always on the brink of some misunderstanding or other, if not a downright quarrel. Was it a shortcoming in her? Or did she choose the wrong people to be drawn to? There was some darkness in Monk which every so often would close her out. It seemed unbreachable. And yet there were moments when she knew, as surely as she knew anything on earth, that he wanted never to hurt her, whatever the cost to himself.

"Absolutely and without reservation," Dagmar said wistfully, cutting across Hester's thoughts. "He adored her. One always knew where she was in a room, because every now and then his eyes would go to her, even if he was talking to someone else.

"And he was so proud of her, her grace, and wit, and the way she carried herself, her elegance and style of dress. He expected everyone to like her. He was so happy if they did, and could not understand it if they did not."

"Were there many who did not?" Hester asked. "Why did the Queen dislike her so intensely? And, it seems, the Countess Rostova?"

"I don't know of any reason, except that, of course, the Queen wanted him to marry Brigitte von Arlsbach," Dagmar explained. "Gisela did encourage him to kick over the traces rather." She smiled at some memory. "He was very used to doing everything he was told. Royal protocol is pretty rigid. There was always some equerry or adviser to remind him of the proper attitude, the correct behavior, whom he should speak to, spend time with, compliment, and who should be ignored, what was improper. Gisela would just laugh and tell him to please himself. He was Crown Prince; he should do as he liked."

She shrugged. "Of course, that is not the way it is. The higher one's calling, the more one must obey one's duty. But she was not born even to aristocracy, let alone royalty, so she did not understand that. I think for him that was a great deal of her charm. She offered him a kind of freedom he had never known. She poked fun at the courtiers who ruled his life. She was witty and outrageous and full of fun." Dagmar took a deep breath and let it out in a snort. "To Ulrike she was only irresponsible, selfish and ultimately a danger to the throne."

"But would she not have grown out of such behavior were she to have married him?" Hester asked. "I mean, with the Queen's approval?"

"I don't know," Dagmar answered ruefully. "The approval was never given."

The leaves were falling gently in the garden. A swirl of wind carried a handful against the window. Dagmar looked anxiously towards Robert.

"Did Brigitte love Friedrich?" Hester said quickly.

Dagmar looked back. "I don't think so. But she would have married him, as her duty, and, I expect, made a good queen."

"The Countess Rostova must hate Gisela passionately to make such an accusation." Hester was learning nothing that was the slightest help. All this would make Rathbone's case worse, not better. "It must be more than merely envy. Do you think she is being prompted by someone else who has a deeper motive?" She leaned forward a little. "Who does she know who might receive some personal gain from making a charge which cannot possibly be proved?"

"I have wondered that myself," Dagmar said, frowning. "And I have racked my brain to think of an answer. Zorah was always an extraordinary creature, willful and eccentric. Once she was nearly killed trying to defend some quite mad revolutionary. It was in '48. The wretched man was making a ridiculous speech in the street, and a crowd attacked him. Zorah strode in shouting like a . . . a barrack room soldier. Called them terrible names and fired a pistol over their heads. Heaven only knows where she got it from, or how she knew how to use it!" Her voice rose in incredulity. "The most absurd thing about it all was that she didn't even agree with what the man was saying." She shook her head. "And yet she can be most kind as well. I have known her to take time and trouble to care for people no one else would bother with, and do it so discreetly I knew only by accident."

Hester found herself liking Zorah in spite of herself. She did not wish to. Zorah had beguiled Rathbone into an impossible situation. Hester resented her doubly for having the skill to intrigue him so he lost his sense of judgment, something she had seen no one else do, and for the danger she had led him into. If she wished to ruin herself, that was her privilege, but to ruin someone else was inexcusable.

But Hester must concentrate on the present need. What she did or did not feel about Zorah personally was irrelevant.

"Could she be in love with someone who is using her in this?" she asked, regarding Dagmar with intelligent interest.

Dagmar considered. "It is the sort of thing she would do," she agreed after a moment. "In fact, some mistaken love, or misplaced idealism, is about the only thing which makes any sense. Perhaps she trusts him to come forward with some fact which will rescue her at the last moment." Her eyes softened. "Poor Zorah. What if he doesn't? What if he is merely using her?"

"To what purpose? Perhaps we are beginning at the wrong end. We should be considering who would benefit from this trial. Who will?"

Dagmar was silent for so long Hester thought she might not have heard.

"Who will benefit politically?" Hester asked again.

"I don't see how anyone can," Dagmar answered thoughtfully. "I have racked my head, but the situation doesn't seem to affect anything that I can think of. I am afraid it is just a stupid mistake made by a woman who has allowed her imagination and her envy to overrule her sense, and it will destroy her. I am very sorry about it."

Bernd's opinion was quite different, when Hester managed to speak to him alone and introduce the subject, this time a trifle more skillfully. She had just returned from an errand in the rain and was brushing the water off her skirt where her cloak had not covered it when Bernd crossed the hall, a newspaper in his hand.

"Oh, good afternoon, Miss Latterly. I see you got wet. There is a good fire in the withdrawing room if you wish to warm yourself. I am sure Polly would bring you some tea, and perhaps crumpets if you wish."

"Thank you," she accepted eagerly. "Will I not disturb you?" She glanced at the newspaper.

"No, not at all." He shook it absently. "I've finished. Full of scandal and speculation, mostly."

"I am afraid now that the trial is nearing, people are beginning to wonder a great deal," she said quickly. "The story is romantic, and although the charge seems unfounded, one cannot help wondering what is the truth behind it."

"I should imagine revenge," he replied with a frown.

"But how can she be revenged when she will lose the case?" Hester argued. "Could it have to do with the Queen?"

"In what way?" He looked puzzled.

"Well, apparently the Queen strongly dislikes Gisela. Is Zorah a great friend of the Queen's?"

Bernd's face hardened. "Not that I am aware." He started towards the withdrawing room as though to end the conversation.

"You don't think the Queen's dislike could be behind this, do you?" Hester asked, hurrying after him. It was an idea which had a glimmer of sense. Ulrike had apparently never forgiven Gisela, and perhaps now she felt Gisela was somehow to blame for Friedrich's death—if not directly, then indirectly. "After all," she continued aloud as they went into the withdrawing room and Bernd pulled the bell rope, rather hard, "he might never have had the accident in the first place if he had not been in exile. And even if he had, he would have received different treatment had he been at home. Maybe, in her mind, she had convinced herself from one step to another, until now she really believes Gisela capable of murder. Maybe . . ." She swung around in front of him as he sat down, her wet skirts cold against her legs. "She has probably not seen Gisela for twelve years. She knows only what other people have told her and what she imagines."

The maid answered the summons of the bell, and Bernd ordered afternoon tea for two and hot buttered crumpets.

"I think it unlikely," he said when the maid had gone and closed the door. "It is a very unpleasant affair, but not one in which I have any part. I would prefer to discuss your opinion of how we may best help my son. He does appear in these last few days to be better in spirits . . . although I do not wish him to become too dependent on the young woman, Miss Stanhope. She is not strong enough to employ on any permanent basis, and also, I think, not suitable."

"Why did the Queen hate Gisela even before she married Friedrich?" Hester said desperately.

His face froze. "I do not know, Miss Latterly, nor do I care. I have sufficient grief in my own family not to be concerned with the self-inflicted misfortune of others. I should appreciate your advice upon what sort of person to employ to be with Robert permanently. I thought you might know of a young man of good character, gentle disposition, perhaps one with a leaning towards reading and study, who would like a position which offers him a home and agreeable company in return for such help as Robert needs."

"I shall make inquiries, if you wish," she replied with a sinking heart, not only for Rathbone but for Victoria. "There may well be someone the job would suit very nicely. Is that what Robert wishes?"

"I beg your pardon?"

"Is that what Robert wishes?" she repeated.

"What Robert wishes cannot be obtained," he said, his voice tight with pain. "This is what he requires, Miss Latterly."

"Yes, Baron Ollenheim," she conceded. "I will make inquiries."

7

MONK SET OUT on his journey northward with far more pleasure than the situation warranted. Evelyn was on the same train, and he looked forward to time in her company. She was delightful, elegant, always feminine. She carried her enjoyment of life and people in such a manner it spilled over onto all around her. Her humor was infectious, and he found himself laughing as well.

He left Venice with regret. Its beauty made it unlike any other city, and he would never again see light on rippling water without thinking of it. But there was also a sadness there. It was a city in decay, and occupied by a foreign army, a society looking to the past and disturbed and angry, fighting for the future. The people were divided among Venetians, who were crushed and resentful, awaiting the moment to strike back; Austrians, who knew they were away from home, in an old and lovely culture which did not want them; and expatriates, who belonged nowhere and lived on memories and dreams which even they no longer believed.

He had tried to express this to Evelyn when he met her briefly at the train station, but she was concerned about the comfort of travel arrangements and had no interest in such reflections. Klaus was gloomy, his huge figure looming in the background, shoulders a little hunched, mind preoccupied with what he would do when he reached Felzburg. He was impatient with railway officials, short-tempered with his own servants, and did not appear even to see Monk.

Evelyn rolled her eyes expressively and gave Monk a dazzling smile, as if the whole performance were somehow funny. Then she followed after her husband with an outward semblance of duty, but also a little swagger to her step, and a glance backward over her shapely shoulder at Monk before stepping up into her carriage.

They were several hours north, and Monk drifted off to sleep watching the countryside roll past. He woke with a jolt, both physical and of memory. For a moment he could not recall where he was traveling to. He had Liverpool in mind. He was going there to do with shipping. Huge Atlantic clippers filled his inner vision, a tangle of spars against a windy sky, the slap of water at the dockside, the gray stretch of the Mersey River. He could see the wooden sides of ships riding on the tide, towering above him. He could smell salt and tar and rope.

There was immense relief in him, as of rescue after terrible danger. It had been personal. Monk had been alone in it. Someone else had saved him, and at considerable risk, trusting him when he had not earned it, and it was this trust which had made the difference to him between survival and disaster.

He sat in the train with unfamiliar trees and hills rushing past the windows. The rattle and lurch were comforting. There was a rhythm to them which should have eased him.

But this did not look like any part of England he knew. It was not green enough, and it was too steep. He could not be going to Liverpool. His mind was blurred, as if sleep still clung to him. He owed an immense debt. But to whom?

The train had high divisions between each row of seats, giving a certain amount of privacy, but he could see that the man on the far side of the aisle was reading a newspaper. It was in Italian. Where would a man buy an Italian newspaper?

Monk glanced up at the luggage rack and saw his own cases. The label which was hanging down said "Felzburg."

Of course. Memory came back quite clearly now. He was trying to find evidence to clear Zorah Rostova of slander, which meant finding proof that Princess Gisela had killed Prince Friedrich. And that was impossible, because she had not only had no reason, she had also had no opportunity.

It was a fool's errand. But he had to do everything he could to help Rathbone, who had been uncharacteristically rash in taking the case in the first place. But it was too late to retreat now.

And Evelyn von Seidlitz was on the train. He smiled as he remembered that. With luck he would see her at dinner. That was bound to be a pleasure; it always was. And if they stopped somewhere agreeable, then the food might be good also. Although he was not looking forward to a night spent in a semireclining seat where it would be extremely difficult to do anything better than take short naps. He seemed to recall that somewhere in the world they had invented a proper sleeping car in the last four or five years. Perhaps it was America. Certainly it was not this train, even though he was traveling in the best accommodation there was.

It felt very natural. That was another discomfort to his mind. Once he had earned the kind of money which had made luxury an everyday thing. Why had he given it up to become a policeman?

This debt he owed was at the heart of it, but rack his mind as he might, it remained clouded. The emotion was sharp enough: obligation, a weight of fear lifted by someone else's loyalty when he had not yet earned it. But who? The mentor and friend he had remembered earlier with such growing clarity and grief? Had he ever repaid that debt, or was it still owing, and that was why it was so sharp now in his mind? Had he walked away from it, leaving it? He wanted to believe that was not possible. He may have been abrupt, at times unfair. He had certainly been overwhelmingly ambitious. But he had never been either a coward or a liar. Surely he had not been without a sense of honor?

How could he know? It was not merely a matter of going back, if that were possible, and paying now. And if it were his mentor, then it was too late. He was dead. That much had come back to him months before. It was necessary he should understand himself, to get rid of the pain of doubt, even if his fears about himself proved to be true. In a sense they were already true, unless he could prove them false. He could not leave this unresolved.

The train stopped regularly to take on coal and water, and for the needs of the passengers. Still, fifty years before, or less, he would have had to make this same journey by coach, and that would have been immeasurably slower and less comfortable.

As he had foreseen, dinner was taken at a hostelry along the way and was excellent. Klaus von Seidlitz had returned to the train a little earlier, in the company of two very solemn, militarily dressed men, so Monk spent a few minutes by the side of the track in the snatched company of Evelyn. He could see her face in the clear mountain starlight, in the sudden red flares of the sparks from the engine, and in the distant torches held by men as they labored to shovel coal and replenish the water for the night's journey northward across France.

He would like to have spoken to her for hours, asked her about herself, told her things he had seen and done which would bring the flash of interest to her face, intrigue her with the mystery and reality of his world. He would like to amuse her.

But Rathbone weighed heavily on his mind. Time was growing short, and he had nothing of worth to take back to the barrister. Was he going to indulge himself, perhaps again, at someone else's expense? Was this the kind of man he was at heart?

He stared up at the sharp, glittering sky with its sweeping darkness, and at the pale clouds of steam windblown across the platform. The heavy noises of coal and steam seemed far away, and he was acutely conscious of Evelyn beside him.

"Has Zorah no friends, no family who could prevail on her to withdraw this insane charge?" he asked.

He heard Evelyn's sigh of impatience, and was furious with circumstances for offering him so much and at the same time preventing him from taking it. Damn Rathbone!

"I don't think she has any family," Evelyn replied sharply. "She always behaved as if she hadn't. I think she's half Russian."

"Do you like her? At least did you, until she did this?"

She moved a step closer to him. He could smell her hair and feel the warmth of her skin near his cheek.

"I don't care about her in the slightest," she replied softly. "I always thought she was a little mad. She fell in love with the most unsuitable people. One was a doctor, years older than herself and as ugly as an old boot. But she adored him, and when he died she behaved atrociously. She simply ignored everyone. Had him burned, of all things, and threw his ashes off the top of a mountain. It was all rather disgusting. Then she went off on a long trip somewhere ridiculous, up the Nile, or something like that. Stayed away for years. Some said she fell in love with an Egyptian and lived with him." Her voice was thick with disgust. "Didn't marry him, of course. I suppose you couldn't have a Christian marriage with an Egyptian anyway." She laughed abruptly.

Monk found all this peculiarly jarring. He remembered Zorah as he had seen her in London. She was an extraordinary woman, eccentric, passionate, but neither overtly cruel nor, as far as he could tell, dishonest. He had liked her. He saw no offense in falling in love out of your generation or with someone of another race. It might well be tragic, but it was not wrong.

Evelyn lifted her face to look at him. She was smiling again. The starlight on her skin was exquisite. Her wide eyes were all softness and laughter. He leaned forward and kissed her, and she melted into his arms.

The train arrived in Felzburg at noon. After several days' travel, Monk was tired and longed to stand in an unconfined space, to walk without turning after three paces, and to sleep stretched out in a proper bed.

But there was little time to be spent on such business. He had a letter of introduction from Stephan, whom he had left in Venice, and went immediately to present himself to Colonel Eugen.

"Ah, I was expecting you!" The man who received Monk was much older than he had imagined, in his middle fifties, a lean, gray-haired soldier who bore the marks of dueling on his cheeks and stood ramrod stiff to welcome his guest. "Stephan wrote to me that you might come. How may I be of help? My home is yours, as is my time and such skill as I possess."

"Thank you," Monk accepted with relief, although he was unsure even of what he was seeking, let alone how to find it. At least he was delighted to accept the hospitality. "That is most generous of you, Colonel Eugen."

"You will stay here? Good, good. You will eat? My man will take care of your luggage. The journey was good?" It was a rhetorical question. Monk had a powerful feeling that the Colonel was a man to whom any journey would be good if he reached his destination alive.

Monk agreed without additional comment and followed his host to where a good luncheon was set out on a dark wood table gleaming with embroidered linen and very heavy silver. A small fire burned halfheartedly in the grate. The paneled walls were hung with swords of varying weights from rapiers to sabers.

"What may I do to assist you?" Eugen asked when the soup had been served. "I am at your disposal."

"I need to learn the truth of the political situation," Monk replied candidly. "And as much of the past as I am able to."

"Do you consider it possible someone murdered Friedrich?" Eugen frowned.

"On the basis of the factual evidence, yes, it is possible," Monk replied. "Does it surprise you?"

He expected shock and anger. He saw neither in Eugen's response, only a philosophical sadness.

"I do not believe it could be Gisela Berentz, but I would not find it hard to believe that someone did it, for political reasons," he answered. "We are on the brink of great changes in all the German-speaking states. We survived the revolutions of '48." He dipped his spoon into his soup and drank without seeming to taste it. "The tide of nationalism is rising all over Europe, and most especially here. Sooner or later, I think we will be one nation. Sometimes principalities like ours survive independently. Some chance of history, or geography, makes them unique, and the large powers are content to let them be. Usually, they are swallowed up. Friedrich believed we could remain as we are. At least," he corrected, "that is what we thought. Count Lansdorff is a strong protagonist for that view, and, of course, so is the Queen. She has dedicated her life to serving the royal dynasty. No duty whatsoever has been too hard for her, no sacrifice too great."

"Except forgiving Gisela," Monk said, watching Eugen's face.

He saw no humor in it, no understanding of irony.

"To forgive Gisela would mean to allow her to return," Eugen answered, finishing his soup and breaking a little bread on his plate. "That is impossible! If you knew Ulrike, you would have understood that from the beginning."

A solitary manservant removed the soup plates and brought in roasted venison and boiled vegetables.

"Why are you prepared to help a foreigner inquire into what can only be a most distressing and unseemly affair?" Monk asked, accepting a generous serving.

Eugen did not hesitate. A shadow crossed his face, and his china-blue eyes flickered with what might have been amusement.

"A percipient question, sir. Because I can best serve my country and her interests if I know the truth."

Monk had a sudden chill rack him, as if the food he had swallowed had been iced. Eugen might just as well have added "That is not to say I will allow it to be repeated!" The meaning was there, for an instant, in his face.

"I see," Monk said slowly. "And what will serve your country? Accidental death? Assassination by a hired man, preferably unknown, or murder by his wife for her own personal motives?"

Eugen smiled coldly, but there was appreciation in his eyes.

"That is an opinion, sir, and mine you do not need to know, nor would it be in my interests that you should. Felzburg is dangerous at the moment. Feelings run very high. We stand at the crossroads of half a millennium of history, perhaps even at the end of it. Germany as a nation, rather than a language and a culture, may be at the beginning of hers."

Monk waited, not wishing to interrupt when he sensed Eugen had more to say. His host's eyes were bright, and there was an eagerness in him which he could not mask.

"Ever since the dissolution of the Holy Roman Empire under Napoleon," Eugen went on, his food now forgotten, "we have been only scores of separate little entities, speaking the same tongue, having the same culture and hoping one day to bring to pass the same dreams, but each in its own way." He was staring at Monk intently. "Some are liberal, some chaotic, some dictatorial and repressive. Some long for freedom of the press, while both Austria and Prussia, the two greatest powers, believe censorship is as necessary to survival and defense as is an army."

Monk felt a faint stirring of memory. News of rebellions all over Europe one spring; men and women at the barricades, troops in the streets, proclamations, petitions, cavalry charging at civilians, shots into the crowd. For a brief spell there had been wild hope. Then despair had closed in as one by one the uprisings had been crushed and a subtler, deeper oppression had returned. But how long ago was it? Was that 1848?

He kept his eyes on Eugen's and listened.

"We had parliaments, briefly," Eugen went on. "Great nationalists arose with liberal ideas, freedom and equality for the vast mass of people. They too were crushed, or failed through their own ineptitude and inexperience."

"Here as well?" Monk asked. He loathed exposing his ignorance, but he had to know.

Eugen helped them both to an excellent Burgundy.

"Yes, but it was brief," he replied. "There was little violence. The king had already granted certain reforms and legislated far better conditions for workers and a measure of freedom for the press." A flicker of a smile crossed Eugen's lean face. It looked to Monk like admiration. "I think that was Ulrike's doing. Some people thought she was against it. She would have an absolute monarchy, if she could. She could rule like your Queen Elizabeth, give orders and chop the heads off those who defied her. But she is three hundred years too late for that, and she is far too clever a woman to overshoot the mark. Better to give them a little and remove the spur of rebellion. You cannot rule a people who hate you, except for a very short time. She has a long vision. She sees generations on the throne, stretching into the future."

"But there are no heirs," Monk pointed out.

"Which brings us to the crux of the matter," Eugen replied. "If Friedrich had returned without Gisela, if he had set her aside and married again, then there would have been." He leaned forward, his face fierce in its intensity. "No man of the Queen's party would ever have killed Friedrich. That is absolute! If he was murdered, then look for someone who is for unification, who does not mind being swallowed by Prussia, Hannover, Bavaria, or any of a score of others strong enough. Or one who had been promised office or possessions by any faction he believes can succeed. There was an attempt in '48 to make one of the Austrian archdukes king of all Germany. It failed, thank God. But that does not mean they could not try again."

Monk's head swam.

"The possibilities are endless."

"No—but they are large." Eugen began to eat hungrily, and Monk copied him. He was surprised how much he enjoyed the food.

"What about Prince Waldo?" Monk asked with his mouth full.

"I will take you to meet him," Eugen promised. "To-morrow."

Eugen kept his word. His valet had pressed Monk's clothes. His evening suit hung in the wardrobe. His shirts were all laun-dered and gleaming white. His studs and cuff links were laid out on the tallboy, as were his brushes and toiletries. He spared a moment to be glad he had had the vanity and extravagance to purchase things of excellent quality at some time in that past he could not remember.

He had got as far as choosing cuff links, agate set in gold, when without warning he remembered vividly doing exactly the same, with these same links, before going to a dinner party in London. He had been accompanying the man who had taught him, sponsored him and sheltered him. He had had for-bearance with Monk's ignorance and lack of polish, his impetuosity and occasional rudeness. With immeasurable patience, he had schooled him not only in the profession of investment banking, but in the arts of being a gentleman. He had taught him how to dress well without being ostentatious; how to tell a good cut, a good art; how to choose a pair of boots, a shirt; even how to treat one's tailor. He had taught him which knife and fork to use, how to hold them elegantly, which wine to select, when and how to speak and when to keep silent, when it was appropriate to laugh. Over a period of years he had made the provincial Northumbrian youth into a gentleman, sure of himself, with that unconscious air of confidence that marks the well-bred from the ordinary.

It was all there in his mind as his hand touched the small piece of jewelry. He was back in his mentor's house in London, twenty or more years before, about to go to dinner. The occasion was important. Something was going to happen, and he was afraid. He had enemies, and they were powerful. It was within their ability to destroy his career, even to have him arrested and imprisoned. He had been accused of something profoundly dishonorable. He was innocent, but he could not prove it . . . not to anyone. The fear gripped ice-cold inside him and there was no escape. It took all the strength he had to quell the panic which rose like a scream in his throat.

But it had not happened. At least he was almost sure of that. Why not? What had prevented it? Had he rescued himself? Or had someone else? And at what cost?

Monk had tried desperately to fight against injustice before, and lost. It had come to him before, a fragment at a time. He had remembered his mentor's wife, her face as she wept silently, the tears running down her cheeks in despair.

He would have given anything he possessed to be able to help. But he had nothing. No money, no influence, no ability that was a shred of use.

He did not know what had happened after that. All he could claw back from the darkness of amnesia was the sense of tragedy, rage and futility. He knew that was why he had given up banking and gone into the police: to fight against injustices like that, to find and punish the cheaters and destroyers, to prevent it happening again, and again, to other innocent men. He could learn the skills, and find the weapons, forge them if necessary.

But what was the debt he had recalled with such a stomach-freezing fear? It was specific, not a general gratitude for years of luridness, but for a particular gift. Had he ever repaid that?

He had no idea . . . no idea at all. There was simply a darkness and a weight in his mind—and a consuming need to know.

The reception was held in a huge hall brilliant with chandeliers hung from a carved and painted ceiling. There must have been a hundred people present, no more, but the enormous skirts of the women, gleaming pale in pastel and muted flower tones, seemed to fill the space. Black-suited men stood like bare trees among clouds of blossom. The light sparked prisms of fire off diamonds as heads and wrists moved. Now and again, above the chatter and occasional laughter, Monk heard the snap as some gentleman bowed and brought his heels together.

Most communications were naturally in German, but as Eugen introduced Monk, in deference to his unfamiliarity with that language, people changed to English.

They spoke of all sorts of trivialities: weather, theater, international news and gossip, the latest music or philosophical notions. No one mentioned the scandal about to break in London. No one even mentioned Friedrich's death. It had happened six months before and it might have been six years, or even the twelve since he had renounced his throne and his country and left forever. Perhaps in their minds he had died then. If they cared whether Gisela defended herself successfully or, indeed, if Zorah Rostova were ruined, they did not mention it.

Now and again conversation did become serious; then it was the aftermath of the conflicts of '48 that was spoken of, and the fiercer oppression which had followed, most especially in Prussia.

All the conversation was of politics, of unification or independence, of social or economic reforms, new freedoms and how they might be won, and above all, like a chill in the air, the possibility of war. Not once did Monk hear Gisela's name mentioned, and Friedrich's came up only in an aside—that he could no longer be a focus for the independence party, and speculating whether Rolf had the popular following to take his place. Zorah was mentioned, but as an eccentric, a patriot. If anyone commented on her accusation, Monk did not hear it.

Towards the end of the evening, Eugen found Monk again and presented him to Prince Waldo, the man who would inherit the crown by default. He saw a man of average height, rather stolid appearance, a face almost handsome but marred by a certain heaviness. His manner was careful. There was little humor about his mouth.

"How do you do, Mr. Monk," he said in excellent English.

"How do you do, sir," Monk answered respectfully, but meeting his eyes.

"Colonel Eugen tells me you have come from London," Waldo observed.

"Yes sir, but more immediately from Venice."

A spark of interest flared in Waldo's dark eyes. "Indeed. Is that coincidence, or are you pursuing some thread in our unfortunate affairs?"

Monk was startled. He had not expected such perception or directness. He decided candor was best. Remembering Rathbone, he had no time to lose.

"I am pursuing a thread, sir. There is a strong suggestion that your brother, Prince Friedrich, did not die solely as a result of his riding accident."

Waldo smiled. "Is that what is known as a British understatement?"

"Yes sir," Monk acknowledged.

"And your interest in it?"

"A legal one, to assist British justice to deal fairly . . ." Monk made a rapid calculation as to which answers would be likely to offend Waldo least. After all, Waldo had had a great deal to gain or lose by Friedrich's decision—not only his personal leadership of the country, but also his vision for the country's future. Friedrich had been for independence. Waldo apparently believed the best hope lay with unification. He could lose his own throne, but perhaps he was genuinely more concerned with the safety and prosperity of his people.

Monk stared at him and tried to make a judgment.

Waldo was waiting. Monk must answer quickly. The swirl of laughter and music continued around them, the hum of voices, the clink of glass. Light shattered into a thousand fragments from jewels.

If Waldo really believed the lives and the peace of his country lay in unification, then he had more reason than anyone to kill Friedrich.

". . . with the issue of slander," Monk finished his sentence.

Waldo's eyes widened. It was not the answer he had expected.

"I see," he said slowly. "It is so serious a matter in England?"

"When it concerns the royal family of another country, yes sir, it is."

A strange flicker of emotion crossed Waldo's face. Monk could not read it. It might have been any of a dozen things. A few yards away, a soldier in resplendent uniform bowed to a lady in pink.

"My brother gave up his duties in his family over twelve years ago, and with it his privileges," Waldo said coolly. "He chose not to be one of us. Gisela Berentz never was."

Monk took a deep breath. He had little to lose.

"If he was murdered, sir, then the question arises as to who did such a thing. With the political situation as it is at present, speculation will touch many people, including those whose views were different from his."

"You mean me," Waldo replied unflinchingly, his brows raised a little.

Monk was startled. "More precisely, sir, someone who holds your views," he corrected hastily. "Not necessarily, of course, with your knowledge or upon your instructions. But it might be difficult to demonstrate that."

"Extremely," Waldo said, his eyes steady and hard, as if already he faced the charge and was steeling himself to it. "Even proof will convince only those who wish to be convinced. It will follow a long path before it reaches the ears of the common man."

Monk changed the subject. "Unfortunately, we cannot prevent the trial. We have tried. We have done everything in our power to persuade the Countess Rostova to withdraw her allegation and apologize, but so far we have failed." He did not know if that was true, but he assumed it would be. Rathbone must have at least that much sense—and desire for his own survival.

A flicker of humor crossed Waldo's face for the first time.

"I could have told you as much," he replied. "Zorah has never been known to back away from anything. Or, for that matter, to count the personal cost of it. Even her enemies have never called her a coward."

"Could she have killed him herself?" Monk asked impulsively.

Waldo did not hesitate an instant, nor did his expression change. "No. She is for independence. She believes we can survive alone, like Andorra or Liechtenstein." Again the shadow of humor crossed his face. "If it had been Gisela who was killed, I would have said certainly she could . . ."

Monk was stunned. The words raced around his head. He tried to grasp their dozen possibilities. Was it conceivable that Zorah had meant to poison Gisela and, through some grotesque mischance, had killed Friedrich instead? This thought opened up vast possibilities. Could Rolf have done it, on his own or for his sister, the Queen? Then Friedrich would have had no impediment to returning to lead the independence party. Or could Brigitte have tried to kill Gisela so that Friedrich could return and she could marry him, to please the country and so she would one day be queen?

Or even Lord Wellborough? He could have been attempting to promote a war which could massively enrich him.

Monk muttered some reply, civil and meaningless, thanked Waldo for having received him, and backed away with his mind still in a tumult.

Monk woke in the night with a jolt, half sitting up in his bed as if someone had startled him. He strained his ears but could hear no sound in the darkness.

The same sense of fear was with him as the one he had felt while putting on his cuff links, an overwhelming isolation, except for one person . . . one person who believed in his innocence and was prepared to risk his own safety in standing by him.

Was there anyone to stand by Gisela, or had she forfeited everything in marrying Friedrich? Was it really "all for love, and the world well lost"?

But it had been a different kind of love which had prompted Monk's one friend to fight for him at any cost, the loyalty that never breaks, the faith which is tested to the last. It had been his mentor who had jeopardized his own reputation on Monk's innocence. He knew that now. He could remember it. He had been accused of embezzlement. His mentor had staked his own name and fortune that Monk was not guilty.

And that had been enough to make them search further, to carry him until the truth was found.

And sitting up in bed with the sweat clammy on his body in the cold night air, he also knew that he had never repaid that debt. When the tide had been reversed, he had not had the ability, or the power. All he possessed was not enough. The man he had most admired had lost everything: home, honor, even, in the end, his life.

And Monk had never been able to repay. It was too late.

He lay back with a feeling of emptiness and a strange aloneness of the irretrievable. Whatever was given, it would have to be to someone else. It could never be the same.

The following afternoon he was presented at court. He needed to know whether it could be that Gisela herself was the intended victim, and he dreaded telling Rathbone.

And yet perhaps of all the possible answers, the one he had thought the worst of all, that Zorah killed him herself, was, in fact, the least appalling. What if it were Prince Waldo, to prevent Friedrich from coming home and plunging the country into war? Or Rolf, on the Queen's behalf, meaning to kill Gisela and thus free Friedrich to return, and he had tragically killed the wrong person?

What would the British legal system, and British society, make of that? How would the Foreign Office and its diplomats at Whitehall extricate themselves from that morass with honor—and European peace?

How much of all of this did Zorah Rostova know or understand?

Queen Ulrike was a magnificent woman. Even after what he had heard of her iron resolve, Monk was unprepared for the force of her presence. At a distance, as he entered the room, he thought she was very tall. Her hair was glittering white, and she wore it swept up high on her head, braided in a natural coronet inside a blazing tiara. Her features were straight and strong, her brows very level. She wore shades of ivory and oyster satins with so slight a hoop that her skirts seemed to fall almost naturally. She stood with her shoulders squared and her gaze straight ahead.

When it was his turn to be introduced, and he walked forward, he saw that she was actually of no more than average height, and closer to, it was her eyes which startled and froze. They were clear aquamarine, neither green nor blue.

His name was announced.

"Your Majesty." He bowed.

"Count Lansdorff tells me you are a friend of Stephan von Emden, Mr. Monk," she said, surveying him with chilly courtesy.

"Yes, ma'am."

"He met you at the home of Lord Wellborough, where my unfortunate son met his death," she continued with no discernible emotion in her voice.

"I stayed there a few days," he agreed, wondering what Rolf had told her and why she had chosen to raise the subject.

"If you are a friend of Baron von Emden's, then possibly you are also acquainted with the Countess Rostova?"

His instinct was to deny it for self-protection. Then he looked at her cool, clear eyes and was startled, even chilled, by the intelligence in them, and by a glimpse of something which might have been emotion, or simply force of will.

"I know her, ma'am, but not well." To such a woman the truth was the only safety. Perhaps she knew it already.

"A woman of dubious tastes but unquestionable patriotism," she said with a ghost of a smile. "I hope she will survive this present storm."

Monk gasped.

"Are you enjoying Felzburg, Mr. Monk?" she continued as if they had been discussing something of equal unimportance. "It is a most agreeable time of year for concerts and theater. I hope you will have the opportunity during your stay here to visit the opera."

It was an indication that the interview was at an end.

"Thank you, ma'am, I am sure I shall find it excellent." He bowed again and withdrew, his head swimming.

* * *

He should have looked forward to the evening immensely. It was a ball to which Eugen had seen he was invited and where he knew Evelyn would also be present. All too soon he would have to return to London and to the reality of his life as it was. Whatever it had been before he had left it to go into the police force, that luxury, that easy acceptance of pleasure, was part of a past he could never relive in memory, much less return to. At least for the time left to him, he would, by act of will, forget the past and the future. The present was everything. He would enjoy it to the fullest, drink the cup of it to the last drop.

He dressed with care, but also with a sense of satisfaction, almost delight. He surveyed himself in the glass and smiled at his reflection. It was elegant and at ease in its beautiful clothes. The face that looked back at him had no diffidence, no anxiety. It was smooth, slightly amused, very sure of itself.

He knew Evelyn found him exciting. He had told her just enough to intrigue her. He was different from any other man she knew, and because she could not understand him, or guess what was really behind the little she could see, he was dangerous.

He knew it as clearly as if she had said it to him in words. It was a game, a delicately played and delicious game, the more to be savored because the stakes were real: not love, nothing so painful or so demanding of the self, but emotion for all that, and one that would not be easily forgotten when he had to leave. Perhaps from now on something of it would be echoed in every woman who woke a hunger and a delight in him.

He arrived at the magnificent home of the host for the ball and strode up the steps. Only a sense of dignity stopped him from racing up two at a time. He felt light-footed, full of energy. There were shimmering lights everywhere: torches in wrought iron holders outside, chandeliers inside blazing through the open doors and beyond the tall windows. He could hear the hum of conversation almost as if the music were already playing.

He handed in his invitation and hurried across the hallway and up the stairs to the reception room. His eyes swept over the crowded heads to find the thick, dark hair of Klaus von Seidlitz. It took him a moment or two. Then someone turned, taller than the others, and he saw Klaus's face with its broken nose and heavy features. He was talking to a group of soldiers in bright uniform, recounting some tale which amused him. He laughed, and for a few moments he was a different man from the brooding, almost sullen person Monk had seen in England. In repose his face had seemed cruel; now it was genial, and merely crooked.

Monk searched for Evelyn and could not see her.

Rolf was standing not more than a dozen yards from him. He looked polite and bored. Monk guessed he was there from duty rather than pleasure, perhaps courting a political interest. Now that Friedrich was dead, where did the independence party pin its hopes? Rolf had the intelligence to lead it. Perhaps he would have been the person behind the throne if a plan to reinstate Friedrich had succeeded. Maybe he had always intended to rule.

Who would be the rallying point now, the person with the popularity, the image people would follow, would sacrifice their money, their houses, even their lives for? That kind of loyalty attaches only to someone with either a royal birthright or a character of extraordinary valor and passion—or to someone who can be seen as a symbol of what the people most desire. It does not matter whether that loyalty is born of truth or fiction, but it must ignite a belief in victory that overrides the defeats and the disappointments, the weariness and the loss.

Rolf had not that magic. Standing on the last step and looking across the heads of the guests at his strong, careful face, Monk knew it, and he imagined Rolf did too.

How deep did Rolf's plans run? Staring at his steady, fixed

gaze, his square shoulders and ramrod back, Monk could believe they might well be deep enough to have murdered Gisela and created out of Friedrich the hero he needed—the rightful heir, bereaved, repentant, returned to lead his people in their hour of greatest peril.

Only the plans had gone disastrously wrong; it was not Gisela who had died, but Friedrich himself.

"Mr. Monk?"

It was a woman's voice, soft and low, very pleasing.

He turned around slowly to see Brigitte smiling at him with interest.

"Good evening, Baroness von Arlsbach," he said a little more stiffly than he had intended. He remembered feeling sorry for her at Wellborough Hall. She had been very publicly rejected by Friedrich. Hundreds of people must have known how deeply the royal family had wanted him to marry her, and that she had been willing, even if only as a matter of duty. But he had steadfastly refused, and then had been prepared to sacrifice everything for love of Gisela.

And Brigitte was still unmarried, a most unusual circumstance for women of her age and station. He looked at her now, standing a few feet away from him. She was not beautiful, but there was a serenity in her which had a loveliness that was perhaps more lasting than regularity of feature or delicacy of coloring. Her eyes were steady and straight but had none of the ice of Ulrike's.

"I did not know you were in Felzburg," she continued. "Have you friends here?"

"Only new friends," he replied. "But I am finding the city most exhilarating." It was true, even if it was due to Evelyn's presence in it rather than any qualities of the city itself. The industrial cities of northern England would have been exhilarating for him had Evelyn been there.

"That is the first time I have heard it described so," she said with amusement. She was a big woman with broad shoulders, but utterly feminine. He noticed how flawless her skin was, and how smooth her neck. She was wearing a king's ransom in jewels, an unusual necklace of cabochon star rubies and pearls. She must hate Gisela, not only for the personal humiliation but also for what she had taken from the country in luring away Friedrich, who would fight for independence, and leaving Waldo, who seemed genuinely to believe in unification. And she had been at Wellborough Hall.

The thought was repellent, but it could not be swept away, no matter how hard it was to believe, standing there on the steps overlooking the ballroom and seeing the peace in her face.

"You don't find it so?" he asked. He thought of sounding surprised, then changed his mind. She would think it affected, perhaps even sarcastic. She was as aware as he, perhaps more so, that it was a very small city compared with the great capitals of Europe, and almost provincial in nature.

As if reading his thoughts, she answered. "It has character and individuality." Her smile widened. "It has a vigor of life. But it is also old-fashioned, a little resentful of sophisticated people from our larger neighbors, and too often suspicious because we dread being overshadowed. Like most other places, we have too many officials, and they all seem to be related to one another. Gossip is rampant, as it is in all small cities. But on the other hand, we are hospitable and generous, and we do not have armed soldiers in the streets." She had not said she loved it, but it was there far more eloquently in her eyes and her voice. If he had been uncertain of her loyalty to independence before, he was not now.

Suddenly *exhilarating* seemed a false word to have used. He had been thinking of Evelyn, not the city, and it was patronizing to speak falsely of thousands of people's lives and homes.

She was looking at him curiously. Perhaps she saw something of his thoughts reflected in his face.

"I wish I could stay longer," he said, and this time he was sincere.

"Must you leave?"

"Yes. Unfortunately, I have business in London which will not wait." That was truer than she could know. "Perhaps you will do me the honor of allowing me to accompany you in?"

"Thank you." She took his proffered arm and began down the steps. He was about to tell the footman who he was when the man bowed deferentially to Brigitte and took Monk's card.

"The Baroness von Arlsbach . . . and Mr. William Monk," he announced.

Immediately there was a hush as heads turned, not to Monk, but to Brigitte. There was a murmur of respect. A way parted for them to enter the crowd. No one pushed forward or resumed their previous conversation until the couple had passed.

Monk realized with a rush of heat to his face how presumptuous he had been. Brigitte had very possibly not aspired to be queen, as apparently Gisela had, but her people had wished it. She was revered next only to Ulrike, and perhaps better loved.

His earlier pity for her faded. To be one man's passionate love was perhaps a quirk of nature no one could create or foresee. To be loved by a country was a mark of worth. No one who held it should be thought of slightly.

The music was beginning in the room beyond. Should he invite her to dance? Would it be insulting now if he did not, or would it be a further presumption if he did? He was not used to indecision. He could not remember ever having felt so gauche before.

She turned to face him, holding out her other hand. It was gracefully done, an unspoken acceptance before he had time to make either mistake.

He found himself smiling with relief, and led her onto the floor.

It was another half hour before he was able to find Evelyn. She was as light in his arms as a drift of silk, her eyes full of laughter. They danced as if there were no one else in the huge room. She flirted outrageously, and he reveled in it. The night would be far too short.

He saw Klaus looking melancholy and rather bad tempered, and all he could feel was a vague distaste. How could such a miserable man expect to hold a creature like Evelyn, who was all wit and happiness?

An hour later, dancing with her again, he saw Klaus talking earnestly with an elderly man Evelyn told him was a Prussian aristocrat.

"He looks like a soldier," Monk agreed.

"He is," she replied, shrugging her lovely shoulders. "Almost all Prussian aristocrats are. For them it is practically the same thing. I dislike them. They are terribly stiff and formal, and have not an atom of humor between them."

"Do you know many of them?"

"Far too many!" She made a gesture of disgust. "Klaus often has them in the house, even to stay with us in our lodge in the mountains."

"And you don't care for them?"

"I can't bear them. But Klaus believes we will ally with Prussia one day quite soon, and it is the best thing to make them your friends now, before everyone else does and you have lost your advantage."

It was a peculiarly cynical remark, and for a moment the laughter faded a little, the lights seemed sharper, glittering with a harder edge, the noise around him shriller.

Then he looked at her face, and the laughter in it, and the moment passed.

But he did not forget her story of Klaus's deliberate courting of the Prussians. Klaus was for unification, perhaps not for his country's sake but for his own. Did he hope to emerge from such forced union with greater power than he now held? Friedrich's return would have compromised that. Had he feared it, and killed Friedrich to prevent it? It was not impossible.

The more Monk considered the idea, the more feasible did it seem.

But it hardly helped Rathbone. Then again, nothing that seemed even possible, let alone likely, would help Rathbone. The only person who seemed to care about Zorah was Ulrike. That curious remark of hers came back to his mind.

At midnight he was drinking champagne. The music was lilting again, strictly rhythmic, almost willing him to dance. Until he could find Evelyn, he asked the nearest woman to him, and drifted out onto the floor, swirled and lost in the pleasure of it.

It was nearly one when he saw Evelyn and contrived to end the dance close enough to her, and she had equally contrived to be away from Klaus and had laughingly passed by her previous partner before he could invite her again.

They came together moving to the music as if it were an element of nature and they simply were carried upon it, as foam upon a current of the sea. He could smell the perfume of her hair, feel the warmth of her skin, and as they spun and parted and came together again, see the glow in her cheeks and the laughter in her eyes.

When at last they stopped for breath, he lost count of how many dances later, it was at the edge of a group of others, some fresh from the floor, some sipping champagne, light winking in the glasses, flashing fire on diamonds in hair and on ears and throats.

Monk felt a sudden surge of affection for this tiny, independent state with its individual ways, its quaint capital, and its fierce desire to remain as it was. Maybe the only common sense, the only provident way forward, was to unite with all the other states into one giant nation. But if they did so then something irreparable would be lost, and he mourned its passing. How much more must these for whom it was their heritage and their home mourn?

"You must hate the thought of Prussia marching in here and

taking over," he said impulsively to Evelyn. "Felzburg will be simply a provincial city, like any other, ruled from Berlin, or Munich, or some other state capital. I can understand why you want to fight, even if it doesn't seem to make sense."

"I can't!" she replied with a flicker of irritation. "It's a lot of effort and sacrifice for nothing. We can always go to Berlin. It will be just as good there . . . maybe better."

A footman passed by with a tray of champagne, and she took a glass and put it to her lips.

Monk was stunned. He looked beyond Evelyn to Brigitte, who was smiling with her mouth, but her eyes were aching with sadness, and even as Monk watched she blinked and he saw her breast rise as she breathed in deeply, and the moment after turned to the woman next to her and spoke.

Surely Evelyn must see that. She could not be as shallow as she had sounded.

"When are you going back to London?" Evelyn asked, her head a little on one side.

"I think tomorrow, perhaps the next day," Monk answered with regret.

Evelyn looked at him, her brown eyes wide. "I suppose you have to go?"

"Yes," he replied. "I have a moral obligation to a friend. He is in considerable difficulty. I must be there when his time of crisis comes."

"Can you help him?" It was almost a challenge in her voice.

Beyond her a woman laughed, and a man proposed a toast to something or other.

"I doubt it, but I can try," Monk replied. "At the very least I can be beside him."

"What purpose is there, if you can't help?" Evelyn was looking very directly at him, and there was an edge of ridicule in her voice.

He was puzzled. It seemed a pointless question. It was

simply a matter of loyalty. One did not leave people to suffer alone.

"What sort of trouble is he in?" she pressed.

"He made a misjudgment," he replied. "It seems as if it will cost him very dearly."

She shrugged. "Then it is his own fault. Why should you suffer for it?"

"Because he is my friend." The answer was too simple to need elaboration.

"That's ridiculous!" She was half amused, half angry. "Wouldn't you rather be here with us—with me? At the weekend we go to our lodge in the forest. You could come. Klaus will be busy with his Prussians most of the time, but you shall find plenty to do. We ride in the forest, have picnics and wonderful nights by the fire. It is marvelously beautiful. You can forget the rest of the world."

He was tempted. He could be with Evelyn, laugh, hold her in his arms, watch her beauty, feel her warmth. Or he could return to London and tell Rathbone that if Friedrich had been the intended victim, then Gisela could not have killed him, but Klaus could have. However, it was far more likely that actually it was Gisela who was meant to be the one who died, and it was only mischance that it had been Friedrich, which doubly proved her innocence. Lord Wellborough could have been guilty, or someone acting for Brigitte or, far worse, for the Queen. Or Zorah could have done it herself.

He could attend the trial and watch Rathbone struggle and lose, watch helplessly as the lawyer damaged his reputation and lost all he had so carefully built in his professional life.

Of course, Hester would be there. She would be trying every last instant there was, racking her brain for anything to do to help, lying awake at night, worrying and hurting for him.

And when it was all over, even if he was criticized, ridiculed and disgraced for his foolishness, his alliance against the establishment, she would be there to stand beside him. She would help to defend him to others, even if in private she castigated him with her tongue. She would urge him to get up and fight again, face the world regardless of its anger or contempt. The greater his need, the more certainly would she be there.

He recalled with a surge of warmth how she had knelt in front of him in his own worst hour, when he was terrified and appalled, how she had pleaded with him, and browbeaten him into the courage to keep on struggling. Even at the very darkest moment, when she must have faced the possibility of his guilt, it had never entered her mind to abandon him. Her loyalty went beyond trust in innocence or in victory, it was the willingness to be there in defeat, even in one which was deserved.

She had none of Evelyn's magic, her beauty or glorious charm. But there was something about her clean courage and her undeviating honor which now seemed infinitely desirable—like ice-cold pure water when one is cloyed with sugar and parched with thirst.

"Thank you," he said stiffly. "I am sure it is delightful, but I have a duty in London . . . and friends . . . for whom I care." He bowed with almost Germanic formality, touching his heels. "Your company has been utterly delightful, Baroness, but it is time I returned to reality. Good night . . . and good-bye."

Her face dropped slack with amusement, then tightened into a blazing, incredulous rage.

Monk walked back towards the staircase and the way out.

8

ON THE LONG and tedious journey home, Monk turned over in his mind what he could tell Rathbone that could be of any service to him in the case. He reviewed it in his mind over and over again, but no matter how many times he did, there was nothing of substance that could be used to defend Zorah Rostova. Whichever of the couple had been the intended victim, there was no way in which Gisela could be guilty.

The only mitigating fact was the extreme likelihood that Friedrich had indeed been murdered.

On arrival in London, Monk went straight to his rooms in Fitzroy Street and unpacked his cases. He had a steaming bath and changed his linen. He requested his landlady to bring him a hot cup of tea, something which he had not had since leaving home over two weeks before. Then he felt as ready as he could be to present himself at Vere Street. He dreaded delivering such news, but there was no alternative.

Rathbone did not pretend any of the usual preliminary courtesies. He opened his office door as soon as he heard Monk's voice speaking to Simms. He looked as perfectly dressed as always, but Monk saw the signs of tiredness and strain in his face.

"Good afternoon, Monk," he said immediately. "Come in."

He glanced at the clerk. "Thank you, Simms." He stood aside to allow Monk past him into the office.

"Shall I bring tea, Sir Oliver?" Simms asked, glancing from one to the other of them. He knew the importance of the case and of the news which Monk might bring. He had already read from Monk's manner that it was not good.

"Oh . . . yes, by all means." Rathbone was looking not at Simms but at Monk. He searched Monk's eyes and saw defeat in them. "Thank you," he added, his voice carrying his disappointment, too heavy for his self-mastery to conceal it.

Inside, he closed the door and walked stiffly around his desk to the far side. He pulled his chair back and sat down.

Monk sat in the nearer one.

Rathbone did not cross his legs as usual, nor did he lean back. His face was calm and his eyes direct, but there was fear in them as he regarded Monk.

Monk saw no purpose in telling the story in chronological order. It would only spin out the tension.

"I think it very probable Friedrich was murdered," he said flatly. "We have every cause to raise the issue, and we may even be able to prove it, with good luck and considerable skill. But there is no possibility that Gisela is guilty."

Rathbone stared back without replying.

"There really is none," Monk repeated. He hated having to say this. It was the same feeling of helplessness again, carrying all the old sense of watching while someone you ought to save was suffering, losing. He owed Rathbone nothing, and it was entirely his own fault that he had taken such an absurd case, but all that touched his reason, not his emotions.

He took a deep breath. "Friedrich was her life. She did not have a lover, and neither did he. Friend and enemy alike knew that they adored each other. They did nothing apart. Every evidence I found indicates they were still as deeply in love as in the beginning."

"But duty?" Rathbone urged. "Was there a plot to invite him back to Felzburg to lead the fight for independence, or not?"

"Almost certainly—"

"Then . . ."

"Then nothing!" Monk said tartly. "He didn't bow to duty twelve years ago, and nothing whatever suggests there has been the slightest change."

Rathbone clenched his fist on the desk, his knuckles shining. "Twelve years ago his country was not facing forced unification with the rest of the German states. Surely he had that much honor in him—that much patriotism and sense of who he was. Damn it, Monk, he was born to be king!"

Monk heard the rising desperation in Rathbone's voice. He could see it in his eyes, in the spots of color in his cheeks. He had nothing whatever with which to help. Everything he knew made it worse.

"He was a man who gave up everything for the woman he loved," he said clearly and levelly. "And there is nothing . . . absolutely nothing . . . to indicate that he ever, for a moment, regretted that decision. If his people wanted him back, then they would have to take his wife with him. The decision was theirs, and apparently he had always believed they would make it in her favor."

Rathbone stared at him.

The silence in the room was so heavy the clock seemed to bang out the seconds. The muffled clatter of the traffic beyond the windows came from another world.

"What?" Rathbone said at last. "What is it, Monk? What is it that you are not telling me?"

"That there seems to me every possibility that Friedrich was not the intended victim, but Gisela herself," he replied. He was about to go on, explaining why, but he saw the understanding of it already there in Rathbone's face.

"Who?" Rathbone said huskily.

"Perhaps Zorah herself. She is an ardent independent."

Rathbone paled.

"Or anyone else who was of the independent party," Monk went on. "The worst possibility—"

"Worst!" Rathbone's voice was high and sharp with sarcasm. "Worse than my own client?"

"Yes." Monk could not withhold the truth.

Rathbone glared at him with disbelief.

Monk struck the blow. "Count Lansdorff. The Queen's brother, acting on her behalf."

Rathbone tried to speak, but his voice failed him. His face was paper white.

"I'm sorry," Monk said inadequately. "But that is the truth. You can't fight without knowing it. Opposing Counsel will find it out, if he's any good at all. She'll tell him, if nothing else."

Rathbone continued to stare at him.

"Of course she will!" Monk banged the desk impatiently. "Queen Ulrike drove her out in the first place. If Ulrike had been for her, instead of against her, twelve years ago, Gisela might be crown princess now. She knows that. There can't be any love lost on either side. But this time Gisela held the winning hand. If they wanted Friedrich back, it would be on his terms . . . which would include his wife."

"Would it?" Rathbone was clinging to straws. "You think he would insist, even in these circumstances?"

"Wouldn't you?" Monk demanded. "Apart from his love for her, which nobody anywhere questions, what would the world think of him if he abandoned her now? It is an ugly picture of a man setting aside a wife of twelve years, when anyone with brains can see that he doesn't have to. He can't plead duty when he has the power. . ."

"Unless Gisela is dead," Rathbone finished for him. "Yes, all right . . . I see the logic of it. It is unarguable. The Queen had every reason to want Gisela dead, and none at all to want to kill Friedrich. Oh, God! And the Lord Chancellor told me to handle the defense with suitable discretion." He started to laugh, but there was a bitterness in it which was close to hysteria.

"Stop it!" Monk snapped, panic rising inside him too. He was failing again. Rathbone was not only without a defense, he was losing his self-control as well. "It is not your duty to protect the Felzburg royal family. You must defend Zorah Rostova the best way you can . . . now that you've said you will." His tone conveyed his opinion of that decision. "I assume you have done everything you can to persuade her to withdraw?"

Rathbone glared at him. "Quite. And failed."

"Well, we may at least be able to convince a jury that a reasonable person could believe it was murder," Monk said, watching Rathbone's face. "You will be able to put the doctor on the stand and question him pretty rigorously."

Rathbone shut his eyes. "An exhumation?" The words came out between stiff lips. "The Lord Chancellor will love that! Are you sure we have grounds for it? We will need something incontrovertible. The authorities will be very loath to do it. Abdicated or not, he was the Crown Prince of a foreign country."

"He is buried in England, though," Monk replied. "He died here. That makes him subject to British law. And he not only abdicated but was exiled. He was no longer a citizen of his own country." He leaned a little over the desk. "But it may not be necessary actually to exhume the body. Simply the knowledge that we could, and would, might be sufficient to provide some considerably more precise answers from the doctor and from the Wellboroughs and their servants."

Rathbone stood up and walked towards the window, his back to the room. He pushed his hands into his pockets, dragging them out of shape uncharacteristically. His body was rigid.

"I suppose proving that it was murder is about the only course left to me. At least that will show she was not merely mischievous, only grossly mistaken. If it is shown, beyond any doubt, that Gisela is innocent, perhaps she may still apologize. If she doesn't, there is nothing left I can do to help her. I will have taken on a madwoman as a client."

Monk intended to be tactful, and so refrained from comment, but his silence was just as eloquent.

Rathbone turned from the window, the sun at his back. He had regained some command of himself. His smile was rueful and self-mocking.

"Then perhaps you had better try Wellborough Hall again and see if you can find something in more detail than before. The only real victory left would be to discover who did kill him. It would not vindicate Zorah in law, but it might, to some extent, in public opinion, and that is what we are fighting almost as much. Please God it was not the Queen!"

Monk stood up. "Between now and next Monday?"

Rathbone nodded. "If you please."

Monk felt time closing in. He was being asked more than he could possibly do. It frightened him because he wanted to succeed. If he failed, Rathbone was going to lose a great deal, perhaps the glamour and the prizes of his profession. He would not recover his prestige after a loss not due to circumstance but to a misjudgment as grave as this. Zorah was not merely guilty of some crime, she was guilty of a social sin of monumental proportions. She would have offended the sensibilities and beliefs of both the aristocracy and the ordinary people who delighted in a love story and fairy tale come true, and who had believed it for twelve years. It tainted not only the royalty of Europe but their own royalty as well. It was one thing to criticize the establishment in the privacy of one's home or around the dinner tables of friends; it was something quite different to expose their faults in a courtroom for the world to behold. A man who caused that, and protected the woman who was at the root of it, could not easily be forgiven.

If it should turn out to be Ulrike, or someone acting in her interests, with her knowledge or not, it would be catastrophic. Rathbone would become a celebrity, remembered only for this one startling case. Everyone would know his name, but no respectable person would want to be associated with him. His professional reputation would be worthless.

He had no right to place Monk in the position of having to rescue him from his own stupidity. And Monk resented appallingly that he could not do it. It was the same failure over again, and it hurt.

"Perhaps it might help to know what you have learned and achieved over the last two weeks, while I have been chasing over half of Europe to discover Gisela's complete innocence," he said cuttingly. "Apart from failing to persuade Countess Rostova to withdraw her accusation, that is."

Rathbone looked at him with amazement and then intense dislike. "I employ you, Monk," he said icily. "You do not employ me. If the time comes when you do, then you may require me to report my doings to you, but not until."

"In other words, you've done nothing of use!"

"If you don't think you can discover anything useful at Wellborough Hall," Rathbone retaliated, "then tell me. Otherwise, don't waste what little time there is arguing. Get on your way. If you need money, ask Simms."

Monk was profoundly stung, not so much by the slight to his abilities, he could have foreseen that, and perhaps he deserved it, but the reference to money was cruel. It placed him on a level with a tradesman, which was precisely what Rathbone had intended. It was a reminder of their social and financial difference. It was also a mark of how frightened Rathbone was.

"I won't discover anything," Monk said through clenched teeth. "There isn't any damn thing to discover." And he swung on his heels and went out of the door, leaving it swinging on its hinges.

However, he was obliged to go to Simms and ask for more

money, which galled his temper so much he almost did not do it, but necessity prevailed.

It was only when he was outside in the street that he cooled down sufficiently to remember just how frightened Rathbone was. That he would let himself lash out at Monk showed his vulnerability more than anything else he could have done or said.

Monk did not consciously decide to go to see Hester, it simply seemed the natural thing to do, given Rathbone's dilemma and Monk's own feelings of fury and helplessness. When things were at their worst, there was a gentleness in her he could trust absolutely. She would never fail.

He saw a hansom a dozen yards ahead of him along Vere Street as he was striding along the pavement. He increased his pace, calling out. The cab stopped, and he swung up into the seat, calling out the address on Hill Street where he knew Hester had been employed before he had left for Venice, assuming she would still be there. He disliked acknowledging a feeling of urgency to see her, but it filled him till no other thought was possible, and there was a perverse pleasure in the cleanness of it, after the memory of Evelyn.

It was a long way from the area of Lincoln's Inn Fields to Berkeley Square and Hill Street, and he settled back in his seat for the ride. It had been exciting to be in Europe, to see different sights, smell the utterly different smells of a foreign city, hear the sounds of other languages around him, but there was a unique pleasure in being home again amongst what was familiar. He realized only then how tense he had been when he did not understand most of what was being said and he had to concentrate for the occasional word which made sense and to deduce from actions and expressions what was meant. He had been very dependent upon the goodwill of others. There was a great freedom in being back in the surroundings where he had knowledge—and the power that gave.

He had very little idea of what he wanted to say to Hester. It was a turmoil in his mind, a matter of emotion rather than thought. It would fall into order when he needed it to. He was not ready yet.

The cab reached Hill Street, and the driver pulled up the horse and waited for Monk to alight and pay him.

"Thank you," Monk said absently, handing over the coins and tuppence extra. He walked across the footpath and went up the steps. It crossed his mind that it might be inconvenient for Hester to receive callers, especially a man. It might even be embarrassing if her employers misunderstood. But he did not even hesitate in his stride, much less change his mind. He pulled the bell hard and waited.

The door opened, and a footman faced him.

"Good afternoon, sir?"

"Good afternoon." Monk did not feel like exchanging pleasantries, but experience had taught him that it was frequently the fastest way to obtain what he wished. He produced a card and laid it on the salver. "Is Miss Hester Latterly still residing in this house? I have just returned from abroad and must leave again this evening for the country. There is a matter of urgency concerning a mutual friend about which I would like to inform her and perhaps ask her advice." He had not lied, but his words implied a medical emergency, and he was happy to leave the misunderstanding.

"Yes, sir, she is still with us," the footman replied. "If you care to come in, I will inquire if it is possible for you to see her."

Monk was shown to the library, a most agreeable place to wait. The room was comfortably furnished in a rather old-fashioned manner. The leather upholstery was worn where arms had rested on the chairs, and the pattern in the carpet was brighter around the edges, where no one had trodden. A fire burned briskly in the grate. There were hundreds of books from which he could have chosen to read, had he wished, but he was too impatient even to open one, let alone concentrate on the words inside. He paced back and forth, turning sharply every seven paces.

It was over ten minutes before the door opened and Hester came in. She was dressed in deep blue, which was unusually becoming to her. She looked nothing like as tired as the last time he had seen her. In fact, she looked very fresh; there was color in her complexion and a rich sheen on her hair. He was instantly annoyed. Did she not care that Rathbone was on the brink of disaster? Or was she too stupid to appreciate the magnitude of it?

"You look as if you are to have the day off," he said abruptly.

She surveyed his perfectly cut jacket and trousers, his immaculate cravat and extremely expensive boots.

"How nice to see you safely home," she said with a sweet smile. "How was Venice? And Felzburg? That was where you were, was it not?"

He ignored that. She knew perfectly well that it was.

"If your patient is recovered, what are you doing still here?" he asked. His tone of voice made it a challenge.

"He is better than he was," she replied very gravely, looking straight at him. "He is not recovered. It takes some time to accustom yourself to the fact that you will not walk again. There are times when it is very hard. If you cannot imagine the chronic difficulties of someone who is paralyzed from the waist downwards, I shall not violate what is left of his privacy by explaining them to you. Please stop indulging your temper and tell me what you learned that will help Oliver."

It was like a slap in the face, swift and hard, the reminder that she had been dealing with one of the most painful of realities while he was away, the end of a major part of the life and hope of a young man. And yet harder still, and more personal, was the hope in her face that he had been able to accomplish something to help Rathbone, her belief in him that he could, and his own now so familiar knowledge that he had not.

"Gisela did not kill Friedrich," he said quietly. "It was not possible physically, and she had even less reason when it happened than ever before. I can't help Rathbone." As he said it his fury was raw in his voice. He loathed Rathbone for being vulnerable, for being so stupid as to put himself in this position, and for hoping that Monk could get him out of it. He was angry with Hester for expecting the impossible of him, and also for caring so much about Rathbone. He could see it in her face, the endless ability to be hurt.

She looked stunned. It was several seconds before she found words to say anything.

"Was it really just—just his accident?" She shook her head a little, as if to brush away an annoyance, but her face was creased with anxiety and her eyes were frightened. "Isn't there anything which can help Oliver? Some sort of excuse for the Countess? If she believed it . . . there must have been a reason. I mean—" She stopped.

"Of course she had a reason," he said impatiently. "But not necessarily anything she would benefit from announcing in court. It looks more and more like an old jealousy she was never able to forget or forgive, and she had taken this moment of vulnerability to try to settle an old score. That is a reason, but it is an ugly and very stupid one."

Temper flashed in her face. "Are you saying he died by accident, and that is all you have learned? It took you two weeks, in two countries, to discover that? And I assume you used Zorah's money to pay your way?"

"Of course I used Zorah's money," he retorted. "I went in her cause. I can only discover what is there, Hester, just as you can. Do you cure every patient?" His voice was rising with his own hurt. "Do you give back your wages if they die? Perhaps you'd better give them back to these people, since you say their son will never walk again."

"This is stupid," she said, turning away from him in exasperation. "If you cannot think of anything more sensible to say, you had better go!" She swung to face him again. "No!" She took a deep breath and lowered her voice again. "No, please don't. What we think of each other is immaterial. We can quarrel later. Now we must think of Oliver. If this comes to trial and he has nothing with which to defend her, or at least offer an explanation and excuse, he is going to face a crisis in his reputation and career. I don't know if you have seen any of the newspapers lately, I don't suppose you have, but they are very strongly in support of Gisela and already painting Zorah as a wicked woman who is bent not only on injuring an innocent and bereaved woman but also on attacking the good qualities in society in general."

She moved forwards, closer to him, her wide skirt catching on the chairs. "Several of them have already suggested a very lurid life, that she has taken foreign lovers and practiced all sort of things which are better left to the imagination."

He should have thought of that, but somehow he had not. He had seen it only in political terms. Of course, there would be ugly speculation about Zorah and her life and her motives. Sexual jealousy was the first thing that would leap to many people's minds.

It was on his tongue to tell Hester that there was nothing anyone could do to prevent that, but he saw the hurt and the hope in her face. It caught at him as if it had been his own, taking him by surprise. It had nothing to do with her life, and yet she was absorbed in it. Her whole mind was bent towards fighting the injustice—or, in Rathbone's case, even if it should prove just, of trying to prevent the wound and do something to ease the harm.

"There is quite a strong possibility he was murdered," he said grudgingly. "Not by Gisela, poor woman, but by one of the political factions." He could not resist adding, "Perhaps the Queen's brother."

She winced but refused to be crushed. "Can we prove he was murdered?" she said quickly. She used the plural as if she were as much involved as he. "It might help. After all, it would show that she was mistaken as to the person who did it but that she was not imagining there really was a crime. And only her accusation has brought it to light." Her voice was getting faster and rising in tone. "If she had stayed silent, then their prince could have been murdered and no one would have known. That would have been a terrible injustice."

He looked at her eagerness, and it cut him.

"And do you think they would really prefer to have the world know that one of the royal family, possibly at the instigation of the Queen herself, murdered the Prince?" he said bitterly. "If you think anyone is going to thank her for that, you are a great deal stupider even than I thought you!"

This time she was crushed, but not utterly.

"Some of her own people may not thank her," she said in a small voice. "But some of them will. And the jury will be English. We still think it very wrong to murder anyone, especially an injured and helpless man. And we admire courage. We will not like what she has said, but we will know that it has cost her dearly to say it, and we will respect that." She looked straight at him, daring him to contradict her.

"I hope so," he agreed with a lurch of emotion inside him as he realized yet again how intensely she cared. She had never even met Zorah. She probably knew nothing of her, except this one event of her life. It was Rathbone who filled her thoughts and whose future frightened her. He felt a sudden void of loneliness. He had not appreciated that she was so fond of Rathbone. Rathbone had always seemed a trifle aloof towards her, even patronizing at times. And Monk knew how she hated being patronized. He had had a taste of her temper when he had done it himself.

"They are bound to." She sounded positive, as though she were trying to convince herself. "You will be able to prove it, won't you?" she went on anxiously, a furrow between her brows. "It was poison—"

"Yes, of course it was. It would hardly be mistaken for a natural death if he'd been shot or hit over the head," he said sarcastically.

She ignored him. "How?"

"In his food or medicine, I presume. I'm going back to Wellborough Hall tonight to see if I can find out."

"Not how was he poisoned," she corrected impatiently. "Naturally, it was disguised in something he ate. I mean how are you going to prove it? Are you going to have the body dug up and examined? How will you get that done? They'll try to prevent you. Most people feel very strongly about that sort of thing."

He had very little idea how he was going to do it. He was as confused and as worried as she was, except that he did not feel as personally involved with Rathbone as she seemed to. He would be sorry, of course, if Rathbone fell from grace and his career foundered. He would do all he could to prevent it. They had been friends and battled together to win other cases, sometimes against enormous odds. They had cared about the same things and trusted each other without the necessity for words or reasons.

"I know," he said gently. "I hope to persuade them to tell me the truth and avoid that. I think the political implications may be powerful enough to accomplish it. Suspicion can do a great deal of damage. People will do a lot to avoid it."

She met his eyes steadily, her anger vanished. "Can I help?"

"I can't think of any way, but if I do, I shall tell you," he promised. "I don't suppose you have learned anything of relevance about Friedrich or Gisela? No, of course not, or you would have said so." He smiled bleakly. "Try not to worry so much. Rathbone is a better courtroom lawyer than you seem to be giving him credit for." It was an idiotic thing to say, and he winced inwardly as he heard himself, but he wanted to comfort her, even if comfort was meaningless and temporary. He hated to see her so frightened—for her own sake, apart from anything he might feel towards Rathbone, which was a confusion of anxiety, friendship, anger and envy. Rathbone had all Hester's attention; her entire mind was taken up with her care for him. She had barely noticed Monk, except as he might be of help.

"He may be able to elicit all sorts of information on the witness stand," he went on. "And we certainly have enough to compel all the people who were at Wellborough Hall that week to testify."

"Have we?" She seemed genuinely cheered. "Yes, of course you are right. He has made such a disastrous judgment in taking the case that I forget how brilliant he is in the courtroom." She let out her breath in a sigh and then smiled at him. "Thank you, William."

In a few words she had betrayed her awareness of Rathbone's vulnerability and her willingness to defend him, her admiration for him, and how much she cared. And she had thanked Monk so earnestly it twisted like a knife inside him as, startlingly, he perceived in her a beauty far brighter and stronger than the charm of Evelyn which had faded so easily.

"I must go," he said stiffly, feeling as if his protective mask had been stripped from him and she had seen him as nakedly as he had seen himself. "I have a train to catch this evening if I am to be in Wellborough in time to find lodgings. Good night." And almost before she had time to answer, he turned on his heel and marched to the door, flinging it open and walking out.

In the morning, after a poor night spent at the village inn during which he tossed and turned in an unfamiliar bed, he hired a local coachman to take him out to Wellborough Hall and alighted with his case. He had no intention of lying about himself or his purpose this time, whatever Lord Wellborough should say.

"You are what?" his lordship demanded, his face icy, when Monk stood in the morning room in the center of the carpet.

Wellborough straightened up from where he had been leaning against the mantel, taking the largest share of the fire.

"An agent of inquiry," Monk repeated with almost equal chill.

"I had no idea such a thing existed." Wellborough's broad nose flared as if he had swallowed something distasteful. "If one of my guests has committed an indiscretion, I do not wish to know. If it was in my house, I consider it my duty as host to deal with the matter without the like of a . . . whatever it is you call yourself. The footman will show you out, sir."

"The only indiscretion I am interested in is murder!" Monk did not move even his eyes, let alone his feet.

"I cannot help you," Wellborough replied. "I know of no one who has been murdered. There is no one dead to my knowledge. As I have said, sir, the footman will show you to the door. Please do not return. You came here under false pretenses. You abused my hospitality and imposed upon my other guests, which is inexcusable. Good day, Mr. Monk. I presume that is your real name? Not that it matters."

Monk did not look away, let alone move.

"Prince Friedrich died in this house, Lord Wellborough. There has already been a very public accusation that it was murder—"

"Which has been vigorously denied," Wellborough cut across him. "Not that anyone worth anything at all gave it a moment's credence. And as you are no doubt aware, the wretched woman, who must be quite mad, is to stand trial for her slander. I believe in a week or so's time."

"She is not standing trial, sir," Monk corrected. "It is a civil suit, at least technically. Though the matter of murder will be exhaustively explored, naturally. The medical evidence will be examined in the closest detail—"

"Medical evidence?" Wellborough's face dropped. He was at once appalled and derisive. "There isn't any, for God's sake! The poor man was dead and buried half a year ago."

"It would be most unfortunate to have to have the body exhumed," Monk agreed. He ignored the expression of disbelief and then horror on Wellborough's face. "But if suspicion leaves no other alternative possible, then it will have to be done, and an autopsy performed. Very distressing for the family, but one cannot allow an accusation of murder to fly around unanswered . . ."

Wellborough's skin was mottled dark with blood, his body rigid.

"It has been answered, man! Nobody in their right mind believes for an instant that poor Gisela would have harmed him in any way whatever, let alone killed him in cold blood. It's monstrous . . . and totally absurd."

"Yes, I agree, it probably is," Monk said levelly. "But it is not so absurd to believe that Klaus von Seidlitz might have killed him to prevent him from returning home and leading the resistance against unification. He has large holdings of land in the borders, which might be laid waste were there fighting. A powerful motive, and not in the least difficult to credit . . . even if it is, as you say, monstrous."

Wellborough stared at him as if he had risen out of the ground in a cloud of sulfur.

Monk continued with some satisfaction. "And the other very plausible possibility is that actually it was not Friedrich who was intended as the victim but Gisela. He may have died by mischance. In which case there are several people who may have been desirous of killing her. The most obvious one is Count Lansdorff, brother of the Queen."

"That's . . ." Wellborough began, then trailed off, his face losing its color and turning a dull white. Monk knew in that moment that he had been very well aware of the designs and negotiations that preceded Friedrich's death.

"Or the Baroness Brigitte von Arlsbach," Monk went on relentlessly. "And regrettably, also yourself."

"Me? I have no interest in foreign politics," Wellborough

protested. He looked genuinely taken aback. "It matters not a jot to me who rules in Felzburg or whether it is part of Germany or one of a score of independent little states forever."

"You manufacture arms," Monk pointed out. "War in Europe offers you an excellent market—"

"That is iniquitous, sir!" Wellborough said furiously, his jaw clenched, his lips thinned to invisibility. "Make that suggestion outside this room and I shall sue you myself."

"I have made no suggestion," Monk replied. "I have merely stated facts. But you may be quite certain that people will make the inference, and you cannot sue all London."

"I can sue the first person to say it aloud!"

Monk was now quite relaxed. He had at least this victory in his hand.

"No doubt. But it would be expensive and futile. The only way to prevent people from thinking it is to prove it untrue."

Wellborough stared at him. "I take your point, sir," he said at last. "And I find your method and your manner equally despicable, but I concede the necessity. You may question whom you please in my house, and I shall personally instruct them to answer you immediately and truthfully . . . on the condition that you report your findings to me, in full, at the end of every day. You will remain here and pursue this until you come to a satisfactory and irrefutable conclusion. Do we understand each other?"

"Perfectly," Monk replied with an inclination of his head. "I have my bag with me. If you will have someone show me to my room, I shall begin immediately. Time is short."

Wellborough gritted his teeth and reached for the bell.

Monk thought it both polite and probably most likely to be efficient to speak first to Lady Wellborough. She received him in the morning room, a rather ornate place furnished in the French manner with a great deal more gilt than Monk cared for. The only thing in it he liked was a huge bowl of early chrysanthemums, tawny golds and browns and filling the air with a rich, earthy smell.

Lady Wellborough came in and closed the door behind her. She was wearing a dark blue morning dress which should have become her fair coloring, but she was too pale and undoubtedly surprised and confused, and there was a shadow of fear in her eyes.

"My husband tells me that it is possible Prince Friedrich really was murdered," she said bluntly. She must have been in her mid-thirties, but there was a childlike unsophistication about her. "And that you have come here to discover before the trial who it was. I don't understand at all, but you must be wrong. It is too terrible."

He had come prepared to dislike her because he disliked and despised her husband, but he realized with a jolt how separate she was, pulled along in his wake, perhaps unable through circumstance, ignorance or dependence to take a different course, and that this lack had little to do with her will or her nature.

"Unfortunately, terrible things sometimes do happen, Lady Wellborough," he replied almost without emotion. "There was a great deal at stake in his returning to his own country. Perhaps you were not aware how much."

"I didn't know he was going to return," she said, staring at him. "Nobody said anything about it to me."

"It was probably still secret, if it was finally decided at all. It may have been only on the brink of decision."

She still looked anxious and a little confused.

"And you think someone murdered him to prevent him going home? I thought he couldn't anyway, after he deliberately abdicated. After all, he chose Gisela instead of the crown. Is that not what it was all about?" She shook her head and gave a little shrug, still standing in the middle of the floor, refusing or unable to be comfortable, as if it might prolong an interview in which she was unhappy.

"I really can't believe he would have returned without her,

Mr. Monk, even to save his country from unification into a greater Germany, which people say will almost certainly happen one day anyway. If you had seen them here you wouldn't even have had such an idea." Her voice dismissed it as ridiculous; there was even regret in it and a note of envy. "I've never known two people to love each other so much. Sometimes it was almost as if they spoke with one voice." Her blue eyes were focused on something beyond his head. "She would finish what he was saying, or he would finish for her. They understood each other's thoughts. I can only imagine what it would be like to have such utter companionship."

He looked at her and saw a woman who had been married several years, beginning to face the idea of maturity, the end of dreams and the beginning of the acceptance of reality, and who had newly realized that her own inner loneliness was not necessarily a part of everyone's life. There were those who had found the ideal. Just when she had accepted that it did not exist, and came to terms with it, there it was, played out in front of her, in her own house, but not for her.

And then the thought of Hester came to him with startling vividness, the sense of trust he knew towards her. She was opinionated and abrasive. There was much in her that irritated him like torn skin, catching every touch. The moment he thought it was healed, there it was again. But he knew her courage, her compassion and her honesty better than he knew his own. He also knew, with a sense of both anger and infinite value, that she would never intentionally hurt him. He did not want anything so precious. He might break it. He might lose it.

But she might hurt him irreparably, beyond her power to help, if she loved Rathbone other than as a friend. That was something he refused to think about.

"Possibly," he said at last. "But it is most important, for reasons Lord Wellborough no doubt explained to you, that we learn the truth of precisely what did happen and find proof of it.

The alternative is to have the investigation of it forced upon us at the trial."

"Yes," she conceded. "I can see that. You have no need to labor the point, Mr. Monk; I have already instructed all the staff to answer your questions. What is it you believe I can tell you? I have been called by the Princess Gisela's solicitors to testify to Countess Rostova's slander."

"Naturally. During their stay here, did Count Lansdorff see Friedrich alone for any length of time?"

"No." It was plain from her face she understood the implication. "Gisela did not allow him to have visitors. He was far too ill."

"I mean before the accident."

"Oh. Yes. They spoke together quite often. They appeared to be healing some of the rift between them. It was rather prickly and uncomfortable to begin with. They had barely spoken in the twelve years since the abdication and Friedrich's leaving the country."

"But they were at least amicable before the accident?"

"They seemed so, yes. Are you saying Rolf asked him to return and he agreed? If he did, it would have been with Gisela, not without." She said it with complete certainty, and at last she moved over to the large sofa and sat down, spreading her huge skirts with automatic grace. "I saw them too closely to be mistaken." She smiled, biting her lip a little. "That may sound overconfident to you, because you are a man. But it is not. I saw her with him. She was a very strong woman, very certain of herself. He adored her. He did nothing without her, and she knew that."

She looked at him, and a shadow of amusement crossed her eyes. "There are dozens of small signs when a woman is uncertain of a man or when she feels she needs to make tiny efforts, listen, be obedient or flattering in order to hold him. She loved him, please do not doubt that for an instant. But she also knew the depth of his love for her, and that she had no cause to question any part of it." She shook her head a little. "Not even duty to his country would have made him leave her. I would even say he needed her. She was very strong, you know. I said that before, didn't I? But she was."

"You say it in the past," he observed, sitting as well.

"Well, his death has robbed her of everything," she pointed out, her blue eyes wide. "She has been in seclusion ever since."

Monk realized with surprise that he did not even know where Gisela was. He had heard nothing about her since Friedrich's death.

"Where is she?" he asked.

"Why, in Venice, of course." She was surprised at his ignorance.

He should have known, but he had been too occupied with learning about the past to think of Gisela as she was now. He wondered who had reported Zorah's slander to her. Not that it was important.

"When he was being nursed here, how was his food prepared?" he asked. "Who brought it to him? I presume he always ate in his rooms?"

"Yes, of course. He was too ill to leave his bed. It was prepared in the kitchen . . ."

"By whom?"

"Cook . . . Mrs. Bagshot. Gisela never left his side, if that is what you are thinking."

"Who else visited him?"

"The Prince of Wales was here for dinner one evening." In spite of the nature of the conversation, and her fear for her reputation as a hostess and the notoriety that was about to beset her, there was still a lift of pride in her voice when she spoke his name, or perhaps more accurately, his title. "He went up briefly to visit him."

Monk's heart sank. It was another board for Rathbone's professional coffin.

"No one else?" he pressed. Not that it was really relevant. It would have been simple enough, in all probability, to waylay a maid on the stairs and slip something unseen into a dish or a glass. A tray might even have been left on a side table for a few moments, giving someone the opportunity to drop in a distillation of yew. Anyone could have walked in the garden and picked the leaves—except Gisela.

Making the leaves or bark into a usable poison presented rather more difficulty. They would have to be boiled for a long time and the liquid taken off. It could hardly be done in the kitchen, except at night, when all the staff were in their beds, and then the evidence would have to have been completely removed. Finding anything to indicate that someone had been in the kitchen at night, or that a saucepan had been used by someone other than the cook, would be helpful but probably give no indication as to by whom.

Lady Wellborough had already answered him and was waiting for his next question.

"Thank you," he said, rising to his feet. "I think I will speak to the cook and the kitchen staff."

She paled and almost lurched forward, grasping his arm.

"Please do be careful what you say, Mr. Monk! Good cooks are fearfully hard to come by, and they take offense easily. If you imply she was in even the remotest way possible . . ."

"I shan't," he assured her. He smiled fleetingly. What a totally different world it was where the loss of a cook could create such anxiety and almost terror. But then he did not know Lord Wellborough, and how Lady Wellborough's happiness depended upon his temper, and how that in turn was dependent upon the good cook's remaining. Perhaps she had cause for her fear.

"I shall not insult her," he promised more decidedly.

And he kept his word. He found Mrs. Bagshot, far from his conception of the average cook, standing at the large, scrubbed, wooden kitchen table with the rolling pin in her hand. She was a tall, thin woman with gray hair screwed back into a tight knot. The orderliness of her kitchen spoke much of her nature. Its warm smells were delicious.

"Well?" she demanded, looking him up and down. "So you think that foreign prince was poisoned in this house, do you?" Her voice already bristled with anger.

"Yes, Mrs. Bagshot, I think it is possible," he replied, looking at her steadily. "I think most likely it was done by one of his own countrymen for political reasons."

"Oh." Already she was somewhat mollified, though still on her guard. "Do you, indeed. And how did they do that, may I ask?"

"I don't know," he admitted, governing his voice and his expression. This was a woman more than ready to take umbrage. "My guess would be by someone adding something to his food as it was taken upstairs to his bedroom."

"Then what are you doing here in my kitchen?" Her chin came up. She had an unarguable point, and she knew it. "It weren't one o' my girls. We don't have no truck wi' foreigners, 'ceptin' as guests, an' we serve all guests alike."

Monk glanced around at the huge room with its spotlessly blacked cooking range, big enough to roast half a sheep and boil enough vegetables or bake enough pies and pastries to feed fifty people at a sitting. Beyond it were rows of copper saucepans hung in order of size, every one shining clean. Dressers held services of crockery. He knew that beyond the kitchen there were sculleries, larders . . . one specifically for game; small rooms for the keeping of fish, ice, coal, ashes; a bake house; a lamp room; a room for knives; the entire laundry wing; a pantry; a pastry room; a stillroom and a general storeroom. And that was without trespassing into the butler's domain.

"A very orderly household," he observed. "Everything in its place."

"O' course." She bristled. "I don't know what you're used

to, but in a big house like this, if you don' keep order you'd never turn out a dinner party for people what come 'ere."

"I can imagine—"

"No, you can't," she contradicted him with contempt. "No idea, you 'aven't." She swung around to catch sight of a maid. " 'Ere, Nell, you get them six dozen eggs I sent for? We'll need them fer tomorrow. An' the salmon. Where's that fish boy? Don't know what day it is, 'e don't. Fool, if ever I saw one. Brought me plaice the other day w'en I asked fer sole! Not got the wits 'e were born with."

"Yes, Mrs. Bagshot," Nell said dutifully. "Six dozen 'en's eggs like you said, an' two dozen duck eggs in the larder. An' I got ten pounds o' new butter an' three o' them cheeses."

"All right then, off with yer about yer business. Don't stand there gawpin' just 'cos we got a stranger in the kitchen. It isn't nothing to do with you!"

"Yes, Mrs. Bagshot!"

"So what is it you want from me, young man?" Mrs. Bagshot looked back at Monk. "I got dinner to get. Put the pheasant in the larder, George. Don't hang 'em in 'ere for 'eaven's sake!"

"Thought you might want to see them, Mrs. Bagshot," George replied.

"What for? Think I never seen a pheasant? Out with yer, before yer get feathers everywhere! Fool," she added under her breath. "Well, get on with it!" she said to Monk. "Don't stand there all day with yer foot in yer mouth. We got work, even if you don't."

"If anyone came into your kitchen at night and used one of your saucepans, would you know about it?" Monk said instantly.

She considered the matter carefully before replying.

"Not if they cleaned it proper and put it back 'zactly where they found it," she said after a moment. "But Lizzie'd know if anyone'd stoked the fires. Can't cook nothin' on a cold stove, if cookin's what yer thinkin' of. What you think was cooked, then? Poison?"

"Yew leaves or bark to make a poisonous liquor," he agreed.

"Lizzie!" she shouted.

A dark-haired girl appeared, wiping her hands on her apron.

"How many times have I told you not to do that?" the cook demanded crossly. "Dirty 'ands shows on white! Wipe 'em on yer dress. Gray don't show! Now, I want yer to think back to when that foreign prince was 'ere, him what died when he fell off 'is 'orse."

"Yes, Mrs. Bagshot."

"Did anyone stoke up your stove at night, like they might 'ave cooked summink on it, boiled summink? You think real careful."

"Yes, Mrs. Bagshot. Nobody done that. I'd 'a knowed 'cos I know 'zactly 'ow much coals I brung in."

"You sure, now?"

"Yes, Mrs. Bagshot."

"Right. Then get back to them potatoes." She turned to Monk. "Them coals is 'eavy. Takes sticks and coals to light fires, an' yer got to know just 'ow to do it. Isn't a matter o' just pushing it all in an' 'oping. Don't always draw first time, and the damper's 'ard to reckon right if yer in't used to it. There's not a lady nor a gentleman yet what could light a decent fire. And there isn't one born 'oo'll shovel coals nor replace what 'e's used." She smiled grimly. "So your poison weren't cooked in my kitchen."

Monk thanked her and took his leave.

He questioned the other servants carefully, going over and over details. A sharper picture of life at Wellborough Hall emerged than he had seen before. He was amazed at the sheer volume of food cooked and wasted. The richness and the choice awoke in him a sharp disapproval. With bread and potatoes added, it would have fed a middle-sized village. What angered him more was that the men and women who cooked it, served it and cleaned away afterwards, accepted all the waste without apparently giving it thought, much less question or rebellion. It was taken by everyone as a matter of course, not worthy of observation. He had done so himself when he had stayed there before. He had certainly done it in Venice and again in Felzburg.

He also heard from each servant individually of the glamour, the laughter and the excitement of the weeks Prince Friedrich had been staying.

"Terrible tragedy, that was," Nell, the parlormaid, said with a sniff. "Such a beautiful gentleman, he were. Never saw a man with such eyes. An' always lookin' at 'er 'e was. Melt your 'eart, it did. Ever so polite. Please an' thank you for everything, for all 'e were a prince." She blinked. "Not that the Prince o' Wales in't ever so gracious too, o' course," she added quickly. "But Prince Friedrich were . . . such . . . such a gentleman." She stopped again, realizing she had made it worse rather than better.

"I'm not going to repeat what you say," Monk assured her. "What about the Princess Gisela? Was she as gracious?"

"Oh, yes . . . well . . ." She looked cautiously at him.

"Well?" he prompted. "The truth, please, Nell."

"No, she weren't. Actual, she were a right cow. Oh!" She looked mortified. "I shouldn't 'a said that . . . the poor lady being bereaved, an' all. I'm terrible sorry, sir. I did'n' mean it."

"Yes you did. In what way was she a cow?"

"Please, sir, I shouldn't never 'ave said that!" she begged. "I daresay where she come from folks are different. An' she is a royal princess, an' all, an' them people in't like us."

"Yes they are," he said angrily. "She's born just the same way you are, naked and screaming for breath—"

"Oh, sir." She gasped. "You shouldn't ought to say things like that about them as is quality, let alone royal!"

"She's only royal because a petty European prince married

her," he said. "And gave up his crown and his duty to do it. What has she ever done in her life that was of use to anyone? What has she made or built? Who has she helped?"

"I dunno what yer mean, sir." She was genuinely confused. "She's a lady."

That, apparently, was sufficient explanation to her. Ladies did not work. They were not expected to do anything except enjoy themselves as they saw fit. It was not only improper, it was meaningless to question that.

"Did the other servants like her?" he asked, changing his approach.

"In't up to us to like nor dislike houseguests, sir. But she weren't no favorite, if that's what you mean."

It seemed a moot point. He did not quibble.

"What about the Countess Rostova?" he asked instead.

"Oh, she were fun, sir. Got a tongue on 'er like a navvy what mends the railways, she 'as, but fair. Always fair, she were."

"Did she like the Princess?"

"I should say not." The idea seemed to amuse her. "Look daggers at each other, them two. Not but what the Princess usually got the best of it, one way or another. Made people laugh, she did. Got a wicked way wi' mocking people. Knew what their weaknesses was and made fun o' them."

"What was the Countess's weakness?"

She did not hesitate. "Oh, 'er fondness for the young Italian gentleman—Barber something."

"Florent Barberini?"

"Yes, that's right. Terrible 'andsome, 'e were, but taken with the Princess, like 'e thought she were something out of a fairy story . . . which I suppose she were." For a moment her eyes softened. "Must be wonderful to fall in love like that. I suppose the Prince and Princess'll be remembered through all 'istory—like Lord Nelson and Lady 'Amilton, or Romeo and Juliet—tragic lovers what gave up the world for each other."

* * *

"Stuff and nonsense," Lady Wellborough's maid said briskly. "She's bin reading them penny books again. I dunno why the mistress lets 'em into the house. Fill young girls' heads with a lot of silliness. Bein' married in't all gin an' gaspers, like my mother used to say. There's the good an' the bad. Men is real, just like women is. They get sick an' 'ave ter be looked after." She sniffed. "They get tired and bad tempered, they get frightened, they're mortal untidy, half o' them snore enough to wake the dead. And once you're in marriage there in't no getting out of it—no matter what. Them daft young girls wants to think a bit before they go chasin' dreams because they read a silly book. Don't do to teach some o' them reading."

"But surely the Prince and Princess were ideally happy?" Monk pressed, not hoping for a reply of any value, just being argumentative.

They were standing at the stairhead, and below them in the hall a parlormaid giggled and a footman said something under his breath. There was a sound of rapid footsteps.

"I expect so, but they 'ad their quarrels like anyone else," the lady's maid said briskly. "Leastways, she did. Ordered 'im about something chronic when they were alone, an' even sometimes when they wasn't. Not that 'e seemed to mind, though," she added. " 'E'd rather 'ave been sworn at by 'er than treated to sweetness by someone else. I s'pose that's what bein' in love does to you." She shook her head. "For me, I'd 'ave given a piece o' my mind to anyone who spoke to me like that. An' maybe paid the consequences for it." She smiled ruefully. "Maybe as well fallin' in love in't for the likes o' me."

It was the first Monk had heard of any quarrels, apart from the brief episode of the Verdi performance in Venice, which seemed to have been over almost before it began—with unqualified victory to Gisela, and apparently without rancor on either side.

"What did they quarrel about?" He was unashamedly direct. "Was it to do with returning to Felzburg?"

"To where?" She had no idea what he was talking about.

"Their own country," he explained.

"No, nothing of that sort." She dismissed the idea with a laugh. "Weren't about anything particular. Just plain bad temper. Two people on top of each other all the time. Quarrel about anything and nothing. Couldn't stand it, meself, but then I'm not in love."

"But she didn't flirt or pay attention to anyone else?"

"Her? She flirted something rotten! But never like she meant to be taken up on it. There's a bit o' difference. Everyone knew she were just 'avin' fun. Even the Prince knew that." She looked at Monk with patient contempt. "If you're thinking as she murdered him 'cos she was fancying someone else, that just shows how much you don't know. Weren't nothing like that at all. There's plenty as did. Right high jinks went on here. I could tell you a story or two, but it'd be more 'an my job's worth."

"I would prefer not to know," Monk said sourly, and he meant it.

He questioned the other servants and learned only the same facts as before, corroborated by a dozen other serious and frightened people. Gisela had never left their suite after Friedrich's accident. She had stayed with him, at his side, except for brief respites taken for a bath or a short nap in the nearby bedroom. The maid had always been within earshot. Gisela had ordered his food in meticulous detail, but she had never gone to the kitchen herself.

However, almost everyone else in the house had moved about freely and could have found a dozen opportunities to pass a servant on the stairs carrying a tray and divert the servant's attention long enough to slip something into the food. Friedrich had eaten only beef broth to begin with, then bread and milk and a little egg custard. Gisela had eaten normally, when she had eaten at all. A footman remembered passing Brigitte on the landing when he was carrying a tray. A parlormaid had left a tray for several minutes when Klaus was present. She stared at Monk with dark, frightened eyes as she told him.

It all added to Rathbone's dilemma and Zorah's condemnation. Gisela physically could not be guilty, and nothing Monk had heard altered his conviction that she had no motive.

Nor was there proof beyond doubt that any other specific person had murdered Friedrich, but suspicion pointed an ugly finger at either Brigitte or Klaus. Once Monk would have been satisfied by that for Evelyn's sake; now that hardly mattered. As he left Wellborough to return to London, his thoughts were filled with Rathbone and how he would have to tell Hester that he had failed to find any real answer.

9

LATE IN OCTOBER, the day before the trial began, Rathbone was joined at his club by the Lord Chancellor.

"Afternoon, Rathbone." He sank gently into the seat opposite and crossed his legs. Immediately, the steward was at his elbow.

"Brandy," the Lord Chancellor said agreeably. "Got some Napoleon brandy, I know. Bring a spot, and for Sir Oliver, too."

"Thank you," Rathbone accepted with surprise—and a little foreboding.

The Lord Chancellor looked at him gravely. "Nasty business," he said with a very faint smile which did not reach his eyes. They were steady, clear and cold. "I hope you are going to be able to handle it with discretion. Can't predict a woman like that. Have to tread very warily. Can't get her to withdraw, I suppose?"

"No sir," Rathbone confessed. "I've tried every argument I can think of."

"Most unfortunate." The Lord Chancellor frowned. The steward brought the brandy, and he thanked him for it. Rathbone took his. It could have been cold tea for any pleasure he had in it. "Most unfortunate," the Lord Chancellor repeated, sipping at the balloon glass in his hands and then continuing to warm the liquid and savor its aroma. "Still, no doubt you have it all in control."

"Yes, naturally," Rathbone lied. No point in admitting defeat before it was inevitable.

"Indeed." The Lord Chancellor was apparently not so easily satisfied. "I trust you have some means of preventing her from making any further ill-considered remarks in open court? You must find some way of convincing her not only that she has nothing to gain, but that she still has something to lose." He regarded Rathbone closely.

There was no avoiding a reply, and it must be specific.

"She is most concerned in the future of her country," he said with assurance. "She will not do anything which will further jeopardize its struggle to retain independence."

"I do not find that of any particular comfort, Sir Oliver," the Lord Chancellor said grimly.

Rathbone hesitated. He had had it in mind that he should at least prevent Zorah from implicating Queen Ulrike, either directly or indirectly. But if the Lord Chancellor had not thought of that disaster, he would not put it into his way.

"I shall persuade her certain charges or insinuations would be against her country's welfare," Rathbone replied.

"Will you," the Lord Chancellor said doubtfully.

Rathbone smiled.

The Lord Chancellor smiled back bleakly and finished his brandy.

His words were echoing in Rathbone's head the following day when the trial began. It was expected to be the slander case of the century, and long before the judge called the court to order, the benches were packed and there was not even room to stand at the back. The ushers had the greatest possible difficulty in keeping the aisles sufficiently clear to avoid hazard to safety.

Before entering the courtroom, Rathbone tried one last time to persuade Zorah to withdraw.

"It is not too late," he said urgently. "You can still admit you were overcome by grief and spoke without due thought."

"I am not overcome," she said with a self-mocking smile. "I spoke after very careful thought indeed, and I meant what I said." She was dressed in tawny reds and browns. Her jacket was beautifully tailored to her slender shoulders and straight back, and the skirt swept out in an unbroken line over its hoops. Her attire was devastatingly unsuitable for the occasion. She did not look remotely penitent or consumed by grief. She looked magnificent.

"I am going into battle without weapons or armor." He heard his voice rise in desperation. "I still have nothing!"

"You have great skill." She smiled at him, her green eyes bright with confidence. He had no idea whether it was real or assumed. As always, she took no notice whatever of what he said, except to find a disarming reply. He had never had a more irresponsible client, or one who tried his patience so far.

"There is no point in being the best shot in the world if you have no weapon to fire," he protested, "and no ammunition."

"You will find something." She lifted her chin a little. "Now, Sir Oliver, is it not time for us to enter the fray? The usher is beckoning. He is an usher, is he not, that little man over there waving at you? That is the correct term?"

Rathbone did not bother to answer but stood aside for her to precede him. He squared his shoulders and adjusted his cravat for the umpteenth time, actually sending it slightly askew, and went into the courtroom. He must present the perfect image.

Instantly the hum of conversation ceased. Everyone was staring, first at him, then at Zorah. She walked across the small space of the open floor to the seats at the table for the defendant, her head high, her back stiff, looking neither right nor left.

There was a dull murmur of resentment. Everyone was

curious to see the woman who could be so unimaginably wicked as to make such an accusation as this against one of the heroines of the age. People craned forward to stare, their faces hardened with anger and dislike. Rathbone could feel it like a cold wave as he followed her, held the chair for her as she sat with extraordinary grace and swept her huge skirts about her.

The murmur of sound started again, movement, whispered words.

Then a moment later there was silence. The farther door opened and Ashley Harvester, Q.C., held it while his client, the widowed Princess Gisela, came into the court. One could sense the electric excitement, the indrawn breath of anticipation.

Rathbone's first thought was that she was smaller than he had expected. There was no reason for it, but he had imagined the woman who had been the center of the two greatest royal scandals in her nation's history to be more imposing. She was so thin as to look fragile, as if rough handling would break her. She was dressed in unrelieved black, from the exquisite hat with the widow's veil and the perfectly cut jacket bodice, emphasizing her delicate shoulders and waist, to the huge taffeta skirt which made her body seem almost doll-like above it, as if she would snap off in the middle were anyone to be ungentle with her.

There was a sigh of outgoing breath around the crowd. Spontaneously, a man called out "Bravo!" and a woman sobbed "God bless you!"

Slowly, with black-gloved hands, Gisela lifted her veil, then turned hesitantly and gave them a wan smile.

Rathbone stared at her with overwhelming curiosity. She was not beautiful, she never had been, and grief had ravaged her face until there was no color in it at all. Her hair was all but invisible under the hat, but the little one could see was dark. Her forehead was high, her brows level and well marked, her eyes large. She stared straight ahead of her with intelligence and dignity, but there was a tightness in her, especially about the mouth. Considering her total bereavement, and this fearful accusation on top of it, the fact that she had any composure at all was to her credit. If she were tense while facing a woman who was so passionately her enemy, who could be surprised or critical?

After that one gesture to the gallery, she took her seat at the plaintiff's table without looking left or right, and markedly avoided letting her eyes stray anywhere near Rathbone or Zorah.

The crowd was so fascinated they barely noticed Ashley Harvester as he followed and took his place. He had sat down before Rathbone looked at him. And yet it was Harvester who was his adversary, Harvester's skill he would have to try to counter. Rathbone had not faced him in court before, but he knew his reputation. He was a man of intense convictions, prepared to fight any battle for a principle in which he believed and ready to take on any foe. He sat now with his long, lean face set in an expression of concentration which made him look extremely severe. His nose was straight, his eyes deep-socketed and pale, his lips thin. Whether he had the slightest shred of humor Rathbone had yet to learn.

The judge was an elderly man with a curious appearance. The flesh covering his bones seemed so slight one was unusually aware of the skull beneath, and yet it was the least frightening of countenances. At first glance one might have thought him weak, perhaps a man holding office more by privilege of birth than any skill or intelligence of his own. In a gentle voice, he called for order and he obtained it instantly—not so much by authority as from the fact that no one in that packed room wished to miss a word of what was said by the protagonists in this extraordinary case.

Rathbone looked across at the jury. As he had said to his father, they were, by definition, men of property—it was a qualification for selection. They were dressed in their best dark suits, stiff white collars, sober waistcoats, high-buttoned coats.

After all, there was royalty present, even if of a dubious and disowned nature. And there was certainly a great deal of noble blood and ancient lineage, either here in the court or to be called. They looked as solemn as became the occasion, expressions grave, hair and whiskers combed. Every one of them faced forward, barely blinking.

In the gallery, reporters for the press sat with their pencils poised, blank pages in front of them. No one moved.

The hearing commenced.

Ashley Harvester rose to his feet.

"My lord, gentlemen of the jury." His voice was precise, with a faint accent from somewhere in the Midlands. He had done his best to school it out, but it lingered in certain vowels. "On the face of it, this case is not a dramatic or distressing one. No one has received a grievous injury to his or her person." He spoke quietly and without gestures. "There is no bloodstained corpse, no mangled survivor of assault to obtain your pity. There is not even anyone robbed of life's savings or of prosperity. There is no business failed, no home in smoldering ruins." He gave a very slight shrug of his lean shoulders, as if the matter held some kind of irony. "All we are dealing with is a matter of words." He stopped, his back to Rathbone.

There was silence in the room.

In the gallery, a woman caught her breath and started to cough.

A juror blinked several times.

Harvester smiled mirthlessly. "But then the Lord's Prayer is only words, is it not? The Coronation Oath is words . . . and the marriage ceremony." He was talking to the jury. "Do you regard these things as light matters?" He did not wait for any kind of reply. He saw all he needed in their faces. "A man's honor may rest in the words he speaks, or a woman's. All we are going to use in this court today, and in the days that follow, are words. My learned friend"—he lifted his head a little towards Rathbone—"and I shall do battle here, and we shall have no weapons but words and the memory of those words. We shall not raise our fists to each other."

Someone gave a nervous giggle and instantly choked it off.

"We shall not carry swords or pistols," he continued. "And yet on the outcome of such struggles as these have hung the lives of men, their fame, their honor and their fortunes."

He turned slowly so he was half facing the jury, half the gallery.

"It is not lightly that the New Testament of Our Lord states that 'In the beginning was the Word—and the Word was with God—and the Word was God.' Nor is it by chance that to take the name of God in vain is the unutterable sin of blasphemy." His voice altered suddenly until it was grating with anger, cutting across the silence of the room. "To take any man's or woman's name in vain, to bear false witness, to spread lies, is a crime that cries out for justice and for reparation!"

It was the opening Rathbone would have used had he been conducting Gisela's case himself. He applauded it grimly in his mind.

"To steal another's good name is worse than to steal his house, or his money, or his clothes," Harvester went on. "To say of another what has been said of my client is beyond understanding, and for many, beyond forgiveness. When you have heard the evidence, you will feel as outraged as I do—of that, I have no doubt whatever."

He swung back to the judge.

"My lord, I call my first witness, Lord Wellborough."

There was a murmur in the gallery, and several scores of people craned their necks to watch as Lord Wellborough came through the doors from the outer chamber where he had been waiting. He was not immediately an imposing figure because he was of fractionally less than average height and his hair and eyes were pale. But he carried himself well, and his clothes spoke of money and assurance.

He mounted the steps to the witness stand and took the oath.

He kept his eyes on Harvester, not looking at the judge—nor at Zorah, sitting beside Rathbone. He seemed grave but not in the least anxious.

"Lord Wellborough," Harvester began as he walked out into the small space of open floor in front of the witness stand and up its several steps, almost like a pulpit. He was obliged to look upward. "Are you acquainted with both the plaintiff and the defendant in this case?"

"Yes sir, I am."

"Were they both guests in your home in Berkshire at the time of the tragic accident and subsequent death of Prince Friedrich, the plaintiff's late husband?"

"They were."

"Have you seen the plaintiff since she left your home shortly after that event?"

"No sir. Prince Friedrich's funeral was held in Wellborough. There was a memorial service in Venice, where the Prince and Princess spent most of their time, so I believe, but I was unable to travel."

"Have you seen the defendant since that time?" Harvester's voice was mild, as if the questions were of no more than social interest.

"Yes sir, I have, on several occasions," Wellborough replied, his voice sharpening with sudden anger.

In the gallery, several people sat a little more uprightly.

"Can you tell me what happened at the first of these occasions, Lord Wellborough?" Harvester prompted. "Please do describe it with a modicum of detail, sufficient so that the gentlemen of the jury, who were naturally not present, may perceive the situation, but not so much as to distract them from what is germane to the case."

"Most certainly." Wellborough turned to face the jury.

The judge's face so far wore an expression of unemotional interest.

"It was a dinner party given by Lady Easton," Wellborough

told the jurors. "There were about two dozen of us at the table. It had been a very agreeable occasion and we were in good spirits until someone, I forget who, reminded us of the death of Prince Friedrich some six months earlier. Immediately we all became a trifle somber. It was an event which had saddened us all. I and several others spoke of our sorrow, and some of us also spoke of our grief for the widowed Princess. They expressed concern for her, both her devastating loss, knowing how deeply and utterly they had cared for each other, and also for her welfare, now that she was completely alone in the world."

Several of the jurors nodded. One pursed his lips.

There was a murmur of commiseration from the gallery.

Harvester glanced at Gisela, who sat motionless. She had removed her gloves, and her hands lay on the table in front of her, bare but for the gold wedding ring on her right hand and the black mourning ring on the left. Her hands were small and strong, rather square.

"Proceed," Harvester said softly.

"The Countess Zorah Rostova was also present among the dinner guests," Wellborough said, his voice thick with distaste, and there flickered across his eyes and mouth something which could have been anxiety.

Rathbone thought of Monk's last trip to Wellborough, and wondered precisely how he had elicited Wellborough's cooperation, almost fruitless though it had proved.

Harvester waited.

The room was silent except for the slight whispers of breathing. A woman's whalebone corset creaked.

"Countess Rostova said that she had no doubt that Princess Gisela would be well provided for and that the grief would be assuaged in time," Wellborough continued. His mouth tightened. "I thought it a tasteless remark, and I believe that someone else passed a comment to that effect. To which she replied that considering Gisela had murdered Friedrich, the remark was really very mild."

He was prevented from going any further by the gasps and murmurs from the body of the court.

The judge did not intervene but allowed the reaction to run its course.

Rathbone found his muscles clenching. It was going to be every bit as hard as he had feared. He looked sideways at Zorah's powerful profile, her long nose, eyes too widely spaced, subtle, sensitive mouth. She was insane, she must be. It was the only answer. Was insanity a plea in cases of slander? Of course not. It was a civil case, not a criminal one.

He did not mean to look at Harvester, least of all to catch his eye, but he found himself doing it. He saw what he thought was a flash of rueful humor, but perhaps it was only pity and knowledge of his own unassailable case.

"And what was the reaction around the table to this statement, Lord Wellborough?" Harvester asked when the noise had subsided sufficiently.

"Horror, of course," Wellborough answered with anxiety. "There were those who chose to assume she must mean it in some kind of bizarre humor, and they laughed. I daresay they were so embarrassed they had no idea what else to do."

"Did the Countess Rostova explain herself?" Harvester raised his eyebrows. "Did she offer a mitigation as to why she had said such an outrageous thing?"

"No, she did not."

"Not even to Lady Easton, her hostess?"

"No. Poor Lady Easton was mortified. She hardly knew what to say or do to cover the situation. Everyone was acutely uncomfortable."

"I should imagine so," Harvester agreed. "You are quite sure the Countess did not apologize?"

"Far from it," Wellborough said angrily, his hands gripping

the edge of the railing of the box as he leaned forward on it. "She said it again."

"In your hearing, Lord Wellborough?"

"Of course in my hearing!" Wellborough said. "I know better than to repeat something in court which I do not know for myself."

Harvester's composure was unruffled. "Are you referring to that same dinner party or to some other occasion?"

"Both . . ." Wellborough straightened up. "She made the statement again that evening when Sir Gerald Bretherton remonstrated with her, protesting that she surely could not mean such a thing. She assured him that she did—"

"And what was the reaction to her charge?" Harvester interrupted. "Did anyone argue with her, or did they dismiss it as bad behavior, possibly the act of someone overwrought or who had indulged too much?"

"They tried to do that," Wellborough agreed. "Then she made the same charge again about a week later, at a theater party. The play was a drama. I cannot remember the title, but she said again that the Princess Gisela had murdered Prince Friedrich. It was an appalling scene. People tried to pretend they had not heard, or that it had been somehow a wretched joke, but it was perfectly apparent that she meant precisely what she said."

"Are you aware, Lord Wellborough, of whether anyone gave the charge the slightest credence?" Harvester spoke softly, but his words fell with great deliberation and clarity, and he glanced towards the jury and then back again at the witness stand. "Please be most careful how you answer."

"I shall be." Wellborough did not take his eyes off Harvester's face. "I heard several people say it was the most malicious nonsense they had ever heard, and of course there could be no question of there being an atom of truth to it."

"Hear, hear!" a man called from the gallery, and was met with immediate applause.

The judge gave the audience a warning look, but he did not intervene.

Rathbone's jaw tightened. His best hope might have been a strong and subtle judge. But perhaps he was being foolish to believe he had a hope at all. The Lord Chancellor's words rang in his ears. Was this discretion or simply absolute surrender?

Beside him, Zorah was impassive. Maybe she still did not realize her position.

"From those who knew her, of course," Wellborough said, still answering the question. "And from a great many who did not. But there were those who repeated it, and the ignorant began to question. There were servants who spread tittle-tattle. It caused much distress."

"To whom?" Harvester said quietly.

"To many people, but the Princess Gisela in particular," Wellborough said slowly.

"Did you meet anyone personally for whom her reputation had suffered?" Harvester pressed.

Wellborough shifted his weight from one foot to the other.

"Yes, I did. I heard ugly remarks on several occasions, and when the Princess wished to return to England for a short stay, it became impossible to employ acceptable staff to look after a small house for her."

"How very unpleasant," Harvester sympathized. "Have you reason to believe this occurred as a result of these accusations by the Countess Rostova?"

"I am quite sure it did," Wellborough replied coldly. "My butler attempted to employ a household so she could stay peacefully for a few months during the summer, to get away from the heat of Venice. She wished to retire here away from public life, quite naturally in the circumstances. This fearful business has made it impossible. We were unable to obtain a satisfactory staff. Rumor had already spread by word of mouth of the ignorant."

There was a murmur of sympathy from the gallery.

"How distressing." Harvester shook his head. "So the Princess was unable to come?"

"She was obliged to stay with friends, which did not offer her either the privacy or the seclusion which she had desired in her bereavement."

"Thank you, Lord Wellborough. If you could remain where you are, my learned friend may have questions to ask you."

Rathbone rose to his feet. He could almost feel the tension crackle in the air around him. He had racked his brain to think of anything to say to Wellborough, but everything that came to his tongue could only have made matters worse.

The judge looked at him inquiringly.

"No questions, thank you, my lord," he said with a dry mouth, and resumed his seat.

Lord Wellborough moved down the steps, walked smartly to the door and went out.

Harvester called Lady Wellborough.

She took the stand nervously. She was dressed in a mixture of dark brown and black, as if she could not make up her mind whether she should be in mourning or not. A death was being discussed, a murder was being denied.

"Lady Wellborough," Harvester began gently, "I do not have many questions to ask you, and they all concern what may have been said by Countess Rostova and what effect it had."

"I understand," she replied in a small voice. She stood with her hands folded in front of her and her eyes wandering to Gisela, then to Zorah. She did not look at the jury.

"Very well. May I begin by taking your mind back to the dinner party you and Lord Wellborough attended at Lady Easton's house in London? Do you recall that occasion?"

"Yes, of course."

"Did you hear the Countess Rostova make the reference to Princess Gisela and Prince Friedrich's death?"

"Yes. She said that the Princess had murdered him."

Rathbone looked across to where Gisela sat. He tried to read the expression in her face and found himself unable to. She appeared unmoved, almost as if she did not understand what was being said. Or perhaps it was that she did not care. Everything that had passion or meaning for her was already irretrievably in the past, had died with the only man she had loved. What was being played out in the courtroom barely impinged on her consciousness—a farce with no reality.

"Did she say it once or several times?" Harvester's voice brought Rathbone's attention back.

"She repeated it again on at least three other occasions that I know of," Lady Wellborough answered. "I heard it all over London, so heaven knows how many times she said it altogether."

"You mean it became a subject of discussion—of gossip, if you like?" Harvester prompted.

Her eyes widened. "Of course. You can hardly hear something like that and not react to it."

"So people repeated it whether they believed it or not?"

"Yes . . . yes, I don't think anyone believed it. I mean . . . of course they didn't." She colored. "It's preposterous!"

"But they still repeated it?" he insisted.

"Well . . . yes."

"Do you know where the Princess was at the time, Lady Wellborough?"

"Yes, she was in Venice."

"Was she aware of what was being said about her?"

She colored faintly. "Yes . . . I . . . I wrote and told her. I felt she should know." She bit her lip. "I hated doing it. It took me over an hour to compose a letter, but I could not allow this to be said and go uncontested. I could defend her by denying it, but I could not initiate any proceedings." She stared at Harvester as she said it, a slight frown on her brow.

Rathbone thought she seemed very concerned that Harvester should understand her reasons, and it occurred to him that perhaps he had coached her to give this answer, and she was watching him to see if she had done so correctly. But it was a fact that was of no use. There was nothing he could make of it to help Zorah.

"You gave her the opportunity to defend herself in law," Harvester concluded. "Which she is now taking. Did you receive a reply to your letter?"

"Yes, I did."

There was a murmur of approval from the gallery. One of the jurors nodded gravely.

Harvester produced a piece of pale blue paper and offered it to the usher.

"My lord, may I place this letter into evidence and ask the witness to identify it?"

"You may," the judge agreed.

Lady Wellborough said that it was the letter she had received, and in a slightly husky voice, she read it aloud to the court, quoting the date and the plantiff's address in Venice. She glanced at Gisela only once and met with the merest acknowledgment.

" 'My dear Emma,' " she began in an uncertain voice " 'Your letter shocked and grieved me beyond words. I hardly knew how to set pen to paper to write you a sensible answer.' "

She stopped and cleared her throat without looking up from the paper.

" 'First may I thank you for being such a true friend to me as to tell me this terrible news. It cannot have been easy even to think how to say it. Sometimes the cruelty of life seems beyond bearing.

" 'I thought when my beloved Friedrich died there was nothing else left to hope or fear. For me it was the end of everything that was happy or beautiful or precious in any way. I truly did not think any other blow could wound me. How very wrong I was. I cannot begin to describe how this hurts. To imagine that anyone at all, any human being with a heart or a soul, could think that I could have injured the man who was the love and core of my life, is a pain I do not think I can bear. I am beside myself with grief.

" 'If she does not withdraw absolutely, and confess she was intoxicated or mad, I shall have to take her to court. I shall loathe every second of it, but I have no choice. I will not have Friedrich spoken of so—I will not have our love defiled. To my everlasting grief and loneliness, I could not save his life, but I will save his reputation as the man I loved and adored above all others. I will not, I will not have the world suppose I betrayed him.

" 'I remain your indebted friend, Gisela.' "

She let the paper rest on the railing and looked up at Harvester, her face white, struggling to keep her composure.

No one was looking at her; almost every eye was on Gisela, even if all they could see was her profile. Several women in the gallery sniffed audibly, and one juror sat staring fixedly and blinking rapidly. Another blew his nose unnecessarily hard.

Harvester cleared his throat.

"I think we can safely assume that Princess Gisela was deeply distressed by this turn of events, and it caused her even greater pain above that which she already suffered in her bereavement."

Lady Wellborough nodded.

Harvester invited Rathbone to question the witness.

Rathbone declined. He heard the rustle of surprise from the gallery, and his eye caught the movement of a juror and the disbelief in his face. But there was nothing at all he could do. In such a desperate situation anything he said would only give Lady Wellborough the opportunity to repeat her evidence.

The judge adjourned the court for luncheon, and Rathbone strode past Harvester and went immediately to the private room where he could speak to Zorah alone, almost dragging her with him, leaving the ugly mutters or grumbles of the crowd as the gallery was cleared.

"Gisela did not kill Friedrich," he said the moment the door was closed. "I have no evidence to make your charge even seem reasonable, let alone true! For heaven's sake, withdraw now. Admit you spoke out of emotion and were mistaken—"

"I was not mistaken," she said flatly, her green eyes calm and perfectly level. "I will not abandon the truth simply because it has become uncomfortable. I am surprised that you think I might. Is this the courage in the face of fire which earned you an empire?"

"Charging into the enemy's guns may make you a name in history," he said acidly. "But it is an idiotic sacrifice of life. It's all very poetic, but the reality is death, agony, crippled bodies and widows weeping at home, mothers who never see their sons again. It is more than time you stopped dreaming and looked at life as it is." He heard his voice growing higher and louder and he could not help it. He was clenching his fists until his muscles ached, and without being aware of it, he chopped his hand up and down in the air. "Did you not hear that letter? Didn't you look at the jurors' faces? Gisela is a heroine, the ideal of their romantic imagination! You have attacked her with a charge you cannot prove, and that makes you a villain. Nothing I can say is going to change that. If I counterattack it will make it worse."

She stood quite still, her face pale, her shoulders squared, her voice low and a little shaky.

"You give up too easily. We have barely begun. No sensible person makes a decision when he has heard only one side of a story. And sensible or not, the jury is obliged to wait and hear us as well. Is that not what the law is for, to allow both sides to put forward their case?"

"You have no case!" he shouted, then instantly regretted losing his self-control. It was undignified and served no purpose whatever. He should never have allowed himself to become so uncontrolled. "You have no case," he repeated in a calmer voice. "The very best we can do is present evidence indicating that Friedrich was murdered by someone, but we cannot possibly prove it was Gisela! You will have to withdraw and apologize sooner or later, or suffer the full punishment the law may decide, and it may be very high indeed. You will lose your reputation . . ."

"Reputation." She laughed a little nervously. "Do you not think I have lost that already, Sir Oliver? All I have left now is what little money my family settled on me, and if she takes that, she is welcome. She cannot take my integrity or wit, or my beliefs."

Rathbone opened his mouth to argue, and then conceded the total pointlessness of it. She was not listening. Maybe she had never really listened to him.

"Then . . ." he began, and realized that what he was about to suggest was futile also.

"Yes?" she inquired.

He had been going to advise her to keep her bearing modest, but that would no doubt be a wasted request. It was not in her nature.

The first witness of the afternoon was Florent Barberini. Rathbone was curious to see him. He was extremely handsome in a Latin fashion, somewhat melodramatic for Rathbone's taste. He was inclined not to like the man.

"Were you at Wellborough Hall at the time of Prince Friedrich's death, Mr. Barberini?" Harvester began quite casually. He chose to use an English form of address, rather than the Italian or German forms.

"Yes, I was," Florent replied.

"Did you remain in England afterwards for some time?"

"No, I returned to Venice for Prince Friedrich's memorial service. I did not come back to England for about six months."

"You were devoted to Prince Friedrich?"

"I am Venetian. It is my home," he corrected.

Harvester was unruffled.

"But you did return to England?"

"Yes."

"Why, if Venice is your home?"

"Because I had heard word that the Countess Rostova had made an accusation of murder against Princess Gisela. I wished to know if that were so, and if it was, to persuade her to withdraw it immediately."

"I see." Harvester folded his hands behind his back. "And when you arrived in London, what did you hear?"

Florent looked down, his brow furrowed. He must have expected the question, but obviously it made him unhappy.

"That apparently the Countess Rostova had quite openly made the charge of which I had heard," he answered.

"Once?" Harvester pressed, moving a step or two to face the witness from a slightly different direction. "Several times? Did you hear her make it yourself, or only hear of it from others?"

"I heard her myself," Florent admitted. He looked up, his eyes wide and dark. "But I did not meet anyone who believed it."

"How do you know that, Mr. Barberini?" Harvester raised his eyebrows.

"They said so."

"And you are sure that was the truth?" Harvester sounded incredulous but still polite, if only just. "They disclaimed in public, as is only civil, perhaps only to be expected. But are you as sure they still thought the same in private? Did not the vaguest of doubts enter their minds?"

"I know only what they said," Florent replied.

Rathbone rose to his feet.

"Yes, yes," the judge agreed before he spoke. "Mr. Harvester, your questions are rhetorical, and this is not the place for them. You contradict yourself, as you know perfectly well. Mr. Barberini has no possible way of knowing what people thought other than as they expressed it. He has said all those whom he knew spoke their disbelief. If you wish us to suppose they thought otherwise, then you will have to demonstrate that for us."

"My lord, I am about to do so." Harvester was not in the least disconcerted. Neither would Rathbone have been in his place. He had every card in the game, and he knew it.

Harvester turned with a smile to Florent.

"Mr. Barberini, do you have any knowledge of injury this accusation may have caused the Princess Gisela, apart from emotional distress?"

Florent hesitated.

"Mr. Barberini?" Harvester prompted.

Florent raised his head.

"When I returned to Venice I heard the rumors repeated there—" He stopped again.

"And were they equally disbelieved in Venice, Mr. Barberini?" Harvester said softly.

Again Florent hesitated.

The judge leaned forward. "You must answer, sir, to the best of your knowledge. Say only what you know. You are not required to guess—indeed, you must not speculate."

"No," Florent said very quietly, so the jurors were obliged to lean forward a little and every sound ceased in the gallery.

"I beg your pardon?" Harvester said clearly.

"No," Florent repeated. "There were those in Venice who openly wondered if it could be true. But they were very few, perhaps two or three. In any society there are the credulous and the spiteful. The Princess Gisela has lived there for some years. Naturally, as a woman leading in society she has made enemies as well as friends. I doubt anyone truly believed it, but they took the opportunity to repeat it to her discredit."

"It did her harm, Mr. Barberini?"

"It was unpleasant."

"It did her harm?" Suddenly Harvester's voice rose sharply. He was a lean figure, leaning a little backwards to stare up at the witness, but there was no mistaking the authority in him.

"Do not be evasive, sir! Did she cease to be invited to certain houses?" He spread his hands. "Were people rude to her? Were they slighting or offensive? Was she insulted? Did she find it embarrassing in certain public places or among her social equals?"

Florent smiled. It took more than even the best barrister to shake his nerve. "You seem to have very slight understanding of the situation, sir," he answered. "She went into deep mourning as soon as the service of remembrance was over. She remained in her palazzo, seldom receiving visitors or even being seen at the windows. She went out nowhere, accepted no invitations and was seen in no public places. I do not know whether fewer people sent her flowers or letters than would have otherwise. And if they did, one can only guess the reasons. It could have been any of a hundred things. I know what was said, nothing more. Whatever the rumor, there will always be someone to repeat it." His expression did not change at all. "Ugo Casselli started a story of having seen a mermaid sitting on the steps of the Santa Maria Maggiore in the full moon," he added. "Some idiot repeated that, too!"

There was a titter of laughter around the gallery which died away instantly as Harvester glared at them.

But Rathbone saw with a sudden, reasonless lift of his heart that the judge was smiling.

"You find the matter humorous?" Harvester said icily to Florent.

Florent knew what he meant, but he chose to misunderstand.

"Hilarious," he said with wide eyes. "There were two hundred people out in the lagoon next full moon. Business was marvelous. I think it might have been a gondolier who started it."

Harvester was too clever to allow his temper to mar his performance.

"Most entertaining." He forced a dry smile. "But a harmless fiction. This fiction of the Countess Rostova's was anything but harmless, don't you agree, even if as absurd and as untrue?"

"If you want to be literal," Florent argued, "it is not of equal absurdity, in my opinion. I do not believe in mermaids, even in Venice. Tragically, women do sometimes murder their husbands."

Harvester's face darkened, and he swung around as if to retaliate.

But the rumble of fury from the gallery robbed him of the necessity. A man called out "Shame!" Two or three half rose to their feet. One of them raised his fist.

Several jurors shook their heads, faces tight and hard, lips pursed.

Beside Rathbone, Zorah put up her hands to cover her face, and he saw her shoulders quiver with laughter.

Harvester relaxed. He had no need to fight, and he knew it. He turned to Rathbone.

"Your witness, Sir Oliver."

Rathbone rose to his feet. He must say something. He had to begin, at least to show that he was in the battle. He had fought without weapons before, and with stakes as high. The judge would know he was playing for time, so would Harvester, but the jury would not. And Florent was almost a friendly witness. He was obviously disposed to make light of the offense. He had once glanced at Zorah with, if not a smile, a kind of softness.

But what could he ask? Zorah was wrong, and she was the only one who did not accept it.

"Mr. Barberini," he began, sounding far more confident than he felt. He moved slowly onto the floor, anything to give him a moment's time—although all the time in the world would not help. "Mr. Barberini, you say that, to your knowledge, no one believed this charge the Countess Rostova made?"

"So far as I know," Florent said guardedly.

Harvester smiled, leaning back in his chair. He glanced at

Gisela encouragingly, but she was staring ahead, seemingly unaware of him.

"What about the Countess herself?" Rathbone asked. "Have you any reason to suppose that she did not believe it to be the truth?"

Florent looked surprised. Obviously, it was not the question he had expected.

"None at all," he answered. "I have no doubt that she believed it absolutely."

"Why do you say that?" Rathbone was on very dangerous ground, but he had little to lose. It was always perilous to ask a question to which you did not know the answer. He had told enough juniors never to do it.

"Because I know Zorah—Countess Rostova," Florent replied. "However absurd it is, she would not say it unless she firmly believed it herself."

Harvester rose to his feet.

"My lord, belief of a truth of a slander is no defense. There are those who sincerely believe the world to be flat. The depth of their sincerity does not make it so, as I am sure my learned friend is aware."

"I am also quite sure he is aware of it, Mr. Harvester," the judge agreed, "although it does go to malice. If he should try to persuade the jury it is so, I shall inform them to the contrary, but he has not yet attempted such a thing. Proceed, Sir Oliver, if you have a point to make?"

There was another ripple of amusement in the gallery. Someone giggled.

"Only to establish that the Countess was speaking from conviction, as you have observed, my lord," Rathbone replied. "And not from mischief or intent to cause damage for its own sake." He could think of nothing to add to it. He inclined his head and retreated.

Harvester stood up again.

"Mr. Barberini, is this opinion of yours as to the Countess's sincerity based upon knowledge? Do you know, for example, of some proof she may possess?" The question was sarcastic, but its tone was still just within the realm of politeness.

"If I knew of proof I should not be standing here with it," Florent replied with a frown. "I should have taken it to the proper authorities immediately. I say only that I am sure she believed it. I don't know why she did."

Harvester turned and looked at Zorah, then back to Florent.

"Did you not ask her? Surely, as a friend, either of hers or the Princess's, it would be the first thing you would do?"

Rathbone winced and went cold inside.

"Of course I asked her," Florent said angrily. "She told me nothing."

"Do you mean she told you she had nothing?" Harvester persisted. "Or that she said nothing in reply to you?"

"She said nothing in reply."

"Thank you, Mr. Barberini. I have no more to ask you."

The day finished with journalists scrambling to escape with their reports and seize the first hansoms available to race to Fleet Street. Outside, crowds filled the pavements, jostling and elbowing to see the chief protagonists. Cabs and carriages were brought to a halt in the street. Coachmen were shouting. Newsboys' voices were lost in the general noise. No one wanted to hear news about the war in China, Mr. Gladstone's financial proposals, or even Mr. Darwin's blasphemous and heretical notions about the origins of man. There was a passionate human drama playing itself out a few yards away, love and hate, loyalty, sacrifice and an accusation of murder.

Gisela came out of the main entrance, escorted down the steps by Harvester on one side and a large footman on the other. Immediately, a cheer went up from the crowd. Several people threw flowers. Scarves fluttered in the brisk October air, and men waved their hats.

"God bless the Princess!" someone called out, and the cry was taken up by dozens, and then scores.

She stood still, a small, thin figure of immense dignity, her huge black skirt seeming almost to hold her up with its sweeping stiffness, as if it were solid. She waved back with a tiny gesture, then permitted herself to be assisted up to her carriage, plumed and creped in black and drawn by black horses, and moved slowly away.

Zorah's departure was as different as could be. The crowds were still there, still pressing forward, eager for a glimpse of her, but their mood had changed to one of ugliness and abuse. Nothing was thrown, but Rathbone found himself clenching as if to dodge and instinctively placing himself between Zorah and the crowd.

He almost hustled her to the hansom, and climbed in after her rather than leave her alone, in case the crowd should bar the way and the cabby be unable to make a path into the clearway of the street.

But only one woman pushed forward, shouting unintelligibly, her voice shrill with hatred. The horse was startled and lunged forward, knocking her off balance. She shrieked.

"Get outta the way, yer stupid cow!" the cabby yelled, frightened and taken by surprise himself as the reins were all but yanked out of his grasp. "Sorry, ma'am," he apologized to Zorah.

Inside the vehicle, Rathbone was jolted against the sides, and Zorah bumped into him and kept her balance only with difficulty.

A moment later they were moving smartly and the angry shouts were behind them. Zorah regained her composure swiftly. She looked straight ahead without rearranging her skirts, as though to do so would be to acknowledge a difficulty and she would not do that.

Rathbone thought of a dozen things to say, and changed his mind about all of them. He looked sideways at Zorah's face. At first he was not sure if he could see fear in it or not. A dreadful thought occurred to him that perhaps she sought this. The rush of blood, the excitement, the danger might be intoxicants to her. She was the center of attention, albeit hatred, rage, a will to violence. There were some people, a very few, to whom any sort of fame is better than none. To be ignored is a type of death, and it terrifies, it is an engulfing darkness, an annihilation. Anything is better, even loathing.

Was she mad?

If she was, then it was his responsibility to make decisions for her, in her best interest, rather than to allow her to destroy herself, as one would govern a child too young to be answerable. One had a duty to the insane, a legal obligation apart from a humanitarian one. He had been treating her as someone capable of rational judgment, a person able to foresee the results of her actions. Perhaps she was not. Perhaps she was under a compulsion and he had been quite wrong to do so, remiss in his duty both as a lawyer and as a man.

He studied her face. Was that calm he saw in her an inability to understand what had happened and foresee it would get worse?

He opened his mouth to speak, and then did not know what he was going to say.

He looked down at her hands. They were clenched on her skirt, the leather gloves pulled shiny across the knuckles, both hands shaking. He looked up at her face again and knew that the eyes staring straight ahead, the set of the jaw, were not born of indifference or unawareness but were the manifestations of fear even deeper than his own—and a very good knowledge that what was to come would be both ugly and painful.

He sat back and looked ahead, even more confused than before and more confounded as to what he should do.

He had been at home for over two hours when his servant announced that Miss Hester Latterly had called to see him. For a second he was delighted, then his spirits sank again as he realized how little he could tell her that was good, or even clear enough in his mind to be put into words.

"Ask her to come in," he said rather sharply. It was a cold night. She should not be kept waiting.

"Hester!" he said eagerly when she entered. She looked lovelier than he had remembered. There was color in her cheeks and a gentleness in her eyes, a depth of concern which smoothed out the tension in him and even made the fears recede for a space. "Come in," he went on warmly. He had already dined, and he assumed she would have also. "May I offer you a glass of wine, perhaps Port?"

"Not yet, thank you," she declined. "How are you? How is Countess Rostova? I saw how ugly it was when you were leaving the court."

"You were there? I didn't see you." He moved aside so that she might warm herself by the fire. It was only after he had done so that he realized what an extraordinary action it was for him. He would never consciously have yielded a place by the fire to a woman, least of all his own fire. It was a mark of the turmoil in his mind.

"Hardly surprising," she said with a rueful smile. "We were crammed in like matches in a box. Who can you call to help? Has Monk found anything even remotely useful? What on earth is he doing?"

As if in answer to her question, the manservant returned to announce that Monk also had arrived, only instead of waiting in the hall or the morning room, he was following hard on the man's heels so that the servant all but bumped into Monk when he turned.

Monk's overcoat was wet across the shoulders, and he handed a wet hat to the manservant before he withdrew.

Hester retained her place closest to the fire, moving her skirts slightly aside so some of the warmth could reach him. But she did not bother with pleasantries.

"What have you learned in Wellborough?" she said immediately.

Monk's face pinched with irritation. "Only substantiation of what we already assume," he said a trifle tersely. "The more I think of it, the more likely does it seem that Gisela was the intended victim."

Hester stared at him, consternation mixing with anger in her face.

"Can you prove it?" she challenged.

"Of course I can't prove it! If I could, I wouldn't have said 'I think,' I would simply have stated that it was so." He moved closer to the fire.

"Well, you must have a reason," she argued. "What is it? Why do you think it was Gisela? Who did it?"

"Either Rolf, the Queen's brother, or possibly Brigitte," he replied. "They both had excellent reason. She was the one thing standing between Friedrich and his return home to lead the independence party. He wouldn't have gone without her, and the Queen would not have had her back."

"Why not?" she said immediately. "If she was so determined to fight for independence, why not have Gisela back? She might dislike her, but that's absurd. Queens don't murder people just out of dislike—not these days. And you'll never get a jury to believe that. It's preposterous."

"An heir," Monk replied tersely. "If he put Gisela aside . . . or she was dead, he could marry again, preferably to a woman from a rich and popular family who would unite the country, give him children, and strengthen the royal house rather than weaken it. I don't know—maybe she has designs on the throne of all Germany. She has the gall—"

"Oh . . ." Hester fell silent, the magnitude of it suddenly striking her. She turned to Rathbone, her face furrowed with anxiety. Unconsciously, she moved a little closer to him, as if to support or protect. Then she lifted her chin and stared at

Monk. "How has Zorah got caught up in it? Did she stumble on the plot?"

"Don't be fatuous," Monk said crossly. "She's a patriot, all for independence. She was probably part of it."

"Oh, I'm sure!" Now Hester was sarcastic. "That's why when it all went wrong and Friedrich died instead, she started to draw everyone's attention to the fact that it was murder, not natural death, as everyone had been quite happy to believe until then. She wants to commit suicide but hasn't the nerve to pull the trigger herself. Or has she changed sides, and now she wants the whole thing exposed?" Her eyebrows rose. Her voice was growing harsher with every word, carrying her own pain. "Or better still—she's a double agent. She's changed sides. Now she wants to ruin the independence party by committing a murder in their name and then being hanged for it."

Monk looked at her with intense dislike.

Rathbone turned sharply, an idea bursting in his mind.

"Perhaps that is not so lunatic as it sounds," he said with urgency. "Perhaps it did all go wrong. Perhaps that is why Zorah is making a charge she knows she cannot prove. To force an examination of the whole affair so the truth can come out, and perhaps she is now prepared to sacrifice herself for it, if she believes it is for her country." He was talking more and more rapidly. "Maybe she sees a fight for independence as a battle that cannot be won but can only lead to war, destruction, terrible loss of life, and in the end assimilation not as an ally but as a beaten rebel, to be subjugated, and her own customs and culture wiped out." The idea seemed cleaner and more rational with every moment. "Isn't she the sort of idealist who might do exactly that?" He stared at Monk, demanding the answer from him.

"Why?" Monk said slowly. "Friedrich is dead. He can't go back now, whatever happens. If she, or one of the unification party, murdered him to prevent him going back, she has accomplished her aim. Why this? Why not simply accept victory?"

"Because someone else could take up the torch," Rathbone replied. "There must be someone else, not as good, maybe, but adequate. This could discredit the party for as long as matters. By the time a new party can be forged and the disgrace overcome, unification could be a fait accompli."

Hester looked from one to the other of them. "But was he going back?"

Rathbone looked at Monk. "Was he?"

"I don't know." He faced the two of them, standing unconsciously close together—and, incidentally, entirely blocking the fire. "But if you are even remotely close to the truth, then if you do your job with competence, let alone skill, it will emerge. Someone, perhaps Zorah herself, will make certain it does."

But Rathbone was far from comforted when he entered court the next day. If Zorah were harboring some secret knowledge which would bring about her purposes, whatever they were, there was no sign of it in her pale, set face.

Zorah had taken her seat, but Rathbone was still standing a few yards from the table when Harvester approached him. When he was not actually in front of a jury his face was more benign. In fact, had Rathbone not known better, he would have judged it quite mild, the leanness of bone simply a trick of nature.

"Morning, Sir Oliver," he said quietly. "Still in for the fight?" It was not a challenge, rather more a commiseration.

"Good morning," Rathbone replied. He forced himself to smile. "Isn't over yet."

"Yes, it is." Harvester shook his head, smiling back. "I'll stand you the best dinner in London afterwards. What the devil possessed you to take such a case?" He walked away to his own seat, and a moment later Gisela came in wearing a different but equally exquisite black dress with tiered skirts and tight bodice, fur trim at the throat and wrists. Not once did she glance towards Zorah. She might not have known who she was for any sign of recognition in her totally impassive face.

The shadow of a smile flickered across Zorah's mouth and disappeared.

The judge brought the court to order.

Harvester rose and called his first witness, the Baroness Evelyn von Seidlitz. She took the stand gracefully in a swish of decorous pewter-gray skirts trimmed with black. She managed to look as if she were decently serious, not quite in mourning, and yet utterly feminine. It was a great skill to offend no one and yet be anything but colorless or self-effacing. Rathbone thought she was quite lovely, and was very soon aware that every juror in the box thought so too. He could see it written plainly in their faces as they watched her, listening to and believing every word.

She told how she too had heard the accusation repeated as far away as both Venice and Felzburg.

Harvester did not press the issue of reaction in Venice, except that it was at times given a certain credence. Not everyone dismissed it as nonsense. He proceeded quite quickly to reactions in Felzburg.

"Of course it was repeated," Evelyn said, looking at him with wide, lovely eyes. "A piece of gossip like that is not going to be buried."

"Naturally," Harvester agreed wryly. "When it was repeated, Baroness, with what emotion was it said? Did anyone, for example, consider for an instant that it could be true?" He caught Rathbone's movement out of the corner of his eye and smiled thinly. "Perhaps I had better phrase that a little differently. Did you hear anyone express a belief that the accusation was true, or see anyone behave in such a manner as to make it apparent that they did?"

Evelyn looked very grave. "I heard a number of people greet

it with relish and then repeat it to others in a less speculative way, as if it were not slander but a fact. Stories grow in the telling, especially if the people concerned are enemies. And the Princess's enemies have certainly received great pleasure from all this."

"You are speaking of people in Felzburg, Baroness?"

"Yes, of course."

"But the Princess has not lived in Felzburg for over twelve years and is hardly likely ever to do so again," Harvester pointed out.

"People have long memories, sir. There are those who have never forgiven her for taking Prince Friedrich's love—and, in their eyes, for having induced him to leave his country and his duty. She is like all people who have risen to great heights; there are those who are jealous and would be only too delighted to see her fall."

Harvester glanced at Zorah, hesitated as if he were considering asking something further, then changed his mind. His meaning was abundantly clear, and yet Rathbone could not object. Nothing had been said.

Harvester looked up at the stand. "So this appalling charge has a possibility of causing great harm to the Princess through the agency of the envious and the bitter, who have long disliked her for their own reasons," he concluded. "This has put a weapon into their hands, so to speak, now of all times, when the Princess is alone and at her most vulnerable?"

"Yes." Evelyn nodded. "Yes, it has."

"Thank you, Baroness. If you would remain where you are, Sir Oliver may have a question or two to ask you."

Rathbone rose, simply not to allow the whole issue to go by default. His mind was racing over the thoughts that had come to him the previous evening. But how could he raise them with a witness with whom Harvester had been so circumspect? All he had was the right to cross-examine, not to open new and entirely speculative political territory.

"Baroness von Seidlitz," he began thoughtfully, looking up at her grave and charming face. "These enemies of the Princess Gisela that you speak of, are they people with power?"

She looked surprised, uncertain how to answer.

He smiled at her. "At least in England, and I believe in most places," he explained, "we are inclined to be very romantic about people involved in a great love story." He must be extremely careful. Anything the jury saw as an attack on Gisela would instantly prejudice them against him. "We may wish we were in their place. We may even envy them their worldly good fortune, but only those who have actually been personally in love with the other party bear them real ill will. Is that not so in your country as well? And certainly I could believe it true in Venice, where the Princess has lived most of the time since her marriage."

"Well . . . yes," she conceded, her brow furrowed. "Of course we love a lover . . ." She laughed a little uncertainly. "All the world does, doesn't it? We are no exception. But there is still resentment among a few that Prince Friedrich should have abdicated. That is different."

"In Venice, Baroness?" he said with surprise. "Do the Venetians really care?"

"No . . . of course they . . ."

Harvester rose to his feet. "My lord, is there really some point to my learned friend's questions? I fail to see it."

The judge looked regretfully at Rathbone.

"Sir Oliver, you are presently eliciting information already within our knowledge. Please proceed to something new, if you have it."

"Yes, my lord." Rathbone plunged on. As before, he had so little to lose. The risk was worth it. "The enemies you referred to who might in some way harm the Princess Gisela, you said they were in Felzburg, is that right?"

"Yes."

"Because in Venice they do not care. Venice is, if you will

pardon me, full of royalty no longer possessing thrones or crowns for one reason or another. Socially, a princess is still a princess. You said yourself that people of any worth did not believe it there. And anyway, the Princess is in retirement, and one invitation or another will make no difference to her. Her friends, which is all she will care about, are totally loyal to her."

"Yes . . ." Evelyn was still at a loss for his meaning. It was clear in her face.

"Would I be correct in supposing that these enemies, who are able to harm her, are not merely the odd disappointed past women admirers of Prince Friedrich, still holding a bitter envy, but people of some power and substance, able to command the respect of others?"

Evelyn stared at him wordlessly.

"Are you sure you wish this question answered, Sir Oliver?" the judge said anxiously.

Even Harvester looked puzzled. Rathbone would seem to be hurting Zorah rather than helping her.

"Yes, if you please, my lord," Rathbone assured him.

"Baroness . . ." the judge prompted.

"Well . . ." She could not contradict herself. She looked at Harvester, then away again. She regarded Rathbone with open dislike. "Yes, some of them are people of power."

"Perhaps political enemies?" Rathbone pressed. "People to whom the fate of their country is of the utmost importance? People who care desperately whether Felzburg remains independent or is absorbed into a unified and greater Germany, losing her individual identity and, of course, her individual monarchy?"

"I . . . I don't know . . ."

"Really!" Harvester protested, rising again to his feet. "Is my learned friend now suggesting some kind of political assassination? This whole argument is nonsense! By whom? These imaginary political enemies of Princess Gisela? It is the

Princess herself that his client has accused." He waved his arm derisively at Zorah. "He is making confusion worse confounded."

"Sir Oliver?" the judge said with a slight frown. "Precisely what is it you are seeking to draw from this witness?"

"The possibility, my lord, that there are grave political issues at stake in the charges and countercharges which are flying," he answered. "And that it is the fate of a country which has fueled the emotions we see here today, and not simply a long-standing jealousy of two women who dislike each other."

"That is a question the witness cannot possibly answer, my lord," Harvester said. "She is not privy to the thoughts and motives of Countess Rostova. Indeed, I don't think anyone is. With respect, perhaps not even Sir Oliver."

"My lord," Rathbone said quietly. "Baroness von Seidlitz is an intelligent woman of political astuteness who spends her time largely in Venice and Felzburg. Her husband has considerable interests in many parts of Germany and is aware of the aspirations of nationalism, the prospects for unification or independence. He is familiar with many of the powerful men of the country. The Baroness's political opinions are informed and not to be dismissed lightly. I asked her if she believed a political motive possible, not if she knew the Countess Rostova's mind."

"You may answer the question, Baroness," the judge directed. "In your opinion, is a political motive possible in this tragic affair? In other words, are there political issues which may be affected by the Prince's death or by what happens in this court?"

Evelyn looked most uncomfortable, but without forswearing what she had already said, and appearing a fool, she could not deny it.

"Of course there are political issues," she admitted. "Friedrich had abdicated, but he was still a prince of the royal house, and there were old loyalties."

Rathbone dared not press it further.

"Thank you." He smiled as if her admission meant something, and returned to his seat. He was aware of Harvester's amusement, and of Zorah's eyes on him with curiosity. The gallery was fidgeting, wanting more drama, more personal passion.

In the afternoon they were satisfied at last. Harvester called Gisela herself. The room was in such a state of expectancy the holding of breath was audible. No one spoke. No one intentionally moved as she rose, crossed the floor and mounted the steps to the stand. A bench creaked as a single person shifted weight. A corset bone snapped. Someone's reticule slipped out of her hands and slithered to the floor with a clunk of coins.

One of the jurors sneezed.

Zorah looked at Rathbone, then away again. She did not speak.

Gisela faced them, and for the first time Rathbone was able to look at her without appearing to stare. In the box behind the rail, she looked even smaller, her shoulders more delicate, her head even a trifle large with its broad forehead and strong brows. No one could deny it was a face of remarkable character, and perhaps an illusion of beauty more meaningful than mere coloring or symmetry of features. She faced Harvester directly, unwaveringly, waiting for him to begin once she had sworn in a low, very pleasing voice as to her name. Her accent also was very slight, her use of English easy.

Harvester had obviously made the appropriate inquiries beforehand and knew better than to use her royal form of address. She had never been crown princess; such title as she had was courtesy.

"Madam," he began, his tone respectful of her widowhood, her legendary love, if not her status. "We have heard testimony in this court that the Countess Zorah Rostova has on several occasions made a most vile and appalling accusation against you, and that she has done it repeatedly, in private and in public places. She herself has never denied it. We have heard from friends of yours that they were aware that very naturally it caused you great grief and distress."

He glanced briefly towards the gallery. "We have heard Baroness von Seidlitz say that it has provided fuel for enemies you may have in your native country who still bear you envy and ill will because of your marriage to the Prince. Would you please tell the court how your husband died? I do not desire to harrow your emotions by raising what can only be devastating memories for you. The briefest description will serve."

She gripped the railing with black-gloved hands as if to steady herself and stood silent for several seconds before summoning the strength to reply.

Rathbone groaned inwardly. It was worse than he had anticipated. The woman was perfect. She had dignity. Tragedy was on her side, and she knew not to play it too much. Perhaps it was Harvester's advice, perhaps her own natural good taste.

"He fell from his horse while out riding," she said quietly, but her voice was distinct, falling into the silence with all the burden of loss. Every word was perfectly audible throughout the room. "He was very seriously injured. His foot was caught in the stirrup iron, and he was dragged." She took a deep breath and let it out softly. She lifted her strong, rather square chin. "At first we thought he was getting better. It is very difficult for even the best doctor to tell how serious an internal injury may be. Then suddenly he relapsed . . . and within hours he was dead."

She stood absolutely immobile, her face a mask of hopelessness. She did not weep. She looked as if she were already exhausted by grief and had nothing left inside her but endless, gray pain, and ahead only an untold number of years of loneliness which no one could reach.

Harvester allowed the court to sense her tragedy, her utter bereavement, before he continued.

"And the doctor said the cause of death was his internal injuries?" he said very gently.

"Yes."

"After the funeral you returned to Venice, to the home you had shared with him?"

"Yes."

"How did you hear of the Countess Rostova's extraordinary charge?"

She lifted her chin a little. Rathbone stared at her. It was a remarkable face; there was a unique serenity in it. She had been devastated by tragedy, and yet the longer he looked, the less did he see vulnerability in the line of her lips or the way she held herself. There was something in her which seemed almost untouchable.

"First, Lady Wellborough wrote and told me," she answered Harvester. "Then other people also wrote. To begin with I assumed it was merely an aberration, perhaps spoken when . . . I do not wish to be uncharitable . . . but I have been left no choice . . . when she had taken too much wine."

"What motive can you imagine Countess Rostova having to say such a thing?" Harvester asked with wide eyes.

"I should prefer not to answer that," Gisela said with icy dignity. "Her reputation is well-known to many. I am not interested in it."

Harvester did not pursue the point further. "And how did you feel when you heard of this, ma'am?"

She closed her eyes. "I had not thought after the loss of my beloved husband that life could offer me any blow which I should even feel," she said very softly. "Zorah Rostova taught me my mistake. The pain of it was almost beyond bearing. My love for my husband was the core of my life. That anyone should blaspheme it in such a way is . . . beyond my ability to express."

She hesitated a moment. Throughout the room there was utter silence. Not one person looked away from her face, nor did they seem to consider the word *blaspheme* out of place. "I shall prefer to not, and indeed I cannot, speak of it if I am to retain my composure, sir," she said at last. "I will testify in this court, as I must, but I will not display my grief or my pain to be a spectacle for my enemies, or even for those who wish me well. It is indecent to ask it of me . . . of any woman. Permit me to mask my distress, sir."

"Of course, ma'am." Harvester bowed very slightly. "You have said quite enough for us to have no doubt as to the justice of your cause. We cannot ease your grief, but we offer you our sincerest sympathies and all the redress that English law allows."

"Thank you, sir."

"If you will remain there, ma'am, it is conceivable Sir Oliver may have some questions to ask you, although I cannot imagine what."

Rathbone rose. He could feel the hatred of the court like electricity in the air, crackling, making the hairs on his neck stand on end. If he even remotely slighted her, was less than utterly sympathetic, he could ruin his own cause far more effectively than anything Harvester could achieve.

He faced Gisela's steady, dark blue eyes and found them oddly unnerving. Perhaps it was the exhaustion of grief, but there was something dead about her gaze.

"You must have been stunned by such a devastating accusation, ma'am?" he said deferentially, trying not to sound too unctuous.

"Yes." She did not elaborate.

He stood in the center of the floor looking up at her.

"I imagine you were not in the best of health after the shock of your bereavement," he continued.

"I was not well," she agreed. She stared at him coldly. She was waiting for an attack. After all, he represented the woman who had accused her of murder.

"In that season of shock and grief, did you have the time, or the heart, to consider the political happenings in Felzburg?"

"I was not in the least interested." There was no surprise in her voice. "My world had ended with my husband's death. I hardly know what I did. One day was exactly like the next . . . and the last. I saw no one."

"Very natural," Rathbone agreed. "I imagine we can all understand that. Anyone who has lost someone very dear knows the process of mourning, let alone a grief such as yours."

The judge looked at Rathbone with a frown.

The jurors were growing restive.

He must reach the point soon or it would be too late. He knew Zorah was watching him. He could almost feel her eyes on his back.

"Had it ever occurred to you, ma'am, to wonder if your husband had been murdered for political reasons?" he asked. "Perhaps regarding your country's fight to retain its independence?"

"No . . ." There was a lift of surprise in Gisela's voice. She seemed about to add something else, then caught Harvester's eye and changed her mind.

Rathbone forced a very slight smile of sympathy to his lips.

"But with a love as profound as yours, now that the possibility has been raised, I should not think you can allow the question to go unanswered, can you? Do you not care even more fervently than anyone else here that, if it was so, the culprit must be caught and pay the price for so heinous and terrible a crime?"

She stared at him wordlessly, her eyes huge.

For the first time there was a rumble of agreement from the court. Several of the jurors nodded gravely.

"Of course," Rathbone said, answering his own question vehemently. "And I promise you, ma'am"—he waved his hand to encompass them all—"this court will do everything in its power to discover that truth, to the last detail, and expose it." He bowed very slightly, as if she had indeed been royalty. "Thank you. I have no more questions." He nodded to Harvester and then returned to his seat.

10

"THE NEWSPAPERS, SIR." Rathbone's manservant handed them to him as he sat at breakfast, the *Times* on top.

Rathbone's stomach tightened. This would be the measure of public opinion. In the pile of newsprint would lie what he was really fighting against, the hope and the fear of what faced him today and for as long as the trial lasted.

That was not the whole truth. It would last a lot longer than that. In people's minds he would always be connected with it.

He opened the *Times* and scanned the pages to find the report. There was bound to be one. It was inconceivable they would ignore such a trial. Everyone in Europe would be following it.

There it was. He had almost missed it because the headline did not mention Gisela's name, or Friedrich's. It read TRAGIC ACCIDENT—OR MURDER? Then it went on to summarize the evidence so far with extreme sympathy for Gisela, describing her in detail, her ashen face, her magnificent dignity, her restraint in refusing to blame others or play on the emotions of the crowd. Rathbone nearly tore the paper on reading that. His hands shook with frustration. She had played superbly. Whether by chance or design, she had done it with consummate brilliance. No actress could have done better.

It went on to speak of Rathbone's own probing of the

situation, calling it desperate. Indeed that was true, but he had hoped it was not so obvious. But the burden of the article sent his heart racing with a surge of hope. They wrote that it was now imperative that the truth be known exactly how Prince Friedrich had died.

His eyes scanned the rest of the column, mouth dry, pulse thumping. It was all there, the political summary of the questions of continued independence versus unification, the interests involved, the risks of war, the factions, the struggle for power, their idealism, even reference to the revolutions across Europe in 1848.

The story ended by extolling the British legal system and demanding that it fulfill its great opportunity, and responsibility, to discover and prove to the world the truth as to whether Prince Friedrich had died by accident or there had indeed been a royal murder committed on English soil. Justice must be done, and for that the truth must be known, however difficult or painful to some. Such a heinous crime could not be kept secret to avoid embarrassment, no matter to whom.

He cast the *Times* aside and turned to the next paper. Its tone was a little different. It concentrated on the more human aspect, and reiterated its cry from the previous day that in the emotion of politics and murder, it must not be lost sight of that the case was about slander. In the very depth of her grief, a tragic and noble woman had been accused of the most appalling of crimes. The court existed not only to discern truth and explore issues which might affect tens of thousands but also, and perhaps primarily, to protect the rights and the good name of the innocent. It was the only recourse they had when falsely accused, and they had the right, the absolute and sacred right, to require it at the hands of all civilized peoples.

Harvester could not have been better served if he had written the story himself.

Rathbone closed the paper with his exhilaration considerably sobered. He had merely begun. He had accomplished the first step, no more.

The seal of displeasure was set upon the remainder of his breakfast by the arrival of the morning post, which included a short note from the Lord Chancellor.

My dear Sir Oliver,

May I commend you upon the tact with which you have so far conducted a most difficult and trying case. We must hope that the weight of evidence will yet persuade the unfortunate defendant to withdraw.

However, I am asked by certain persons at the Palace, who have grave interest in continued good relations in Europe, most especially with our German cousins, to advise you of the delicacy of the situation. I am sure you will in no way allow your client to involve, by even the slightest implication, the dignity or honor of the present royal family of Felzburg.

Naturally, I answered the gentleman in question that all fears in that direction were without foundation.

I wish you good fortune in the negotiation of this miserable matter.

Yours faithfully

The letter was signed with his name but not his title.

Rathbone put it down with a stiff hand, his fingers shaking. He no longer wished even tea or toast.

Harvester began the day by calling Dr. Gallagher to the stand. Rathbone wondered whether he had intended calling him even before the question of murder arose late the previous day. Possibly he had foreseen the newspaper's reaction and been prepared. Harvester did not seem anxious. But then he was far too good an actor to show what he did not wish to have seen.

Gallagher, on the other hand, looked extremely uncomfortable. He climbed the steps to the stand awkwardly, tripping on the last one, only saving himself by grasping the railing. He faced the court and took the oath, coughing to clear his throat. Rathbone felt a certain pity for him. The man had probably been nervous attending the Prince in the first place. It had been a very serious accident, and he might well have expected to lose his patient and be blamed for his inability to perform a miracle. He must have been surrounded by people in deep anxiety and distress. He had no colleagues upon whom to call, as he would have had in a hospital. He must be wishing that he had demanded a second opinion, someone from London, so he would not now have to bear the responsibility alone—and, if there were to be any, the blame.

He looked white; his brow was already beaded with sweat.

"Dr. Gallagher," Harvester began gravely, striding out to the middle of the floor. "I regret, sir, having to place you in this position, but you are no doubt aware of the charges that have been made regarding the death of Prince Friedrich, whether mischievously or with sincere belief. The fact remains that since they have been made in public, we cannot now allow them to go unanswered. We must find the truth, and we cannot do that without your full testimony."

Gallagher started to speak and ended coughing. He pulled out a white handkerchief and put it to his mouth, then when he had finished, kept it in his hand.

"Poor man," Zorah whispered beside Rathbone. It was the first comment she had passed upon any witness.

"Yes, sir, I understand," Gallagher said unhappily. "I will do all that lies in my power."

"I am sure you will." Harvester was standing with his hands behind his back—what Rathbone had come to realize was a characteristic stance. "I must take you back to the original accident," Harvester continued. "You were called to attend Prince Friedrich." It was a statement. Everyone knew the answer.

"Where was he and what was his condition when you first saw him?"

"He was in his rooms in Wellborough Hall," Gallagher replied, staring straight ahead. "He was on a board which had been brought upstairs because they feared the softness of the bed might cause the bones to scrape against each other were he unable to be absolutely flat. The poor man was still conscious and perfectly sensible to all his pain. I believe he had requested this himself."

Rathbone glanced at Zorah and saw her face stiff with knowledge of the Prince's suffering, as if in her mind it still existed. He steeled himself to search for guilt as well, but he saw no shadow of it.

He turned to look across at Gisela. Her expression was totally different. There was no life in her face, no turmoil, no anguish. It was as if every emotion in her were already exhausted. She had nothing whatever left.

"Indeed," Harvester was saying somberly. "A very distressing affair altogether. What was your diagnosis, Dr. Gallagher, when you had examined him?"

"Several ribs were broken," Gallagher answered. "His right leg was shattered, broken in three places very badly, as was his right collarbone."

"And internal injuries?" Harvester looked as grim as if the pain and the fear were still alive and present among them all. In the gallery, there were murmurs of pity and horror. Rathbone was acutely aware of Zorah beside him. He heard the rustle of her skirts as her body twisted and became rigid, reliving the horror and uncertainty of that time. He did not mean to look at her again, but he could not help it. There was a mixture of feelings in her features, the extraordinary nose, too long, too strong for her face, the green eyes half closed, the lips parted. At that moment he found it impossible to believe she could have caused the death which followed after.

But he still had no idea how much she knew or what were

her true reasons for making the charge of murder, or even if she had loved Friedrich or merely felt pity for any human suffering. She was as unreadable to him as she had been the first day he had met her. She was exasperating, possibly more than a little mad, and yet he could not see her as villainess, and he could not dislike her. It would make things a great deal easier if he could. Then he might discharge his legal duty to her and feel excused, instead of caring what happened to her, even if it was entirely her own doing.

Gallagher was describing the internal injuries he was aware of—or, in his best medical opinion, guessed.

"Of course, it is impossible to know," he said awkwardly. "He seemed to be recovering, at least his general health. I think he would have remained severely incapacitated." He took a deep breath. "Now it appears I missed something which may have ruptured when he moved or perhaps coughed severely. Sometimes even a sneeze can be very violent."

Harvester nodded. "But the symptoms as you observed them were entirely consistent with death from injury, such as those he sustained in what was a very bad fall indeed?"

"I . . . I believed so at the time." Gallagher fidgeted, turning his chin as if to loosen a collar which was choking him, but he did not move his hands from where they gripped the rail in front of him. "I signed the certificate according to my honest belief. Of course—" He stopped. Now his embarrassment was abundantly plain to every man and woman in the room.

Harvester looked grim. "You have second thoughts, Dr. Gallagher? Upon reading in the newspapers of Sir Oliver's suggestion in yesterday's hearing—or earlier than that, may I ask?"

Gallagher looked wretched. He kept his eyes on Harvester's face, as if he dared not glance away in case he should meet Gisela's gaze.

"Well . . . really . . . I suppose mostly since reading the newspapers. Although a private inquiry agent spoke to me some little time ago, and his questions were rather disturbing, but I gave it little credence at the time."

"So your thoughts were prompted by others? Would this agent be in the employ of Sir Oliver and his client, by any chance?" He made a slight, almost contemptuous, gesture towards Zorah.

"I . . ." Gallagher shook his head. "I have no idea. He gave me to understand he was charged with protecting the good name of the Princess and of Lord and Lady Wellborough."

There was a murmur of anger from the crowd. One of the jurors pursed his lips.

"Did he! Did he indeed?" Harvester said sarcastically. "Well, that may be so, but I can tell you without doubt, Doctor, that he has no connection whatever with the Princess Gisela, and I shall be amazed if he had any with Lord and Lady Wellborough. Their reputations are in no danger, nor ever have been."

Gallagher said nothing.

"On reflection, Doctor," Harvester continued, walking a few paces and turning back, "do you now still feel that your original diagnosis was correct? Did Prince Friedrich die as a result of injuries sustained in his accident, and possibly exacerbated by a fit of coughing or sneezing?"

"I really do not know. It would be impossible to be certain without an autopsy on the body."

There was a gasp around the room. A woman in the gallery shrieked. One of the jurors looked extremely distressed, as if it were about to happen right in front of him, there and then.

"Is there anything to prove it cannot have been an injury which was the cause, Dr. Gallagher?" Harvester demanded.

"No, of course not! If there were I should not have signed the certificate."

"Of course not," Harvester agreed vehemently, spreading his hands. "Oh, one more thing. I assume you called upon the Prince very regularly while he was recuperating?"

"Naturally. I went every day. Twice a day for almost the first week after the accident, then as he progressed well and the fever abated, only once."

"How long after the accident did he die?"

"Eight days."

"And during that time, who, to your knowledge, cared for him?"

"Every time I called, the Princess was there. She appeared to attend to his every need."

Harvester's voice dropped a fraction and became very precise. "Nursing need, Doctor, or do you mean that she also cooked his food?"

There was silence in the room. It hammered in the ears. The chamber was so crowded with people they were jammed together in the seats, fabric rubbing on fabric, the wool gabardine of gentlemen's coats against the taffeta and bombazine of women's gowns, suits and wraps. But for all the sound they might have been waxworks.

"No," Gallagher said firmly. "She did not cook. I was led to understand she did not have the art. And since she was a princess, one could hardly have expected it of her. I was told she never went to the kitchens. Indeed, I was told she never left the suite of rooms from the time he was brought to them until after he had died . . . in fact, not for some days after that. She was distraught with grief."

"Thank you, Dr. Gallagher," Harvester said graciously. "You have been most clear. That is all I wish to ask you presently. No doubt Sir Oliver will have some point to raise, if you will be so good as to remain where you are."

Gallagher turned to face Rathbone as he rose and came forward. Monk had mentioned the yew trees at Wellborough to him, and he had done his research. He must not antagonize the man if he wished to learn anything of use. And he must forget Zorah, leaning forward and listening to every word, her eyes on him.

"I think we can all appreciate your position, Dr. Gallagher," he began with a faint smile. "You had no cause whatever to suppose the case was other than as you were told. No one expects or foresees that in such a household, with such people, there will be anything that is untoward or other than as it should be. You would have been criticized for the grossest offensiveness and insensitivity had you implied otherwise, even in the slightest manner. But with the wisdom of hindsight, and now having some idea of the political situation involved, let us reexamine what you saw and heard and see if it still bears the same interpretation."

He frowned apologetically. "I regret doing this. It can only be painful for all those present, but I am sure you perceive the absolute necessity for having the truth. If murder was done, it must be proved, and those who are guilty must account."

He looked quite deliberately at the jury, then at Gisela, sitting bleak-faced and composed next to Harvester.

"And if there were no crime at all, simply a tragedy, then we must prove that also, and silence forever the whispers of evil that have spread all over Europe. The innocent also are entitled to our protection, and we must honor that trust."

He turned back to the witness stand before Harvester could complain that he was making speeches.

"Dr. Gallagher, what precisely were the symptoms of Prince Friedrich's last few hours and of his death? I would spare everyone's feelings if I could, most of all those of his widow, but this must be."

Gallagher said nothing for a moment or two. He seemed to be marshaling his ideas, setting them right in his mind before he began.

"Do you wish to refer to notes, Dr. Gallagher?" the judge inquired.

"No, thank you, my lord. It is a case I shall not forget." He drew in a deep breath and cleared his throat huskily. "On the day the Prince was taken more seriously ill, I was summoned earlier than I had expected to call. A servant from Wellborough Hall came to my house and requested that I come immediately, as Prince Friedrich was showing symptoms of considerable distress. I asked what they were, and he told me he was feverish, had a very severe headache and was nauseous, and was experiencing great internal pain. Of course, I went immediately."

"You had no patients at that time?"

"One. An elderly gentleman with the gout, a chronic condition for which I could do little but advise him to abstain from Port wine. Advice he declined to take."

There was a nervous titter around the gallery, and then silence again.

"And how did you find Prince Friedrich when you saw him, Dr. Gallagher?" Rathbone asked.

"Much as the manservant had said," Gallagher replied. "By then he was in severe pain and had vomited. Unfortunately, in the cause of decency the vomitus had not been kept, so I was unable to ascertain the degree of blood in it, but the Princess told me it was considerable. She feared he was bleeding heavily, and she was in very great distress. Indeed, she seemed to be in greater agony of emotion than he was of body."

"Did he vomit again while you were there?"

"No. Very shortly after I arrived he fell into a kind of delirium. He seemed very weak. His skin was cold to the touch, clammy, and of a blotchy appearance. His pulse was erratic, insofar as it could be found at all, and he was in great internal pain. I admit I . . . I was in fear for his life from that time on. I held very little hope he could recover." He was ashen himself, and looking at his rigid stance and agonized face, Rathbone could well imagine the scene as Gallagher had struggled desperately to help the dying man, knowing he was beyond all human aid, watching his suffering and unable to relieve it. It was a profession Rathbone could never have followed himself. He vastly preferred to deal with the anguish and injustices of the mind, the complications of the law and its battles.

"I imagine everyone here can conceive your distress, Doctor," he said aloud and with sincere respect. "We can only be grateful we were not in your place. What happened next?"

"Prince Friedrich failed rapidly," Gallagher answered. "He grew colder and weaker. The pain seemed to subside, and he slipped into a coma from which he did not recover. He died at about quarter to four that afternoon."

"And you concluded from what you had seen, and what you already knew of the case, that he had bled to death internally?"

"Yes."

"A not-unnatural conclusion, given the circumstances as they were then," Rathbone agreed. "But tell me, Dr. Gallagher, looking back now, is there anything whatever in those symptoms which is indicative not of internal bleeding but of poison? For example, the poison from the bark or leaves of the yew tree?"

There was a sharp intake of breath around the room. Someone gave a little squeal. A juror looked very distressed.

Zorah fidgeted and frowned.

As always, Gisela remained impassive, but her face was so bloodless she might have been dead herself, a marble figure of a woman.

Rathbone put his hands in his pockets and smiled sadly, still facing the witness. "In case you have had no occasion recently to remind yourself of what those are, Doctor, let me enumerate them—for the court, if not for you. They are giddiness, diarrhea, dilation of the pupils of the eyes, pain in the stomach and nausea, weakness, pallor of the skin, convulsions, coma and death."

Gallagher closed his eyes, and Rathbone thought he swayed a little in the stand.

The judge was staring at him intensely.

One of the jurors had his hand up to his face.

Gisela sat like stone, drained as if all that mattered to her, all that gave her life, had already left her.

In the gallery, a woman was weeping quietly.

Zorah's face was pinched with unhappiness. She looked as if she had lived through the pain and grief of the day all over again.

"There was no diarrhea," Gallagher said very slowly. "Unless it occurred before I arrived and I was not told. There were no convulsions."

"And dilation of the pupils, Dr. Gallagher?" Rathbone almost held his breath. He could feel his own pulse beating.

"Yes . . ." Gallagher's voice was little more than a whisper. He coughed, and coughed again. "Yes, there was dilation of the pupils of the eyes." He looked wretched.

"And is that a symptom of bleeding to death, Doctor?" Rathbone kept all criticism from his voice. It was easy . . . he did not feel it. He doubted any man in Gallagher's place would have thought of it.

Gallagher breathed out with a sigh. "No. No, it is not."

There was a gasp in the gallery.

The judge's face tightened, and he watched Rathbone gravely.

"Dr. Gallagher," Rathbone said in the prickling silence, "are you still of the opinion that Prince Friedrich died as a result of bleeding to death from the wounds sustained in his fall?"

The jurors stared at Gisela and then at Zorah.

Zorah clenched her fists and moved forward an inch.

"No sir, I am not," Gallagher answered.

There was a shriek from the gallery and the gasping of breath. Apparently someone fainted, because several people started to rise to their feet and jostle to make space.

"Give her air!" a man commanded.

"Here! Smelling salts," someone else offered.

"Burn a feather!" came the call. "Ushers! Water!"

"Brandy! Has anyone a flask of brandy? Oh, thank you, sir!"

The judge waited until the woman had been assisted, then gave Rathbone leave to continue.

"Thank you, my lord," Rathbone acknowledged.

"Can you name the cause of death, Dr. Gallagher, in your best judgment? So long after the event, and without any further examination, we appreciate you can only guess."

The movement in the gallery ceased abruptly. The fainting woman was ignored.

"I would guess, sir, that it was the poison of the yew tree," Gallagher said wretchedly. "I profoundly regret that I did not realize it at the time. I tender my apologies to Princess Gisela and to the court."

"I am sure no person of sensibility blames you, Doctor," Rathbone said frankly. "Which of us would have thought on the death of a prince, in the home of a respected member of the aristocracy, to look for poison? I most certainly would not, and if any man here says he would, I would beg leave to take issue with him."

"Thank you," Gallagher said painfully. "You are very generous, Sir Oliver. But medicine is my duty and my calling. I should have observed the eyes and had the courage and the diligence to pursue the discrepancy."

"You have had the courage now, sir, and we are obliged to you for it. That is all I have to ask you."

Harvester rose to his feet. He looked pale and less certain than at the beginning of the day. He did not move with the same ease.

"Dr. Gallagher, you are now of the opinion that the poison of the yew tree was the cause of Prince Friedrich's death. Can you tell us how it was administered?"

"It would have been ingested," Gallagher replied. "In either food or drink."

"It is pleasant to the taste?"

"I have no idea. I should imagine not."

"What form would it take? Liquid? Solid? Leaves? Fruit?"

"A liquid distilled from the leaves or the bark."

"Not the fruit?"

"No sir. Curiously enough, the fruit is the one part of the yew tree which is not poisonous—even the seeds themselves are toxic. But in any case, Prince Friedrich died in the spring, when trees do not fruit."

"A distillation?" Harvester persisted.

"Yes," Gallagher agreed. "No one would eat yew leaves or bark."

"So it would have been necessary for someone to gather the leaves, or the bark, and boil them for a considerable time?"

"Yes."

"And yet you told us that the Princess never went to the kitchens. Did she have apparatus in her rooms in which she could have done such a thing?"

"I believe not."

"Could she have done it over the bedroom fire?"

"No, of course not. Apart from anything else, it would have been observed."

"Was there a hob on the bedroom fire?"

"No."

"Did she go out and gather the bark or the needles of the yew trees?"

"I don't know. I believe she did not leave the Prince's side."

"Does it seem to you reasonable to suppose that she had either the means or the opportunity to poison her husband, Dr. Gallagher? Or, for that matter, any motive whatsoever?"

"No, it does not."

"Thank you, Dr. Gallagher." Harvester turned away from the witness stand to face the courtroom. "Unless the Countess Rostova knows some major fact of which we are unaware, and she has chosen to keep it from the authorities, it would seem she cannot believe so either, and her accusation is false, and she knows it as well as we do!"

* * *

Henry Rathbone had been in court that day, as he had the day before. Oliver visited him in the evening. He had an intense desire to get out of the city and as far away as was practical from the courtroom and all that had happened in it. He rode through the sharp, gusty late autumn evening towards Primrose Hill. The traffic was light, and his hansom made swift progress.

He arrived a little after nine and found Henry sitting beside a blazing fire and looking at a book on philosophy, upon which he seemed unable to concentrate. He put it down as soon as Oliver entered the room. His face was bleak with concern.

"Port?" he asked, gesturing towards the bottle on the small table beside his chair. There was only one glass, but there were others in the cabinet by the wall. The curtains were drawn against the rain-spattered night. They were the same brown velvet curtains that had been there for the last twenty years.

Oliver sat down. "Not yet, thank you," he declined. "Maybe later."

"I was in court today," Henry said after a few moments. "You don't need to explain it to me." He did not ask what Oliver was going to do next.

"I didn't see you. I'm sorry." Oliver stared into the fire. Perhaps he should have taken the Port. He was colder than he had thought. The taste would have been good, its heat going down his throat.

"I didn't want to distract you from your task," Henry replied. "But I thought you might want to talk about it later. Easier if I had been there. It isn't only what is said, it's the way people react to it."

Oliver looked across at him. "And you are going to tell me that the crowd is with Gisela . . . the poor bereaved widow. I know. And as far as I can see, they are right. Monk thinks it is political and whoever did it actually intended to kill Gisela, to free Friedrich to return home and lead the party for independence, but somehow the plan misfired and the wrong person took the poison."

"Possibly," Henry said with a frown puckering his forehead. "I hope you aren't going to say anything so foolish in court?"

"I don't think it's foolish," Oliver said immediately. "I think he's probably right. The Queen hated Gisela with a passion, but she had an equal passion to have Friedrich back, both to lead the party of independence and to marry a wife who would give him an heir to the throne. The other son has no children."

Henry looked puzzled. "I thought Friedrich had several sisters."

"Doesn't pass through the female line," Oliver replied, easing himself a little more comfortably in the chair.

"Then change it till it does!" Henry said impatiently. "A lot simpler and less dangerous than murdering Gisela and trying to deal with a bereaved Friedrich and put more backbone into him to make him lead a battle which will take all the courage and skill and determination anyone could have. And even then which may be a lost cause. You need a miracle for that, not a man who has just lost the love of his life and who may well be intelligent enough to realize who was responsible for that."

Oliver stared at his father speechlessly. He had not thought so far ahead. If they had succeeded in killing Gisela, surely Friedrich would have at the very least been suspicious of them?

"Maybe it was not the Queen, or Rolf, but some fanatic without the brains to foresee what would happen?" he said hesitantly.

Henry raised his eyebrows. "And were there many of them at Wellborough Hall with access to the Prince's food?"

Oliver did not bother to reply.

The fire caved in with a shower of sparks, and Henry picked up the tongs and placed several more coals in it, then sat back again.

"Who will Harvester call tomorrow?" he asked, fishing for

his pipe and putting it absentmindedly into his mouth without even pretending to light it.

"I don't know," Oliver replied, his mind almost numb.

"Could Gisela be guilty?" Henry pressed. "Is there any way in which it is possible . . . even supposing she did indeed have motive?"

"The servants," Oliver said, answering the earlier question. "Harvester'll call the household servants from Wellborough Hall. They'll almost certainly testify that after the accident Gisela never left the suite of rooms they had."

"Truthfully?"

"Yes . . . I think so."

Henry took the pipe out of his mouth. His slippers were so near the fire the soles were beginning to scorch, but he had not noticed, his mind was so intent on the problem.

"Then she cannot be guilty," he said frankly. "Unless one supposes she habitually carries distillation of yew about with her, or else that she planned this from before the accident. Either of which supposition would require total proof before anyone at all is even going to entertain it."

"I know," Oliver conceded quickly. "It wasn't she."

They sat in silence again except for the ticking of the tall clock against the wall and the comfortable flickering of the fire.

"Your feet are burning," Oliver remarked absently.

Henry moved them, wincing as he became aware of the hot soles.

"Then you must find out who it was," the older man said.

"Either Rolf or Brigitte, if it was meant to be Gisela in order to free Friedrich to return home, or Klaus von Seidlitz, if Friedrich was the right victim—to prevent his return."

"You have not yet proved that there was a conspiracy," Henry pointed out. "You can't leave that to assumption. The jury won't return any verdict which indicates that if you don't show it."

"It doesn't matter," Oliver said miserably. "The charge is

slander, and they can only bring in a verdict that she is guilty, because she is guilty. I might manage to persuade them she did it to expose the fact that he was murdered and she dared not accuse anyone else—or that somehow she originally imagined it could have been Gisela, although I can't think anyone would believe that. One would only have to ask her why she thought so; she does not provide a single coherent answer."

He got up and went over to the cabinet, opened it and took out a glass. He returned to the fire, filled his glass with Port, and sat down.

"I daren't call her to the stand. She'll hang herself."

Henry stared at him.

"Sorry," Oliver apologized for the exaggeration. Henry hated overstatement. "Would you like some more?" He gestured towards the decanter of Port.

"She may indeed." Henry ignored the Port as if he had not heard. "She may do exactly that, Oliver, if you are not very careful. If you don't prove a plot to return Friedrich, and even if you do, the question is going to arise: Did Zorah kill him herself? Did she have the opportunity?"

"Yes." Even the Port could not help the deepening chill inside him.

"Could she have obtained the yew and distilled it?"

"She could certainly have obtained it. Anyone could, except Gisela. We haven't found out yet how it was distilled. That is the biggest break in the chain of evidence. The kitchen staff seem quite sure no one used the kitchen for it. But she is no better or worse than anyone else in that aspect."

"Had she the motive?"

"I don't know, but it won't be hard to suggest several, from personal jealousy and resentment for Gisela's marrying Friedrich twelve years ago," Oliver answered, "to political hatred because Gisela was the one person stopping Friedrich from returning home to lead the battle for independence—or, for that matter, stopping him from having filled his duty to be king in the first place."

"So the answer is very much that she had a motive—the oldest in the world and the easiest to understand." Henry shook his head. "Oliver, I am afraid you and your client have created for yourself an extremely unpleasant situation. You are going to be very fortunate indeed if she escapes the threat of the gallows in this."

Oliver said nothing. He knew it was true.

As Rathbone had foreseen, Harvester spent the entire next day calling the servants from Wellborough Hall. He must have been prepared for the necessity, unless he had sent someone for them the day before, after court adjourned, and they had traveled all night—assuming there were trains at night from that part of Berkshire.

It all confirmed Rathbone's worst expectations. Servant after servant took the stand, very sober, very frightened, dressed in their Sunday best, transparently honest, twisting their hands in embarrassment.

The Princess Gisela had at no time left the suite of rooms she occupied with the Prince, God rest his soul. No one had ever seen her on the other side of the green baize door. She had certainly never been into the kitchens. Cook swore to that, so did the kitchen maid, both scullery maids, the pastry cook, the bootboy and three of the footmen, the butler and the housekeeper, two parlormaids, four housemaids and two tweenies. One lady's maid spoke on behalf of three upstairs maids, a valet and three laundresses.

The Princess Gisela had been seen outside her rooms by no one at all, and there was almost always someone about.

On the other hand, there were unquestionably yew trees in the gardens, several of them.

"And could any person who walked in the gardens have

access to these yew trees?" Harvester asked the housekeeper, a comfortable, good-tempered woman with graying fair hair.

"Yes sir. The yew walk is a most agreeable place, and a natural way to it if one wishes a little time alone. It leads up towards the best views across the fields."

"So it would not occasion surprise to see anyone there, even walking alone?" Harvester said cautiously.

"No sir."

"Did you ever see or hear of anyone in particular walking there?"

"I'm far too busy with a house full of guests to be looking out of windows seeing who's out walking, sir. But a good sunny day, an' it was a very nice spring, most of the guests would be out at one time or another."

"Except the Princess Gisela?"

"Yes sir, 'cept her, poor lady."

"The Countess Rostova, for example?"

"Yes sir," she said more cautiously. "Liked a good walk. Not a lady to sit inside the house on a fine day."

"And after his accident, were the Prince's meals taken up from the kitchen to his rooms regularly?"

"Always, sir. He never came out. Sometimes it was no more than a little beef tea, but it was always sent up."

"Carried by a maid or a footman?"

"Maid, sir."

"And might such a maid pass another guest on the stairs or on the landing?"

"Yes sir."

"And would automatically stand aside and make way for such a guest?"

"Of course."

"Guests might pass closely enough on the stairs for something to be surreptitiously added to a dish by sleight of hand?"

"I don't know, sir. Dishes should be covered on a tray, and a cloth over them as well."

"But possible, Mrs. Haines?"

"I suppose so."

"Thank you." Harvester turned to Rathbone. "Sir Oliver?"

But Rathbone could make no argument of any value. There was nothing to contradict. He himself had proved that Friedrich was poisoned. Harvester had proved that it could not have been by Gisela. Rathbone could not implicate anyone else. It would be an act of desperation to suggest a name, and looking at the jurors, he was wise enough to know any attempt to lay specific blame could rebound against him. He had not yet irrefutably argued a plot to restore Friedrich, and it would be a plot, because it would automatically depose Waldo. No one was going to admit to it in the present climate. It would be political suicide, and anyone passionate enough about the struggle might sacrifice himself or herself in its cause, but never sacrifice the cause itself, and certainly not to save Zorah.

Harvester smiled. He had sought to protect Gisela by proving her innocence, and thus Zorah's guilt of slander. Now he was on the brink of seeing Zorah indicted, at least in the public mind, of murder. And unless Rathbone found some way of proving the contrary, it might be in law as well.

By the time the day was ended, Henry Rathbone was correct—Zorah herself was close to the shadow of the gibbet.

As the court rose, press reporters burst through the doors and raced for the hansoms outside, shouting out to drivers to take them to Fleet Street. The crowds craned their necks and surged forward to see Gisela and cheer her, shout out blessings and encouragement, praise and admiration.

For Zorah, there were cries of hatred. Rotten fruit and vegetables were thrown. More than one stone cracked sharply against the wall behind her, and she made her way, ashen-faced, head high, eyes terrified, to where Rathbone had ordered a coach to wait. He knew he dared not trust to finding a hansom in that enraged throng which was now threatening physical violence.

"Hang 'er!" someone yelled. "Hang the murderin' bitch!"

" 'Ang 'er!" the crowd roared. " 'Ang 'er! 'Ang 'er by 'er neck! Send 'er ter the rope!"

It was only with great difficulty and some buffeting that Rathbone managed to guide her to the coach and help her up into it, bruised and breathless.

She sat close beside him as the coach lurched forward and the horses stepped and jibbed, trying to make their way through the pressing bodies. Hands reached up for the harness, and the driver cracked his whip. There was a howl of rage, and the coach plunged forward again, throwing Zorah and Rathbone off balance. Without thinking, he put out his hand to steady her and kept hold of her. He could not think of anything to say. He wanted to be able to tell her it would be all right, somehow or other he would rescue them both, but he knew of no way, and she would not have been comforted by a lie, only angered.

She looked at him gratefully but without hope.

"I did not kill him," she said, her voice barely audible over the rattling of the wheels and the roaring of the crowd behind them, but perfectly steady. "She did!"

Rathbone felt a chill of despair settle over his heart.

Hester also traveled home from the court in a state of profound misery. She was deeply afraid for Rathbone, and the more desperately she tried to think of a way out for him, the less could she see one.

She went in through the front door at Hill Street shivering with cold, although it was quite a mild afternoon; she felt so crushed she had no heart to give herself energy.

She did not want to speak to either Bernd or Dagmar, and she was sure they would have arrived home before she did. They had their own carriage, and they had not stayed to the bitter end to see Rathbone and Zorah mobbed as they left, bearing the rage and the hatred of the crowd.

She went straight upstairs to her room, and after taking off her outer cape, knocked on Robert's door, which was ajar.

"Come in?" he said immediately.

She opened the door and was surprised to see Victoria sitting in the easy chair and Robert in his wheelchair, not on the bed. They looked at her eagerly, but there was no tension in them, and their chairs were close together, as though they had been talking earnestly before she knocked. Robert's face was not pale anymore. The late autumn sun and wind had given him color as he had sat out in the garden, and his hair, flopping forward over his brow, was shining. It really was time they had a barber in to cut it.

"What happened?" he asked. Then he frowned. "It wasn't good, was it? I can see it in your face. Come and tell us." He indicated a second bedroom chair. His eyes were full of concern.

She was aware of the warmth of his feeling. Suddenly she was furious that someone she liked so much should be crippled, confined to a chair, almost certainly for the rest of his life, denied the chance of a career, of love and marriage, the things his peers expected as a matter of course. She found herself almost choked with emotion.

"Was it really as bad as that?" Robert said gently. "You'd better sit down. Would you like me to ring for a tray of tea? You look pretty upset."

She tried to force a smile and knew she had failed.

"You don't have to pretend," Robert went on. "Is the verdict in already? It can't be, can it?"

"Did she withdraw?" Victoria asked, puzzled.

"No. No, she didn't withdraw," Hester replied, sitting down. "And the verdict is a long way off yet. Sir Oliver hasn't even started. But I can't see that it will help when he does. It has reached the stage now where Zorah will be fighting to keep from the gallows herself . . ."

Thcy both stared at her.

"Zorah?" Robert said aghast. "But Zorah didn't kill him! If she had, she would be the last person to mention murder. She'd be only too happy they all thought it was accidental. That doesn't make any sense!"

"Perhaps they don't think she is sensible," Victoria pointed out. "They may think she's a fanatic, or hysterical. I know that they are saying she is very eccentric, and that she dresses in men's clothes and has been to all sorts of unsuitable and indecent places. And of course they are suggesting that her morals are appalling."

Hester was startled that Victoria should be aware of such things. How on earth did she know? Then she remembered Victoria's drastically altered circumstances. She must have come down so far in the world that she no longer had anything like the life of the young lady she had been before her family's disgrace, and no doubt now also financial dependency upon relatives. She was probably far better acquainted with the harsher side of life and its realities than Robert was.

He was staring at Victoria, and she colored unhappily.

"Who is saying that?" he asked her. "That's totally unjust."

"When people are angry, justice has very little part in it," she replied quietly.

"Why should they be angry?" He frowned. "She may have injured Gisela, but the verdict isn't in yet. And if it was murder, then they should be grateful to her, whoever is guilty. At least she has brought the truth about that to light. It seems to me they are doing exactly what they are blaming her for . . . jumping to conclusions without hearing the facts, and condemning people without evidence. That's totally hypocritical."

Victoria smiled. "Of course it is," she agreed gently. Her eyes were soft and bright as she looked at him.

Robert turned to Hester. "What about your friend, Sir Oliver? How is he? He must be feeling very badly that he cannot help, especially if it is as serious for her as you say."

"I don't think he has any idea what to do for the best,"

Hester said frankly. "He has to prove it was someone else to save the Countess, and we haven't any proof."

"I'm sorry."

Victoria rose to her feet, moving with great awkwardness as the pain caught her, then straightening again and hiding it so Robert should not see. "It is getting late, and I should leave. I am sure you must be tired after the disasters of the day. I shall leave you to talk. Perhaps some idea may come to you." She looked at Robert, hesitating a moment, blinking, and then making herself smile again. "Good night." And then quite suddenly she turned on her heel and went out of the door, closing it behind her clumsily. The expression in her eyes and in her voice, the color in her face, had betrayed her feelings, and Hester had read them as plainly as if they had been spoken in words, perhaps more plainly. Words can lie.

She looked at Robert. His mouth was pinched, and his eyes were dark with pain. He stared down at his legs, placed on the chair for him by the footman. One foot was a trifle crooked, and he was powerless even to straighten it. Hester saw it, but to lift it for him would be an intolerable reminder at this moment.

"Thank you for bringing me Victoria," he said quickly. "I think I shall always love her. I wish I had anything on earth I could give her that compared with what she has given me." He breathed out. "But I haven't." He hesitated. "If I could walk . . . If I could only stand!" His voice broke, and for long, aching moments he had to fight to retain his self-control.

Hester knew that Victoria had told him nothing of her own griefs. It was an acutely private thing, and yet Robert was suffering, and perhaps he would allow both their happiness to slip away from them because he believed they were so unequal and he was worth nothing to her.

Hester spoke very quietly. Perhaps this was a mistake, an irretrievable error, the breaking of a trust, but she told him.

"You can give her love. There is no gift as great—"

He swung his shoulders around, glaring at her with rage and

frustration and pain in his eyes, and something agonizing which she thought was shame.

"Love!" he said bitterly. "With all my heart . . . but that's hardly enough, is it? I can't look after her. I can't support or protect her. I can't love her as a man loves a woman! 'With my body I thee worship!' " His voice cracked with unshed tears and loneliness and helplessness. "I can't give her love; I can't give her children!"

"Nor can she give such things to you," Hester said softly, longing to touch his hand and knowing it was not the time. "She was raped as a girl, and as a result of that had a backstreet abortion. It was very badly done, and she has never healed. That is the cause of her affliction, her constant pain, and at some times of the month it is worse than at others. She cannot ever have marital relations, and she certainly could not bear a child."

He was ashen white. He stared at her with horror so great his body shook, his hands clenched and unclenched in his lap, and she thought for a moment he was going to be sick.

"Raped?" he choked. His face filled with feelings of such violence and horror she hated herself for having told him. He despised Victoria. Like so many others, he felt she was unclean, not a victim but somehow a vessel which had invited and deserved its own spoiling. In telling him she had made a fearful misjudgment, irreparable.

She looked at Robert again.

His eyes were brimming with tears.

"She suffered that!" he whispered. "And all the time she was here, she was thinking of me . . . How . . . how could you have let me be so selfish?"

Now without thinking she grasped his hand and held it. "It wasn't selfishness," she said urgently. "You couldn't know, and really I had no right to tell you. It is a very private thing. I . . . I couldn't bear you thinking—" She stopped. That would certainly be better unspoken.

He smiled at her suddenly. "I know."

She did not know whether he knew or not, and she was certainly not about to put it to the test.

"I shan't tell her you told me," he promised. "At least not yet. It would embarrass her, wouldn't it." That was a statement, not a question. "And I shall not tell my parents. It is not my secret to share, and I think they may not see it as it should be seen."

She knew he was certainly right about that. Bernd did not consider Victoria Stanhope a suitable friend for his son in any permanent sense, let alone more than that. But relief overwhelmed her like a great and blessed warmth, a taste of sweetness.

"Isn't she the most beautiful woman you've ever seen?" Robert said earnestly, his eyes bright and gentle. "Thank you for bringing her to me, Hester. I shall be grateful to you forever for that."

11

RATHBONE BEGAN HIS DEFENSE of Zorah Rostova with a kind of despair. At the beginning, his worst fear had been that he would not be able to save her from disgrace and possibly a considerable financial punishment. He had hoped to be able to mitigate it by showing that her intention had been mistaken but honorable.

Now he was struggling to save her from the rope.

The court was packed till the room seemed airless, the people so tightly crammed together one could hear the rub of fabric on fabric, the squeak of boots, the creak of whalebone as women breathed. He could smell damp wool from a thousand coats come in from the rain. The floor was slippery with drips and puddles. Every scrap of air seemed already to have been breathed before. The windows steamed up with the exhalation.

Pressmen sat elbow to elbow, hardly able to move sufficiently to write. Pencils were sharp, licked ready. Paper was damp in shaking hands.

The jury was somber. One man with white whiskers fidgeted constantly with his handkerchief. Another smiled fleetingly at Gisela and then looked quickly away again. None looked at Zorah.

The judge instructed Rathbone to begin.

Rathbone rose to his feet and called Stephan von Emden.

The usher repeated the name, and his voice was swallowed by the thick, crowded room. There was no echo.

Everyone waited, necks craned. Their eyes followed him as he came in, crossed the floor and climbed the steps to the stand. Since he had been called for the defense, it was assumed he was in Zorah's favor. The animosity could be felt in a wave of anger from the gallery.

He was sworn in.

Rathbone moved forward, feeling more vulnerable than he could ever remember in all the countless times he had done this. He had had bad cases before, clients about whom he felt dubious, clients in whom he believed but felt inadequate to defend. Never before had he been so aware of his own misjudgments and his own fallibility. He did not even feel confident he would not add to them today. The only thing he believed in totally was Hester's loyalty to him, not that she thought he was right but that she would be there at his side to support him regardless, whatever the nature or degree of his defeat. How blind of him to have taken so long to see that beauty in her—or to realize its worth.

"Sir Oliver?" the judge prompted.

The court was waiting. He must begin, whatever he had to say, of how much or how little use. Had they any idea how lost he was? Looking at Harvester's lean face and the expression on it, he was sure the other lawyer knew very well. There was even a kind of pity in him, though without the slightest suggestion he would stay his hand.

"Baron von Emden"—Rathbone cleared his throat—"you were staying at Wellborough Hall when Prince Friedrich met with his accident, and during the time of his apparent convalescence, and then his death, were you not?"

"Yes sir, I was," Stephan agreed. He looked calm and very grave with his clear hazel eyes and the smooth tawny hair which fell a little forward over his right brow.

"Who else was there?" Rathbone asked. "Apart from the household staff, of course."

"The Baron and Baroness von Seidlitz, Count Rolf Lansdorff—"

"He is the brother of Queen Ulrike, is he not?" Rathbone interrupted. "The uncle of Prince Friedrich?"

"Yes."

"Who else?"

"Baroness Brigitte von Arlsbach, Florent Barberini and the Countess Rostova," Stephan finished.

"Please continue," Rathbone said.

Stephan went on. "Colonel and Mrs. Warboys from one of the neighboring houses were guests for dinner two or three times, and their three daughters, and Sir George and Lady Oldham, and one or two others whose names I forget."

Harvester was frowning, but he had not so far interrupted. Rathbone knew he would, if he did not make some relevant point soon.

"Did it surprise you to find Baroness von Arlsbach and Count Lansdorff invited to the same house party with Prince Friedrich and Princess Gisela?" he asked. "It was well known that when Prince Friedrich left his own country the feeling was not entirely kind towards him, especially from the royal household, and indeed from the Baroness, whom it is said the country would have liked for queen. Is that untrue?"

"No," Stephan answered with obvious reluctance. It was an embarrassing subject, one which for both personal and patriotic reasons he would rather not have discussed publicly, and his emotions showed in his face.

"Then were you surprised?" Rathbone pressed, some future scene with the Lord Chancellor playing itself out in his mind like an execution.

"I would have been, were the political situation not as it is," Stephan answered.

"Would you please explain that?"

Harvester rose to his feet. "My lord, the guest list is not an issue. There is no question as to who was present, or was not. Sir Oliver is desperate and wasting time."

The judge turned his bland face towards Harvester. "It is up to me to decide how the court may use its time, Mr. Harvester. I am disposed to allow Sir Oliver a little latitude in the matter, so long as he does not abuse it, given that this is an adversarial system. I am still primarily interested in establishing the truth as to whether Prince Friedrich was murdered, and if so, by whom. When we know that, we can then apportion blame appropriately to the Countess Rostova regarding her accusation."

But Harvester was far from satisfied. "My lord, we have already proved that the one person who could not be guilty is my client, the Princess Gisela. Quite apart from her devotion to her husband, her utter lack of motive, we have also demonstrated that she was the one person who had not the means or the opportunity."

"I have been present all the time the evidence has been given, Mr. Harvester," the judge replied. "Do you imagine I have not been directing my mind to it?"

There was a distinct mutter of amusement around the gallery, and several jurors smiled.

"No, my lord! Of course not!" Harvester was in some discomposure. It was the first time Rathbone could recall ever seeing him thus.

The judge smiled very slightly. "Good. Proceed, Sir Oliver."

Rathbone inclined his head in acknowledgment, but he was under no illusion that the latitude would be wide.

"Baron von Emden, would you explain to us the alteration in the political situation which made the guest list understandable to you?"

"Twelve years ago, when Friedrich abdicated in favor of his younger brother, Waldo, so he could marry Gisela Berentz, whom the royal family would not accept as crown princess, the feeling against him was strong. It was even stronger against her," Stephan said in a calm, level voice, but one in which the memory of pain and embarrassment was sharp. "The Queen, in particular, did not forgive the injury it did to the royal house. Her brother, Count Lansdorff, shared her feelings very deeply. So did the Baroness von Arlsbach. As you observed, many in the country had wished and expected Friedrich to marry her. It was embarrassing for her because there was every indication that she would have obeyed her duty and accepted him."

He looked unhappy, but he did not hesitate. "Baron and Baroness von Seidlitz, on the other hand, went frequently to Venice, where Prince Friedrich and Princess Gisela had made their principal home, with the result that they were not in any true sense accepted at court in Felzburg."

"Are you saying that the feelings of resentment, betrayal, or whatever you will, were so deep that even after twelve years, it is still impossible to be a true friend of both parties?" Rathbone asked.

Stephan thought for a moment.

The judge was watching him.

The room was almost silent. There was the occasional creak or rustle of shifting in seats.

Gisela sat rigid. For once there was emotion in her face, as if mention of that old humiliation still tore open a wound. There was tightening of her lips. Her gloved hands clenched. But there was no way of knowing whether it was her rejection or Friedrich's which she remembered.

"It was not entirely a matter of feelings from the past," Stephan answered, looking directly at Rathbone. "New political situations have arisen which make all the old issues of very urgent, current importance."

Harvester moved uncomfortably, but he knew it was useless to object. He would only mark it more clearly in the mind.

"Would you explain, please?" Rathbone pressed.

"My country is one of a large number of German states,

principalities, and electorates." Stephan addressed the court in general. "We have a language and a culture in common, and there is a movement gathering strength for us to unite under one king and one government. Naturally, in all the separate entities there are those who can see the benefits such a unity would bring and those who will fight with all they possess to retain their individual character and independence. My own country is as divided as any. Even the royal family is divided."

Now he had their total attention. Several jurors were shaking their heads. As citizens of an island nation, they could understand, at least with their heads, the passion for independence. With their hearts, they had no concept of the fear of being swallowed. It had not happened to them in fifty generations.

"Yes?" Rathbone prompted him.

Stephan obviously disliked having to expose the division in public, but he knew there was no alternative.

"The Queen and Count Rolf are passionately for independence," he replied. "Crown Prince Waldo is for unification."

"And the Baroness von Arlsbach?"

"Independence."

"Baron von Seidlitz?"

"Unification."

"How do you know this?"

"He has made no secret of it."

"He has advocated it?"

"Not openly, not as far as that. But he has argued its possible merits. He has become friends with many of those who are highly placed in Prussia."

There was a murmur of disapproval in the court. It was perhaps emotional rather than a matter of considered thought.

"And what were Prince Friedrich's feelings on the subject?" Rathbone asked. "Did he express any that you are aware of?"

"He was for independence."

"Sufficiently so to act towards that end?"

Stephan bit his lip. "I don't know. But I do know that this is why Count Lansdorff came to Wellborough Hall to speak to him. Otherwise he would normally have declined any invitation to be in the same house with Friedrich."

The judge's face pinched with concern, and he looked very steadily at Rathbone as if he were on the brink of interrupting him, but he did not.

"Did he initiate the meeting or did Prince Friedrich, do you know?" Rathbone asked, acutely aware of what he was doing.

"I believe it was Count Lansdorff."

"You say you believe it. Do you not know?"

"No, I don't know, not beyond doubt."

"And Baron von Seidlitz, why was he there, if his views were opposite? Was some kind of debate planned, an open discussion?"

Stephan smiled briefly. "Of course not. It is all only speculation. I don't know if any talks took place at all . . . which is probably why Klaus von Seidlitz was there . . . in order to conceal the political aspects of the occasion."

"What about Countess Rostova and Mr. Barberini?"

"They are both for independence," Stephan replied. "But Barberini is half Venetian, so he appeared a natural person to invite since Friedrich and Gisela live in Venice. It gave it the appearance of an ordinary spring house party."

"But it was—in reality, beneath the festivities, the parties and picnics, the hunting, the theatrical evenings, the music and the dinner parties—a deeply political gathering?"

"Yes."

He knew Stephan could not say any offer had been made to Friedrich, or any plea, so he did not ask.

"Thank you, Baron von Emden." He turned to Harvester.

Harvester rose, his expression a curious mixture of anger and anxiety. He strode onto the floor as if he had intense purpose, his shoulders hunched.

"Baron, were you party to these conspiracies to invite Prince Friedrich to return to his country and usurp his brother?"

Rathbone could not object. The language was pejorative, but he had laid the foundation for it himself.

Stephan smiled. "Mr. Harvester, if there was a plan to ask Prince Friedrich to return and lead a battle for retaining our independence, I was not a party to it. But providing it was to do that, and that only, had I known, I would gladly have joined. If you think it was a question of usurping, then you have demonstrated that you do not understand the issues. Prince Waldo is prepared to abdicate his throne and his country's independence and have us be swallowed up as part of a larger state."

He leaned forward on the railing, addressing Harvester as if he were the only other person in the room. "There would be no throne left in Felzburg, no crown to argue over. We should be a province of Prussia, or Hannover, or whatever the resulting conglomerate of states was called. No one knows who would be king, or president, or emperor. If Friedrich was indeed asked to come home, and he had accepted, it would be to preserve a throne in Felzburg, whoever sat on it. Perhaps he would not have wished to. Perhaps he would have lost the battle anyway, and we would still have been swallowed into a greater whole. Perhaps it would have meant war, and we would have been conquered. Or possibly the other minor liberal states would have allied with us rather than be consumed by the reactionaries. Now we will never know, because he is dead."

Harvester smiled bleakly.

"Baron, if this was the purpose of the visit to Wellborough Hall, and I am sure that you believe it was, then perhaps you will answer a few questions which arise from that supposition. If Friedrich had declined the invitation, would that have given anyone motive to wish him dead?"

"Not so far as I am aware."

"And if he had accepted?"

Stephan's mouth tightened with distaste at being forced to express his beliefs aloud, but he would not equivocate.

"Possibly Baron von Seidlitz."

"Because he was for unification?" Harvester's eyebrows rose. "Is it so likely Prince Friedrich, single-handedly, could have achieved that end? You made it sound far more difficult, problematical, in your earlier answers. I had not realized he still commanded such power."

"He might not have achieved our continued independence," Stephan said patiently. "He might well have achieved a war for it, and war is what von Seidlitz dreads. He has far too much to lose."

Harvester looked amazed. "And have not you all?" He half turned towards the gallery, as if to include them in his surprise.

"Of course." Stephan took a deep breath. "The difference is that many of us also believe that we have something to gain. Or perhaps I should say, more correctly, to preserve."

"Your identity as an independent state?" Harvester's voice was not mocking, not even disrespectful, but it did probe with a hard, unrelenting realism. "Is that truly worth a war to you, Baron von Emden? And in this war, who will fight?" He gestured in angry bewilderment. "Who will lose their homes and their lands? Who will die? I do not see it as an ignoble thing to wish your country to avoid war, even if it is a horrific thing to murder your prince in that cause. At least most of us here could understand that, I find it easy to believe."

"Possibly," Stephan agreed, his face suddenly alight with a passion he had kept tightly in control until now. "But then you all live in England, where there is a constitutional monarchy, a Parliament in which to debate, a franchise in which men can vote for the government they wish. You have the freedom to read and write what you wish." He did not move his hands, but his words embraced everyone in the room. "You are free to assemble to discuss, even to criticize, your betters and the laws they make. You may question without fear of reprisal. You may form a political party for any cause you like. You may worship any God in any manner you choose. Your army obeys your politicians, and not your politicians the army. Your queen would never take orders from her generals. They are there to protect you from invasion, to conquer weaker and less fortunate nations, but not to govern you and suppress you should you threaten to assemble in numbers or protest your state or your labor laws, your wages or your conditions."

There was not a murmur in the gallery. Hundreds of faces stared at him in amazement—and in silence.

"Perhaps if you lived in some of the German states," he went on, his voice now raw with sadness, "and could remember the armies marching in the streets a decade ago, see the people manning the barricades as suddenly hope flared that we too might have the liberties you take so lightly, and then afterwards see the dead, and the hope ended in despair, all the promises broken, you would be prepared to fight to keep the small privileges Felzburg has." He leaned forward. "And in memory of those who fought and died elsewhere, you would offer your life too, for your children and your children's children . . . or even just for your country, your friends, for the future, whether you see them, know them, or not, simply because you believe in these things."

The silence prickled in the ears.

"Bravo!" someone cried from the gallery. "Bravo, sir!"

"Bravo!" A dozen more shouted, and they began to stand up one by one, then a dozen, then a score, hands held up, faces alight with emotion. "Bravo!"

"God save the Queen!" a woman called out, and another echoed her.

The judge did not bang his gavel or make the slightest attempt to restore order. He allowed it to run its course and subside on its own. Once watched, the wave of passion had spent itself, emotion had passed.

"Mr. Harvester?" he said inquiringly. "Have you further points to ask of Baron von Emden?"

Harvester's face was puzzled and unhappy. Obviously, Stephan's evidence had opened up a vehemence the lawyer had not foreseen. The issue had ceased to be political in any dry and objective sense and became a thing of raging urgency which touched everyone. The emotional balance had been altered irrevocably. He was not yet sure where it would lead.

"No, my lord, thank you," he answered. "I think the Baron has demonstrated most admirably that feelings ran very high during the meeting at Wellborough Hall, and many may have believed that the fate of a nation hung on the return, or not, of Prince Friedrich." He shook his head. "None of which has the slightest relevance to the Countess Rostova's accusation against Princess Gisela and its demonstrable untruth." He looked for a moment towards Rathbone, and then returned to his seat.

It was perfectly timed. Rathbone knew it as well as Harvester did. He had not defended Zorah from the charge of slander, he had not even defended her from the unspoken charge of murder. If anything, Stephan might unwittingly have made things worse. He had shown how very much was at stake and sworn that Zorah believed in independence. She could never have wished Friedrich dead, but she might very easily have tried to kill Gisela and counted it an act of supreme patriotism. That was now believable to everyone in the room.

"What the devil are you doing, Rathbone?" Harvester demanded as they passed each other when leaving for the luncheon adjournment. He looked confused. "Your client is as likely to be guilty of a mistake in victim as anybody." His voice dropped in genuine concern. "Are you sure she is sane? In her own interests, can you not prevail upon her to withdraw? The court will pursue the truth now, whatever she says or does. At least protect her by persuading her to keep silent, before she incriminates herself . . . and, incidentally, drags you down with her. You have too many rogue witnesses, Rathbone."

"I have a rogue case," Rathbone agreed ruefully, falling into step with Harvester.

"I can imagine the Lord Chancellor's face!" Harvester skirted around a group of clerks in intense discussion and rejoined Rathbone as they went down the steps into the raw, late October wind.

"So can I." Rathbone meant it only too truthfully. "But I have no alternative. She is adamant that Gisela killed him, and short of abandoning the case, for which I have no grounds, I have to follow her instructions."

Harvester shook his head. "I'm sorry." It was commiseration, not apology. He would not stay his hand, nor would Rathbone had their roles been reversed, as he profoundly wished they were.

When they returned in the afternoon, Rathbone called Klaus von Seidlitz, who was obliged to substantiate what Stephan had said. He was reluctant to concede it at first, but he could not deny that he was for unification. When Rathbone pressed him, he argued the case against war and its destruction, and his large, crooked face filled with growing passion as he described the ruin created by marching armies, the death, the waste of the land, the confusion and loss to the border regions, the maimed and bereaved. There was something dignified in his shambling figure as he told of his lands and his love for the little villages, the fields and the lanes.

Rathbone did not interrupt him. Nor, when Klaus had finished, did he make any implication that he might have murdered Friedrich to prevent him from returning home and plunging their country into just such a war.

If there was anything good in this, it was that there would be no question that there were abundant reasons for Friedrich's murder, or the mischance which had killed Friedrich rather than Gisela. There were passions and issues involved which anyone could understand, perhaps even identify with.

But it was far from enough to help Zorah yet. He must make it last as long as he could, and hope that in probing he unearthed something specific, something which pointed unarguably to someone else.

He glanced to where she sat beside him, pale-faced but at least outwardly composed. He would be the only one who saw her hands clenched in her lap. He had never been aware of knowing so little of the true mind of a client. Of course, he had been duped before. He had been convinced of innocence, only to find the ugliest, most callous guilt.

Was it so with Zorah Rostova?

He looked at her now, at her turbulent face, so easily ugly or beautiful as the light or the mood caught it. He found her fascinating. He did not want her to be guilty, or even deluded. Perhaps that was part of her skill? She had made herself matter to him. He had not the faintest idea what was passing through her mind.

He asked to recall Florent Barberini to the witness stand. The judge made no demur, and his single look in Harvester's direction silenced any objection. The jury was sitting bolt upright, waiting for every word.

"Mr. Barberini," Rathbone began, walking slowly out onto the floor. "I formed the opinion from your previous testimony that you are aware of the political situation both in the German states and in Venice. Since you were on the stand before, many further facts have come to light which make the politics of the situation relevant to the death of Prince Friedrich and to our attempt to discover exactly who brought that about, either intentionally or in a tragic and criminal accident—when, in fact, they had meant to murder Princess Gisela instead . . ."

There was a gasp around the room. Someone in the gallery stifled a scream.

Gisela winced, and Harvester put out his hand as if to steady her, then, at the last moment, changed his mind. She was not an approachable woman. She sat as if an invisible cordon of isolation were wrapped around her. She seemed only peripherally aware of the drama playing itself out in the thronged room. She wore her grief more visibly than simply clothes of black, mourning jewelry or a black-veiled hat. She had retreated to some unreachable place within herself. Rathbone knew the jury was acutely sensitive to it. In a way, it was a louder proclamation of her injury than anyone else's words could have been. Harvester had an ideal client.

Zorah was at the opposite pole. She was full of turbulent color and energy, completely alien, challenging far too many of the assumptions upon which society rested its beliefs.

Rathbone returned to Florent as the murmuring died down.

"Mr. Barberini, the crux of this case hangs on the question of whether there was indeed a plan to ask Prince Friedrich to return to his country to lead a party to fight to retain its independence from any proposed unification into a greater Germany. Was there such a plan?"

Florent did not hesitate or demur.

"Yes."

There were a hundred gasps in the gallery. Even the judge tensed and moved forward a little, staring at Florent. Zorah let out a long sigh.

Rathbone felt the relief flood through him like a blast of warmth after an icy journey. He did not mean to smile, but he could not help it. He found his hands shaking, and for a moment he could not move, his legs were weak.

"And . . ." He cleared his throat. "And who was involved in this concern?"

"Count Lansdorff principally," Florent replied. "Assisted by the Baroness von Arlsbach and myself."

"Whose idea was it?"

This time Florent did hesitate.

"If that is politically compromising," Rathbone interjected, "or if honor forbids you to mention names, may I ask you if you believe the Queen would have approved your cause?"

Florent smiled. He was extraordinarily handsome. "She would have approved Friedrich's return to lead the party for independence," he replied. "Providing it met with her terms, which were absolute."

"Are you aware what they were?"

"Naturally. I would not be party to negotiating any arrangement which did not meet with her approval." His face relaxed into a kind of black humor. "Apart from any loyalty to her, no such plan could work."

Rathbone relaxed a little as well, giving a slight shrug. "I assume the Queen is a woman of great power?"

"Very great," Florent agreed. "Both political and personal."

"And what were her terms, Mr. Barberini?"

Florent answered intently, with no pause, no consciousness of the jury, the judge or the gallery listening.

"That he come alone," he said. "She would not tolerate the Princess Gisela's coming with him as his wife. She was to remain in exile and be put from him."

There was a gasp around the court and a sigh of exhaled breath.

Gisela lifted her head a little and closed her eyes, refusing to look at anyone.

Harvester's face was grim, but there was nothing for him to say. There was no legal objection.

Zorah remained expressionless.

Rathbone was again obliged to break all his own rules. He must ask a crucial question to which he did not know the answer, but there was no alternative open to him.

"And were these terms made known to him, Mr. Barberini?"

"They were."

Again there was a rustle from the crowd, and someone hissed disapproval.

"Are you certain of that?" Rathbone pressed. "Were you present?"

"Yes, I was."

"And what was Prince Friedrich's answer?"

The silence prickled the air. A man in the very last seat in the gallery moved, and the squeak of his boots was audible from where Rathbone stood.

The bleakest of smiles flickered over Florent's face and disappeared.

"He did not answer."

Rathbone felt the sweat break out on his skin.

"Not at all?"

"He argued," Florent elaborated. "He asked a great many questions. But the accident happened before the discussions were concluded irrevocably."

"So he did not refuse outright?" Rathbone demanded, his voice rising in spite of his efforts to control it.

"No, he put forward his own counterproposals."

"Which were?"

"That he should come and bring Gisela with him." Unconsciously, Florent omitted the courtesy title of Princess, betraying his thoughts of her. To him she would always be a commoner.

"And did Count Lansdorff accept that?" Rathbone asked.

"No." It was said without hesitation.

Rathbone raised his eyebrows. "It was not open to negotiation?"

"No, it was not."

"Do you know why? If the Queen, and the Count Lansdorff, feel as passionately about the freedoms of which you spoke, and if those who would form any political fighting force do also, surely the acceptance of Princess Gisela as Friedrich's wife is a small price to pay for his return as leader? He could rally the forces as no one else could. He is the King's eldest son, the natural heir to the throne, the natural leader."

Harvester did rise this time.

"My lord, Mr. Barberini is not competent to answer such a question—unless he makes some claim to speak for the Queen, and can demonstrate such authority."

"Sir Oliver"—the judge leaned forward—"do you propose

to call Count Lansdorff to the stand? You cannot have Mr. Barberini answer for him. Such an answer will be hearsay, as you know."

"Yes, my lord," Rathbone replied gravely. "With your lordship's permission, I shall call Count Lansdorff to the stand. His aide informed me he is reluctant to appear, which is understandable, but I think Mr. Barberini's evidence has given us no choice in the matter. Reputations, and perhaps lives, depend upon our knowing the truth."

Harvester looked unhappy, but to object would make it appear that he believed Gisela could not afford the truth, and that was tantamount to defeat, in public opinion if not in law. And by now the law was only a small part of the issue. It hardly mattered what could be proved to a jury; it was what people believed.

The court adjourned for the night in a bedlam of noise. Newspapermen scrambled over each other, even knocking aside ordinary pedestrians, to make their way outside and clamber into hansoms, shouting the names of their newspapers and demanding to be taken there immediately. No one any longer knew what to think. Who was innocent? Who was guilty?

Rathbone took Zorah by the arm and hurried her, half pushing her bodily, past the front row of public seats, towards the door and out into the corridor. Then he paced as rapidly as he could towards a private room and a discreet exit. Only afterwards was he surprised that she could keep up with him.

He expected her to be exultant, but when he turned to face her he saw only a calm, guarded courage. He was confused.

"Is this not what you thought?" he said, then instantly wished he had not, but it was too late not to go on. "That Friedrich was invited home on condition he left her behind, and she was so afraid he would take the offer, she killed him rather than be put aside? It does begin to look conceivable that someone in her sympathy may have done it for her. Or that she may have connived with someone, each for his own purpose."

Her eyes filled with black humor, part self-mockery, part anger, part derision.

"Gisela and Klaus?" she said contemptuously. "She to keep her status as one of the world's great lovers, he to avoid a war and his own financial loss? Never! If I saw it with my own eyes I still wouldn't believe it."

He was dumbfounded. She was impossible.

"Then you have nothing!" He was almost shouting. "Klaus alone? Because she didn't do it . . . that has been proved! Is that what you want . . . or are you trying to bring down the Queen for murder?"

She burst into laughter, rich, deep-throated and totally sincere.

He could happily have hit her, were such a thing even thinkable.

"No," she said, controlling herself with difficulty. "No, I do not want to bring down the Queen. Nor could I. She didn't have anything to do with it. If she wanted Gisela dead she would have done it years ago, and done it more efficiently than this! Not that I think she mourns Friedrich's death as she might have thirteen or fourteen years ago. I think in her mind he has been dead since he chose Gisela before his duty and his people."

"Count Lansdorff?" he asked.

"No. I like you, Sir Oliver." She seemed to say it simply because it occurred to her. "She killed him," she went on. "Gisela killed him."

"No, she didn't!" He was totally exasperated with her. "She is the only person who could not have. Haven't you listened to the evidence at all?"

"Yes," she assured him. "I just don't believe it."

And he could achieve nothing more with her. He gave up, and went home in a furious temper.

* * *

In the morning, Count Rolf Lansdorff took the stand. He did so grimly, but without protest. To show his displeasure would have been beneath the dignity of a man who was not only a soldier and a statesman, but brother to the most formidable queen in the German states, if not in Europe. Looking at him as he stood upright, head high, shoulders back, eyes level and direct, one was not likely to mistake him.

"Count Lansdorff," Rathbone began with the utmost politeness. The man was already an enemy, simply by the act of Rathbone's having called him to stand witness and be questioned like a common man. He did not know whether it was a mitigating circumstance, or one which added to the offense, that it had not happened in the Count's own country. It was not the law which had compelled him to be here, but the necessity of answering public opinion, of defending himself, and then his dynasty, before the bar of Europe's history.

Rolf was listening.

"Mr. Barberini has told us that while you were at Wellborough Hall this spring you met a number of times with the late Prince Friedrich," Rathbone began again, "in order to discuss the possibility of his returning to his country to lead a fight to retain independence, rather than be swallowed up in a unified Germany. Is this substantially correct?"

Rolf's muscles tightened even more until he was standing rigid, like a soldier on parade in front of a general.

"It is . . ." he conceded. "Substantially."

"Are there details in which it is . . . inadequate or misleading?" Rathbone kept his tone almost casual.

There was not a sound in the room.

He turned and took a step or two, as though thinking.

Gisela sat with an expressionless face. Rathbone was startled how strong it was in repose, how pronounced the bones. There was no softness in her mouth, no vulnerability. He wondered what inner despair filled her that she could look so impervious to what was going on around her. It seemed as if truly, now that Friedrich was dead, nothing could touch her. Perhaps it was only for his sake, for his memory, that she had brought this action at all.

Rolf's lips closed in a thin, delicate line. He took a deep breath. His expression was one as of a man biting into something that had turned sour.

"The offer was conditional, not absolute," he replied.

"Upon what, Count Lansdorff?"

"That is a political matter, and a family matter, both of delicacy and confidentiality," Rolf replied coolly. "It would be crass to discuss it in public, and extremely insensitive."

"I am aware of that, sir," Rathbone said gravely. "And we all regret that it should be necessary . . . absolutely necessary, in order that justice should prevail. If it is any service in sparing your feelings, may I ask you if the condition was that Prince Friedrich should divorce his wife and return alone?"

Rolf's face tightened till the light shone on the smooth planes of his cheeks and brow and his nose seemed like a blade.

The judge looked deeply unhappy. It occurred to Rathbone with a jolt that doubtless the Lord Chancellor had sent a word of warning to him, too.

"That was the condition," Rolf said icily.

"And did you have hopes that he would meet it?" Rathbone pressed relentlessly.

Rolf was startled. It was obviously not the question he had expected. It took him an instant to collect his thoughts and reply.

"I had hoped that I would be able to prevail upon whatever sense of honor he had left, sir." He did not look at Rathbone but at some point on the wooden paneling in the wall far above the lawyer's head.

"Had he given you indication of that before you came to England, Count Lansdorff? Or was there some other circumstance or event which led you to believe that he had changed his mind since his original abdication?" Rathbone pursued.

Rolf still stood like a soldier on parade, but now one who heard the steps of the firing squad come to a halt.

"Sometimes one's obsession with love subsides into something of better proportion with time," he replied with intense dislike. "I had hoped that when Friedrich learned of his country's need, he would set aside his personal feelings and follow the duty for which he was born and groomed, and whose privileges he was happy to accept for the first thirty years of his life."

"It would be a great sacrifice . . ." Rathbone said tentatively.

Rolf glared at him. "All men make sacrifices for their country, sir! Does any Englishman whom you respect answer the call to arms by saying he would rather remain at home with his wife?" His voice almost choked it was so thick with disgust. "Damn the invader or the foreign army which would trample his land! Let someone else fight him. He would rather dance in Venice and float around in a gondola making love to some woman! Would you admire such a man, sir?"

"No, I would not," Rathbone replied with a sudden sense of the shame which burned in the man in front of him. Friedrich was not only his prince but his sister's son, his own blood. And Rathbone had forced him to this conclusion in front of a courtroom of ordinary people of the street—a foreign street at that. "Did you put this to him at Wellborough Hall, Count Lansdorff?"

"I did."

"And his reply?"

"That if we needed him so profoundly in order to fight to retain our independence, then we should make the allowance and accept that woman as his wife."

There was a wave of emotion around the room like the backwash of a tide.

For once Gisela too reacted. She winced as if she had been threatened with a blow to the face.

"And considering how much might ride on his return, were you willing to accept those terms?" Rathbone asked in the silence.

Rolf's chin rose a fraction. "No sir, we were not."

There was a sigh across the gallery.

"You say 'we,' " Rathbone said. "Who else do you mean, Count Lansdorff?"

"Those of us who believe the best future for our country lies in our continued independence and the laws and privileges which we presently enjoy," Rolf answered. "Those who believe that the alliance with other German states, in particular Prussia or Austria, will be a step back into a darker and more repressive age."

"And have they declined you as their leader?" Rathbone inquired.

Rolf looked at him as if he had spoken in an unintelligible language.

Rathbone moved a little across the floor, to command his attention again.

"Is your sister, Queen Ulrike, of that conviction, Count Lansdorff?"

"She is."

"And your nephew, Crown Prince Waldo?"

Rolf's face remained almost expressionless, only an increased rigidity in his shoulders betraying his feelings.

"He is not."

"Naturally, or he would lead the party and Friedrich's return would not be necessary. I understand the health of His Majesty the King gives cause for great concern?"

"The King is extremely ill. He is failing," Rolf agreed.

Rathbone turned again, facing slightly the other way.

"Your motives for wishing Prince Friedrich's return are very easily understandable, sir. Indeed, I imagine almost every man or woman here could sympathize with you and, given the same circumstances, would probably do as you have done. What is far harder to understand—in fact, for me it is impossible—is why your hatred of Princess Gisela ran so deeply as to make her abandonment a condition of Prince Friedrich's return. It does not seem to make sense."

He turned his head to glance momentarily at Gisela. "She is a charming and attractive woman, and has proved an excellent wife to Prince Friedrich—loyal, dignified, witty, one of the most successful hostesses in Europe. There has never been a word even whispered against her reputation in any sense. Why were you prepared to jeopardize your battle for independence simply to see that she did not return home with her husband?"

Rolf stood stiffly in the box. He did not move his hands from his sides but remained at attention.

"Sir, the situation is an old one, of some twelve-odd years. You know nothing of it except the last few months. For you to assume that you could possibly understand it is ridiculous."

"I need to understand it," Rathbone assured him. "The court needs to."

"You do not!" Rolf contradicted. "It has nothing to do with Friedrich's death or with the Countess Rostova's slander."

The judge looked at Rolf, a slight frown creasing his forehead, but when he spoke his voice was still infinitely polite.

"You are not the jury in this matter, Count Lansdorff. You are in an English court now, and I will decide what is necessary and what is not, according to the law. And those twelve gentlemen"—he indicated the jury—"will deliberate and decide what they believe to be true. I cannot force you to answer Sir Oliver's questions. I can only advise you that should you fail to do so, you will invite an adverse opinion as to the reason for your silence. And murder is a capital crime. This particular murder was committed on English soil and is subject to English law, whoever the man or woman who committed it may be."

Rolf looked ashen.

"I have no idea who killed Friedrich or why. Ask your questions." He did not add "and be damned," but it was in his face.

"Thank you, my lord," Rathbone acknowledged, then turned back to Rolf.

"Was the Princess Gisela aware of your negotiations, Count Lansdorff?"

"Not from me. Whether Friedrich told her or not, I don't know."

"You could not deduce from her behavior?" Rathbone said with surprise.

"She is not a woman whose thoughts or feelings are readily visible in her expression," Rolf answered coldly and without even glancing towards Gisela. "Whether her continued"—he searched for the word—"enjoyment of the party was due to ignorance of our mission or to confidence that Friedrich would never leave her, I have no way of knowing."

"Had you ever joined such a party before, Count Lansdorff?"

"Not if Friedrich was there, no. I am the Queen's brother. Friedrich chose to go into exile rather than fulfill his destiny." The damnation was complete in his expression and in the tone of his hard, precise voice.

"So we may deduce that Gisela believed Friedrich would not leave her?"

"You may deduce what you please, sir."

Harvester smiled bleakly. Rathbone caught it out of the corner of his eye. He tried another approach.

"Were you empowered to make any decisions regarding terms or concessions to Prince Friedrich, Count Lansdorff? Or did you have to refer back to the Queen?"

"There were no concessions to make," Rolf answered with a frown. "I thought I had made that plain, sir. Her Majesty would not countenance the return of Gisela Berentz, either as crown princess or as consort. If Friedrich did not accept those terms, then another leader for the cause would be sought."

"Who?"

"I do not know."

Rathbone thought that was a lie, but he could see from Rolf's face that it was the only answer he would receive.

"It is a very extreme hatred the Queen has for the Princess Gisela," he said thoughtfully. "It seems contrary to the best interests of her country to allow such a personal emotion to govern her actions." It was not really a question, but he hoped it would sting Rolf into a defensive response.

He was successful.

"It is not a personal hatred!" Rolf said. "The woman was unacceptable as Friedrich's wife . . . for many reasons, none of which are merely personal." He used the term with the utmost derision.

Rathbone deliberately turned and stared at Gisela as she sat beside Harvester. She was a picture of grief, a perfect victim. Harvester did not need to defend her from Rolf, her own demeanor did it better than any words of his could have. He looked angry, but satisfied.

Zorah was sitting upright, tense, her face white.

Rathbone turned back to Rolf.

"She seems eminently suitable to me," he said innocently. "She has dignity, presence, the admiration, even the love or the envy, of half the world. What more could you wish?"

Rolf's mouth twisted with an emotion which was as much pain as scorn.

"She has the art to seduce men, the wit to make herself the center of attention, and the style to dress well. That is all."

There was a hiss from the gallery. One of the jurors let out an exclamation of horror.

"Oh, come sir . . ." Rathbone protested, his pulse suddenly racing, his mouth dry. "That seems, at the very kindest, ungallant and highly prejudiced—at the worst, as if founded in some acutely personal hatred—"

Rolf lost his temper. At last he unbent and leaned forward over the railing, glaring across at Rathbone.

"That you should be ignorant of her nature, sir, is hardly your fault. Most of Europe is ignorant of it, thank God. I would that they could have remained so, but you force my hand. Like any other royal house, we need an heir. Waldo will not provide one, through no fault of his own. That is not a matter I can or will discuss. Gisela is childless of her own choice—"

There was a wave of reaction from the gallery.

Harvester half rose in his seat, but his protest was lost in a general noise.

The judge banged his gavel for silence and a return to order.

Rathbone looked at Rolf, then at Gisela. She seemed almost bloodless, her eyes huge and hollow, but he had no idea whether it was fear, horror, mortification at such public disclosure, or an old grief reawakened.

The noise still had not subsided. He turned to Zorah.

She seemed as surprised and confused as anyone.

The judge banged his gavel again. Order returned.

"Count Lansdorff?" Rathbone said distinctly.

Rolf would not now be stopped. "Had Friedrich put her aside, he could have married a more suitable woman, one who would have given the country an heir," he continued. "There are many young women of noble birth and spotless reputation, pleasing enough in manner and appearance." He did not look away from Rathbone, but his face tightened in reluctance. "The Baroness von Arlsbach would have been perfect; she would always have been perfect. The Queen begged him to marry her. She had every virtue, and is deeply loved by the people. Her family is unblemished. Her own reputation grows higher by the month."

He ignored the people, even the jurors, every set of eyes scanning the benches to see if she was present. "She has dignity, honor, the loyalty of the people and the respect of all those who meet her, native and foreigner alike," he continued. "But he chose that woman instead." His eyes flickered for a moment to Gisela and away again. "And we are left barren!"

"That is a tragedy which has affected many dynasties, Count Lansdorff," Rathbone said sympathetically. "We are not unfamiliar with it here in England. You will have to amend your constitution so the crown may pass laterally through the female line." He ignored Rolf's expression of incredulity. "But you could not know when Prince Friedrich married Gisela that that union would be childless, and it is unjust to be so certain that it is Gisela's doing, and willfully so."

He lowered his voice a little. "Many women long desperately to have a child, and when they do not have one, they put a brave face to the world and hide their grief by pretending it is not there. It is a very private and deeply personal affliction. Why should anyone, even a princess, parade it for the public to see, or to pity?"

Rolf said with tense, almost sibilant bitterness, "Gisela's barrenness is of her own choosing. Do not ask me how I know it!"

"I must ask you," Rathbone insisted. "It is a harsh charge, Count Lansdorff. You cannot expect the court, or anyone, to believe you unless you can substantiate it!" He smiled a trifle wryly at the irony.

Rolf remained silent.

Harvester rose to his feet, his face flushed. "My lord . . . this is iniquitous! I . . ."

"Yes, Mr. Harvester," the judge said quietly. "Count Lansdorff, you will either retract your remarks about the Princess Gisela, and admit them to be untrue, or you will explain your grounds for making them and allow the court to decide whether they believe you or not."

Rolf stood to attention again, straightening up and squaring his shoulders. He looked beyond Rathbone and the plaintiff's and defendant's tables to somewhere in the gallery, and without thinking, Rathbone turned and looked also. The judge followed Rolf's eyes, and the jury swiveled to stare.

Rathbone saw Hester, and next to her a young man in a wheelchair, his fair brown hair catching the light. Behind him, also in the aisle, were an older man and woman of unusually handsome appearance. Presumably, from the way they regarded him, they were his parents. This was the patient Hester had spoken of. She had said they were from Felzburg. It was not unnatural they should feel compelled to come to the trial, after what the newspapers had said.

Rathbone turned back to the witness stand.

"Count Lansdorff?"

"Gisela is not barren," Rolf said between his teeth. "She had a child from an illicit affair many years before she married Friedrich—"

There was a gasp of indrawn breath around the room so sharp it was a hiss. Harvester shot to his feet, then found he had no idea what to say. Beside him, Gisela was as white as paper.

One of the jurors coughed and choked.

Rathbone was too stunned to speak.

"She did not want it," Rolf went on, his voice stinging with contempt. "She wanted to get rid of it, abort it—" Again he was forced to stop by the noise in the courtroom. The gallery erupted in anger, revulsion and distress. A woman screamed. Someone called out curses, random, indiscriminate.

The judge banged his gavel, his eyes puckered with distress.

Harvester looked as if he had been struck in the face.

Rolf's voice, harsh and loud, cut across them all.

"But the father wanted the child, and told her he would expose her if she destroyed it, but if she bore it, alive, he would take it and love it."

There was sobbing in the gallery.

The jurors were ashen-faced.

"She gave birth to a son," Rolf said. "The father took it. He struggled for a year to care for the boy himself, then he fell in love with a woman of his own rank and station, a woman of gentleness and nobility who was prepared to raise the boy as her own. Conceivably, the boy has never known he was not hers."

Rathbone had to clear his throat before he could find his voice.

"Can you prove that, Count Lansdorff? These are terrible charges."

"Of course!" Rolf's lips curled in scorn. "Do you imagine I would make them from the witness stand if I could not? Zorah Rostova may be a fool . . . but I am not!

"Her second child was not so fortunate," he continued, his voice like breaking ice. "She conceived to Friedrich, and this one she succeeded in aborting herself. Apparently, she had some knowledge of herbs. It is an art some women choose to cultivate—for health or cosmetic reasons, among others. And to concoct aphrodisiacs or procure abortions. She was ill after this, and was attended for a short time by a doctor. I do not know if you can force him to testify, but he would not lie to you under oath. The matter distressed him profoundly." His face was contorted with emotion. "But if his profession seals his tongue, ask Florent Barberini. He will swear to it, if you press him. He has no such binding loyalties." He stopped abruptly.

Rathbone had no alternative. The court was hanging on a breath.

"But the child you say she bore, Count Lansdorff? Gisela's son! That is surely provable?"

Rolf looked one more time at the judge.

The judge's face was filled with regret but unyielding.

"I am sorry, Count Lansdorff, but the charge you make is too terrible to go unproved, true or false. You must answer if you can."

"The affair was with Baron Bernd Ollenheim," Rolf said

huskily. "He took his child, and when he married, his wife loved the boy as her own."

He had nothing else to say, but the emotion of the court would not have permitted him to speak anyway. As suddenly as the breaking of a storm, their adoration for Gisela had turned to hatred.

Harvester looked like a man who had witnessed a fatal accident. His face was bereft of color, and he made half movements and then changed his mind, opened his mouth as though to speak and found he had no words.

Gisela herself sat like a woman turned to stone. Whatever she felt, there was no reflection of it written on her features. There was nothing that seemed like regret. Not once did she turn to see if she could recognize Bernd Ollenheim in the gallery, and she could hardly have failed to realize he was there—from Rolf's steady gaze, filled with pity, and from the movement of the crowd as it too realized at whom he had gazed.

Rathbone looked at Zorah. Had she known this? Had she been waiting for Rolf to expose it, hoping, trusting it would come?

From the motionless amazement in her face he could only deduce that it was as shocking to her as it was to everyone else, except Gisela herself.

It was seconds, minutes, before the hubbub died down sufficiently for Rathbone to be heard.

"Thank you, Count Lansdorff," he said at length. "We appreciate that must have been painful for you to have to reveal, in your regard for the innocent. However, it explains Queen Ulrike's undying contempt for Gisela . . ." He too almost unconsciously omitted her title. "And the reason she could not, in any circumstances, permit her to return to Felzburg and become queen. Were this to become public knowledge after that event, the scandal would be devastating.

It could bring down the throne. It was not possible that she should permit that."

He took a step back, turned, and then faced Rolf again. "Count Lansdorff, was Prince Friedrich aware of this past tragedy and of Gisela's son?"

"Of course," Rolf said bleakly. "We told him when he first sought to marry her. He disregarded it. He had an ability not to see what he did not wish to."

"And the later abortion? I presume that is why she has not since conceived a child?"

"You presume correctly. She now cannot. I doubt you will get the doctor to testify to that, but it is true."

"And was Prince Friedrich aware that his child was killed in the womb?"

There was a gasp around the room. In the center of the gallery, a woman was weeping. The jurors were like a row of men at an execution.

Rolf blanched even further.

"I don't know. I did not tell him, although I knew it then. I doubt she told him. Unless Barberini did. I think that unlikely."

"You did not use it to persuade him to leave his wife? I confess, I believe I would have."

"I would have too, Sir Oliver," Rolf said grimly. "But only as a last resort. I did not want a broken man. As it happened, I did not have the opportunity, and after his accident it would have been brutal. It might have killed him. Whether I would have told him later, had he recovered, I cannot tell you. I do not know."

"Thank you, Count Lansdorff. I have no further questions for you. Please remain, in case Mr. Harvester has."

Harvester rose, swayed a little, as if caught in a great wind, and cleared his throat.

"I . . . I assume, Count Lansdorff, that this monstrous story is one you could, and would, prove in this court if required to?" He attempted to sound brave, even defiant, but his ability failed him. He was obviously as appalled as anyone in the room. He was a man quietly devoted to his own wife and daughters, and his emotions had been too profoundly outraged for him to conceal it.

"Of course," Rolf said dryly.

"You may be required to do so. Naturally, I shall take instruction." There was nothing he could say to rebut the charge, and to have spoken now of its irrelevance to Zorah's slander would have been ridiculous. No one cared. No one was even listening. He sat down again a changed man.

The judge looked at Rathbone, his face pinched with sadness.

"Sir Oliver, I feel, regrettably, that you had better provide whatever substantiation is open to you. We do not impugn Count Lansdorff's testimony, but so far it is still only his word. I think it were better the issue were closed now, if that is a chance available to us."

Rathbone nodded. "I call Baron Bernd Ollenheim to the stand."

"Baron Bernd Ollenheim!" the usher repeated.

Very slowly, Bernd rose to his feet and made his way forward from the gallery, across the floor and up the steps of the witness stand till he turned at the top and faced the court. He was white, his eyes sick with distress. He looked over Rathbone's head towards Gisela as if she were something that had crept out of a cesspool.

"Would you like a glass of water, sir?" the judge asked him gently. "I can send an usher for one with no difficulty."

Bernd recalled himself. "No . . . no, thank you, my lord. I shall be quite in command of myself."

"If you wish for assistance, you may request it," the judge assured him.

Rathbone felt like a man stripping another naked. He did it only because the question must be answered now, and finally.

"Baron Ollenheim, I shall not keep you long." He took a

deep breath. "I regret the necessity for calling you at all. I simply wish to ask you either to substantiate or to deny the testimony of Count Lansdorff regarding your son. Is he indeed also the son of Gisela Berentz?"

Bernd had difficulty in speaking. His throat seemed to have closed. He struggled to fill his lungs with air, and then to master the anguish which overwhelmed him.

The entire courtroom was silent in shared distress.

"Yes . . ." he said at last. "Yes, he is. But my wife . . . my wife has always loved him . . . not only for my sake, but for his own. No . . ." He gasped again, his face twisted with the pain of memory—and fear for her now. "No woman could love a child more."

"We do not doubt it, sir," Rathbone said quietly. "Nor the agony this must have cost you, both then and now. Is Count Lansdorff also correct that Gisela Berentz wished to destroy the child"—he used the word intentionally, but having seen Robert Ollenheim through Hester's eyes, it came easily—"but that you forced her to carry it to term and to give birth?"

The silence deafened the room.

"Yes . . ." Bernd whispered.

"I ask your pardon for the intrusion into what should have been able to remain a purely personal grief," Rathbone apologized. "And I assure you of our respect for you and your family. I have nothing further I need to ask you. Unless Mr. Harvester has, that is all."

Harvester rose. He looked wretched.

"No, thank you. I do not believe that Baron Ollenheim has anything relevant to the issue at hand which he could tell us."

It was a brave attempt to remind the court that the case was one of slander between Zorah and Gisela, but no one cared anymore. The issues were abandonment, abortion and murder.

The day ended in uproar. Police had to be called in to escort Gisela to the carriage and protect her from the fury of the crowd, now surging in on her with an even fiercer rage and potential for violence than they had showed towards Zorah just two days before. They were shouting, pelting Gisela with refuse; some of them even hurled stones. One rock clattered against the carriage roof and ricocheted against the wall beyond. The cabby shouted back at the crowd, afraid for himself and his horse, and lashed his whip over their heads.

Rathbone stood on the outside of Zorah and hustled her away, fearing that she too would be a focus for their wrath. It was she who had instigated this entire collapse of dreams, and she would be hated for it.

Robert Ollenheim had asked his parents for privacy, at least for an hour, and it was Hester who sat in the carriage next to him on the way home to Hill Street. Bernd and Dagmar had stood by helplessly as the footman assisted him up and then Hester after him, but they made no attempt to argue or remonstrate.

He sat immobile, staring ahead as the horses picked up speed. The footman rode on the box. The young man and Hester were alone, moving through the milling, jostling streets.

"It's not true!" he said over and over again, grating the words between his teeth. "It's not true! That . . . woman . . . is not my . . ." He could not even bring himself to say the word *mother*.

Hester put her hand over his, and felt it balled into a fist under the blanket which covered his knees. It was extremely cold in the carriage, and for once he did not resent being tucked up.

"No, she isn't," she agreed.

"What?" He turned to look at her, his face puzzled and slack with disbelief. "Didn't you hear what my father said? He said that woman . . . that woman . . ." He took a difficult, jerky breath. "Even before I was born, she didn't want me! She wanted to have me . . . destroyed!"

"She isn't your mother in any sense that matters," Hester

said gravely. "She gave up that right. Dagmar Ollenheim is your mother. She is the one who reared you, who loved you and wanted you. You are the only child she has. You simply have to think of her at any time during all the years you have been alive to know how deeply she loves you. Have you ever doubted it before?"

"No . . ." He was still having difficulty catching his breath, as if something were crushing his chest. "But that . . . that other woman is still my mother! I'm part of her!" He glanced at Hester with wide, agonizing eyes. "That's who I am! I can't get away from it, I can't forget it! I came from her body! From her mind!"

"Her body," Hester corrected. "Not her mind. Your mind and your soul are your own."

A new horror dawned on him.

"Oh, God! What will Victoria think of me? She'll know! She'll read it on some . . . some sandwich board, hear it from a newsboy in the street. Someone will tell her! Hester . . . I've got to tell her first!" His words tumbled over each other. "Take me to where she lives! I've got to be the one to tell her. I can't let her find out from anyone else. Where does she live? I never even asked her!"

"She has lodgings in Bloomsbury. But you can't go there now. You must wait for her to come to you—"

"No! I must tell her. I can't bear . . ."

"You must," she said firmly. "Think of your mother . . . I mean Dagmar, not that other woman, who has no claim on you at all. Think how Dagmar must be feeling now. Think of your father, who loved you even before you were born, who fought for your life! They need your support. They need to know that you are all right and that you understand."

"But I must tell Victoria before—"

She held his hands hard. "Robert! Do you not think Victoria would most want you to do what is right, what is gentle and honorable and loving to those who have loved you all your life?"

It was minutes before he relaxed. They lurched and swayed through the darkening streets. The level of light in the carriage flickered as they passed the lampposts and moved into the mist and shadows between.

"Yes . . . I suppose so," he conceded at last. "But I must see her tonight. I must send a message to her. I must see her before she hears it somewhere else. Otherwise I may never have the chance to tell her I love her. She will know my mother is . . . God knows what! I am . . . I am part of that woman and I don't want to be, so desperately I almost wish I had never been born. How can it happen, Hester? How can it be that you can be born part of someone you loathe and abhor? It is so unfair it is unbearable."

"You are not part of her," Hester said firmly. "You are you . . . whatever you choose to be. Whatever she has done, it is not your fault. It is wretched for you, because people can judge cruelly—and you are right, it is unfair. But you should know better than to blame yourself."

She waited a moment while a dray rattled past them. "Nothing she is has anything to do with who you are, unless you want it to," she went on. "Sin is not an inherited disease. You cannot pass it from parent to child. Nor can you pass the blame. That is one thing about responsibility . . . you cannot ever take anyone else's, no matter how you love them, and no one can give you theirs. We each stand alone. Whatever Gisela did, and she couldn't have killed Friedrich, you are not answerable to anyone for it . . . not to society, not to Victoria, and not to yourself."

Her grip tightened on his arm. "But listen to me, Robert! You are responsible for what you do now, for how you treat your father, or Dagmar. You are responsible if you think now only of your own pain and confusion, and turn away from theirs."

He bent his head in total weariness, and she put her arms around him, holding him as tightly as she could, reaching up and touching his hair with her hand, gently, as if he had still been ill, or a child.

She told the coachman to go slowly, so Bernd and Dagmar would get to Hill Street before them.

When they arrived and pulled up, Robert was ready. The door was flung open and Bernd stood there, white-faced, Dagmar a step behind him.

"Hello, Father," Robert said calmly, the ravages of emotion not visible in his face in the rain-spattered lamplight. "Would you give me a hand down? It's fearfully cold in here, in spite of the rug. I hope there's a decent fire in the withdrawing room."

Bernd hesitated, searching Robert's eyes as if he could barely believe it. Then he almost fell forward and put his arms out to lift him, awkwardly at first, trying to look as if he were only helping him, but in the coach light the tears were bright on his cheeks and his hands trembled.

Robert looked beyond him at Dagmar.

"You'd better go inside, Mother," he said clearly. "You'll freeze standing out here. There's a fog rising." He forced himself to smile at her, then gradually it became real, filled with light, memories of all the tenderness he had known as surely as he knew anything at all.

Hester climbed out after him and followed them up the steps and inside. She was unaware of the night air, chill around her, or of the facts that the edge of her skirt was wet from the gutter and her feet were numb with cold.

Victoria left for Robert's side as soon as she received the letter—in fact, she returned with the coach the footman had taken to deliver it. Robert saw her alone. For once the door was closed, and Hester waited in the withdrawing room with Bernd and Dagmar.

Bernd paced the floor, turning at either end of the room, his face pale, his eyes returning each time to the door.

"What will she do?" he demanded, staring at Hester. "What will she say to him? Will she be able to accept him or speak of his . . . parentage?" He too could not bring himself to call Gisela the boy's mother.

"Considering who her father was, she of all people will understand," Hester said quietly but with total assurance. "Will Robert be able to accept that?"

"Yes," Dagmar said quickly, but she was smiling. "One is not answerable for one's father's sins. And he loves her, more than he ever would an ordinary woman who had no trials or sorrows of her own. I hope he has the courage to ask her to marry him. And I hope she will have the faith to accept him. Will she, do you think?" She did not even glance at Bernd to see if he approved. She had no intention of allowing him to disapprove.

"Yes," Hester said firmly. "I believe she will of her own accord. I think he will persuade her. But if she should doubt, then we shall give her the strength."

"Of course we shall," Dagmar agreed. "They will have a different kind of happiness from most people's, but it will be every bit as profound . . . perhaps more so." She looked up at Bernd and held out her hand.

He stopped pacing and took it, holding it hard, so tightly she winced, but she did not move to withdraw it. He smiled at Hester and nodded his head a little jerkily.

"Thank you . . ."

12

THE FOLLOWING MORNING was Saturday, and Hester slept in. She awoke with a jolt, remembering that the case was far from over. They still did not have any idea who had killed Friedrich. Legally, if not morally, Gisela remained the injured party, and Zorah had slandered her by saying that she was guilty of murder. The jury would have no alternative but to find for Gisela, and she would have nothing to lose now by asking for punitive damages. She had no reputation to enhance by mercy. She was a ruined woman and might need every ha'penny she could wrest from anyone. She might find her only solace in vengeance against the person who had brought about this whole disaster.

And with Zorah's defeat would go Rathbone's. At worst, Zorah could even be charged with Friedrich's murder herself.

Hester rose and dressed in the best gown she had with her, a plainly tailored dark rust red with a little black velvet at the neck.

It was not that she felt her appearance mattered to the issue, it was simply that the act of taking care, of doing her hair as flatteringly as possible, of pinching a little color into her cheeks, was an act of confidence. It was like a soldier shining his boots and putting on his scarlet tunic before going into battle. It was all morale, and that was the first step towards victory.

She arrived at Rathbone's rooms at five minutes after eleven, and found Monk already there. It was cold and wet outside, and there was a comfortable fire in the grate, and lamps burning, filling the room with warmth.

Monk, dressed in dark brown, was standing by the fireplace, his hands up as if he had been gesturing to emphasize a point. Rathbone sat in the largest armchair, his legs crossed, buff-colored trousers immaculate as always, but his cravat was a little crooked and his hair poked out at the side where he had apparently run his fingers through it.

"How is Ollenheim?" Monk asked, then looked at her clothes and the flush in her cheeks with a critical frown. "I assume from your demeanor that he is taking it quite well. Poor devil. Hard enough discovering your mother regarded you as such an embarrassment to her social ambitions she first tried to abort you, then the moment you were born, gave you away, without having to sit in a courtroom while half London discovers it at the same time."

"And what about the Baroness?" Rathbone asked. "Not an easy thing for her either, or the Baron, for that matter."

"I think they will be very well," she replied decisively.

"You look uncommonly pleased with yourself." Monk was apparently annoyed by it. "Have you learned something useful?"

It was a hard reminder of the present which still faced them.

"No," she admitted. "I was happy for Robert, and for Victoria Stanhope. I haven't learned anything. Have you?" She sat down in the third chair and looked from Monk to Rathbone and back again.

Monk regarded her unhappily.

Rathbone was too exercised with the problem to indulge in any other emotions.

"We have certainly made the jury regard Gisela in a very different light . . ." he began.

Monk let out a bark of laughter.

"But that doesn't substantiate Zorah's charge," Rathbone continued with a frown, deliberately ignoring Monk and keeping his eyes on Hester. "If we are to prevent Zorah from facing the charge of having murdered Friedrich herself, then we need to know who did, and prove it." His voice was quiet, so subdued as to be lacking its usual timbre. Hester could feel the defeat in him. "She is a patriot," he went on. "And perfectly obviously hates Gisela. There are going to be many people who think at this critical point in her country's fate, she took the opportunity of trying to kill Gisela but made a devastating mistake, and Friedrich died instead." He looked profoundly unhappy. "I could believe it myself."

Monk looked at him grimly.

"Do you?"

Hester waited.

Rathbone did not reply for several moments. There was no sound in the room but the snapping of the fire, the ticking of the tall clock, and the beating of the rain on the windows.

"I don't know," he said at last. "I don't think so. But . . ."

"But what?" Monk demanded, turning towards him. "What?"

Rathbone looked up quickly, as if to make some remark in retaliation. Monk was questioning him as if he were a witness on the stand. Then he changed his mind and said nothing. That he gave in so easily was a measure of his inner turmoil, and it worried Hester more than any admission in words could have done.

"But what?" Monk repeated sharply. "For God's sake, Rathbone, we have to know. If we don't get to the bottom of this the woman could hang . . . eventually. Friedrich was murdered. Don't you want to know who did it . . . whoever it was? I'm damn sure I do!"

"Yes, of course I do." Rathbone sat farther forward. "Even if it is Zorah herself, I want to know. I don't think I shall ever sleep properly again until I know what actually happened at Wellborough Hall, and why."

"Somebody took advantage of the situation and picked yew bark or leaves, made poison of them, and slipped it to Friedrich," Monk said, shifting his weight a little and leaning against the mantel. "Whether they meant to kill Friedrich or Gisela is probably the most important thing we need to know." He was standing too close to the fire, but he seemed unaware of it. "Either the poison was meant for Friedrich, to stop him from returning, in which case it was most probably Klaus von Seidlitz—or possibly . . . his wife." A curious flicker of emotion crossed his face and as quickly vanished again. "Or else it was intended for Gisela, and for some reason she gave the food or the drink, whatever it was, to Friedrich. If that were so, then it could be anyone who was for independence: Rolf, Stephan, Zorah herself, even Barberini."

"Or Lord Wellborough, for that matter," Rathbone added. "If he had a sufficient financial stake in arming someone for the fighting which would follow."

"Possible," Monk conceded. "But unlikely. There are enough other wars. I can't see him taking that kind of risk. I am sure this is a crime of passion, not profit."

Hester had been thinking, trying to visualize it in purely practical terms.

"How did they do it?" she said aloud.

"Simple enough," Monk replied impatiently. "Distract the servant carrying the tray. Have the distillation of yew in a small vial or whatever you like. A hip flask would serve. Just pour it into the beef tea, or whatever was on the tray that you know is for either Friedrich or Gisela, depending on which one you mean to poison. He was too ill to have been eating the same food as she did. He had mostly infusions, custards and so on.

She ate normally, if not very much. The kitchen staff and the footmen all testify to that."

"Have you ever tried to make an infusion of leaves or bark?" she asked with a frown.

"No. Why? I know it must have been boiled." A crease furrowed his brow. "I know the cook says it wasn't done in the kitchen. It must have been done over a bedroom fire. All the bedrooms have fires, and in spring they will have been lit. Anyone would have had all night to do it in privacy. That's what must have happened." His body relaxed again as he concluded. He became aware and moved away a step. "Anyone could have picked the leaves. They all went up and down the yew walk. I did myself. It's the natural way to go if you want to take the air for any distance."

"In what?" Hester asked, refusing to be satisfied.

Both men were staring at her.

"Well, if you are going to boil something half the night on your bedroom fire, you have to do it in something," she explained. "No pans were taken from the kitchen. Do you suppose somebody just happened to bring a saucepan along in their luggage . . . in case they might need it?"

"Don't be stupid!" Monk said angrily. "If they'd thought of poisoning someone before they came, they'd have brought the poison with them, not a saucepan to boil it. That's idiotic!"

"Are we sure it's a crime of impulse?" Rathbone asked no one in particular. "Could Rolf not have made provision to get rid of Gisela if Friedrich would not agree to his terms?"

"Possibly . . ." Monk conceded.

"Then he's an incompetent," Hester said with disgust. "And that would be idiotic. Why kill Gisela when he didn't even know if Friedrich was going to recover or what his answer would be? He would have waited."

"We've only Rolf's word he hadn't answered," Monk pointed out. "Perhaps he did refuse."

Hester started to think aloud. "Perhaps he already had

someone else to take his place? And he needed Friedrich more as a martyr than as a prince who refused to come home?"

Again both men stared at her, but this time with dawning incredulity and then amazement.

"You could be right," Monk said, his eyes wide. "That could be!" He turned to Rathbone. "Who else would he choose? With the natural heir gone, who is next? A political hero? A figurehead who has everyone's love? Barberini? Brigitte?"

"Maybe . . . yes, maybe either of those. With their knowledge, do you think?" He put his hands up and ran them through his hair. "Oh, damn! That takes us right back to Zorah Rostova! I'd swear she would have the nerve to do that if she thought it right for her country . . . and then try to see Gisela hanged for it!"

Monk jammed his hands into his pockets and looked miserable. For once he refrained from telling Rathbone his opinion of having accepted such a client. In fact, from the set of his face, Monk looked to Hester as if he had even resisted making the judgment in his mind. His expression was one of trouble, even of pity.

"What does Zorah say herself?" she asked. "I haven't even met her. It is strange to be talking about someone so central to everything when I have never spoken to her, or seen her face except fleetingly, as she turned around, and at a distance of at least twenty feet. And of course I've never spoken to Gisela either. I feel as if I know nothing about the people in this case."

Monk laughed abruptly. "I'm beginning to think none of us do."

"I'm going to leave personal judgments and try to apply my intelligence to reasoning it through." Rathbone reached for the poker and prodded the fire. It settled with a crackle, and he carefully placed a few more coals onto it, using the brass fire tongs. "My judgments of people in this case do not seem to have been very perceptive." He colored very slightly. "I really believed in the beginning that Zorah was right and that somehow or other Gisela had poisoned him."

Monk sat down opposite Rathbone, leaning forward, elbows on his knees. "Let us consider what we know beyond question to be true and what we can deduce from it. Maybe we have been assuming things we should not have. Reduce to the unarguable, and let us start again from there."

Rathbone responded obediently. It was another mark of his despair that he did not resent Monk's giving him orders. "Friedrich fell and was injured very seriously," he said. "He was treated by Gallagher."

Monk ticked the points off on his fingers as Rathbone outlined them.

"He was cared for by Gisela," Rathbone went on. "No one else came or went apart from servants—and one visit from the Prince of Wales."

"He appeared to be recovering," Monk interposed. "At least, as far as anyone could tell. They must all have thought so."

"Important," Rathbone agreed. "It must have seemed as if the plan were viable again."

"But it wasn't," Hester contradicted. "His leg was broken in three places . . . shattered, Gallagher said. At that point Gisela had already won. He wouldn't have served the independence party except as a figurehead, and they needed a lot more than that. An invalid, dependent, in pain, easily tired, would be no use to them."

They both stared at her, then turned slowly to stare at each other.

Rathbone looked beaten. Even Monk looked suddenly exhausted.

"I'm sorry," Hester said very quietly. "But it's true. At the time he was killed, the only ones it makes sense should want him dead are the people of the independence party, so that they could legitimately find a new leader."

They remained in silence for minutes. The fire burned up, and Monk rose and took a step away from it.

"But no one was alone with him, apparently," he said finally. "The servants were there coming and going. The doors were not locked. Everyone agrees Gisela never left the suite."

"Then the food was poisoned between the kitchen and the bedroom," Rathbone said. "We knew that before. It may have been poisoned with yew. We knew that also. It could have been anyone in the house, except for the difficulty of knowing how they prepared it."

"Unless they brought it with them," Monk continued. "They might fairly safely assume that a large country house like Wellborough Hall would have a yew tree, either on the grounds or in a nearby churchyard. Unless if Rolf brought it with him, intending to use it if Friedrich refused . . . and then lay the blame on Gisela?"

"Only it is all going wrong," Hester said quietly. "Because the court is insisting on having the chain of evidence, and that is going to lead back to Rolf . . . or Brigitte . . . or Florent or Zorah . . . and it could not have been Gisela! He is not nearly as clever, or as thorough, as he supposes."

They sat in silence for several more minutes, Rathbone staring into the fire, Monk frowning in thought, Hester looking from one to another of them, knowing the fear was only just beneath the surface, as it was in her, tight and sick and very real.

They were engaging their minds in reason, but the knowledge of failure, and its cost, was ready to overwhelm them the moment they let go of that thin, bright light of logic.

"I think I shall go and see Zorah Rostova," she said, rising to her feet. "I would like to talk to her myself."

"Feminine intuition?" Monk mocked.

"Curiosity. But if you have both met her, and not had your judgment addled, why shouldn't I? I can hardly do worse."

* * *

She found Zorah in her extraordinary room with the shawl pinned on the wall, a roaring fire sending flames halfway up the chimney and reflecting on the blood red of the sofa. The bearskins on the floor looked almost alive.

Zorah remained seated where she was and surveyed Hester with only the slightest interest. "Who did you say you were? You mentioned Sir Oliver's name to my maid, otherwise I would not have let you in." She was perfectly candid without intending to be offensive. "I am really not in a disposition to be polite to guests. I have neither the time nor the patience."

Hester was not put out. In the same circumstances, from what she knew of them, she would have felt the same. She had stood in the dock, where Zorah might yet stand if Rathbone were unsuccessful, which looked frighteningly like an inevitability now.

She looked at Zorah's highly individual face with its beautiful green eyes too widely spaced, its nose too long and too prominent, its sensitive mouth, delicate lipped. She judged her to be a woman capable of consuming passion, but far too intelligent to allow it to sweep away her perception or her understanding of other people, of law, or of events.

"I said I was a friend of Sir Oliver's because I am," Hester answered. "I have known him well for some time." She met Zorah's gaze squarely, defying her to question precisely what that might mean.

Zorah looked at her with growing amusement.

"And you are concerned that this case will cause him some professional embarrassment?" she deduced. "Have you come to beg me, for his sake, to recant and say that I was mistaken, Miss Latterly?"

"No, I have not," Hester replied tartly. "If you would not do it before, I cannot see any reason why you would now. Anyway, it would hardly help things as they are. If Sir Oliver does not find who killed Friedrich, and prove it, you will be in the dock yourself, sooner or later. Probably sooner."

She sat down without being invited. "And I can tell you, it is an extremely unpleasant place. You cannot imagine quite how unpleasant until you have been there. You may put a brave face on it, but inside you will be terrified. You are not stupid enough to fail to realize that losing there does not mean a financial loss or a little unpleasantness socially. It means the hangman's rope."

Zorah's face tightened a little. "You don't mince words, do you, Miss Latterly? Have you come on Sir Oliver's behalf? What is it you want?" She still regarded her visitor with a faint contempt.

Hester did not know if that contempt was for her plainer, very conventional dress, so much more predictable and less dashing, less individual and certainly less flattering than Zorah's own. Possibly it was a countess's contempt for a woman of very moderate breeding who was obliged to earn her own living. If it was the contempt of a woman of courage and adventurous spirit for a woman who stayed at home and busied herself with suitable feminine occupations, she could match Zorah stride for stride any day.

"On the assumption that you are telling the truth, as far as you know it," Hester responded, "I want you to exercise your intelligence, instead of merely your strength of will, and start trying to work out what happened at Wellborough Hall. Because if we do not succeed in that, it is not only Sir Oliver's career which will suffer for having made a serious misjudgment in taking on a highly unpopular case, but it will be your life in jeopardy. And what I think may actually be more important to you, it will ruin the reputation and honor of that group of men and women in your country who are prepared to fight for Felzburg's continued independence. Now, I need your attention. Countess Rostova?"

Slowly Zorah sat up, a look of surprise and dawning disbelief on her face.

"Do you often address people in this fashion, Miss Latterly?"

"I have not recently had occasion to," Hester admitted. "But in the army I frequently exceeded my authority. Emergencies have that effect. One is forgiven for it afterwards, if one succeeds. If one fails, it is the least of one's problems."

"The army . . ." Zorah blinked.

"In the Crimea. But that is all quite irrelevant to this." She brushed it away with a gesture of her hand. "If you would be good enough to turn your mind to Wellborough Hall?"

"I think I could like you, Miss Latterly," Zorah said quite seriously. "You are eccentric. I had no idea Sir Oliver had such interesting friends. He quite goes up in my esteem. I confess, I had thought him rather dry."

Hester found herself blushing, and was furious.

"Wellborough Hall," she repeated, like a schoolmistress with a refractory pupil.

Obediently, and with a very tight smile, Zorah began to recount the events from the time of her own arrival. Her tongue was waspish, and at times extremely funny. Then, when she spoke of the accident, her voice changed and all lightness vanished. She looked somber, as if even at the time she had realized that it would lead towards Friedrich's death.

Abruptly, she called the maid and requested luncheon, without referring to Hester or asking what she might like. She ordered thin toast, Beluga caviar, white wine, and a dish of fresh apples and a variety of cheeses. She glanced once at Hester to see her expression, then, finding satisfaction in it, dispatched the maid to carry out her duties.

She continued her tale.

Every so often Hester stopped her, asking to hear some point in greater detail, a room described, a person's expression or tone of voice recollected more sharply.

When Hester left late in the afternoon her mind was in turmoil, her brain crowded with impressions and ideas, one in particular which she needed to inquire into in minute detail, and for it she must see an old professional colleague, Dr. John Rainsford. But that would have to wait until tomorrow. It was too late now. It was nearly dark, and she needed to order her thoughts before she presented them to anyone else.

A lot depended upon the judgment she had formed of Zorah. If Zorah was right, then the whole case hung on that one tiny recollection of fact. Hester must verify it.

She returned to Rathbone's rooms on Sunday evening. She had sent a note by a messenger asking that Monk be there also. She found them both awaiting her, tense, pale-faced and with nerves strained close to the breaking point.

"Well?" Monk demanded before she had even closed the door.

"Did she tell you something?" Rathbone said eagerly, then swallowed the next words with an effort, trying to deny his hope before she could destroy it for him.

"I believe so," she said very carefully. "I think it may be the answer, but you will have to prove it." And she told them what she believed.

"Good God!" Rathbone said shakily. He swallowed hard, staring at her. "How . . . hideous!"

Monk looked at Hester, then at Rathbone, then back to Hester again.

"Do you realize what he is going to have to do to prove that?" he said huskily. "It could ruin him! Even if he succeeds . . . they'll never forgive him for it."

"I know," she said softly. "I didn't create the truth, William. I merely believe I may have found it. What would you prefer? Allow it to go by default?"

They both turned to Rathbone.

He looked up at them from where he was sitting. He was very white, but he did not hesitate.

"No. If I serve anything at all, it must be the truth. Sometimes mercy makes a claim, but this is most certainly not one of those times. I shall do all I can. Now tell me this again, carefully. I must know it all before tomorrow."

She proceeded to repeat it detail by detail, with Monk occasionally interrupting to clarify or reaffirm a point, and Rathbone taking careful notes. They sat until the fire burned low and the wind outside was rising, gusting with blown leaves against the window, and the gas lamps made yellow pools in the room with its browns and golds and burnt sugar colors.

On Monday morning the court was filled and people were crowded fifteen and twenty deep outside, but this time they were silent. Both Zorah and Gisela came in under heavy escort, for their own protection and to avoid the likelihood that an eruption of emotion would turn into violence.

Inside also there was silence. The jurors looked as if they too had slept little and were dreading the necessity of making a decision for which they still could see no unarguable evidence. They were harrowed by emotions, some of them conflicting, shattering their beliefs of a lifetime, the assumptions about the world, and people, upon which their evaluations were based. They were profoundly unhappy and aware of a burden they could not now evade.

Rathbone was quite candidly afraid. He had spent the night awake as much as asleep. He had dozed fitfully, every hour up and pacing, or lain staring at the dark ceiling, trying to order and reorder in his mind the possibilities of what he would say, how he would counter the arguments which would arise, how to defend himself from the emotions he would inevitably awaken, and the anger.

The Lord Chancellor's warning was as vivid in his mind as if he had heard it yesterday, and he needed no effort to imagine what his reaction would be to what Rathbone must do today. For the first time in twenty years he could see no professional future clearly ahead.

The court had already been called to order. The judge was looking at him, waiting.

"Sir Oliver?" His voice was clear and mild, but Rathbone had learned there was an inflexible will behind the benign face.

He must make his decision now, or the moment would be taken from him.

He rose to his feet, his heart pounding so violently he felt as if they must see his body shake. He had not been as nervous as this the very first time he stood up before a court. But he had been far more arrogant then, less aware of the possibilities of disaster. And he had had immeasurably less to lose.

He cleared his throat and tried to speak with a resonant, confident tone. His voice was one of his best instruments.

"My lord . . ." He was obliged to clear his throat again. Damnation! Harvester must know how frightened he was. He had not even begun, and already he had betrayed himself. "My lord, I call the Countess Zorah Rostova to the stand."

There was a murmur of surprise and anticipation around the gallery, and Harvester looked taken aback but not alarmed. Perhaps he thought Rathbone foolish, or knew he was desperate, probably both.

Zorah rose and walked across the short space of floor to the steps with an oddly elegant stride. And it was a stride, as if she were in open country, not inside a public hall. She moved as if she were in a riding habit rather than a crinoline skirt. She seemed unfeminine compared with the fragility of Gisela, and yet there was nothing masculine about her. As on every day of the trial before, she wore rich autumnal tones, reds and russets which flattered her dark skin but were highly inappropriate to such a somber occasion. Rathbone had failed at the outset to persuade her to look and behave with decorum. There was no point in adopting such a pattern now. No one would believe it.

For an instant, clear as sunlight on ice, she looked at Gisela, and the two women's eyes met in amazement and hatred; then she faced Rathbone again.

In a steady voice, she swore as to her name and said she would tell the truth and the whole truth.

Rathbone plunged in before he could lose his courage.

"Countess Rostova, we have heard several people's testimony of the events at Wellborough Hall as they saw them or believed them to be. You have made the most serious charge against Princess Gisela that one person can make against another, that she deliberately murdered her husband while he lay helpless in her care. You have refused to withdraw that charge, even in the face of proceedings against you. Will you please tell the court what you know of the events during that time? Include everything you believe to be relevant to the death of Prince Friedrich, but do not waste your time or the court's with that which is not."

She inclined her head very slightly in acknowledgment and began in a low, clear voice of individuality and unusual beauty.

"Before the accident we spent our time in the ordinary pursuits of the best kind of country house party. We rose when we pleased. It was spring, and occasionally still quite cold, so often we did not come downstairs until the servants had the fires lit for some little while. Gisela always breakfasted in her room anyway, and Friedrich frequently remained upstairs and kept her company."

There was a brief flicker of amusement on the faces of two of the jurors, and then it died immediately to be replaced by a swift flush of the color of embarrassment.

"Then the gentlemen would go out riding or walking," Zorah continued. "Or if the weather were unpleasant, would go into the smoking room and talk, or the billiard room, the gun room or the library and talk. Rolf, Stephan and Florent spoke together quite often. The ladies would walk in the gardens if it was fine, or write letters, paint, play a little music, or sit and read or exchange stories and gossip."

There was a murmur from the gallery, perhaps of envy.

"Sometimes luncheon would be a picnic. Cook would pack

a hamper and one of the footmen would take a dogcart with everything for us. We could join him whenever we fancied, beside a river, or a glade in the wood, or an open field by a copse of trees, wherever seemed most attractive."

"It sounds charming . . ." Rathbone put in.

Harvester rose to his feet. "But irrelevant, my lord. Most of us are acquainted with how the wealthy spend their time when in the country. Countess Rostova is surely not suggesting this most pleasant way of life is responsible for the Prince's death?"

"I shall not allow our time to be wasted too far, Mr. Harvester," the judge replied. "But I am inclined to allow Countess Rostova to paint a sufficient picture for us to perceive the household more clearly than we do so far." He turned to the witness stand. "Proceed, if you please. But be guided, ma'am. We require that this shall pertain to the Prince's death before much longer."

"It does, my lord," she replied gravely. "If I may describe one day in detail, I believe it will become understandable. You see, it is not one domestic incident which was the cause, but a myriad of tiny ones over a period of years, until they became a burden beyond the will to bear."

The judge looked puzzled.

The jurors were obviously utterly confused.

People in the gallery shifted in anticipation, whispering to one another, excitement mounting. This was what they had come for.

Harvester looked at Zorah, then at Rathbone, then at Gisela.

Gisela sat, pale as ice, without responding. For any change in her expression, she might not have heard them.

"Then proceed, Countess Rostova," the judge ordered.

"It was before the accident, I cannot remember exactly how many days, but it is immaterial," she resumed, looking at no one in particular. "It was wet and there was quite a sharp wind. I rose early. I don't mind the rain. I walked in the garden. The daffodils were magnificent. Have you smelled the wet earth after a shower?" This remark seemed directed towards the judge, but she did not wait for any reply. "Gisela rose late, as usual, and Friedrich came down with her. Indeed, he was so close behind her he accidentally trod on the hem of her skirt when she hesitated coming in through the door. She turned and said something to him. I cannot remember exactly what, but it was sharp and impatient. He apologized and looked discomfited. It was somewhat embarrassing because Brigitte von Arlsbach was in the room, and so was Lady Wellborough."

Rathbone took a deep breath. He had seen the look of surprise and distaste on the jurors' faces. He did not know whether it was for Zorah or for Gisela. Whom did they believe?

Please God that Hester was right. Everything rested upon one fact and all she had deduced from it.

"Please continue, Countess Rostova," he said with a crack in his voice. "The rest of this typical day, if you please."

"Brigitte went to the library to read," Zorah resumed. "I think she was quite happy alone. Lady Wellborough and Evelyn von Seidlitz spent the morning in the boudoir, talking, I imagine. They both love to gossip. Gisela asked Florent to accompany her to the village. I was surprised, because it was raining, and she hated the rain. I think he does too, but he felt it would be ungallant to refuse her. She had asked him in front of everyone, so he could not do so politely. Friedrich offered to take her, but she said rather tartly that since Rolf had already expressed a desire to talk with him, he should stay and do so."

"She did not appear to mind that Friedrich should spend time talking with Count Lansdorff?" Rathbone said with affected surprise.

"On the contrary, she practically instructed him to," Zorah replied with a little shake of her head, but there was no hesitation in her voice.

"Can she have been unaware of Count Lansdorff's purpose in coming to Wellborough Hall?" Rathbone asked.

"I cannot imagine so," Zorah said frankly. "She has never been a foolish woman. She is as aware as any of us of the political situation in Felzburg and the rest of Germany. She lives in Venice, and Italy is also on the brink of a struggle for unification and independence from Austria."

"We have heard that she is uninterested in politics," Rathbone pointed out.

Zorah looked at him with ill-concealed impatience.

"To be uninterested in politics in general is not at all the same thing as being unaware of something that is going on which may affect your own survival," she pointed out. "She has never been uninterested in what may ruin her."

There was a murmur in the gallery. One of the jurors leaned forward.

"Ruin her?" Rathbone raised his eyebrows.

Zorah leaned a little forward. "If Friedrich had returned to Felzburg without her, she would be a divorced wife, publicly set aside, and have only the worldly means he chose to give her. And even that might not lie entirely within his power to decide. His personal fortune comes from royal lands at home. Many of them are on the Prussian borders. If there were a war to retain independence, Klaus von Seidlitz would not be the only one to lose the majority of his possessions. She was always aware of that."

A chilly smile crossed her face. "Just because a person spends her life in the pursuit of pleasure, dresses sublimely, collects jewels, mixes with the rich and the idle, does not mean she is unaware of the source of the money or does not keep a very sharp mind to its continuing flow."

Again there was the rumble from the gallery, and a man raised his voice in ugly comment.

"Is that deduction, Countess Rostova?" Rathbone inquired, ignoring the crowd. "Or do you know this of your own observation?"

"I have heard Friedrich mention it in her presence. She did

not wish to know details, but she is very far from naive. The reasoning is inescapable."

"And yet she was happy—in fact, eager—that Friedrich should spend time alone in conversation with Count Lansdorff?"

Zorah looked puzzled, as if she herself did not understand it, even in hindsight.

"Yes. She instructed him to."

"And did he?"

"Of course."

The gallery was silent now, listening.

"Do you know the outcome of their discussion?"

"Count Lansdorff told me Friedrich would return only on condition he could bring Gisela with him as his wife, and in time as his queen."

One of the jurors let out a sigh.

"Did Count Lansdorff hold out any hope that he could be prevailed upon to change his mind?" Rathbone pressed.

"Very little."

"But he intended to try?"

"Naturally."

"To your knowledge, did he succeed?"

"No, he did not. At the time of the accident Friedrich was adamant. He always believed the country would have them both back. He believed that all his life. Of course, it was not true."

"Did he express any belief that Count Lansdorff would yield?"

"Not that I heard. He simply said that he would not consider going without Gisela, whatever the country's need or anybody's conception of his duty. He thought he could face the issue." She said it with little expression in her voice, but her face was twisted with contempt and it was beyond her control to hide it.

Harvester turned to Gisela and whispered something, but she did not appear to answer him, and he did not interrupt.

"I see," Rathbone acknowledged. "And the rest of the day, Countess Rostova?"

"The weather improved. We had luncheon, and then some of the men went riding over the open country. Gisela suggested that Friedrich go with them, but he preferred to remain with her, and I believe they walked in the gardens, then had a game of croquet."

"Just the two of them?"

"Yes. Gisela asked Florent Barberini to join them, but he felt he would be intruding."

"Prince Friedrich seems to have been very devoted to his wife. How can Count Lansdorff, or anyone, seriously have believed he would set her aside and return to Felzburg to spend the rest of his life without her?"

"I don't know," she said with a little shake of her head. "They did not live in Venice. They had not seen them closely for years. It was something you would not accept as true unless you had seen it. Friedrich seemed hardly able to do anything without her. If she left the room, one was aware he was waiting for her to return. He asked her opinion, waited for her praise, depended upon her approval."

Rathbone hesitated. Was it too soon? Had he laid sufficient foundation yet? Perhaps not. He must be sure. He glanced at the jurors' faces. They were looking confused. It was too soon.

"So on that day they played croquet together through the afternoon?"

"Yes."

"And the rest of the gathering?"

"I spent the afternoon with Stephan von Emden. I'm not sure about anyone else."

"But you are sure about Friedrich and Gisela?"

"Yes. I could see the croquet lawn from where I was."

Harvester rose to his feet.

"My lord, all the witness is establishing is that Prince Friedrich and Princess Gisela were devoted to each other, which the world already knows. We have all watched their meeting, their romance, their love and the sacrifice it has cost them. We have rejoiced for them and wept for them. And even after twelve years of devoted marriage, we now know that their love had not dimmed in the slightest. If anything, it was even deeper and more total than before. Countess Rostova herself acknowledges that Prince Friedrich would never have returned home without his wife, and she was as abundantly aware of that as was anyone else."

He waved expansively towards Zorah in the witness stand. "She has said that she does not understand how even Count Lansdorff could so delude himself as to keep any hope of his mission's being successful. She has told us she knew of no plans he had to overcome that obstacle, nor did Count Lansdorff himself. Princess Gisela could not physically have poisoned her husband, and she had no possible motive whatever for wishing to. The defense is wasting everyone's time proving my case for me. I am obliged, but it is unnecessary. I have proved it for myself."

"Sir Oliver?" the judge asked. "Surely this expedition of yours cannot be as pointless as it seems?"

"No, my lord. If the court would be patient a little longer?"

"A little, Sir Oliver. A very little."

"Thank you, my lord." Rathbone bowed his head a fraction, then turned back to Zorah. "Countess Rostova, the evening, if you please." He had hoped this would be unnecessary, but now he had no weapon left but this. "What happened in the evening?" he asked.

"There was a dinner party, and we had games to entertain us afterwards. There were several guests. It was an excellent meal, nine or ten courses, and a magnificent choice of wines. All the women wore their best gowns and jewels. As usual, Gisela outshone us all, even Brigitte von Arlsbach. But then

Brigitte was never ostentatious, in spite of being the wealthiest person present."

She looked at the wooden paneling above the heads of the farthest row of the gallery, recalling the party to her mind's eye.

There was complete silence again. Everyone was straining to catch each word.

"Gisela was very entertaining that evening." Her voice was tight in her throat. "She made us all laugh. She became more and more daring in her wit . . . not vulgar, I have never known her to be vulgar. But she could be very outspoken about other people's weaknesses. She had an acute insight into what made people vulnerable."

"That sounds a little cruel," Rathbone observed.

"It is extremely cruel," she corrected. "But when coupled with a sharp enough wit, it can be very funny as well—to anyone except the victim."

"And who was the victim on this occasion?"

"Mostly Brigitte," she answered. "Which was possibly why neither Stephan nor Florent laughed. But everyone else did. I assume they did not appreciate what was involved and knew no better. The wine flowed freely. Why should they care about the feelings of a baroness from some obscure German principality, when one of the most glittering and romantic figures of Europe was holding court at the dinner table?"

Rathbone did not express his opinion. His stomach was knotted tight. This was going to be the worst moment of all, but without it there was no case.

"And after dinner, Countess Rostova?" His voice sounded almost steady. Only Monk and Hester, sitting in the gallery, could guess how he felt.

"After dinner we played games," Zorah answered with a half smile.

"Games? Card games? Billiards? Charades?"

The judge was looking at Zorah, frowning.

Zorah's mouth tightened. "No, Sir Oliver, rather more physical than that. I cannot recall every game, but I know we played blindman's buff. We blindfolded each of the gentlemen in turn. We all fell over rather often and ended on couches or on the floor together."

Harvester rose to his feet.

"Yes, yes," the judge agreed. "The point of all this, Sir Oliver? Young people do play games which to some of us are of a bawdy and somewhat questionable nature."

He was trying to rescue the situation, even to rescue Rathbone from himself, and he knew it.

For a moment Rathbone hesitated. Escape was still possible, and with it defeat, not only for Zorah but for the truth.

"There is a point, my lord," he said quickly. "The rest of the evening, if you please, Countess Rostova."

"We played hunt the thimble," she went on obediently. "It was hidden in some extremely indiscreet places . . ."

"Did anyone object?"

"I don't think so. Brigitte didn't play, nor, I think, did Rolf. Brigitte was rather conspicuous by remaining sober. By about midnight or a little after we were playing horse races."

"Horse races?" the judge inquired, nonplussed.

"The men were on hands and knees, my lord," Zorah explained. "And the ladies rode astride them."

"They raced in that manner?" The judge was surprised.

"Not to any effect, my lord," she said. "That was not really the purpose. There was a great deal of laughter, perhaps a little hysterical by then. We fell over rather often."

"I see." The look of distaste on his face made it apparent that he did indeed see.

"And Princess Gisela joined in with this entertainment?" Rathbone persisted. "And Prince Friedrich?"

"Of course."

"So Gisela was in high spirits? She was totally happy?"

Zorah frowned very slightly, as if thinking before she answered.

"I don't think so."

"But you have said she was involved in the . . . fun!" Rathbone protested.

"She was . . . she rode Florent . . . and fell off."

There was an outburst from the gallery, almost instantly choked off.

"Was Prince Friedrich annoyed or distressed by the attention that was paid to her?" Rathbone asked with dry lips.

"No," Zorah replied. "He loved to see her the center of laughter and admiration. He had no jealousy over her, and if you are thinking he feared she might respond too willingly to anyone's advances, you are mistaken. She never did. Never have I seen her respond unbecomingly to any other man, nor have I heard from anyone else that she did. They were always together, always speaking to each other. Often he would sit so close to her he would reach out and touch her hand."

There was conspicuous movement in the gallery now.

The judge looked totally confused. Harvester was openly perplexed.

"And yet you are not sure that she was happy?" Rathbone said with as much disbelief as he could manage. "Why do you say that? It would seem to me she had everything a woman could desire."

An expression of rage and pity filled Zorah's face, as an emotion entirely new to her swept away all old convictions.

"I saw her alone, standing at the top of the stairs," she answered slowly. "The light was on her face, and I was in shadow at the bottom. She did not know I was there. For a moment she looked utterly trapped, like an animal in a cage. The expression on her face was terrible. I have never seen such despair before in anyone. It was a complete hopelessness . . ."

There was a silence of incredulity in the court. Even the judge was stunned.

"Then a door opened behind me," Zorah went on, almost in a whisper. "And she heard the noise, and the look vanished. She made herself smile again, and came down the stairs with a sort of forced sparkle, her voice brittle."

"Did you know the cause of this emotion, Countess?"

"Not at the time. I imagined then that it was fear that Friedrich would succumb to the pressure of family and duty, and that he would indeed return to Felzburg—and put Gisela aside. Even so, that would not explain the sense of panic I saw, as if she were . . . caged, fighting to escape something which clung and suffocated her." She lifted her chin a little, and her voice was tight in her throat. "She was the last woman on earth I wanted to pity, and yet I could not forget the look I saw in her eyes as she stood there."

There was silence in the court, a tension palpable in the air.

"And the rest of the evening?" Rathbone prompted after a moment.

"We continued drinking, playing games, laughing and making risqué jokes and cruel remarks about people we knew, or thought we did, and went to bed at about four in the morning," Zorah answered. "Some of us went to our own beds, some of us didn't."

There was a growing rumble of disapproval from the gallery and looks of discomfort in the jury box. They did not like having their betters spoken of in such terms; even if some accepted it was true, they preferred not to be forced to acknowledge it. Others looked genuinely shocked.

"And that was a typical day?" Rathbone said wearily.

"Yes."

"There were many like that?"

"They were almost all like that, give or take a detail or two," she replied, still standing very upright, her head high in spite of having to look slightly down to the body of the court. "We ate and drank, we rode on horseback or in carriages or gigs. We raced a little. We had picnics and parties. We played croquet. The men shot birds. We rowed on the river once or twice. We walked in the woods or the garden. If it was wet, or cold, we talked or played the piano, or read books, or looked at pictures. The men played cards or billiards, or smoked. And, of course, they gambled on anything and everything—who would win at cards, or which servant would answer a bell. In the evenings, we had musical entertainment, or theatricals, or played games."

"And Friedrich and Gisela were always as devoted as you have described?"

"Always."

Harvester rose to his feet. "My lord, this is intrusive, unproven and still totally irrelevant."

Rathbone ignored him and hurried on, speaking over the other lawyer's protest, almost shouting him down.

"Countess Rostova, after the accident, did you ever visit Prince Friedrich in his rooms?"

"Once."

"Would you describe the room for us, please?"

"My lord!" Harvester was shouting now as well.

"It is relevant, my lord," Rathbone said even more loudly. "I assure the court, it is critical."

The judge banged his gavel and was ignored.

"My lord!" Harvester would not be hushed. He was now on his feet and facing Rathbone in front of the bench. "This witness has already been impugned by circumstances. Her own interest in the matter is the issue before us. Nothing she says she saw—"

"You cannot impugn it before it is said!" Rathbone cried furiously. "She must be allowed to defend herself—"

"Not by—" Harvester protested.

The judge held up his hands. "Be silent!" he roared.

They both stopped.

"Mr. Rathbone," the judge said, resuming a normal tone. "I hope you are not about to add a further slander to your client's already perilous situation."

"No, my lord, I am not," Rathbone said vehemently. "Countess Rostova will not say anything which cannot be substantiated by other witnesses."

"Then her evidence is not the urgent matter you stated," Harvester said triumphantly. "If other witnesses can say the same thing, why did you not have them do so?"

"Please sit down, Mr. Harvester," the judge requested firmly. "Countess Rostova will continue with her evidence. You will have the opportunity to question her when Sir Oliver has finished. If she makes any remarks detrimental to your client's interests, you have the recourse which you are presently taking. Proceed, Sir Oliver. But do not waste our time, and please do not push us to make moral judgments of issues other than the death of Prince Friedrich and whether your client can substantiate the terrible charge she has made. That is your sole remit here. Do you understand me?"

"Yes, my lord. Countess Rostova, will you please describe Prince Friedrich's bedroom and the suite of rooms he and Princess Gisela occupied during his illness at Wellborough Hall?"

There was a whispering of consternation and disappointment from the crowd. They had expected something far more titillating.

Even Zorah looked a little puzzled, but she began obediently.

"They had a bedroom, dressing room and sitting room. And, of course, they had the private use of a bathroom and water closet, which I did not see. Nor did I see the dressing room." She looked at Rathbone to know if this was what he wished.

"Would you describe the sitting room and bedroom, please." He nodded to her.

Harvester was growing impatient, and even the judge was

beginning to lose his tolerance. The jury were clearly lost. Suddenly the proceedings had degenerated from high tension to total banality.

Zorah blinked. "The sitting room was quite large. It had two bay windows, facing west, I think, over the knot garden."

"My lord!" Harvester had risen to his feet again. "This cannot possibly be of any relevance whatsoever. Is my learned friend going to suggest that Princess Gisela somehow climbed out of the sitting room window and down the wall to the yew walk? This is becoming absurd, and it is an abuse of the court's time and intelligence."

"It is precisely because I respect the court's intelligence that I do not wish to lead the witness, my lord," Rathbone said desperately. "She does not know which piece of her observation pertains to and explains the whole crime. And as far as time is concerned, we would waste a lot less of it if Mr. Harvester did not keep interrupting me!"

"I will allow you another fifteen minutes, Sir Oliver," the judge warned. "If you have not reached some point of relevance by then, I shall entertain Mr. Harvester's objections." He turned to Zorah. "Please make your description as brief as possible, Countess Rostova. Pray continue."

Zorah was quite obviously as confused as everyone else.

"The carpet was French, at least in design, of a variety of shades of wine and pink, as were the curtains. There were several seats, I do not recall how many, all upholstered in matching fabric. There was a small walnut table in the center of the floor, and a sort of bureau over by the farther wall. I don't remember anything else."

"Flowers?" Rathbone asked.

Harvester let out a very clearly audible snort of disgust.

"Yes," Zorah replied with a frown. "Lily of the valley. They were Gisela's favorite. She always had them when they were in season. In Venice she had them forced, so she could have them even in late winter."

"Lily of the valley," Rathbone repeated. "A bunch of lily of the valley? In a vase? A vase full of water?"

"Of course. If they were not in water they would very quickly have died. They were not in a pot, if that is what you mean. They were cut from the conservatory, and the gardener had them sent up for her."

"Thank you, Countess Rostova, that is sufficient description."

There was a gasp of amazement around the room, like the backwash of a tide after a great wave has broken. People looked at each other in disbelief.

The jurors looked at Zorah, then at the judge, then at Harvester.

"That is supposed to be relevant?" Harvester said, his voice rising sharply.

Rathbone smiled and turned back to Zorah.

"Countess, it has been suggested that you were jealous of the Princess because she replaced you twelve years ago in Prince Friedrich's affections, and you have chosen this bizarre way of seeking your revenge. Are you jealous of her because it was she who married him and not you?"

A succession of emotions crossed Zorah's face—denial, contempt, a bleak and bitter amusement; then suddenly and startlingly, pity.

"No," she said very softly. "There is nothing in heaven or earth that would persuade me to change places with her. She was suffocated by him, trapped forever in the legend she had created. To the world they were great lovers, magical people who had achieved what so many of us dream of and long for. She was the reality. It was Antony and Cleopatra without the asp. That was what gave her her fame, her status. It defined who she was, without it she was no one, a sham. No matter how he depended upon her, or clung to her, or drained the life from her, she could never leave him, never even seem to lose her temper with him. She had built an image for herself and she was imprisoned within it forever, being sucked dry, having to smile, to act all the time. I didn't understand that look on her face at the top of the stairs at the time. I knew she hated him, but I did not understand why.

"Then yesterday evening I was speaking with someone, and quite suddenly I saw Gisela trapped forever playing the role she had created so brilliantly, and I knew why she broke out of it the way only she could. She was a cold, ambitious woman, prepared to use a man's love in any way she could, but I could not have wished that living incarceration on anyone. At least . . . I don't think I could. . . . After all, the accident crippled him. He would never again be active, a companion to her. It was the last window of her cell in a final and utter imprisonment with him."

There was silence in the room. No one spoke. Nothing moved.

"Thank you, Countess," Rathbone said softly. "I have no more to ask you."

Then the spell broke, and there was a low rumble of dismay turning to rage, almost a violence of confusion, the pain of breaking dreams.

Harvester spoke to Gisela, who did not answer. Then he rose. "Countess Rostova, has anyone at all—other than yourself, so you say—noticed this profound terror and despair in one of the world's most beloved and fortunate women? Or are you utterly alone in your extraordinary perception?"

"I have no idea," Zorah replied, keeping her voice level and her eyes steady on his face.

"But no one has ever, at any time, given you the slightest indication that he or she saw through the constant, twelve-year-long, day-and-night, fair-weather-and-foul, public and private happiness and love to this tragedy you say was beneath it?" His tone was heavily sarcastic. He did not sink to melodrama, but his voice would have cut flesh.

"No . . ." she admitted.

"So we have only your word for it, your brilliant, incisive sight, which, now you are in the witness stand, morally in the dock, accused and desperate yourself, has shown you, and you alone, this incredible fact?"

She met his gaze without flinching, a very faint smile curling her lips.

"I am the first, Mr. Harvester. I shall be the only one for a very short time. If I can see what you cannot, that is because I have two advantages over you; I have known Gisela far longer than you have, and I am a woman, which means I can read other women as you never will. Does that answer your question?"

"Whether others follow eventually, Countess, remains to be seen," he said coldly. "Here, today, you stand alone. Thank you . . . if not for truth, at least for a most original invention."

The judge looked at Rathbone inquiringly.

"No more questions, thank you, my lord," he answered.

Zorah was excused and returned to her seat.

"I should like to recall Lady Wellborough, if your lordship pleases," Rathbone continued.

Emma Wellborough came from the body of the court, looking pale, startled, and now considerably frightened.

"Lady Wellborough," Rathbone began, "you have been present during Countess Rostova's testimony . . ."

She nodded, then realized that was inadequate and replied in a shaking voice.

"Her description of events in your home, prior to Prince Friedrich's accident, is it substantially true? Is that how you conducted your lives, how you spent your days?"

"Yes," she said very softly. "It . . . it didn't seem as . . . as trivial as she made it sound . . . as . . . pointless. We were not really . . . so . . . drunken . . ." Her voice trailed off.

"We are not making judgments," Rathbone said, and then he knew it was a lie. Everyone in the room was making judgments, not only of her but of all her class and of Felzburg's royal family. "All we need to know," he went on a little hoarsely, "is if those were the pursuits of your time, and if the Prince and Princess had the relationship of closeness Countess Rostova described, forever together, largely at his insistence. She tried to break away, find herself a little time alone or with other company, but he was always there, clinging, demanding?"

She looked bewildered and profoundly unhappy. Had he taken her too far?

She hesitated so long he felt his heart beating, his pulse racing. It was like playing a fish on a line. Even at the last moment he could still lose.

"Yes," she said at last. "I used to envy her. I saw it as the greatest love story in the world, what every girl dreams of . . ." She gave a jerking little laugh that ended almost in a choke. "A handsome prince, and Friedrich was so very handsome . . . such marvelous eyes, and a beautiful voice . . . a handsome prince who would fall passionately in love with you, be prepared to lose the world for your sake, just so long as you loved him." Her eyes were full of tears. "Then sail away and live happily ever after in somewhere as marvelous as Venice. I never thought of it as a prison, as never being free, or even alone again . . ." She stopped, some dark inner thought overwhelming her. "How . . . terrible!"

Harvester had risen to his feet, but he did not interrupt. He sat down again in silence.

"Lady Wellborough," Rathbone said after a moment, "the description Countess Rostova gave of the room where Friedrich and Gisela stayed in your home, is that correct?"

"Yes."

"Did you see the flowers there yourself?"

"You mean the lily of the valley? Yes, she requested them. Why?"

"That is all, thank you. Unless Mr. Harvester has any questions for you, you may go."

"No . . ." Harvester shook his head. "No, not at this time."

"My lord, I call Dr. John Rainsford. He is my final witness."

Dr. Rainsford was a young man with fair hair and the strong intelligent face of an enthusiast. At Rathbone's request, he gave his considerable qualifications as a physician and toxicologist.

"Dr. Rainsford," Rathbone began, "if a patient presented symptoms of headache, hallucinations, cold clammy skin, pain in the stomach, nausea, a slowing heartbeat, drifting into coma, and then death, what would you diagnose?"

"Any of a number of things," Rainsford replied. "I should require a history of the patient, any accidents, what he or she had eaten lately."

"If the pupils of the eyes were dilated?" Rathbone added.

"I would suspect poison."

"By the leaves or the bark of the yew tree, possibly?"

"Very possibly."

"And if the patient had blotches on his skin?"

"Oh . . . that is not yew. That sounds more like lily of the valley—"

There was a hiss of breath around the entire court. The judge leaned forward, his face tense, eyes wide. The jurors sat bolt upright. Harvester broke his pencil with the unconscious tension of his hands.

"Lily of the valley?" Rathbone said carefully. "Is that poisonous?"

"Oh, yes, as poisonous as anything in the world," Rainsford said seriously. "As poisonous as yew, hemlock or deadly nightshade. All of it—the flowers, the leaves, the bulbs. Even the water in which the cut flowers stand is lethal. It causes exactly the symptoms you describe."

"I see. Thank you, Dr. Rainsford. Would you remain there in case Mr. Harvester has anything to ask you."

Harvester stood up, drew in a deep breath, and then shook his head and sat down again. He looked ill.

The jury retired and was absent for only twenty minutes.

"We find in favor of the defendant, Countess Zorah Rostova," the foreman announced with a pale, sad face. He looked at the judge first, to see if he had fulfilled his duty, then at Rathbone with a calm, grave dislike. Then he sat down.

There was no cheering in the gallery. Perhaps they did not know what they had expected, but it was not this. It left them unhappy—with truth, but no victory. Too many dreams were soiled and broken forever.

Rathbone turned to Zorah.

"You were right, she did murder him," he said with a sigh. "What will happen to the fight to keep independence now? Will they find a new leader?"

"Brigitte," she answered. "She is well loved, and she has the courage, and the belief, and the dedication to her country. Rolf and the Queen will be behind her."

"But when the King dies, Waldo will succeed him. Then Ulrike will have far less power," Rathbone pointed out.

Zorah smiled. "Don't believe it! Ulrike will always have power. The only one who is remotely a match for her is Brigitte, in her own way. They are on the same side, but unification will come; it is simply a matter of when and how."

She rose to her feet amid the shifting and muttering of the crowd as they moved to leave. "Thank you, Sir Oliver. I fear my defense has cost you dearly. You will not be loved for what you have done. You have shown people too much of what they would prefer not to have known. You have made the wealthy and the privileged see themselves, however briefly, a great deal more clearly than they wished to, parts of themselves they would have preferred to ignore.

"And you have disturbed the dreams of ordinary people who like, even need, to see us as wiser and better than we are. In future it will be harder for them to look on our wealth and idleness and bear it with equanimity—and they have to do that, because too many are dependent upon us, one way or another. And neither will we forgive them for having seen our faults."

Her face tightened. "I think perhaps I should not have spoken. Maybe it would have been better if I had allowed her to get away with it. It might have done less harm in the end."

"Don't say that!" He clasped her arm.

"Because it was a hard battle?" She smiled. "And we paid too much to win? That had nothing to do with it, Sir Oliver. How much it costs has nothing to do with how much it is worth."

"I know that. I meant don't believe that it is better to allow a helpless man to be murdered by the person he trusted above all others, and for it to go unquestioned. The day we accept that, because it will be uncomfortable to look at the truth it exposes, we have lost all that makes us worth respecting."

"How very proper—and English," she replied, but with a sudden tenderness in her voice. "You look exactly as if you would say such a thing, with your striped trousers and stiff, white collar, but perhaps you are right, for all that. Thank you, Sir Oliver. It has been most entertaining to know you." And with that she smiled more widely, with a warmth and radiance he had not seen in her before, and turned and left in a swirl of scarlet and russet skirts.

The room was darker without her. He wanted to go after her, but it would have been foolish. There was no place for him in her life.

Monk and Hester were at his elbow.

"Brilliant," Monk said dryly. "Another astounding victory—but Pyrrhic, this time. You will have lost more than you gained. Good thing you got your knighthood already. You'd not get it now."

"I don't need you to tell me that," Rathbone replied sourly. "I would not have done it, had not the alternative been even worse." But his mind was on Zorah, the brimming life in her, the recklessness and the courage. Perhaps honoring her was worth the cost and the sense of loss now.

Monk sighed. "How could such a love end like that? He gave up everything for her. His country, his people, his throne. How could the greatest love story of the century end in disillusion, hatred and murder?"

"It wasn't the greatest love," Hester answered him. "It was two people who needed what the other could give. She wanted power, position, wealth and fame. He seemed to want constant admiration, devotion, someone to be there all the time, to live his life for him. He hadn't the courage to stand without her. Love is brave and generous, and above all it springs from honor. In order to love someone else, you must first be true to yourself."

Rathbone looked at her and slowly his face creased into a smile.

Monk frowned. His eyes filled with intense dislike, then anger, then as he fought with himself, he lost the battle, and his body eased.

Deliberately, he put his arm around Hester.

"You are right," he said grudgingly. "You are pompous, opinionated and insufferable—but you are right."

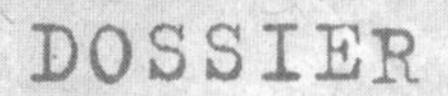

Weighed in the Balance

Anne Perry

Acclaimed writer Anne Perry channeled her beloved character William Monk to answer some hard-hitting questions about his life and work.

Mortalis: All your readers see how busy you are solving crimes. Do you think violent crime has become more rampant during Victorian times than it was in the past? Are the police getting better at solving it?

William Monk: Very definitely better. Believe it or not, in the 1700s it was worse. As for police getting better at solving it—in the 1600s, 1700s—what police?

M: Do you prefer working for the police force or as a private investigator?

WM: I am now in the police force again, and apart from the challenges of having command of men, trying to live up to their expectations of a leader, and being answerable to superiors whom I do not always admire, I prefer the financial security of police work for my family. I would rather worry about crime than money. Also I don't have to look for work, it comes to me. And I am growing to like and trust my superior, Inspector Orme.

On the downside I cannot refuse a case, no matter how I may dislike it. But then I couldn't afford to before, at any rate.

M: How do you think Hester's experience in the Crimean War prepared her for solving mysteries now?

WM: I'm not sure that it did directly. It contributed to making her who she is, and that helps everything. I think she would always have been a crusader for something, but ultimately her time in Crimea was the ideal thing for her in regards to her courage and compassion, her anger against injustice and with the frequent stupidity of those in authority. I don't think it chose her, she chose it.

M: If you could go back in time and erase the coach accident that caused your amnesia, would you?

WM: Never! It was painful and confusing, but it gave me the chance to start over, to see myself from the outside. It was an opportunity for clarity that few people ever have. Without it I would have continued in all my arrogance and with many mistakes. This way at least I have the chance to address them.

M: What is the worst part of your job?

WM: Knowing that I am answerable to my superiors, and they can countermand me due to political pressures on them. It happens sometimes.

M: What has been your most frightening experience?

WM: Physically—being underground in the total darkness of the sewers, not knowing which way to go or if I could get out. Emotionally—not knowing myself, or what I might have done during the time I can't remember.

M: What is your favorite possession?

WM: I don't know yet.

M: What do you do to relax?

WM: I walk with Hester in the park near my home, and look across at the river.

PHOTO: © DIANE HINDS

ANNE PERRY is the bestselling author of two acclaimed series set in Victorian England: the William Monk novels, including *Execution Dock* and *Dark Assassin,* and the Charlotte and Thomas Pitt novels, including *Buckingham Palace Gardens* and *Long Spoon Lane.* She is also the author of the World War I novels *No Graves As Yet, Shoulder the Sky, Angels in the Gloom, At Some Disputed Barricade,* and *We Shall Not Sleep,* as well as seven holiday novels, most recently *A Christmas Promise.* Anne Perry lives in Scotland. Visit her website at www.anneperry.net.